THE WASTE LAND

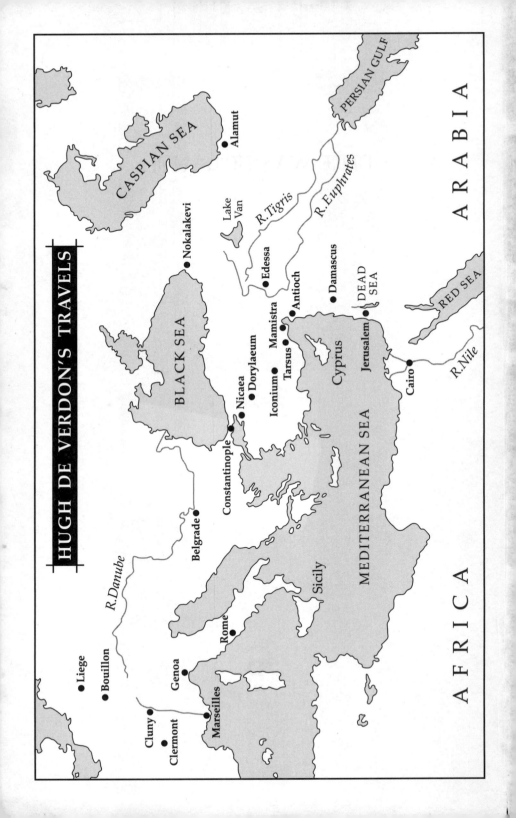

HUGH DE VERDON'S TRAVELS

Liege
Bouillon
Cluny
Clermont
Marseilles
Genoa
Rome
Belgrade
Constantinople
Nicaea
Dorylaeum
Iconium
Tarsus
Mamistra
Antioch
Edessa
Nokalakevi
Damascus
Jerusalem
Cairo
Alamut

CASPIAN SEA
BLACK SEA
MEDITERRANEAN SEA
RED SEA
PERSIAN GULF
DEAD SEA
Lake Van
R. Tigris
R. Euphrates
R. Nile
R. Danube
Sicily
Cyprus
ARABIA
AFRICA

THE WASTE LAND

An Entertainment

by

Simon Acland

Charlwood Books

Charlwood Books
42 Charlwood Road
London SW15 1PW
www.charlwoodbooks.com

Published by Charlwood Books 2010
Copyright © Simon Acland 2010
Reprinted 2011
Distributed by Gardners Books, 1 Whittle Drive, Eastbourne,
East Sussex, BN23 6QH
Tel: +44(0)1323 521555 | Fax: +44(0)1323 521666

A CIP catalogue record for this book is available from the British Library

ISBN-978-0-9561472-0-2

Typeset in Caslon by Amolibros
This book production has been managed by Amolibros
Printed and bound by T J International Ltd, Padstow, Cornwall, UK

ABOUT THE AUTHOR

Simon Acland spent over twenty years as a venture capitalist. When his company was sold in 2007 he took the opportunity to turn to writing. His interest in the myths and legends surrounding the Holy Grail stems from studying twelfth and thirteenth century French grail romances at university.

The Waste Land is his first novel. It will shortly be followed by a sequel, *The Flowers of Evil*.

Simon has also written a non-fiction book about venture capital, entitled *Angels, Dragons and Vultures – how to tame the venture capital beasts.*

You can find more information about the genesis of *The Waste Land* on the website www.simonacland.com.

What Other Writers Say About The Waste Land

Catherine Bailey "An intriguing tale…"

Douglas Hurd "The Waste Land will be thoroughly enjoyed by anyone with a taste for rollicking adventure laced with a subtle dose of literary learning."

Stanley Johnson "Sex, violence and more than a dash of romance: Simon Acland's gripping First Crusade mystery thriller rivals the Da Vinci Code for interest and suspense."

Giles MacDonogh "I found it utterly gripping."

Juliette Mead "Simon Acland's debut novel is a potent cocktail: take one part First Crusade historical romance, one part modern academic satire – and add three jiggers of coming-of-age, Grail-questing, spur-winning Knight's tale. A rollicking, galloping read from a highly individual story teller."

Tim Waterstone "Highly original and a most enjoyable read."

For Tiresias

ACKNOWLEDGEMENTS

I am very grateful to Ranjit Bolt for his translation of Ovid, to Wayne Barron for his help with my Greek, and to Noonie Minogue for her help with my Latin. Thank you to John Vernon Lord for permission to use his splendid illustration on the cover, to Dennis Hall for his design advice, to Richard Unthank for his maps, and to Jane Tatam for making this publication a reality.

I would like to thank everyone who read various drafts of this book and gave a nervous first-time author ideas and encouragement, especially my family, Peter and Claire Ainsworth, Hugh Barnes, Candida Brazil, Felicity Bryan, Robert Dudley, Douglas Hurd, Stanley Johnson, Katie Lee, Giles MacDonogh, Julie Mead, Jack Tenison, Chris Wakling and Tim Waterstone. Thank you to them, and to Susannah and Martin Fiennes, Caroline and Simon Clarke, Mark Hudson, Patrick Seely and Julia Kreitman for the helpful introductions they made.

DRAMATIS PERSONAE IN ORDER OF APPEARANCE

Although the nature of every person in this book is imaginary, the following characters are based on actual historical figures:

Hugh de Semur (1024-1109), sixth Abbot of Cluny from 1049 (known as "the Great"), canonised 1120

Otto de Lagery (1042-1099), Prior of Cluny until 1078, then Cardinal Bishop of Ostia, elected Pope Urban II in 1088

Adhemar de Monteil (d. 1098), Bishop of Le Puy, representative of Pope Urban II on the First Crusade

Godfrey de Bouillon (c. 1058-1100), Duke of Lower Lorraine from 1087, Advocatus Sancti Sepulchri from 1100

Eustace de Boulogne (c. 1055-c. 1125), elder brother of Godfrey, Count of Boulogne from 1087

Baldwin de Boulogne (c. 1059-1118), younger brother of Godfrey, Count of Edessa from 1098, King of Jerusalem from 1100

Godehilde (d. 1098), Baldwin's wife, daughter of Ralph de Conches

Bagrat (dates uncertan), Baldwin's Armenian friend and guide

Walter Sans Avoir (d. 1097) Lord of Boissy, a leader of the first wave of the First Crusade

Hugh de Vermandois (1053-1101), son of Henry I of France

Alexios Comnenos (1048-1118), Byzantine Emperor 1081-1118

Peter the Hermit (d. 1115), a leader of the First Crusade

Bohemond of Taranto (c. 1058-1111), son of Robert Guiscard, from 1099 Prince of Antioch

Raymond de Saint Gilles (c. 1041-1105), from 1094 Count of Toulouse, Duke of Narbonne and Margrave of Provence

Tatikios (dates unknown), trusted general of Emperor Alexios

Tancred (1072-1112), nephew of Bohemond, later Prince of Galilee

Hasan-i Sabbah (c. 1058-1124), founder of the Assassins, known as the Old Man of the Mountains

Mohammed (dates unknown), his son

Peter Bartholomew (d. 1099), a soldier in the service of Provençal knight William de Cunhlat

Guillermo Embriaco and his brother (dates unknown), Genoese sea captains

Geldemar Carpenel (d. 1101), a knight under Godfrey's command, later Lord of Haifa

PROLOGUE

The Master of St Lazarus' College was annoyed. His guest of honour for dinner at high table was late. The Master remembered that the Best-Selling Author had been a poor timekeeper as an undergraduate at the college. When he had turned up for anything at all, that was. Still, a little inconvenience could be suffered if it proved possible to extract the coveted donation to the College's funds.

The other members of the Senior Common Room stayed well out of the Master's way, even though this meant loitering in the colder corners of the classically proportioned room, away from the fire blazing under the Adam mantelpiece. They had all learned to read the expression of irritation in those harsh eyes, magnified and distorted by the hard steel-rimmed bifocals. The Master's temper had not been improved by five years away from the college presiding over an obscure branch of the intelligence service. An unacademic brusqueness had entered his manner. This now notched with his undeniable intellect to fire cruel shafts of sarcasm that were hard to bear before a couple of glasses of sherry.

Had the College Fellows been given to kindly thoughts, they might have blamed the parlous state of the College finances for the Master's moods. His frosty eyes glanced with scorn around the room. What did they know about the real world outside, where cold winds blew? Did they even begin to understand the threat to their comfortable lives if he could not raise the millions needed to make good the damage to the College Foundation by a series of disastrous private equity investments? Gah. What did he care about keeping them lazy in their cosy chambers? Why on earth had he taken on the task of dragging the most backward of colleges into the modern age? St. Lazarus indeed! If ever an institution needed to be raised from the dead it was this one. But what really mattered was his peerage. Everyone recognised that it was richly deserved, but it would still elude him if he failed in his task and instead became the first Master to preside over the bankruptcy of an ancient college. It would make no difference that those foolish investments had been made before his time.

This painful reverie was interrupted by the door to the Common Room. It opened to reveal the Best-Selling Author wearing an unaccustomed expression of shame-faced apology under his affectedly tousled leonine hair.

"I'm so sorry, dreadful traffic. My driver, lost in the one way system. All very different to my day."

"Well, there we are. There's just time for a quick glass of sherry before dinner. Dry?"

The Best-Selling Author brightened at the offer of a drink. He perked up even more when he saw that he was the focus of the room's attention. The bloody College had taken his scholarship away – justifiably maybe as he had done no work and ended up with a Third – but now they were fawning over him.

The critics had never exactly focused their praise on the Best-Selling Author's sensitive understanding of third party characters. Plot yes, excitement yes, definitely hard to put down. Plenty of page-turning Boy's Own action. Some quite good sex. But subtle characterization? No, not really. In fact not at all. So it was no surprise that the Best-Selling Author basked in the Senior Common Room's attention under a misapprehension.

For in fact the fellows hid critical appraisal behind their bland expressions. Each was busy matching the Best-Selling Author's features to the publicity photographs so well-known from the back cover of his books. Not one of them would have owned up to buying the Best-Selling Author's *oeuvre*. Of course not. Too low brow by far. But the truth was that curiosity had conquered their intellectual snobbery. Each had surreptitiously plucked a gaudy volume from a bookstand in airport or railway station before paying at the counter with the shamefaced bravado normally reserved for purchases of pornography.

"Airbrushed," thought the History Don caustically. "The true facts eliminated. The source material rewritten and distorted by the addition of more, thicker, darker curls."

"How cruel the passage of time," thought the Chaplain with a modicum of Christian charity. "How the lines have deepened and the cheeks have sagged."

"What a clever point of view," thought the Professor of English. "A neat perspective created by showing only the head, not the loose decaying spread of the body underneath."

"A poor translation," thought the Modern Languages Tutor. "An inaccurate rendering."

"The adjective does not agree with the noun," thought the Classics Fellow. "Definitely the wrong case."

And then there was just time to arrange the smiles, extend the hands, and murmur appreciation at their introduction to the celebrity, before dinner was announced. They all marched to their stations in the oak-panelled hall.

High Table was the battlefield across which the dons were accustomed to ride their hobby-horses, jousting with whichever lance their research or teaching had that day provided.

"At least he has not written a holy grail book yet," remarked the Chaplain with *sotto voce* mischief to his neighbour the Professor of History. "I hate all that cod religion. As far as I'm concerned, it's downright blasphemous."

As the Chaplain had intended, the Modern Languages Tutor overheard and looked affronted. *Modern* Languages was not quite the right way to describe his subject because he was a medieval specialist and believed that no French literature was worth reading after Rabelais – except Nerval perhaps.

"Actually Chrétien de Troyes' '*Roman de Perceval*' shows a great poetic imagination. There is nothing specifically Christian about Chrétien's grail, if you'll excuse the pun. The word *graal* in the original just translates as dish – the sort of dish in which you'd serve a large fish."

The Chaplain snickered slightly because just at that moment one of the ancient college servants began to pass round a plattered poached salmon. The Modern Languages Tutor ignored him with as much scorn as he could muster.

"All the religious stuff was tacked on later by Robert de Boron and the rest. If Chrétien had only lived to finish his story the grail would never have become holy, much less a popular mystery."

The Professor of English leant forward aggressively. "I'd take issue with the idea that there is any real originality in the grail romances at all. Most of the imagery is just recycled from earlier fertility legends. I know that it is fashionable these days to rubbish Jessie Weston but nobody who has read Frazer's '*Golden Bough*' can really doubt the arguments in her '*From Ritual to Romance*'. The real poet of imagination was Eliot, whose genius melded the grail stuff with Ovid and the earlier myths. '*The Waste Land*' is simply the last word on the subject."

The History Don intervened quickly because he knew from past experience that the misty expression now creeping over the Professor of English's face presaged a torrent of quotation. "It's all a load of nonsense. Simply not rooted in fact. A waste of time."

The Classics Fellow liked the last word to be his, like the proper thump of a Latin verb at the end of a sentence. "Just comparing the crudeness and lack of sophistication of the grail romances with the magnificent achievements of Homer, Virgil appreciate not just their size but also the beauty of the huge honeyed stones locked together in tight precision. Countless stout round towers butted forward, proudly wearing belts of ochred orange brick. The poor huts and hovels huddled before them served only to accentuate the height rearing above, like thickets at the base of a great tree. If ten tall men had been able to stand on each others' shoulders they might have just touched the top. Then I saw that such a measurement could not have been made even by the best acrobats, for the whole was protected by a wide water-filled moat which lapped the base of the ramparts. This liquid girdle stretched out as far as I could see, choking off the whole neck of land that contained the city.

'Thank God we come here in peace, not war,' I thought in grateful optimism. My own astonishment was reflected in different shades across the features of my companions as they came to appreciate the city's insuperable position. To the south, whence we had come, it was protected by the Sea of Marmara. That in itself was a matter of wonder to me, for I had never seen the sea before, and could scarcely believe that such an expanse of water existed.

And to the north stood guard a thinner stretch of water known poetically as the Golden Horn. It was in this direction that we were shepherded by a sharp-helmeted imperial escort. Our route along the walls showed off the full extent of their Emperor's formidable fortifications. Perhaps it had been deliberately chosen to awe us. I counted four main gates, each guarded by square crenellated towers still more massive than their round cousins between. Before each gate seethed a diverse throng of travellers and merchants, seeking entry for the Nativity feast day. I longed to pass with them through those gates to gain news of Blanche and to view the unimaginable riches beyond. But instead I had to make do with whatever glimpses I could catch from outside, as we were firmly guided to the northernmost end of the fortifications.

no four years. It takes a long time for these things to reach the shop shelves, you know. Sometimes I wonder what my publisher does all day. And the advance was spent a long time ago. My agent negotiated such a good deal up front that there is no chance of any royalties coming through. Now I just seem to have run out of ideas. I can't get any good plots going."

A deep gloom fell as the diners silently contemplated their problems. The fire at the side of the hall burned too far distant to cast any warmth, and instead just flickered ominous shadows on the hammer beam ceiling. The dark corners of the ancient room closed in menacingly around the small pools of light cast on the table under the heavy silver candelabra. A breath of cold air whispered through the chamber, guttering the candles and chilling the dons under their gowns. One or two of them glanced over their shoulders, as if to see what had caused the draught, but in reality anxious to check that nothing was creeping up behind them. The ancient spirits of long-dead fellows seemed to circle the room in threatening disapproval.

A voice, harsh and nasal, cut the silence. It came from the dark shadows beyond the candles' range.

"I think the time has come for me to share what I have been working on these past few months."

The Fellows started at this unexpected intrusion. They had forgotten the insignificant Research Assistant, who now leaned forward into the light. The other members of the Senior Common Room shuddered as the candles lit up the livid red scar which so grotesquely disfigured one side of his twisted face. The Chaplain felt some Christian pity for the Modern Languages Tutor who had to supervise this monstrosity.

"A few months ago I made the most extraordinary discovery in the library. I found a parchment manuscript, written partly in old French, interspersed with medieval Latin and occasional koine Greek. It was stuck in the middle of an uninteresting palimpsest – probably the reason it had not been spotted before. I'd date it to the first half of the twelfth century. It certainly predates Chrétien de Troyes. One really interesting thing is that there are bits of it that Chrétien must have drawn on for his *Perceval*. I've deciphered virtually all of it now. It seems to be the journal of some Crusader monk who claims to have discovered the truth of the Holy Grail. It is an extraordinary story, as gripping as anything that our honoured guest has ever devised."

The Best-Selling Author gathered himself to challenge such an outrageous statement. But the History Don got his blow in first.

"Does it fit with the facts? Does it match the contemporary chronicles, the reliable sources? Although that could hardly be accurately ascertained by a member of the Modern Languages faculty, could it?"

The History Don looked round the table for support. Cautiously the Chaplain intervened.

"Does it touch on religious matters too? I imagine it nails all the silly old heresies surrounding the grail and eternal life."

"How do you know that you have translated the Latin and the Greek correctly? Before you go making a fool of yourself and circulating your findings you had better allow me to check the manuscript over." The Classics Fellow's offer was prompted less by charity than by academic greed.

"And of course I can help you to render the translation into elegant prose," oozed the Professor of English.

Now it was the Master's turn. Perhaps his preprandial dissatisfaction with his college colleagues, his frustration at the Best-Selling Author's excuses, and the lure of the old port had encouraged greater alcoholic self-indulgence than was his wont. Or perhaps there was just something strange in the air that night. In any case, his fancy took off on an atypical flight.

"I have an idea. I think I have a solution to our problems. The manuscript, college property of course, could provide our friend here with his new plot. He will write it in his inimitable style, and share the royalties with the College. It will kick-

Chapter One

THE ROOTS THAT CLUTCH

"Hugues de Verdon semme,
Et cil est mon histoire.
Ni conte ni roman est
Quoi qu'il soit bien etrange,
Mais est un vrai histoire."

"Hugh de Verdon is my name,
and this is my story.
No tale or romance is this,
however strange it may seem;
it is a true story."

I come of a family of knights which held land near Verdun under
the Dukes of Lorraine. I was born in the year of the Lord 1077.
Or so I was told. My birth is the only event in my story which I
do not remember witnessing myself. So that much at least I have
to take on trust, and pass on to you in that spirit.

Why should I trouble to chronicle this history? Well, for a start,
I have too much time on my hands. And the important truths in
this document should not die with me, however much some might
so wish. Read this manuscript with care and discretion. So much
of my suffering stems from my own illicit reading. I would not wish
my fate on you.

I know you want me to move on quickly to tell of battlefields

*and adventure. But first I must set out some events from my early
life so that you may understand what made me the man that I am.
My male kin died when I was young. To protect me from the same
fate, my mother placed me in the great monastery of Cluny.*

✳

When I look back all those years it seemed almost that I had
two childhoods. The first was set inside the warm dark cocoon
of my mother's chamber. The loudest noise came from the
crackling of her fire, the brightest light from its flames and
their reflections dancing on the walls. I would listen with half
an ear to my mother's quiet, soothing voice, as she sat
conversing over needlework with her maids, her moist eyes,
dark with care and occasional reproach, following me round
the room as I played.

But it was the light-filled world outside that held my
attention. My ears pricked up whenever I heard horses clatter
into the yard. Silent hope turned to secret thanks when my
mother's door burst open. There stood my father, filling the
doorway, his deep-set eyes sparkling with vigorous good
humour.

"What is my boy doing in this dark roomful of women?
Does he not come of a family of knights who take their descent
from the great Emperor Charlemagne?"

I flushed with excitement, and then twinged with guilt as
I tried to ignore my mother's sighs. I knew they were directed
at me, for my ill-concealed glee, as much as at her husband,
for the interruption and his attention on son not wife. As my
father gathered me up, I tried not to flinch away from the
bristling tickle of his beard. I filled with excitement as he
rushed me outside through the great hall, threw me onto a
horse and rode off to hunt. My two elder brothers complained
bitterly that their young sibling would slow the party down

and spoil their sport. My exuberance overcame my fear of the pummelling that they would mete out to me later, as I pulled triumphant faces and stuck out my tongue at them when my father's back was turned.

I was anyway determined not to give grounds for their gripes. I was far too eager to impress and to earn my next outing. Any fear that I might have had of hurt and pain was washed away by excitement. I took many tumbles but by the time I was ten it was hard to shake me out of a saddle and I could skilfully handle a lance and a bow to kill boar and deer. This much my brothers tacitly acknowledged when their remonstrations ceased and I became a member of the party by right.

Sometimes my father and brothers went after more dangerous quarry. Called to avenge a theft, or to erase a slight, they donned their mail coats, strapped on their long swords and gripped their shields. Their brows encased in the shells of their helmets, grimly closed away behind their noseguards of steel, they set off after two-legged game, hard-faced and tense with a greater excitement. I begged to go too but was told that I was too young, that my time would come. My mother then gazed on me in unspoken reproach and when I squirmed with guilty discomfort, she turned to watch painfully until my father and my two elder brothers were out of sight.

A day arrived in late autumn, the mournful season, after the leaves but before the first bright fall of snow, when instead of hooves clattering into the yard there came the dolorous rumble of an ox cart. A servant panicked into the hall and shrilled for my mother.

"My lady, my lady, I beg you, come at once."

Catching the urgent fear in that call, she threw her needlework aside with an uncharacteristic lack of heed. All the colour had washed from her face. She passed into the court, rushing forward and slowing, then rushing forward again, as her anxiety tore at her desire to maintain the appearance of dignity. I followed forgotten behind.

My childish unconcern froze to horror at the chilling wail that broke from my mother's throat. Never had I heard such a sound. Never had I imagined that her calm composure could conceal such passion, such pain.

The cart was heaped with the broken bodies of the three familiar knights. The keening lamentation of mother and wife rose and fell as she clutched and clawed at her beloveds' remains. The carcasses were already grotesquely stiff, rigidly rejecting her caresses. Limbs jutted out at odd angles like the legs of the stags and boar we used to bring home from the hunt. My mother's howls were tossed back without sympathy by the cold walls of the courtyard. Slowly they subsided into low racking sobs.

Our family steward, hurt too, dishevelled and bloodied, struggled to lower his portly frame from his horse. The jovial expression that he always showed me was now wiped over with pain and grief. The magic arm that used to pluck tasty sweetmeats for me from behind my left ear now dangled limp and useless.

"They caught us in an ambush. First we knew was a hail of arrows from the trees. That knocked many of us down."

He paused in a grimace of pain and drew breath.

"Your sons were almost the first to fall. My lord charged forward. He always did. This time his luck deserted him. The spear went up under his mail and deep into his guts. After a rough fight we scattered them and chased them off. When I came back, I found him lying pierced on the field. We carried him back to the place where his – your – sons lay. We found one dead and already food for crows and ravens. The other was almost gone. My lord's groans were awful to hear. As your second son gave up his spirit, so he too swooned away and we heard his death rattle."

Hesitantly my mother's maids tried to pull her away. At

first she resisted angrily but then her shoulders sank in broken resignation and she allowed herself to be turned from the scene. Ignored, I stood still by the cart and gazed at those bodies which I remembered shortly before so full of life and vigour. Gripped by some macabre fascination, my hand trembled out to touch them. I felt the clamminess of death on their faces. I shuddered at my elder brother's eye sockets, one pitted and pocked by the ravens and crows which had just begun their meal, the other red and empty where the vicious beaks had pecked their fill. Something irresistible pulled my hand and forced my fingers into the slimy cavity. The other well-known faces seemed to turn on me disapproving expressions of vacant agony and fear. I span and ran, full of pity and fright, but whether for them or for myself I could not tell. There were so many unanswered questions that I had wanted to ask of my father. One thing I did know then without doubt was that my life, previously running its course so cheerfully and so predictably, had ruptured, as a fracture in the rock under a river causes a waterfall, and was now pouring in an unexpected direction.

No more hunting and hopes of knightly adventure for me; from all that I was disinherited. My grief-broken mother intended at all costs to protect me from the fate of the husband and sons she had loved so well. Her youngest, dearest child was to be a monk, safely cloistered away from danger and death. She gave grateful thanks for our kinship with Hugh de Semur, the sixth abbot of the great monastery at Cluny. She wrote to beg him to take me in as one of a small number of boys who would train from an early age to become novices and then full members of the Benedictine order. For herself, she begged leave to enter Cluny's sister convent at Marcigny.

The turn of the years 1087 and 1088 was the darkest winter I had seen. My mother wore sepulchral mourning. Ironically her hair, once jet black, began to grey and lighten as if in protest at her funereal clothes. The pools of her eyes took on infinite depths, darker and harder to fathom than the night sky, whose stars were mirrored in miniature by the pricks of light scattering through her tears. Her sorrow and her grief deadened her quiet to a conventual silence. Now the fire in the grate in her chamber seemed to smoulder and smoke rather than crackle and blaze as of old. The bursts of energy brought to my life by my father were gone. Through that winter I became wan and listless. All my zest had been stripped away.

"Dear son," my mother would say, sighing lugubriously, "you must promise me to learn well what you are taught. You must lead a life dedicated to God and to your duty. Promise me. Don't think of the life led by your father and your brothers as knights. If you follow that path you will destroy not just yourself but your poor mother as well. Your father and brothers died with blood on their hands. They received no absolution. They enjoyed no remission of their sins. We must save them from the eternal fires of hell. Without our constant prayers they will burn there forever."

And at that solemn thought her hands met, and her eyes rolled upwards in supplication. My faith was secured by the callowness of youth, so I could only agree that my mother's wishes were meet and fitting. I had been stirred by the stories of Our Lord Jesus Christ, his disciples and the old prophets told to me by my mother's fire. I almost felt proud to be asked to subsume my own hopes and ambitions into a life of monastic abstinence. I had not been allowed to protect my kin with the strength of my arm; perhaps now I could save their immortal souls through the power of my prayers.

When it was time to journey to Cluny, at least spring had come. As nature came back to life and the green leaves began to bud from their branches, so my youthful high spirits tried to push forth again. But the change in season also made me sadder that my father's lands would be left untended and barren instead of bursting with vitality.

14

As our retinue reached the abbey's double-doored entrance, my emotions seethed in a maelstrom. The excitement of my first journey drained away and the unknown life lurking behind those high walls stirred fear into my curiosity. The dark monks scared me as they worked the surrounding orchards and fields, scratching at the soil like a flock of rooks, their white faces beaking out under their black cowls. The abbey awed me; it was in itself the largest town I had seen, ringed by a thick wall broken by occasional narrow windows, with the houses of the village scattered around outside. By the wall loomed the skeleton of a building greater than I had dreamed possible, clad in wooden scaffolding. The ribbed bones of huge arches made me think of the great fish which had swallowed up holy Jonah.

The entrance was guarded by a solid gatehouse. It squatted on the walls with menace. I realised that it hunched there as much to close the inhabitants in as to keep strangers out. Above the gates was carved the Cluniac coat of arms – two large keys crossed over a single heavenwards pointing sword. It pictured to me an uncompromising message: 'Here forever you will be locked away from your childhood knightly ambition.' Fear had now conquered my curiosity, hollowing my belly and spreading through it in a thick cold soup. Our steward hammered on the gate with his left arm – for his right still hung useless, and I knew that the magic which had once delighted me was vanished for ever – calling forth at the grille a pale face which asked our business. Presumably the answer was satisfactorily provided, for the heavy oak door swung wide and my mother and I were shown to a small room at one side of the entrance.

"Welcome, my lady," said the monk in charge of the portal, "you are expected. Wait while I send for my Lord Abbot. Stay here – no woman may pass beyond the inner gate," indicating a thick door bound stoutly with black iron. I took in little of his appearance save the rough black habit and the round shaven tonsure, which made me shudder and reach up to check the soft hair on the top of my own head.

That dark room by the gate was furnished only with two hard chairs and a wooden settle. Like penitents we waited in discomfort for a while. We did not speak; what little I had to say had been already said. My mother sat very straight, watching me standing, quivering with anticipation, too tense to sit but too overawed by the stark surroundings to run about. The walls had been washed white and their only ornament was a crucifix from which Christ looked down. Thinking Jesus' expression tinged with pity, I whispered a brief inner prayer as my mother had taught me. A single shaft of sunlight shone through the narrow barred window, illuminating a funnel of dust down to a cross of shadow in a bright rectangle on the flagstone floor. As if the outside world were mocking my plight, denying my prayer, a cloud passed over the sun, closing out the beam of light and plunging the room into a gloom still deeper. Just at that moment the door swung open to reveal a tall, commanding figure. He bowed with respect to my mother, keeping his arms folded and his hands hidden deep in his habit's wide sleeves, as if he did not want to risk contact with female flesh. She stood and returned his salute with a curtsey.

"Cousin Hugh...My Lord Abbot..."

The Abbot contemplated her in silence. I wondered if he too were thinking a prayer. How could he not feel sympathy for this lady whose grief was etched so plainly in new lines over her beautiful face? And then a warm smile lit the Abbot's gaunt face.

"Yes, Lady Claire. Yes, you do have a look of your mother about you. I am now in my sixty-fifth year, so it is a long time ago, but I still remember her gentleness to me as a child in Semur at my father's court."

'At least he remembers what it was to be a child,' I thought. I gained some courage from this notion as I met his gaze as

16

firmly as I could. I felt myself transfixed, pierced through, by the Abbot's grey eyes. They carried out their examination from deep beneath unruly eyebrows. They were not unkind; indeed even in that moment of anxiety I could not mistake their humanity. Somehow, though, they seemed to read my innermost soul. Before I gave away all my secrets, I averted my face towards the floor in a gesture that I hoped showed respect, not subservience.

"Well, Hugh, we share our given name. Perhaps when we both die they will dry our bones and turn them into tools for making shoes too, eh? For that was the fate of the first Saint Hugh the shoemaker."

I felt very small and awkward and could find no response to make. I breathed a quiet sigh of relief when the Abbot turned back to my mother.

"So you wish your Hugh to become a monk? To devote his life to the service of Our Lord, disinherited? To eschew a knight's life and all worldly pleasures, just as my own mother desired for me? I wanted it as much as my mother. I was only fourteen when I renounced my title of Count and my rights to my father's lands. Then I began my novitiate. My full vows came the following year. I was unusually young – I do not know that we would allow it again. Eight or ten years are normally required to learn the ways of the abbey, and to establish that a vocation to a life in the service of Our Lord is real. A false calling only leads to corruption and sin. The rule of Blessed Saint Benedict is too strict to follow without a true vocation. Our Holy Father the Pope was himself prior here. He has now entrusted us with the duty of stamping out improper practices in our Mother Church. So we have to maintain the highest standards. I am afraid that we have many enemies who view our power with suspicion and jealousy. To withstand their attacks we must place ourselves beyond reproach. Then achieve our task we will, to the greater glory of Our Lord Jesus Christ, to whom we owe so much."

The Abbot stopped abruptly, perhaps realising that his enthusiasm was running away. It seemed to me almost that he was unaccustomed to speaking for so long.

"You must go now. Say goodbye…for the last time."

I hesitated, unsure how to behave and fearing embarrassment in front of this forbidding figure. But then emotion overcame my reticence and I threw myself into my mother's arms. I felt sure then that I would never again feel their embrace. I caught a murmur of maternal lamentation. We kissed. I fought to hold back my tears. I pulled away, hoping to see my mother's cheeks wet, but her self-control was unbroken. Then the inner gate opened. I passed through into a strange new world where the future held unknown tests and challenges. Glancing back, I saw my mother now in a swoon on the floor. I felt guilty at leaving her thus, but also strangely gladdened at last to see such a clear demonstration of affection. Before I could consider further, and before my gratitude for this proof of my mother's love could turn to shame for my own selfishness, the door shut with a firm thud.

With it closed the chapter of my childhood.

ST LAZARUS' COLLEGE

"Now do you see why I am so excited?"

The Research Assistant was perched uncomfortably in the Modern Language Tutor's untidy rooms on the only upright chair which was not piled with books and papers. The perpetrator of this mess was hiding in a greasy brown velvet wing chair, a dry martini in one hand and a half-smoked cigarette in the other. He was carefully positioned to the right of the younger man so that he did not have to see the awful mark which scarred the far side of his face. From here, he thought, the fellow looks almost human. This uncharacteristically compassionate reflection was broken by the harsh, nasal voice emanating from the object of his pity.

"It *must* have been Chrétien's *Urtext*. There are just too many similarities with *Perceval*. It can't be a coincidence. Take the death of the father and the brothers for a start, the way their eyes are pecked out by crows and ravens. Then there are the words the mother uses to address her son – *biax fix* – dear Son – and her swoon when she leaves her. Later in the manuscript you'll find that the young man's description of Blanche follows Chrétien almost word for word – sorry, the other way round I mean. I tell you, Chrétien copies the young man's description nearly verbatim. That Hugh must have been quite a poet himself, you know. Near the very end of the manuscript he describes the falling of the wounded goose in the snow with exquisite lyricism. Chrétien must have liked the image and lifted it."

The Research Assistant leaned forward, bringing the scarred side of his face into view. The Modern Languages Tutor shuddered, causing the long tail of ash on his cigarette to fall to the floor. He thought of the lower body wound suffered by the boy Hugh's father, his unasked questions, the lands going to waste. That was the Fisher King all right. Yes, perhaps the Research Assistant was on to something. His attention was dragged back again by the unpleasant nasal voice.

"I must be allowed to publish. I must. It will be the most important advance in grail scholarship for decades. It is my big chance. For once and for all the arguments about the legend's source material will be laid to rest. Forget Loomis and the others. My reputation will be made."

The Modern Languages Tutor sighed and took a last long drag on his cigarette. He drained his martini to signal the end of the interview.

"You know perfectly well that the Master will never allow it. He won't give you the manuscript back. Not for a long time after his precious bestseller is finished at any rate. I am almost as keen as you – after all I am your supervisor. My name would be on the publication in front of yours. We would share the glory. But for the time being I just don't see what we can do."

The Research Assistant's eyes widened and then narrowed, their expression of twisted surprise turning to ill-concealed hatred. He stood abruptly and left the room.

CHAPTER TWO

BETWEEN TWO LIVES

Were you patient, I could tell you much about my years at Cluny. I might detail the hardships imposed by the rules of silence, obedience and humility. At the start my faith was so strong that I could ignore those privations. But I will spare you and provide just as much of an account as you will need to follow the rest of my history. Indeed all you really need to know is that I acquired the normal skills of a monk, learning to read and write in the languages required to understand the Holy Scriptures.

That door closed me out of my childhood and into a prison of relentless routine. My mother's solemn words about the need to save my father and brothers from eternal damnation echoed and re-echoed in my head. So I prayed to God for their salvation with all the fervour that I could muster. My unquestioning faith carried me through those early years of monastic life. But even so, sometimes when I thought of my father and brothers, my mind slipped from careful prayer to careless memories of the joys that life had once offered but which were now denied to me, and had to be dragged protesting back.

Under our saintly abbot, the regime at Cluny was not

21

intentionally cruel. Only later in my life was I fated to discover and understand the real meaning, the deliberate nature of true cruelty. Hard was an better word for my life at Cluny. The timetable was hard, starting well before dawn for Nocturns, the first of eight long services on a normal day. The work was hard, whether in the gardens and fields, in the kitchen and refectory, or on the building site of the new church whose incomplete arches had fancifully echoed to me the ribs of Jonah's whale. The very fabric of the abbey was hard, right down to the thin straw-stuffed mattress at the end of the long stone dormitory on which I laid my weary body after Compline. But normally I was too tired to notice.

The communal life of the abbey permitted no privacy but created isolation. The only relationship that counted was with God. We monks might as well have been ants in a heap, workers in a common cause yes, but showing no more apparent feeling for each other than a busy insect. Our hands were our antennae, for we communicated by sign, not sound. It was unusual for me to speak to another human being above twice a week. Since that was in the confessional with the Abbot, or in his absence with the Major Prior, it could hardly count as a familic interaction. My voice's sole purpose was to praise God in prayer or song. As one of the boys in the abbey, ranking below even novices in the hierarchy, my main duty was to sing in the chapel. I gained some solace from the plaintive sound of my clear treble reverberating beneath the vaulted ceiling. But there were times when that echo brought back the horror of my mother's screams ringing around the courtyard of our old home.

Loneliness drove me to draw what pleasure I could from learning. My routine every day save Sundays and Feast Days was to attend the library with the other boys immediately after Prime and to spend the morning under the tuition of Brother Anselm, the Chief Librarian. The library held a spectacular collection of works – indeed in all my travels I would only see one better. The Holy Scripture, of course, was its cornerstone. It formed the foundation of my faith. Then there were works of history and philosophy by all the great Christian writers – Saints Augustine, Ambrose, Jerome and Gregory and the Venerable Bede. Their wisdom – the great Augustine's in particular – cemented my belief so that I thought it could never be shaken. I also read some of their earlier counterparts – Cicero, and fragments of Aristotle translated into Latin by Boethius. A few works even still survived in their original Greek; all this made a vast storehouse of knowledge to be pillaged to fill my empty young mind.

Naturally, before I could savour these delicious works I had to learn to read and to understand the languages in which they were written. This skill came quickly to me. Perhaps in some way the linguistic challenge became a conduit for my dammed-up energy. Perhaps I was unusually gifted. In any case, before long I had outstripped the other boys, even those who had been at Cluny for several years more than I. In the outside world this might have earned me respect at the price of jealousy. In the abbey's superficially unemotional atmosphere I could scarcely tell how the others felt towards me, and I scarcely bothered to care. How different to life at home, where my brothers' feelings had been communicated in an instant with a blow, a laugh, a shout or a cuff.

We used Latin of course as our daily language in chapel and in readings to avoid the confusing Babel of our different vernaculars, for the fame of Cluny attracted devotees from far and wide. Regular usage soon made the Roman language as natural to me as my Northern French. But I also culled some Greek from the fragmentary texts that survived in the library. Perhaps if I had had knowledge of how this would determine my fate in the years ahead, I would have been more cautious about acquiring this unusual scholarship.

The library soon became my favourite place. I enjoyed the relative comfort provided by the thick walls, for they kept out

23

some of the heat in summer and excluded some of the winter cold. I warmed to the yellow pools of friendly candlelight and the mysteries they created of the dark corners beyond their reach. I was soothed by the hushed turning of parchment and the scratching of quills in the scriptorium. In later life, for better or for worse, the gentle musty smell surrendered by ancient documents alongside their secrets always carried me back to those days at Cluny.

When one day flows after another with little change of routine, when a week, a month, a year drifts sluggishly by, an unusual event stands out like a great rock rearing up from a quiet river. So it was when I received a summons from the Abbot. Unaccustomed emotions – surprise, interest, curiosity – ran across the face of the monk who signed me the message. I felt the same expressions skating over my own, pursued by nervous apprehension. Pressing my clammy palms tightly together to prevent them shaking, I examined my conscience, but could think of no sin deserving of punishment. I hurried to the spartan room that served the holy head of my order as bedchamber and study. Outside the oak door I paused to compose myself and to steady my breathing. Then I knocked.

Inside I heard a single word. I pushed the door open and found myself caught in the Abbot's piercing gaze. I felt him measuring me, perhaps against his memory of the boy he had welcomed three years before. I wondered what he saw in my face. He had the better of me, for I had caught only indistinct glimpses of a pale oval reflection in the abbey fish pool, or stretched and bent in the silver chalices that I polished in the sacristy. I felt a sudden flash of resentment that I could not even know my own appearance. Then the Abbot's face brightened in a gentle smile. Whatever he had seen in me must have pleased him. Warm compassion emanated towards me, and I relaxed. He made the Sign of the Cross in blessing and soothed me with his tone of ethereal spirituality, so familiar from the confessional.

"Brother Hugh, I find it hard to believe that you have now been with us for three full years. You have learnt so much in that time. I can only say that your progress has been exemplary."

I stood straighter in pleasure and surprise. The Abbot's smile broadened.

"Indeed, Brother Anselm tells me not just of your talents in Latin. He says that your mastery of Greek is now unequalled in the abbey – praise indeed from a monk as learned as he in an ancient scholarship, and one so nearly lost to us. I hear your knowledge of the Scriptures and many important Commentaries is excellent too. Brother Anselm has asked me to appoint you as his junior assistant. I told him I would be pleased to accede to his request, so long as he would spare me some of your time to perform occasional secretarial duties for me. Well done. Your mother would indeed be proud of you."

I remembered the rule of humility and fought to cover my rising pride. Still, I could do nothing to hold back the warmth that flushed up my neck. The Abbot seemed to read my mind.

"Your satisfaction is natural. But you must remember that your achievement has only been made possible by God's grace. Remember the parable of the talents. Continue to put to work the skills that Our Lord has given to you for His greater glory."

My pride now dampened, I signed my thanks and backed out of the room.

As junior assistant to Brother Anselm, one of my new tasks was to find texts requested by monks for their reading. Occasionally, with the Librarian's approval, I might even recommend works to them. This created for me the opportunity – indeed the duty – to improve my own knowledge of the full contents of the library, and to extend my own reading material. I began to use this privilege to follow through lines of argument in one work back to the philosopher who had provoked the original controversy. So from Saint

Augustine's treatise *De libero arbitrio* about free choice and the origin of evil, I was able to reach back to the work which prompted it – the *Enneads* of Plotinus. Thus I learned that Saint Augustine's view that the weakness of the soul formed the root of all evil had emerged as a counter-argument to Plotinus's opinion that wickedness began in matter. Each scholar put a powerful case. I could of course not doubt the great Augustine, but I did gain the first glimmerings of understanding that a different point of view might be arguable. I realised that perhaps if I had been able to read Pelagius's lost works in the original – lost I assumed because they were nowhere to be found in the great library – rather than just Saint Augustine's refutation of those views – I might have wrestled still more with those awkward contradictions in the Augustinian belief that Man possessed free will in spite of God's omniscience.

Concerns thus began to creep into my awakening mind. Once unshakeable certainties came under threat. I longed to express my disquiet in the confessional with Abbot Hugh. Week after week I attended my interview with him determined to pour out my worries. Then I looked up at his ascetic profile as he knelt in front of me, and was unable to summon the courage to do so. Instead I resorted to muttering banalities about how I had allowed my mind to wander in chapel, or been unable to control my greed by longing for an extra helping of soup at supper. Afterwards I would go away more troubled than ever, my discomfort now mixed with dissatisfaction at my own timidity and lack of frankness.

Little by little, as I carried out more secretarial work for the Abbot, our relationship tightened. Eventually the day came when my courage did not fail me and my doubts poured out.

"My Father Abbot, my mind is troubled. Saint Augustine tells us to greatly cherish intellect. He says we should apply reason to our faith. Yet when I do so I get confused. There are so many conflicting arguments. If God is all-powerful and all-knowing, why does he allow evil in the world? How can I have free will of my own if God knows what I am going to do before I have even done it?"

Lesser men might have belittled my worries and told me brusquely to limit the range of my reading. But I thought I detected in my Father Confessor's sighs that my own adolescent intellectual stirrings were not totally unfamiliar to him. He turned his wise eyes towards me and this time I was able to meet and hold his penetrating gaze.

"Hugh, my son, philosophy is no substitute for faith. It never can be. The true love of God counts for more than all the metaphysical hair-splitting in the world. Remember... remember that there is no absolute truth outside the Holy Scripture. Even the wisest commentator falls far, far short of the all-encompassing wisdom of God. Read and believe. Do not always expect to understand."

For a while I gained comfort from the absolute security of his belief. And I think that the Abbot was satisfied that he had been able to return my searching mind to the straight and narrow path, and that I had moved on along it. The tenor of our confessional reverted to the uneventful. He entrusted me with still more secretarial work and ended the sharp looks of concern that once shot from under his bushy eyebrows to discomfit me with their searching diagnosis of my spiritual health.

And indeed I had moved on. In the library I had discovered reading material of a quite different nature. One of my duties was to take books from the shelves one by one, to dust them off and clean them carefully before replacing them. My cycle brought me to a forgotten row which was seldom visited, to judge by the thickness of the dust lying there. I tut-tutted to myself under my breath as I took the obscure volumes carefully down, nevertheless throwing up enough of a cloud to make myself choke. As I stifled my coughs, hoping that I had not disturbed my brothers in the library, I noticed that there was another row of volumes tucked behind the first. They were considerably smaller in size. I assumed that they had been placed there to save space. With idle interest at my discovery I pulled one off the shelf and wiped the dust from its cover. I opened it and inside I made out the title '*P. Ovidi Nasonis – Metamorphoses*'. Curious, I rolled around my tongue those unforgettable opening lines:

> *In nova fert animus mutates dicere formas*
> *corpora; di, coeptis (nam vos mutastis et illas)*
> *adspirate meis primaque ab origine mundi*
> *ad mea perpetual deducite tempora carmen!*
>
> *My soul bids me sing of body shapes transformed;*
> *O Gods, you wrought those changes, now shape*
> *my task with inspiration and spin out my song*
> *from creation onwards to my modern times!*

The magic of the ancient gods transported me in a flash to another world. A window opened in the dull grey walls that enclosed me, revealing a thrilling universe bursting with colour. Shaking with excitement and sudden guilt I pushed the book back onto the shelf and hid it again in its double rank. I hardly knew that I had returned to my desk. Librarian Anselm signed a question toward me.

"Brother, do you have a fever?"

I struggled to pull myself back into the real world. For sure I did feel feverish, hot and cold at the same time. I composed my trembling hands enough to indicate in response that a long night of prayer had left me tired and weak. But I just boiled in an irresistible frenzy to read the book that I had found. I wrestled with the problem of how to take it unseen out of the library, utterly ignoring the dreadful consequences of discovery.

One of my other duties as Brother Anselm's junior assistant was to identify damaged works among the delicate volumes

28

in the library. Mostly of course these were parchment, but there were also ancient fragments written in strange scripts on papyrus. I was meant to take them to Brother Anselm for his view about whether they could be repaired, or whether they should be erased and reused as palimpsest. A week or so before I had happened to note that many of the pages of a copy of Saint Victorinus's *Commentary on the Apocalypse of Saint John* had been damaged by moisture and mice. I remembered the occasion especially clearly because an old hole-riddled sheet fell from the volume as I opened it. At first I had been startled lest my lack of care had caused a page to fall loose from its binding. But on bending down to pick up the leaf I had noticed that it was quite different. It was grainy, of papyrus, not smooth like parchment, and covered in a distinctive Greek script – in ink of an unusual colour – the colour of dried blood. Indeed, at the time I had wondered whimsically whether some ancient scribe, in desperate need, had plundered his own veins for his writing material. Then the thought passed, as I was called away to another duty, and I had tucked the sheet back firmly inside the cover.

Now I sought out Saint Victorinus again. To salve my conscience I carefully checked that the volume was well beyond repair. Surreptitiously I removed enough pages to accommodate the slimmer volume of Ovid. I returned to my shelf of temptation while Brother Anselm was otherwise occupied. With shaking hands I reached down my forbidden fruit and concealed it between Saint Victorinus's sympathetic covers. Shocked by my own audacity, I returned to my desk and struggled to sit there until it was time to leave the library. Then I tucked Saint Victorinus under my arm in the normal way. Nobody suspected its cargo of treasure.

My temptation and fall happened in March. I remember the season well, because I recall my impatience as I longed for the daylight hours to lengthen and to extend the time I could read without the help of a candle. During those months

29

of spring and early summer I worked my way through Ovid and other great classics that I found on the shelf beside *Metamorphoses* – the *Iliad* in Baebius Italicus's Latin translation and the *Aeneid*. I had never dreamed that such literature could exist, and even less imagined that a dry book could contain a world so vivid and so exciting. While the flowers in the abbey garden burst open and fruited through that hot summer, so my mind erupted with bright, vibrant colours and bold, violent figures. As my imagination ran riot, all the romantic urges of my pre-monastic boyhood were rekindled. My fear of discovery just sharpened my feverish excitement.

Brother Anselm, kindly and considerate towards me, began to worry more and more about my health. I suppose I must have become paler and paler as the hours when I should have been sleeping were given over to taboo literature. I struggled to dissemble and to stay awake in the library. Then, one fateful morning after a wakeful night given over to *Metamorphoses*, whose humour, passion and extraordinary heroes, heroines and villains had made it my fast favourite, I nodded off at my desk. My dreams of Jason and Medea were shattered by Brother Anselm's solicitous touch on the shoulder. Concern crackled between us – mine lest my catnap had betrayed me, Anselm's for the well-being of the assistant he had chosen. Puzzled to see such an undistinguished commentary as Saint Victorinus still on my desk after many weeks, the Librarian made to pick up the volume. I stood up, desperately wondering how to divert his attention. I signed that I had finished with the apocalyptic commentary and was about to return it to the shelves. Smiling, Anselm indicated that he would gladly perform that simple task for me. We both tried to pick up the heavy book together, and as we fumbled, the smaller concealed volume tumbled to the floor. My nerves exaggerated its thump, which seemed to echo round the library with unnatural noise. Brother Anselm stared at me with surprised inquiry and gathered up the incriminating evidence before I could move. He opened the cover and recoiled in horror when he read there what he held. His kindness melted into hot rage as he seized me by the elbow, marching me off without more ado, to be interviewed by the Abbot.

Whenever I think back, even after all that has happened to me in the intervening years, I still squirm and cringe at the memory of that audience. Brother Anselm's jowled face, normally so friendly and well-intentioned towards me, was now wobbling with purple fury. His outrage was such that he forgot to sign and stammered out loud to the Abbot an explanation of what had happened. I prepared myself for an outburst. Instead the Abbot quietly turned to me and asked if the Librarian's report were true. I hung my head in acquiescent shame. The Abbot then signed to Brother Anselm to leave the room. I quietly thanked God that my reprimand would at least be delivered in private.

My gratitude was driven away by the horror of the expression turned upon me by the Abbot – an expression that I still remember with absolute clarity – an expression not of anger, but just of the deepest disappointment tinged with compassion.

"Hugh, my son, Hugh. You have let yourself down. You have let me down too and have betrayed my trust. You have betrayed your mother and her love for you. Imagine how she would feel if she knew what you had done. Worst of all though, you have betrayed Our Lord Jesus Christ. I had thought that our philosophical discussions in the confessional had come to an end because you had found the straight and narrow path. I thought that you had conquered your doubts. It had even occurred to me that you might be ready to end your novitiate and take your full vows. But now I see that you have been led far, far astray. Your young mind has been filled with poison. There may be no antidote. You see, some books contain such wickedness that they corrupt minds. Few are immune – only those that are fully formed and resolute in Christ. Some books

31

purport to contain knowledge but hold only lies. There are even false Gospels which must be destroyed so that none might read their heresies. This book you have been reading will also be consigned to the flames. No-one else shall be tempted towards hellfire by its contents. Better that it should burn than a soul. And the library will be scoured for any other profanities. They will meet the same fate."

I started, filling with shocked dismay that such precious writings might be wiped forever from human knowledge. For the first time I understood that even a holy man – even this abbot who was the closest thing to a father that I now had – might seek to erase information which did not support his own beliefs. But my unspoken protest died on the sharp point of the Abbot's stare.

"If there is a cure for your pollution it will be long and painful. I have no alternative but to punish you severely. You will receive thirty-six blows of the rod in front of the whole chapter. When you are recovered, you will stand at the furthest end of the nave during each holy office from now to Michaelmas holding in your outstretched arms a copy of the Holy Scriptures – the only book, by the way, that you will in future be permitted to read."

The Abbot's expression relaxed a little. "You have been helpful to me. I have grown fond of you. I will pray for your return to grace."

Tears clouded my eyes until I could scarcely see. I stumbled from the room to pour them out in private. That interview was the worst part of my punishment, worse even than the acute pain of the rod, worse than my humiliation in front of the other monks, and worse than the tiresome week of recovery lying flat on my face in the infirmary while the wounds knitted across my tattered buttocks. It was worse than the hours every day holding the heavy book during all eight holy offices as the weather grew colder through autumn and winter and the icy wind whistled beneath the west door of the chapel around my legs and under my habit. Physically perhaps I benefited, becoming more resilient, more tolerant of pain, and gaining in strength and stamina. Perhaps, for my determination to bear my punishment without complaint, I regained some silent respect from my fellows, several of whom I saw had been far from disappointed by my fall from grace. Throughout those long months I stood at the chapel door as straight as the rod which had left me with scars that I still bear today.

ST LAZARUS' COLLEGE

The Classics Fellow was in an unusually good mood as he warmed himself at the Senior Common Room fire before dinner.

"Well I must say. I like that chapter. The trouble I have in getting my idle students to read *Metamorphoses*! And here is a fine chap actually falling in love with it. I had never heard of someone being flogged for actually reading Ovid, but by God I'd like to be able to flog them for failing to do so!"

The History Don did not share the Classics Fellow's humour.

"Well I don't like it at all. I want to see more facts in the story. How do we know Cluny's precise bibliotheca? The collection was scattered when the abbey was destroyed seven centuries later in the French Revolution. Scant records remain. Why can't we have some more description of what it was like to be a monk at the end of the eleventh century? You skate over the daily routine of the abbey but include various details that are frankly irrelevant."

This last comment was addressed at the Best-Selling Author, who had come up to deliver his latest chapters for inspection and was in a jovial mood thanks to the rapid progress of his story and his third glass of sherry.

"Don't worry, old fellow," he said. "Readers find too much of that monk stuff pretty dull. They want to get on to the battles and romance. But there is a lot of history coming in the next chapter. I promise you. And it will all be very accurate; even the description of the weather is validated by the contemporary chronicles. And the meaning of the bits of information you may think irrelevant will be revealed later on in the story – that blood ink papyrus for example. At this early stage in the book I'm just seeding the plot. We writers call it exposition." And he roared with laughter.

The Professor of English nodded his head sagely. "Exposition. Yes indeed. That's very good. But perhaps you'd let me polish some of your prose later on. I did like the pun about Saint Victor-in-us."

Now it was the Chaplain's turn to bridle with pious indignation. "Pun? What do you mean, pun? Saint Victorinus actually existed. His *Commentary on the Apocalypse of Saint John* really is quite interesting ."

The Research Assistant sat silent in a dark corner, a murderous expression on his twisted face, oozing bitterness at the theft of his precious manuscript and its perversion in the filthy cause of lucre.

CHAPTER THREE

WAITING FOR A KNOCK UPON THE DOOR

I did not forget my reading, nor the scholarship I had acquired. Hard lessons are sometimes the best remembered. That much at least they could not take away from me. My desperation rose – to break loose, to find a place where I could hear laughter, and laugh myself.

The eternal cycle turned through winter and spring, summer and autumn, and back to winter again. I was uncertain if I would have slowed it down if I could, to prevent the waste of my youth, or speeded it up in the hope that fate might have something better in store.

So I reached the beginning of that extraordinary year 1095, seventeen, unhappy and disillusioned. The New Year announced itself in startling fashion. As we monks left Compline on the very first day of January, the night sky was lit by a violent shower of meteors and shooting stars. I ignored the cold to stop in the wintry dark and to gawp at the spectacle. Crackling sheets of green and purple light unfolded on the northern horizon, lending the faces of my brother monks a ghostly hue. How appropriate, I remember thinking, for these creatures are indeed half-dead, scarcely living their lives.

The spectacle continued for hours. This was unquestionably a portent, a sign of great events to come in the year ahead. I sorrowed that they were events in which I could but hope to be involved. What is more, this unusual heavenly activity continued as the months went by. As well as meteor showers and those strangely coloured fires in the north, many bright comets moved across the sky, putting in my mind the holy star which marked the birth of Our Lord Jesus Christ and led the wise Magi to His stable. My bitterness at missing great events grew with each manifestation.

A week into January I was on duty in the kitchens, serving a small group of tattered travellers who had come to seek overnight refuge from the vile weather. Many pilgrims passed through, some coming specifically to pray at Cluny. Others were *en route* to different destinations. The rule of silence did not apply to these visitors, who took their meals in a small chamber at the side of the great room where we ate. The glimpses of the outside world afforded by the travellers' conversations gave me a Jacob's ladder to a happier place. For a time my oppression was lifted by their tales, especially as meals progressed and the pilgrims' loquacity was fuelled by the rich abbey wine. So I looked forward to nothing more than the occasion every three months or so when my turn came to serve them. In winter this was particularly welcome, for the visitors' room was far smaller than our great refectory and better heated by a warm fire, offering temporary escape from the frigid conditions in the larger hall.

On this occasion the focus of attention in the group of five travellers was a small grizzled man with close cropped hair and leathery sun-darkened skin. I started with excitement when I heard the word 'Jerusalem' and gathered that the fellow had recently returned from a pilgrimage to the Holy Sepulchre itself. I hovered round the table, dragging out my tasks, anxious to hear as much of the conversation as I could.

"It was a miracle that we reached the port of Acre on that rat-infested floating sieve. But then we still had over a hundred leagues to cover to the Holy City. We walked mostly at night and rested during the day, because of the heat. And for fear of the infidel. We found precious little to drink and less to eat. Several of our group were unable to make it, let me tell you."

He paused and looked round the table to make sure that he held the attention of all his companions. I saw that like me they were hanging on his words. Satisfied, the storyteller continued, his fluency indicating that he had told his tale many times before.

"We just had to leave them where they fell by the road, for the dogs and beasts. Poor bastards. It was a far cry from years gone by. Apparently then even the damned Musselman might give help and succour to Christian pilgrims. At last, after five weary nights' march, we saw the blessed sight. The Holy City's massive walls were silhouetted against the sun rising beyond in the East – one of the finest sights in all the world, that was. I wish I could say in all Christendom. How we thanked God, for I do not believe we could have managed much more. Then we got lucky. The sentries must have still been half asleep, because we were able to enter by King David's Gate when it opened. Then we made our way to the Church of the Holy Sepulchre, praise be to God. But that was where our troubles really began. We'd just knelt down to pray when we were dragged out by some of those dark heathen bastards. They robbed us and beat us half dead. We were kicked out of the city to bind our wounds and fend for ourselves. I can tell you we were lucky to make it back...those few of us who did."

The storyteller paused to take another gulp from his goblet and I reluctantly moved back towards the kitchen with some empty dishes. By the time I got back, the talk had moved on, but for the next days my head swirled with indignant rage at the desecration of the holy places and the Moslems' cruel treatment of Christian visitors, and filled with notions of making that sacred journey myself. I constructed wild escape plans in my head, thinking of joining up with a group of pilgrims as they travelled on from the abbey, before rejecting such ideas as forlorn, for who would risk the wrath of Cluny by taking with them a renegade novice?

As the year progressed it became clear to those of us working in the abbey fields that the harvest was going to be one of the worst in living memory. April is the cruellest month for nature to rebel, and that spring was marked by days of burning sun soon after the crops had begun to sprout, shrivelling them in the ground, only for the dull roots that remained to be surprised by torrential summer rains that washed away what was left. I prayed with the others for mercy as best I could, but in my heart I knew that my prayers would go unanswered. Surely God was showing His displeasure to us and indicating His wish for His children to avenge the insult given to the places where His Holy Son was made man, had suffered and died for all sinners?

The Abbot returned to Cluny during the course of that burning spring, his latest effort of diplomacy to reconcile Pope and Emperor successful for a while. My spirits lifted a little at the news imparted in the first of the daily addresses that he was accustomed to give to us in the chapter house when he was resident at the abbey.

"My brothers, it saddens me that I have been away from you for so long, but I cannot shun the duties entrusted to me by our Holy Mother Church. Many of you will remember our Holy Father Pope Urban II as Prior Odo de Lagery, when he was a much-loved and trusted member of our humble community here, before he was called away seventeen years ago to serve the Church in Rome. Well, he now intends to pay us the signal honour of visiting in the month of October. He will lead the consecration of our new high altar and will spend a week with us here in prayer and contemplation in preparation for a great council of the Church to be held at Clermont in November."

Such was the excitement aroused by this news that a collective murmur echoed around the vault, before it was stilled by a sharp look from the Abbot.

Abbot Hugh's return also meant that he took charge again of my spiritual well-being. I feared that I would not be able to hide my inner turmoil for long from my Father Confessor's uncanny perception and sensitivity, however bland the words that I placed after the formulaic "Bless me Father Abbot, for I have sinned…" And sure enough, some time toward the middle of that turbid summer, I found myself having another conversation about the future course of my life.

"Hugh, my son," the Abbot said, as I fidgeted under that keen bushy-browed gaze, "I can tell that you are unsettled and uneasy with yourself. You perform your duties well. You present an exterior of humility and obedience, as is meet and fitting. But you are not as frank or open in the confessional with me as you were once. You no longer ask me any questions. Remember that your interior feelings, your innermost self, can be read by God as if written in a book. You are disappointing Him by not revealing them openly to your Father Confessor."

I bowed my head, shamed again by this gentle wisdom. The worries that I had tried to hide away came tumbling out as if an overfilled store had burst open.

"My Father Abbot, I am plagued by doubts about my vocation. I am unworthy, unsuited to complete my novitiate. How can I take my vows to serve God in this monastery? I pray. I read the Bible. I meditate. I try so hard to conquer my inner demons but my inability to put them from me must show how deep the Devil is within. I am seized with a violent restlessness, with a desperate incertitude which shakes the very foundation of my faith. I remember so well the words you spoke the first day I had the honour to meet you. I remember what you said about the need before I took my vows to establish that my vocation was real. You said that a false calling leads to corruption and sin."

My voice began to shake with sorrow and frustration and tailed off into silence.

"Hugh, I remember that day well too, and the words that I spoke. I also remember your mother's desire for you to enter our humble community and to spend your life in prayer."

He sighed.

"I must tell you something. I am sorry, for it is sad. From our sister convent at Marcigny I have just received news that your mother is dead. She suffered a long and painful illness. But she overcame her suffering. She prayed until the end with fortitude and grace. She touched that whole community with her true love of God. May He rest her soul in peace. There is only one place that a woman of her goodness can now be. Surely you cannot desire to let her down and fail to fulfil her dearest wish?"

I turned away to hide unstoppable tears. I knew that the Abbot would watch with compassion the pain of a son at the loss of his mother. But I did not want him to guess that I was in fact quivering with guilt as well as grief as I realised how long it had been since I had given my mother serious thought, except occasionally to resent her role in imprisoning me at Cluny.

Gently the Abbot's voice continued, "I want to keep you close by me. Over this coming time, with preparations practical and spiritual to be made for our former prior's papal visit, and for the great council that will follow, I will again need to make use of your services as secretary. I hope you have not forgotten all the skills you learnt in the library."

Here his voice lightened and I looked up to see the ghost of a smile whispering across his face.

"Yes. I shall want you to accompany me to Clermont. I am determined that you should rediscover your vocation.

I want you to fulfil your mother's ambition and learn to become a steady member of our community. Perhaps when you have seen the perils and privations of the world outside you will find it easier to accept the permanent shelter of these walls."

I was only partly restored by my abbot's wise words. I still felt trapped by what was expected of me, and blocked away from what I wanted to do. My restless desire to escape was aggravated as much as soothed by the shame my mother's memory had awoken. But at least I had new duties to enliven my routine.

As the papal visit approached, the whole rhythm of the abbey became more urgent. Our monastic lives momentarily beat with a stronger pulse. The summer rains gave way to a glorious autumn and the beech trees exchanged their green for a stately golden brown as if in Pope Urban's honour.

At last the great day arrived. We all lined up outside Cluny's double gates beside the west end of the vast church which had been the focus of so much effort for so many years. I felt pride – and tried less to suppress it than once I might have – but also trepidation – to be standing two paces behind the Abbot in my position as his secretary. Then my excitement rose with the dust in the distance. It must be thrown up by the papal retinue, I thought. A few minutes more and I could make out a company of archers uniformed in red and gold, their crossbows slanted over their shoulders. They were followed by a splendid litter slung between two richly caparisoned white mules. On all four sides its scarlet canopy was embroidered with crossed keys in gold and silver. A flock of dignitaries rode alongside the litter, foremost amongst them two cardinals, recognisable by their crimson hats and robes.

As the procession came to a halt, the Abbot raised his hand and dropped it again. At his signal we fell to our knees with military precision. What a shame, I thought, that the Holy Father could not see our display from behind his silken curtain.

Then the canopy was drawn back and Pope Urban II climbed slowly down. He looked a little shaky from the litter's rollicking ride but nevertheless indicated impatiently to his attendants that he did not need the assistance of their outstretched arms. Then the Abbot stepped forward in greeting. The Pope grandly extended his hand, heavy with the gold ring of the fisherman on its first finger. The Abbot knelt to give his kiss of respect, and I realised that it was the first time that I had seen him meet a superior. For once showing his seventy years, he struggled to rise back to his feet. In a gesture which might have projected compassion had it been made with less grandeur, Pope Urban took the Abbot's arm to help him up, before embracing him and exchanging kisses.

"The knees, you know, Holy Father," Abbot Hugh smiled wryly, "they have been bent and unbent a few times too many in the service of Our Lord."

Urban smiled back, looking flattered by the respect discernible beneath this effusion of affection. My heart swelled in that fine moment at the sight of the two strongest pillars of our Mother Church regarding each other outside the largest and finest house of God in Christendom. Both were tall men; I judged that in his youth the Abbot had perhaps been the taller, but the twenty extra years that he carried had reduced his advantage, and now they stood eye to eye. I studied with interest the papal face, and saw plump round cheeks under its neatly trimmed beard. I imagined the Pope experiencing the same discomfort that I felt under the Abbot's clear grey gaze. Anyway, he looked away, pursing into a smile his full purple lips which perhaps attested to the luxuries of Rome.

"I see some little changes since I last was here. Your masons have been busy, I judge. I cannot wait to see inside this great edifice that you have erected to the everlasting glory of God."

Pope and Abbot moved towards the thick oak doors in the austere monumental façade.

"Cluny remains as old-fashioned as ever, I see. None of these new arches *en ogive* for you."

It was the Abbot's turn for a smile, but one which displayed humility and self-deprecation.

"When I have seen them on my travels, I have always felt that there was something aggressive about those sharp ends pointing up at Our Lord in Heaven. I preferred to show Him a smooth round shape, more fitting and more respectful. I wished to glorify God, not indulge the pride of our masons by encouraging them to show off unnecessary new tricks."

"But you have been modern enough to put glass in your windows, I see. You don't find that too new-fangled?"

I wondered why the Pontiff was looking for things to criticise in our fine new church, but the Abbot's gentle smile did not waver.

"Yes, Holy Father, but I feel that does serve the useful purpose of keeping God's weather out of His house whilst letting in His light. And the colours the glaziers have been able to achieve, whilst not quite as bright as I would like, do add to the splendour and so to His glory."

The service to dedicate and consecrate the high altar of the abbey church took place the following day, led by Pope Urban in his three-tiered crown. It was solemn but joyful, dignified yet elated, and towards the front of the congregation I felt more contentment than for a long while. Or perhaps that feeling was prompted by the rapid approach of my trip to Clermont. Against the colours of the painted walls and ceiling, the glowing windows and the magnificent vestments of the papal celebrant and his party, was set the contrast of our black habits, the lungs beneath swelling to fill the choir and nave with glorious plainchant. Many of my brothers' faces were wet with real tears, washed with the emotion released by the end of their long labours. For them this service was the finale to a long crescendo, a fortissimo in their monastic lives which would never be repeated. I feared that unless I could find a way out, it might be the climax of my own life too. I shuddered at the thought of such a wasted existence.

As Abbot Hugh's secretary, I was fortunate enough to be among those silently and discreetly present at many of the discussions that took place between the two men over the course of the Pope's stay in his old abbey. One I must record here.

"Hugh, my old friend," – I jumped to hear the Holy Father speak my name, relaxing again as I realised that it was not me whom he addressed – "you have always been a true guide and a mentor to me. Ever since my days in your house as prior. My role now is a lonely one. I welcome this opportunity to seek your views. At my Council of Piacenza, just this last March, I received ambassadors from the Greek Emperor Alexios. They brought me gifts – the usual fine Byzantine silks and gold, and some carefully chosen holy books which now grace my library in Rome. They also brought a fragment of the True Cross in a magnificent reliquary. I have had it placed behind the altar in Saint Peter's. The Eastern Empire is hard pressed, beset by enemies; the splendour of these gifts reflects the level of Emperor Alexios's concern. The Turk holds Nicaea, the very city where our '*Credo in unum Deo*' was defined. That is only a few leagues from the gates of Constantinople itself. Emperor Alexios already has many Frankish soldiers in his service and has been impressed by their loyalty and bravery. Now he wants more to drive back the infidel and to secure his eastern borders. He wants the help of the Papacy..."

"...to become his recruiting sergeant..." murmured the Abbot beneath his breath.

"For my part," the Pope grandly continued, "one of my greatest sorrows and regrets is to see the sacred places of the Holy Land in the hands of the unbeliever. Our resolute pilgrims now risk being set upon, abused and as like as not killed before they can complete the most sacred journey to the Holy Sepulchre. To be sure, many years have passed since the city of Jerusalem was in our Christian hands. But at least until the Seljuk Turks threw the Fatimids back to Egypt our pilgrims had free and open access to the holy places.

"I also look with deep sadness on the state of affairs here, in my homeland. Here the only law that rules is force. Christian knight fights Christian knight. The common folk live in penury and constant fear of violent death. Perhaps, when so much of our Christian society is in breach of five of the Ten Holy Commandments at once, it is no surprise that God has allowed our enemies to deny the Holy Land to us.

"And even Christian princes fight and squabble with each other. I and my worthy predecessors – God rest their holy souls – have had our differences with the German Emperor, whose ancestors from Charlemagne onwards were once some of the strongest protectors of our Church.

"You know that well, for you have helped me much to calm those disputes with Henry your godson. You have helped him to see how wrong he is to try to curtail my power."

Here the Abbot bowed his head. Urban saw this as an acknowledgement of such gracious papal words. I knew the Abbot well enough to interpret his gesture differently. I could see that he sought to hide his growing discomfort and his disagreement with the Pope's egocentric assessment of the rights and wrongs in his dispute with the Emperor.

"But my lands are still at threat from those turbulent Normans, Bohemond and the rest of the litter of that fox Robert Guiscard. Here I have common cause with Alexios, for they also eye his Dalmatian possessions.

"That is a common cause, but the sees of Rome and Constantinople are less at one than I would like. Rome is not fully acknowledged as 'caput et mater' – head and mother of the Church – by the eastern bishops. The damaging differences of doctrine and practice persist."

Pope Urban had become steadily more urgent and animated

as his discourse had progressed, exciting himself with his own fine words. Now, unable to contain himself any longer, he stood up and started pacing the room. My abbot stood too but the Pope waved him back to his chair.

"I have given these challenges much thought. I have prayed for guidance and God has now shown me the way forward. At Clermont I will announce a great holy war. It will be a war of the Cross, a Crusade. The goal of my Crusade will be the holy city of Jerusalem itself – we will take Jerusalem and once again it will be a Christian city. All the knights and common soldiers who take the Cross will receive from me a dispensation from their sins. Any who die on Crusade will be guaranteed a place in the Kingdom of Heaven. Instead of fighting each other their energies and martial valour will be channelled to the service of Our Lord. Emperor Alexios will receive the succour he seeks. Our full authority will be re-established over the eastern sees of the Church. The position of the Church and the Papacy at the head of the unified army of Christ will be unassailable."

I thrilled with excitement at these fine words, ready to take the Cross and set off to Jerusalem myself. I looked at Pope Urban with renewed respect. He stopped pacing and turned triumphantly to face the Abbot, expecting to see a display of enthusiasm for his brilliant policy. But in fact he encountered a very different reaction – a weary, sorrowful resignation – which made the older man look fully his age.

"Odo, my old friend…" A frisson passed round the room. Never before had I heard the Abbot forget himself with such a breach of protocol.

He corrected himself, bowing deeply, "My most Holy Father, please forgive my indiscretion…"

Pope Urban signalled that he had taken no offence and the Abbot continued, his voice lower, quieter, more spiritual than the Pontiff's temporal eloquence.

"I have seen at close hand – on my journeys to Leon and

Castille – the harm and damage wrought by so-called holy war. Of course Cluny has benefited greatly from the martial successes of old King Ferdinand and his noble son Alfonso – our great church would not have been built without the census they pay from the wealth they have wrested back from the Moslems – but at the cost of much suffering. Our religion is not about this world but about the next. Our Lord Jesus Christ taught us to turn the other cheek. He chided your first antecedent Peter who so rashly struck out and severed the ear of the high priest's servant. He chose to defeat His enemies by rising from the dead, not by preventing His own death in this world. The sixth commandment is unequivocal – it says 'thou shalt not kill' – it does not say 'thou shalt not kill save in a just cause'. With the greatest respect, I must question the righteousness of achieving even worthy goals in this world with promises of salvation in the next. The prayers of my monks are the purer the further they are removed from the actions of the world; the worthier, the closer they are to holy manifestations."

Pope Urban had meanwhile returned to his seat, and he now covered his irritation by reaching out towards a bowl placed on the table between himself and the Abbot which was filled with some of the recent harvest from the Cluny vines. Seeing a shadow flit over his host's face, he pulled his hand away and commented dryly, "Yes, I still struggle with my passion for grapes."

"So is it with me and fish. We all have our weaknesses."

Urban acknowledged this flash of old friendship, but did not look warmed by it, and returned to the serious conversation.

"My Lord Abbot, your response does not surprise me. You have always been otherworldly. I remember when I had to chide you for accepting Hugh of Burgundy as a member of your community here, leaving a hundred thousand Christians without a protector. It is well that you are Abbot of Cluny and that I am Pope in Rome – we are best suited that way. I have to take temporal as well as spiritual considerations into account. Thank you for your advice – I will pray further and meditate. I ask you and your monks to beseech God that I reach the right decision – but my heart tells me that I should stick to my course."

Abbot Hugh silently bowed his head in a dutiful gesture but sadness and disappointment sketched the line of his shoulders.

The papal party left the abbey the following day, and gradually the level of excitement amongst my fellow monks subsided as their ant-life returned to its dull routine. My excitement however moved towards fever pitch as the time for my journey approached. Our preparations were simple. Apart from me, the Abbot took two servants. We were all mounted on mules, and our meagre provisions were packed on a fifth. Our black habits and lack of baggage plainly announced that there would be no rich pickings for any brigands from this group of travellers, and even in those troubled times we could be reasonably sure that we would pass unmolested.

To reach Clermont from Cluny, you travel west to pick up the headwaters of the great River Loire. These we followed briefly before cutting southwards towards the brooding craters of the Auvergne, which I thought of later as ominous symbols of the eruption that the Council of Clermont was to provoke. Now, though, I was elated to be riding, uncloistered at last, for the first time in six years out of sight of the walls of Cluny. My muscles long unaccustomed to gripping a saddle, I would struggle stiffly down from my mule at the end of our day's ride, causing my abbot to comment with gentle mirth that his old legs seemed more supple than mine.

At Clermont was situated one of the many Benedictine priories affiliated to Cluny. There we lodged, a short walk from the cathedral. Its prior made a great fuss of the Abbot, in spite

49

of his efforts to have himself treated like any normal traveller, and I enjoyed basking in his reflected glory.

The first six days of the council's dry church business were of no interest to me, and I can scarcely remember what was discussed. My whole attention was absorbed by the exciting hubbub created in the town by the presence of over three hundred bishops and senior churchmen, and by the busy townsmen catering to their needs. Or if I have to be honest it was the unfamiliar presence of the townswomen that most engaged me. Walking from the priory to the cathedral I could sometimes feel their eyes upon me and if – God forgive me – they were young and pretty, I felt confused and uncomfortable. Under the Abbot's close observation, I knew that either to look or to look away would reveal my turmoil. So I tried to affect an unconcerned nonchalance. I am sure the Abbot saw through it and quietly despaired for his young secretary.

As the council progressed, the town became fuller still, and the crowds changed in character. More noblemen and knights arrived, exciting flashes of colour in the dark lava-stone streets, louder, brasher and noisier than the brown, white or black clad clerics. Also many ordinary people flocked in from the surrounding region. By now Clermont was ringed by a far larger town of tents and temporary shelters. Many common people just slept in the open. Fortunately for them the weather through that autumn month remained unusually dry and mild. The air of anticipation became stronger as the last day of the council approached, for it was to be marked by the Holy Father's address in a field to the north of the town.

It would have taken a team of strong oxen at least three days to plough that field, and yet it was packed to overflowing with an excited throng. The papal throne and pulpit were set on a high dais covered in cloth of red and gold emblazoned prominently with the crossed keys. The greatest churchmen, of whom Cluny's Abbot was of course one, had been provided with seats close to the dais. I stood as straight and tall as I could behind his chair while other bishops and clerics, nobles and knights jostled with each other for the best positions. The common people were pushed to the back, with some even sitting in the oak trees ringing the field so that they could see over the heads of the crowd. The hubbub ceased as the Holy Father came into view wearing his favourite triple crown, walking under a palanquin held at each corner by a crimson-clad archdeacon.

Urban II ascended the pulpit and made a sign of blessing over the utter silence of the expectant crowd.

"My dearest brethren in Christ," he began. His voice rang out powerfully.

"I, Urban II, invested by the mercy and goodness of God with this papal tiara, and spiritual leader over the whole world, over all the bishoprics and sees of Christendom, have come here in this great crisis to you, as a messenger of divine admonition. The perfidious Turk has devastated the Kingdom of God by robbing our eastern brethren of Anatolia. Your Christian Byzantine brothers in the East need your aid. But worse, the Turk has seized and desecrated our holiest places. They foul the towns and streets where Our Holy Lord Jesus Christ was born, lived His life among us, and died for your sins. They stable their horses in the most sacred churches of the city of Jerusalem – yes they allow them to soil the Holy Sepulchre itself."

A roar of outrage began in the crowd, silenced only by Urban raising his arms in a dramatic command for quiet.

"And our pilgrims, those worthy travellers seeking to fulfil their Christian duty and earn their place in Heaven, what of them? The heathen Saracen seize them, torture them most cruelly, putting out their eyes and slicing off their limbs, even making of them human sacrifices to their false and wicked gods.

"Remember the heavenly disturbances throughout this year.

Remember the ruined harvest. Remember the unseasonable heat and the floods. What are they but a sign of Our Lord God's displeasure that His children stand idly by while these appalling crimes are committed? I demand a Holy War – enter on the road to the Holy Sepulchre, wrest Jerusalem, the very navel of the world, from that wicked race. Make it the capital once more of Christendom. Become soldiers of Christ, become crusaders, fighters marked with the Holy Cross."

Finding Abbot Hugh sitting near the front of the crowd, and briefly fixing his eyes, Pope Urban continued.

"To those of you who doubt the justice of this cause, I say…have you forgotten the teaching of Saint Augustine the most wise? Violence can be born of love and is wholly just, if the beloved object of that violence gains from it. Did not Our Lord Jesus Christ throw over the tables of the moneychangers in the Temple, driving them away to a better life? Was not Saint Paul blinded and hurled from his horse by the Holy Ghost on the road to Damascus so that he could come to see the true straight and narrow way? Do we not chastise our children when they stray, so that they may learn to change their direction towards good? So it is right – indeed, it is our solemn Christian duty – to use necessary violence against the Saracen, to convert them by force if need be, and to make them see the error of their ways so that they can be saved from the fires of Hell.

"Victory will be yours, for Christ will be your standard bearer. And sweet though victory in this world may be, for you shall take the riches and possessions of the enemy, sweeter still shall victory be in the next. To all who nobly embark on this solemn quest I promise absolution and remission of your sins, and to any of you who fall on the journey or in battle, whilst wearing the Cross, I promise eternal salvation."

As those two final words echoed around the field in a last crescendo, and the Pope sat back down on his throne, a roar rolled through the crowd, repeated over and over again.

"Deus le volt – God wills it – Deus le volt."

The faces of the secular and ecclesiastical lords at the front of the crowd were mostly suffused with acclaim and excitement at Urban's rousing speech. I too found myself shouting "Deus le volt" until my abbot, quiet almost alone in the crowd, turned his face towards me in an unusually grim, doom-laden expression.

"You too, Hugh?"

I was taken aback and welcomed the distraction of the mitred figure of Adhemar, Bishop of le Puy, throwing himself forward towards the papal throne, kneeling and begging the Holy Father for permission to join the expedition. Many others followed. One especially dashing figure caught my attention, a tall knight with leonine hair and beard. I remember thinking that was the sort of man I wanted to be.

Pope Urban II stood again, basking in the acclaim, unable to banish from his face an expression of smooth satisfaction at a job well done. He scanned the audience, revelling in the fanaticism he had provoked, and then swept back the way he had come.

I could not remember seeing my abbot so troubled and despondent. Back in his lodgings, he struggled to concentrate on the correspondence he was dictating to me. Normally tranquil and full of inner peace, he jumped and started when a knock came at the door of his chamber and a junior prior entered to say that a nobleman, Godfrey de Bouillon, Duke of Lower Lorraine, craved an audience. With a tired gesture the Abbot indicated that he would see the visitor, and the dashing blond knight who had earlier caught my attention entered the room. He bowed peremptorily to the Abbot, paying no attention to me standing a little behind.

"My Lord Abbot, I know that your monastery of Cluny possesses wealth that surpasses any other Christian foundation. I have heard great things of you from my liege lord the Emperor Henry. I need money to raise a great army to take to the East. I wish to sell you my estates at Bouillon."

Wearily the Abbot riposted that he had no wish to acquire land for Cluny so far to the north. Then, at an uncharacteristic loss for what to say next, and casting around for conversation, he turned to me and said, "You and the Lord Duke are cousins, you know. Your father held his land from Duke Godfrey's own father."

So I was connected to this paragon! He was what I aspired to be. My shyness was momentarily stripped off by vainglory. I surprised myself by stepping forward and bowing to the Duke, who was simmering at the Abbot's refusal to consider his request.

"Hugh de Verdon, at your service, my Lord."

"At my service indeed! What service could you do me?"

The Duke spoke gruffly. I supposed he was used to getting his own way and angry to be thwarted in his wish to sell his lands.

For a moment I hesitated and nearly stepped back into the shadows. But the powerful emotions of the moment still held me. Excitement overcame timidity and my words tumbled out almost of their own accord.

"I read and write well, my Lord. I can even speak some Greek, the language of the Byzantines. You will need someone to interpret for you in the East. I have been a good secretary to my Father Abbot…"

Now I turned to the Abbot, my mouth open as I only now fully realised the implication of my own words. I might as well have slapped him across the face, for the expression of shock painted across it.

"What do you mean, Hugh? What do you think you are saying? Are you suggesting that you would ignore your Christian duty? Would you repudiate your vows, and depart on this improper campaign? What would your mother say if she could see you now?"

The Abbot's face coloured and paled as warring emotions fought across it – anger, sorrow, dismay, compassion.

My shoulders slumped in resignation. I nearly succumbed to the force of this protest and to the guilty emotions that poured through me. Then I caught the glimmer of amusement in the Duke's face, amusement, I thought, at my expense. Such a man would never have difficulty in facing down another and doing his own will. Why should I not take this chance to win what I so desperately desired? Why should I return to have my vitality slowly sapped by my half-life at the abbey? My father's knightly pride rose in me. Now I cared more about showing weakness in front of this scornful chevalier than about showing boldness that might anger the Abbot.

I raised my chin and fixed the Abbot's eyes with my own. "My Lord Abbot, I am truly grateful to you for all that you have done. But my father's blood runs in my veins as well as my mother's."

I turned back to the Duke. "Sir…" I fumbled for the right words to use. I wanted to say 'Your Grace' but in front of the holy Abbot such words seemed blasphemous. It was more than I could manage.

"Sir…my father served yours well. He died fighting bravely in your father's interest. He fought to protect his lands against bandits. You owe it to his memory. You owe it to our ancient bonds of blood to take me with you. I swear, I swear" – I wanted to say 'upon my mother's head', but again choked on the words I would have chosen – "…I swear that it is a decision I will never give you cause to regret."

Now it was Duke Godfrey's turn to look uncomfortable. I could see my emotional plea working powerfully upon him, but then he was turning uncertainly towards the Abbot, not wanting to cross the influential churchman. I knew that my fate, my future hung in the balance. That thought – that it was *my* future – furnished me with the courage I needed.

"My Lord Abbot, permit me to remind you again of the

wise words you spoke that very first day we met. Then you said that I needed time to establish that my vocation was real. You said I needed to be sure that a life in the service of Our Lord and the abbey was truly my calling. You said that a false calling leads to corruption and sin. You know...you know how hard I have tried. You have heard my anguish in the confessional. I am my father's son as much as my mother's. It was only the cruel trick of fate that brought about his death, in the service of Lord Godfrey's father" – this for the Duke's benefit again – "and carried me at my mother's behest to your abbey. I beg you now to release me. Let me go."

For what seemed like an age, Abbot Hugh stared silently at me. Then he sighed, lowered his head and sadly said, "If you must go, and if this noble Duke will take you, you may go. I will miss you for you have become dear to me, but I suppose that in my heart of hearts I have known for some time now that your vocation was not strong and that you should not complete your vows."

He looked up and once again – for what I thought would be the last time – I felt the penetrating wisdom of that direct gaze misting my eyes with tears.

Thus it was that I became part of the retinue of Godfrey de Bouillon, Duke of Lower Lorraine, *Advocatus Sancti Sepulchri*, the man who was to be offered the title of King of Jerusalem.

SAINT LAZARUS' COLLEGE

"Well, I do have to concede that in Chapter Three you have succinctly captured the Papacy's main motives for launching the First Crusade. You didn't actually read history here did you? It really isn't a bad summary. I could maybe quibble with a few things. There is no evidence that Duke Godfrey de Bouillon was at Clermont, for example. The audience was almost entirely made up of clerics. But then nor can I point to any evidence that proves he was not there."

The History Don scratched his chin pensively. Buoyed by this unexpected praise, the Best-Selling Author leered at the college servant who was at that moment offering him a dish of overcooked vegetables. 'She is a bit younger and prettier than the old crones they normally have here,' he thought. 'Perhaps I could seek her out after dinner…'

Disconcerted by the wink that accompanied this lascivious thought, the poor girl tipped the serving dish too much, so that a dribble of lukewarm vegetable water ran into her tormentor's lap, somewhat dampening his ardour.

This exchange did not escape the Chaplain's attention, and needled by moral outrage he weighed in.

"I'm sorry but I *do* object to a lot of it. It may be fashionable in the history department to ascribe totally cynical motives to Pope Urban for launching the First Crusade. But I simply cannot accept that his fundamental purpose was other than spiritual and well-intentioned. He was a good Pope, who saw the religious significance of winning back the Holy Land and set about doing so in a way that was perfectly proper for that era. I can just see where the rest of this tale is leading – next we will be hearing about the superiority of Islam over Christianity and the wickedness of the so-called Christian *Jihad* – another ill-founded viewpoint dear to the hearts of the liberal establishment."

"Now, now, Chaplain," intervened the Master. "If you are not careful you will be tarred with the same brush as the good book-burning Abbot. Christianity can stand up for itself against foreign ideas, I am sure. And books cannot be written by committee; if there is a man alive who understands that, after my days in Whitehall I am he. Although I have asked our distinguished Professor here to review the text for errors of English. We cannot allow a book to go out under the college's imprint with grammatical mistakes in it. You know how sloppy the syntax in this type of book normally is."

The Master turned to the Best-Selling Author. "Forgive me, I don't mean to cause offence, but you know how it is."

The Best-Selling Author looked up from dabbing at his moist crotch and shrugged his shoulders in careless acquiescence.

The Professor of English glowed quietly. He knew that the Best-Selling Author was too ignorant, and his colleagues too wrapped up in their own narrow specialisms, to pick up the quotations from his favourite poem with which he planned to spice the text under the pretext of his grammatical review.

CHAPTER FOUR

A FLASH OF LIGHTNING

*At last, at last, I was free. But then I did not know that
we are always bound by one form of servitude or another,
tied up by the past as much as the present. I could not
simply slough off my monkish skin.*

I passed a sleepless night and rose the next morning wan, and
wondering what I had done. I sought out the Abbot and found
him emerging from the priory chapel. From his pale expression
I gathered that he had spent much of the night in prayer. He
put his arm around my shoulders and we walked to the gate
of the priory. There we stopped and I looked at him forlornly.
He smiled back.

"Go with my blessing, Hugh." He made the Sign of the
Cross. "I bless you in the name of the Father, the Son, and
the Holy Ghost. May they watch over you, guide you and
protect you wherever your travels may take you. Remember
what you have learnt. And remember me in your prayers."

I tried to stammer out my thanks but only inarticulate
noises emerged.

"It's all right. I know." The Abbot embraced me. "Go now,
before you unman me."

My fear that I had made an awful mistake was exacerbated when I presented myself timidly at the Duke's lodgings, only to be greeted with a growl which wiped my mind of my carefully prepared speech.

"So you have come after all, little monk cousin. What was I thinking of yesterday? Heaven knows what made me accede to your request. I've just given myself another useless mouth to feed. By the God who is so precious to you, you had better prove your worth to me – if you want to accompany me to Bouillon, let alone all the way to the East. I'd leave you here were it not for the promise I made in front of your churchman. I cannot afford to cross him. I don't suppose you can even stay in a saddle."

All I could do was stammer helplessly in reply.

Nevertheless I was furnished with a fine chestnut mare, a world apart from the dull mule that had carried me from Cluny. My pleasure at the feel of the lively animal between my legs was marred by my fear of being unable to handle her and of looking a fool.

Six years earlier I had ridden south in trepidation at being shut away from the world that I wanted. Now I found myself riding back north churning with apprehension at the prospect of that same world reopening before me. Fatherless, motherless, brotherless, laid safely in a monastic cocoon while I grew up, I had now forced my way through its protective skin. For the first time I had to shake out my adult wings. And I had parted from the Abbot, my guide, my mentor, my confessor – not a relative or a true father perhaps, but closer to being so than anyone else. How different would things be with my new flamboyant master?

The Duke rode with a dozen retainers, clad not in full mail, but in leather jerkins covered by short white overshirts proudly bearing the double orange cross of Lorraine. Godfrey himself was sumptuously arrayed in a finer version of the same outfit, topped by an orange fur-trimmed cloak. In my patched black habit I felt shabby and out of place. I tried to stay out of the way at the back of the troop but with impatience Godfrey beckoned me forward.

"My kin should not ride with the men-at-arms, even, little monk, if they are a step ahead of you and already wear the Cross."

Maybe these words were intended jovially, but they cut me as a harsh jibe. I continued to suffer in mute embarrassment at the Duke's occasional comments, imagining the sniggers they provoked from the men-at-arms behind.

We had ridden for half a day and I felt that I had not yet disgraced myself, handling my mare as if I had hardly been out of the saddle. Suddenly I heard loud crashes through the thick undergrowth to the right of the path.

"Boar," roared Godfrey, "Let's have some sport."

Grabbing a lance from the man to his right, he set spurs to his black stallion and charged forward. I kicked my heels into my mare's side in a rush of instinctive exhilaration that I had not felt since hunting with my father and brothers all those years before. For a moment it was as if I was once again following them, anxious to impress, determined not to be outdone. As I twisted between the trees, ducking my head to avoid the rough clutching fingers of low branches, I saw a family of wild boar running in front. Half a dozen striped boarlets, hard to make out against the sun-dappled leaves on the forest floor, scurried after their grey bristling parents. They scattered. Godfrey gained fast. He ignored the sow and her brood and chased the high-backed boar, leaning forward to make the kill. Just as he thrust, his target jinked to one side. His lance caught the ground instead, and the force sprung him from his horse. I remembered a trick I had learnt from my father. Leaning sideways, I twisted to snatch the quivering spear from the ground. Kicking my heels to get the last burst of speed from my mare, I thrust with all my strength at the boar's high shoulder. To my delight my strike was true, driving right through to the heart so that the pig lurched over onto one side and lay thrashing its legs in its death throes. Panting with hot excitement I turned proudly and trotted my mare back to where the Duke was standing up, winded but otherwise unhurt, and dusting himself off.

A momentary glare of bad temper shone red in his eyes. Had I done the wrong thing? My excitement drained away, leaving dregs of relief at the return of the Duke's boisterous good nature.

"Not bad, little monk, not bad at all. Perhaps after all there is more to you than meets the eye. You certainly wiped mine just then. Good de Bouillon blood will out."

He chuckled as he indicated peremptorily to one of the men behind to bring him his horse, which, well-trained, had stopped a short way off, its shiny sweat-flecked flanks heaving.

"We will all eat well tonight."

'I have passed one test,' I thought to myself as I watched the boar's carcass being slung over the back of one of the packhorses. The horse shied under its gory burden and the men-at-arms fought to control it. For all that, their humour was high, and I felt smiles of praise directed towards me where I had detected sneers before. As we rode on to spend the night in the next town's inn, I basked in the modest respect that I had won from the men around me.

The horses were stabled, the boar was given over to be roasted, and wine was called for. I did not know where to go or how to behave in those unfamiliar surroundings, and stood uncomfortably in the shadows, away from the bustle. But I seemed to be in the Duke's favour, for he beckoned me over.

"So you can stick pigs as well as speaking Greek, can you, little monk?" he said, "Is there anything that you can't do?"

And then he spotted my shy confusion as a young serving woman came forward to place wooden drinking goblets and a large flagon of wine on the table.

"Ha – I'll warrant you can't do much with women."

Godfrey's roar of laughter and the wench's coy smile flushed my cheeks hotter and redder still.

The boar was brought on a great grail and we set to with our knives, greedily slicing off the flesh and licking the juices off our fingers. The room was lit by a large fire at one end. It danced with a companionable light and filled with the strong smells of smoke, roasted pig, and spiced wine. Godfrey called for flagon after flagon and downed the lion's share himself. Even so, I drank far more than I was accustomed to in the abbey, and had to leave the room unsteadily to relieve myself outside.

When I came back some minutes later and pushed open the door, I saw that the company had left save the Duke of Lower Lorraine, who was leant back in his chair, his hose around his knees, jugjugging the serving wench. Her skirts were pulled up and her bodice was pulled down so that her bare breasts danced up and down in the firelight. Her hands pushed down on Godfrey's chest while his hands were clenched round her bare buttocks. She shook her head from side to side to flick the sweaty tendrils of hair out of her eyes. My mouth opened and my tongue dried as I saw her large brown nipples bouncing around and heard her whimpering like an animal, her moans punctuated by Godfrey's deeper grunts as he took his pleasure. He turned his lust-flushed face, which matched the girl's own expression, and grinned over his shoulder, "You can have her, young Hugh, when I have finished." Overcome by embarrassment and disgust, but mixed with burning desire, I turned and fled the room, to commit the sin of Onan violently behind the stables. I was unable to shake that image from my mind for many months to come and for all my prayerful efforts I could not resist defiling myself with that sinful act so firmly forbidden at the abbey.

Godfrey of course was merciless in his mockery.

"Your stomach not strong enough for a course of wench

after all that boar, eh? You are used to different fare in the abbey, are you? A few cups of wine and you cannot perform at all, is that it? Perhaps you have a withered stump, little monk."

My discomfort was increased by the sycophantic sniggers of the men-at-arms at their master's jibes. I feared I had now squandered what respect I had won by spearing the boar.

It was in early December, just before the snows finally came, that we arrived back at Godfrey's stronghold of Bouillon. The fortress perched on a rocky outcrop high above the fish-filled River Semois which wound through the rough forested hills of the Ardennes. The water ran deep and black at the base of its cliff and the towers at its top seemed to spring straight from the rock beneath. Four strong well-shaped towers protected each corner of the quarried stone walls, and in the centre soared the tallest tower of all.

In that stout keep at its heart, the serious work of gathering an army began. I was kept busy writing until my eyes stung and my frozen fingers ached through their numbness. My stamina was fuelled by determination to prove my worth. I would do whatever was needed in order to earn my place at Godfrey's side on the journey east. How I longed to be more than a mere scribe. My abilities were stretched to their limits, for I had to write in both French and Flamand, as to the South the first was spoken and to the North the second. My master prided himself on his ability to communicate in each.

"I was born at the frontier of two nations," he was fond of saying as he strode up and down dictating to me, slapping his baton of office against the palm of his hand, a bearskin robe round his shoulders, "and when I speak and command in the language of either, men listen and obey."

I gained some satisfaction from the messengers carrying letters in my hand in all directions, letters seeking to raise money and men. Greater satisfaction still was mine when I was told to ready myself for a trip with Godfrey through three bitterly cold January days to Liege, to agree the sale of Bouillon and its surrounding estates to Bishop Orbert. After some hard negotiation, strengthened by Godfrey's argument that the money would be used to further God's will, I drew up a contract which stated that the Bishop would pay one thousand three hundred marks of silver and three marks of gold, and that Godfrey's three immediate heirs might repurchase the land for the same price.

"Well, Hugh, that's something. The good Bishop of Liege has made up for your tight-fisted abbot. That should keep us in funds until we are able to capture some Saracen treasure. And somehow I don't think I will be returning to buy back this land."

Two of the early letters that I wrote at Godfrey's dictation were addressed to the Duke's brothers, the elder Eustace, Count of Boulogne, and the younger Baldwin. The unmitigated materialism in the tone of Godfrey's message to them disturbed me. Where now was the fine idealism spoken by Pope Urban in that field at Clermont?

"Come and join me, my dear brother, and take the Cross. I am tired of answering to the Emperor in Lower Lorraine. His interference has left me duke in little more than name. I plan to sell all my possessions. I will raise as much money as I can by every means at my disposal. I go to seek fame and fortune in the Holy Land. Come with me and we will carve out dominions for ourselves from the territory held by the unbelieving Turks. Adventures and booty await us. How often is it that plunder and pillage are endorsed by the Holy See and even bring with them the promise of eternal salvation?"

The brothers soon answered Godfrey's call. Count Eustace was an older, shorter, plumper and altogether more comfortable version of Godfrey. He led only five hundred men-at-arms and no more than fifty knights but he still earned an affable greeting.

"Well, my old brother, I am pleased to see you, even if you have brought with you but a quarter of the men that I have provided from my own lands of Bouillon. With such a paltry crowd at least you will not be able to challenge your younger brother's leadership of this army."

With a friendly slap on the back Godfrey drove away the frown that had threatened to cloud the good nature in Count Eustace's round face.

"Do I detect some reluctance to abandon your comfortable home for too long? You leave your noble Countess behind and plan to hurry back to her at the earliest opportunity, I'll wager, when you have had a bit of sport and done just enough to secure the future of your immortal soul."

Count Eustace noticed me and treated me with courtesy. Told by Godfrey of our distant kinship, he spoke kindly of my father. Though they had never met face to face, he said, he knew of his reputation. I warmed to his politeness.

The reception of the younger brother Baldwin was a very different affair. Godfrey's greeting seemed uncharacteristic to me – guarded, careful, and circumspect.

"Welcome, brother Baldwin. Thank you for joining me. I know that you share my ambition to carve out a great domain for yourself in the East. You and I…we will stand shoulder to shoulder against the Moor…the black-haired and the blond together will take on all comers. But I trust you will remember who has organised this little trip, and who raised the finance to provision it. Do not worry…we will find you enough rich loot to suit your expensive tastes."

Baldwin twisted out a frosty smile that reciprocated the lack of warmth in Godfrey's words.

"You will not be the only ex-churchman in our party." Godfrey gestured in my direction. "That's my secretary, a cousin of ours. He was formerly a Cluniac novice, and is a useful linguist. What's more, he can wield a lance as well as a quill – at least against a wild boar. Let's see his mettle when he is up against Saracens. Their tusks are a little sharper."

My heart leapt with excitement, for this was the first time I had heard Godfrey imply that I might be travelling East as a fighter. My imagination raced away, building adventures, cementing the edifices that I had constructed for myself out of hope when lying awake at night. They all tumbled down again at the chilling sneer that I received from Baldwin, which revealed plainly a thin, cruel mouth beneath the sparse cover of his neatly trimmed beard and moustache. I felt too that Baldwin's scorn was directed at Godfrey, as much as at me, for his kindness in taking me in.

Baldwin had brought few soldiers with him, for he held little land, and as Godfrey's words implied, had indeed been originally destined for a career in the Church. This he had abandoned when his schemes had snared an adequate dowry from his match with Godehilde, daughter of Ralph de Conches, a Norman who had won rich lands in the conquest of England. Godfrey greeted Godehilde with more enthusiasm and unfortunately less caution than he had Baldwin.

"Well, sister, it is so good to see you, more beautiful than ever."

The words broke uncontrolled from his lips as soon as he raised them from kissing her hand for a little longer than was seemly.

"How is it that your radiance is undimmed? Nobody would know that you have already borne my lucky brother three children."

Godehilde curtseyed silently and deeply, lowering her eyes with every outward show of modest propriety. But in spite of my inexperience of women, I could detect the pleasure aroused in her by Godfrey's warm words of welcome. She could not keep a flirtatious smile from dancing along her lips. By lowering her gaze she showed off her long dark eyelashes; with the depth of her curtsey she offered Godfrey a downwards glimpse at her breasts.

"Come. That's enough. You don't have to grovel on the floor. My brother is not some sort of monarch. He is of no higher birth than me."

Baldwin's voice sounded as cold as his eyes looked.

With reluctance Godfrey tore his attention from the voluptuous figure and golden colouring of his sister-in-law and turned to another exotic member of Baldwin's company, a dark Armenian, by the name of Bagrat. Godfrey made a great show of welcome.

"At your service, my friend. We will rely heavily on your knowledge of the foreign lands through which we would pass on our Crusade. And doubtless you speak many tongues, and can interpret for us even better than Cousin Hugh."

Again I saw hard eyes full of scorn turning to meet mine. Bagrat's narrow features were a dark and distorted reflection of his master Baldwin's. I wondered what circumstances could have driven him so far away from home. A taste for cruelty and intrigue was written across that face; some evil skulduggery must have precipitated his banishment. I felt an instinctive loathing for the man. I was sure that my emotion had roots deeper than a mere concern that the Armenian's skills in language might render my own services redundant. 'With whatever tongue he speaks', I thought, 'it will be as forked as Satan's.'

A matter of days after these inauspicious arrivals, another party passed down the wintry Semois valley. This was led by Walter Sans Avoir, Lord of Boissy, another nobleman to whom I had written at Godfrey's dictation. Godfrey had been especially keen to persuade Sans Avoir to join him, for he had a reputation as a formidable warrior. He and his family were therefore welcomed to Bouillon with particular courtesy, and were offered lodgings in the castle itself, in order to provide them with greater comfort than was available among the field of tents mushrooming down the valley.

Sans Avoir looked indeed a ferocious individual, a Goliath, with hands that could have strangled a pig. I imagined another similarity to the Philistine champion, for the blank of his brutish face signalled that his excess of brawn was balanced by a deficit in guile.

But I paid little regard to Sans Avoir, or to his bizarre bodyguard, armed outlandishly with great axes hanging from leather thongs round their necks. My attention was drawn elsewhere in his retinue. With him was a girl – I knew she could not be a daughter, nor scarcely even a distant relation, so utterly different from him was she. She was of similar age to me, and more graceful than a singing bird. Her hair glowed so clear and bright it seemed to be spun of the finest gold. Her forehead was high, white and smooth as if polished by the careful hand of a man who had carved her face from stone or ivory. Her eyebrows were well-shaped, set well apart, and her eyes, brilliant, laughing, were clear and bright. Her nose was straight and long, and tints of crimson and white showed better across her face than scarlet cloth on silver. I felt admiration that dwarfed Godfrey's for Godehilde. And I tried hard to hope that, like the sister-in-law's response to my master, this girl had noted my attraction towards her with a tiny measure of reciprocity. Beside this girl's pure beauty though, Godehilde was already blown and blowzy.

SAINT LAZARUS'S COLLEGE

The Modern Languages Tutor now wished fervently that he had not sought this interview with the Master. It had taken an unexpected and most unpleasant turn.

He had not enjoyed the unusually early start demanded by the Master's tiresome habit of clearing internal College business by ten o'clock in the morning. Normally he did not rise before then and would not leave his chambers until he had been fortified by a couple of stiff preprandial martinis. Nevertheless, he had managed to drag himself blinking mole-like into the early morning light, after masking the sour taste of last night's gin with his first two cigarettes of the day. He had brushed most of the ash off the sleeve of his jacket, before noticing with irritation that the edge of the tweed was frayed. That was the sort of detail that did not escape the Master's hard stare. He knew that it would not help to create a good impression; but anyway he could not do anything about his thinning lank hair, or the cheeks wizened by years of excessive alcohol and tobacco. But, damn it, he was a scholar, and that was what he wanted to talk to the Master about.

Reading the latest chapter of *The Waste Land* – why had the Professor of English been allowed to get away with that title? – in the Common Room the night before, he had come to the shocked realisation that his Research Assistant must be right. The little details that brought the book to life – lifted from the ancient manuscript of course, not created by the self-satisfied Best-Selling Author – definitely contained uncanny echoes of Chrétien de Troyes. The description of the castle at Bouillon matched that of Goornement de Goort, where Perceval learned to fight, far too precisely to be a coincidence. And the first description of Blanche – well the Research Assistant had certainly not been mistaken there. He might be an ugly specimen but he was not completely ignorant.

'Scarlet cloth on silver – *le sinoples sor argent*', and the rest of the description – it was lifted almost word for word from Chrétien's verse; the Best-Selling Author could not possibly have conjured such an identical description by chance.

It had been a very long time since the Modern Languages Tutor's name had appeared on any publication. But once he had been a promising academic. Then he had secured his fellowship, his comfortable rooms, and he had sunk into the laziness borne of his little vices. The possibility of publishing, editing and annotating the manuscript – or having his Research Assistant do the work and taking most of the glory from him – had reawakened his academic ambitions. So he had to get the original manuscript back from the Master, who doubtless kept it locked somewhere, jealously protecting its story.

The Master greeted the Modern Languages Tutor with distaste. To a man who was fastidious about every detail of his own appearance, the untidy seediness of the man, the rank smell of stale smoke and the mole-like bloodshot eyes, were a personal affront. When had he last washed his hair? His mission to modernise the college could not succeed unless he did away with superannuated fossils like this one.

So before the Modern Languages Tutor could state his business, the Master went on the attack. Striking first was a tactic which had served him well in Whitehall.

"Thank you so much for coming to see me. I have been meaning to speak to you for a long time. I know this will come as a shock, but the Fellows have decided to terminate your appointment here. As you know, there are very few students who want to study languages any more, and fewer still who have any interest in your medieval specialities. And I am afraid that your long publication drought is not doing anything to push us up the league tables. You know how short we are of space, and we want to appoint a new Fellow in Computer Science. He will need your rooms. Of course, you will have until the end of the academic year…"

To the Modern Languages Tutor it seemed like a very bad dream and he fumbled in his coat pocket for a cigarette before remembering that in no circumstances would the Master allow anyone to light up in his rooms.

"But, Master, I am planning a publication which will turn the whole world of grail scholarship upside down. It will redound to the great credit of Saint Lazarus. We are sure that the document which furnishes the plot of *The Waste Land* is Chrétien de Troyes' original source for the *Roman de Perceval*. It is the original grail romance. There are just too many similarities for it to be a coincidence. I am sure of it. Think of all the implications. All I ask is access to the manuscript. My Research Assistant has done a lot of the work already. We'll have a preliminary paper out by, let's see, the end of the Michaelmas term at the latest."

"I'm sorry. The decision has been made. It is final. And there is absolutely no question of that manuscript being released before *The Waste Land* is at the top of the bestseller list."

CHAPTER FIVE

THE ROAD WINDING ABOVE

For some days I have not been able to write. The sorrowful memories that came flooding back to me were too strong. Now I have gathered my thoughts once more and have tried to set down the facts of what happened as I remembered them then.

I wandered the cold halls and corridors of Bouillon in a daze, fulfilling my duties for Godfrey like a man whose head was still ringing from a fierce blow on the helm. I found myself making mistakes that before would have cut my pride and made me anxious lest their discovery thwarted my journey East. Now I scarcely cared. I did not even know what she was called. I christened her again and again in my mind but no name that I chose could do her justice. I asked myself how she came to be in the retinue of Walter de Boissy. How could her slender grace be blood-related to his bestial strength? How I wished that I had been dressed like a knight, like a real man, when her gaze swept over me. In my monkish garments I must have been as good as invisible to a girl like her.

Whenever I had the opportunity in between wielding my quill in the Duke's service, I practiced hard with real weapons.

At first I had been driven by eagerness to gain Godfrey's respect as more than his 'little monk' and to win a place as a proper fighting man in his retinue. Now I hoped most that she might somehow come to recognise my prowess. My skills with bow, javelin and spear quickly returned, for they had been well learnt by my father's side at the hunt. So on the training field I worked mainly with the sword, thrusting and slashing at pillows and padded shields and taking part in practice bouts. The sergeant in charge of weapons training was a grizzled veteran by the name of Stephen. He had a look of my father's old steward about him, except that a scar cut the right side of his face, dragging down his lower eyelid. In the cold air, the exposed red rim watered constantly, giving him a comically mournful expression. He might have been one of the gargoyles spouting water from the gutters of Cluny's church. Gruff at first, he seemed to warm to me, perhaps approving my plain enthusiasm for his trade, and appreciating my eagerness to learn. As the weeks passed, my muscles strengthened and I thought my shoulders had noticeably broadened. Certainly the few garments I had brought from the abbey now felt tight across my back and upper arms. I was sure that they had hung loose before.

Late one dark afternoon I had finished all the letters required of me. Freed, I ran down the spiral stairway to the deep courtyard where sword practice took place. I waved at Stephen as I pulled on one of the leather jerkins worn to provide some protection from the training swords. These weapons were blunted to prevent serious injury but could still hurt badly if your guard were penetrated as I knew to my cost from several blows and bruises. Although busy with another fencing partner, Stephen repaid me with a grin that twisted his scarred face more than ever. When his bout was over, he came across. We stood face to face, swords raised, circling warily round, and then set to, cutting and thrusting, blocking and parrying. Perhaps he was treating me kindly, but it seemed to me that I was now a reasonable match for him. I battered at Stephen's guard, trying to find a way through to his body, and soon, in spite of the cold air which misted my breath, sweat was trickling down under my helmet to add to the stains on my jerkin. Then to my consternation I heard a bellow echoing in the stairwell from which I had entered the court.

"Hugh, damn it, where are you? I have work for you to do. What in the Devil's name do you think you are doing, shirking your tasks and skulking off?"

An irate Godfrey burst into the yard. Stephen respectfully lowered his sword and inclined his head. The other sparring couples did the same. I fought now to maintain my composure and to conceal my humiliation and distress.

"Why are you wasting your time here? You are a scribe, damn it, not a knight; a weapon of goose feather is more fitted for your feeble hands than one of steel."

Then a wicked glint came into the Duke's eye.

"Here, I'll teach you a lesson. Sergeant, give me your weapon."

Godfrey quickly donned a padded jerkin and helmet and took his place opposite me in the ready position. Hesitantly I too raised my sword. 'Should I fight to win,' I wondered, 'and incur my patron's greater wrath, or take a battering as bravely as I can before I return in resignation to my inky desk?' Before I could make up my conscious mind Godfrey came at me with a roar, whirring his weapon down in a vicious arc. The second nature born of my training snapped in, and I parried, blocked and parried again. Godfrey was more than a head taller than Stephen, his reach far greater, so his blows rained down from above where Stephen's angled in from the side. As I adjusted I came to realise with excitement that I could protect myself from this man's attacks. I began to relish the challenge. Was there now a hint of surprise in my challenger's expression, a little more wild violence in each blow as our swords rang together with a harsh metallic clash that re-echoed in its turn around the narrow courtyard?

Out of the corner of my eye I saw the pale oval of a face peering down from one of the narrow keep windows. With a jolt, I realised who it was. Now if I lost, she would witness my shame and my humiliation. That thought, and the momentary lapse of concentration that it brought, almost cost me the contest. Just in time I saw my foe's sword arching down. At the last moment I moved sideways far enough for it to miss by a finger. The near miss prompted a bellow of excitement and a charge of renewed vigour. Behind my assailant, I saw Stephen silently mouthing, "Remember your footwork. Move your feet," and as I centred myself again I began to dodge some of the strokes, saving energy and resting my parry-jarred muscles. Frustrated by this agility, my opponent became wilder, wasting his own vigour and clattering his blade right down against the flagstones, where it scattered sparks into the gloom. Was his breathing now a little strained as he raised the heavy sword again? Was he moving a bit more slowly? I tried a couple of swings myself and enjoyed forcing a backwards step from my adversary. This provoked another furious swipe. It hammered downwards at me but I side-stepped briskly. Seeing the enemy off balance, I countered with a hard blow into his ribs. Now my rival bent over, grunting with surprised pain. Before he could undouble himself and raise his sword again, Stephen stepped in.

"That is enough, my Lord. By the rules of the training ground that is the end of the bout."

For a moment I had forgotten whom I was fighting. Instinct and energy, fed by an urgent desire to impress the girl, had blinded me to my opponent's identity. I looked up at the window which held her and imagined a smile on her face as she turned away. But in that very moment of triumph it flooded back on me with horror that I had struck my patron. It was none other than the Duke of Lower Lorraine standing there in front of me, winded, doubled up, cursing with pain. I realised that my journey was over, my hopes scattered. At best it would be back to the monastery, probably after a period clapped in irons in the damp festering dungeon beneath the keep. Out of the corner of my eye I saw Stephen standing rigidly at one side of our master, his drooping lid watering more than ever. The other fencers who had remained to watch, doubtless anticipating my sound thrashing, were now also motionless, gaping too to see what would happen next. For the minutes of the fight, time had flashed past for me, as fast as the blades cutting the air; now it seemed to have stopped as still as the sword I held grounded at my feet. Slowly Godfrey raised his head and straightened himself. The feared red light of anger shone from his eyes but then faded, his face instead splitting in a smile. His roar of laughter now echoed round the courtyard and Stephen and the other onlookers relaxed.

"Well fought. I'll feel that for at least a week."

He clapped his arm around my shoulders.

"Come, we have work to do."

Set free by relief, my thoughts flew after the girl as she turned from the window, and followed her around the castle in my imagination. I constructed unnecessary errands as excuses to wander around in the hope that I might encounter her. And then I hurried along, not daring to tarry in case I met her. Unworthy cause for prayer though I knew it to be, I begged God passionately that I might chance upon her; then, realising that I did not know what words to speak if my supplications were answered, I unsaid them again.

At last I did find her. In one way the encounter was all I might have hoped, for I found her in the room where I was accustomed to write Godfrey's correspondence. 'Can she have come here in search of me?' I thought with the excitement of sudden hope. In another way it was all that I might have feared, for the Duke was there before me. He growled lasciviously as he backed her into a corner.

"Come here, Blanche, my pretty, don't be shy now."

And so I learnt her name. Then I remembered the serving wench with painful clarity. I remembered the lecherous looks lavished on sister-in-law Godehilde. Jealous anger began to erupt from somewhere deep down in my body. Blanche's eyes flashed towards me and I tried to read the message they held – was it fear of Godfrey, annoyance at my arrival, shame, supplication? Later I wondered more, but then I did not stop to think and reacted instinctively with a growl of my own.

"My Lord. Come away from her. I have work to do here."

The Duke must have noticed Blanche's gaze flickering over his shoulder because he had already begun to turn angrily towards the unwelcome intruder. When he saw it was me, his irritation subsided to be replaced with roars of laughter.

"I see, Hugh. So that's how it is! You like her, do you? Well good luck – I'll wager your need is greater than mine."

Blanche, more flushed now than ever, took her chance to run towards the door. As she rushed by I was sure that I felt her fingers brush my right hand. Had it been an accident? After all, the room was small, the passage narrow. But no, I told myself, she moves with such poise, such fluency. That touch could not have been chance.

Godfrey's chortles subsided and my volcanic fury cooled into pumiced lumps of embarrassment. Spring seemed to be coming early for me. My imagination filled with romantic blooms. But then they were blackened and withered by a sudden frost. No sooner had we settled down to work than the doorway to our chamber was filled by the huge frame of Walter Sans Avoir. The thunder of his rumbling voice shattered my clear sky.

"My Lord Duke, you have shown me great courtesy and consideration. You would have me lend my prowess in war to your expedition. But I and my men grow impatient at your lengthy preparations. We are ready. We are eager to travel east. I am used to command, not to fall in behind others. I have received messengers from Germany, from Peter the Hermit. His fervent preaching has gathered together many common people, a rabble that needs to be shaped into an army. He looks for commanders, and offers me a high place in his council. I intend to accept his overtures. I will leave with my force and my household forthwith."

Godfrey flushed with annoyance at the news that his assiduous hospitality had been wasted on Sans Avoir. I had no idea what colour my own face had turned.

"But my Lord de Boissy," I stammered, completely forgetting myself, "Peter the Hermit's rabble might as well be babes in arms for all the hope they have of reaching Constantinople in one piece. They can have no provisions, for last year's poor harvest has yielded too little to feed them. They'll have no discipline, no equipment to speak of. You would do better to stay and wait with us."

Godfrey looked with surprise at me but instead of scolding my impetuosity he agreed.

"My secretary is right. Peter the Hermit and his men will be the first to test the uncertain mood of our friend the Byzantine Emperor. They may well find him less friendly than they expect when he is confronted by their horde on his borders."

But none of Godfrey's arguments could sway the Lord of Boissy. His mind, small in that vast body, was set. I glared with hate after the big man who was taking Blanche away. Godfrey looked at me with amused affection.

"What on earth is the matter? Come, come, it is not so bad. There are plenty of other pretty little fish in the river. And we can make do without Walter Sans Avoir. He and the rabble he goes to lead will prepare the way for us."

I though was utterly disconsolate. Somehow I had to see Blanche alone before she left. Perhaps I could talk her into staying. Perhaps I could offer her my hand. Then I dismissed such a ludicrous idea before it had taken full form. What would she want with a scribe like me, a poor product of the cloister, utterly ignorant of women, penniless? No sooner had I decided that my cause was hopeless, than a ray of spring sunshine shone through my clouds. Eyes modestly downcast, Blanche entered my writing chamber, causing me to start from my chair, almost jerking over the pot of ink on my desk. I realised that I had not heard her voice before. My heart soared at the gentle melody of her tone.

"Sir, forgive my immodest intrusion. I had to thank you for protecting me before I leave."

She raised her eyes shyly and then her modesty made them fall again, but not before I had seen a gentle smile crossing her lips. By now I had managed to disentangle myself from my desk and I was about to reach out to touch Blanche's soft hand when I saw with shame the ink stains on my fingers and thrust their incriminating evidence behind my back. I so wanted her to think me a knight, not a clerk. I was momentarily captivated by the length of her eyelashes but managed to drag my attention back to her words.

"I do not want to go, you know, but my guardian insists. Perhaps you will catch us up in Constantinople. Perhaps we will see each other again there. I do hope so."

I could now feel myself blushing to the roots of my hair. Tongue-tied I muttered something indistinct about how I hoped so too. Then I watched helplessly as Blanche reached out to my writing desk and picked up the knife that I used to sharpen my quills.

"Let me give you something to remember me by."

In a quick movement she cut a hank of hair from one golden tress and then with a sigh turned the knife towards herself. Unable to move, fearing that she might be about to do herself harm, I breathed again as she sliced a small piece of yellow ribbon from her dress. She wound it deftly round the lock of hair, tied it in a neat bow, and held it out to me.

"I'll carry it next to my skin always," I murmured and then

felt a touch on my cheek as she reached up a light kiss. Before I could come to my senses she had turned and left the room.

Now I felt my need to earn a place with Duke Godfrey on the march more viscerally than ever. Love melded with ambition to create a desire greater than I had ever felt before. I thought I had done the Duke's work well, but I still trembled in doubtful insecurity, worrying to the point where I lay in bed at night unable to sleep. So I quaked one fine summer morning when the Duke turned to me in the writing chamber.

"Cousin, you have served me well. I am pleased with you." Were those words the preamble to my final dismissal? Or did I detect some affection in his tone? Perhaps that was just sympathy at the harsh message he was about to deliver?

"Without your help we would have been hard pushed to complete our preparations in time. Really. And I know you've put the rest of your time to good use. I know all too well the result of your efforts in the training lists."

The Duke rubbed his side in rueful memory and I shifted nervously.

"Don't be concerned; I do know that you have taken up the sword only when your work with the quill has been done. I know too – to my cost – how well you have learned to fight. I have a small gift for you."

He turned to open a dark chest behind him, lifting out a sword in a scabbard decorated with fine Venetian embroidery.

"My friend, this sword was meant for you and I want you to have it. Go to the armourer and tell him to issue you with a coat of mail, a shield and a lance. After all, you are my cousin. It is not meet that Charlemagne's blood should run in the veins of a mere clerk. You will travel to the East with me as a proper knight. Of course your duties as my secretary will continue. Your skills in writing and reading are too valuable for me to spare. Your talents with language will serve me well. Brother Baldwin has his interpreter – that shifty Armenian; you shall be mine."

I was too much overcome to speak coherently. I swelled with pleasure. I felt prouder than I could remember since the Abbot had praised me and made me his secretary, but now that I was unbound by the vow of humility I did not have to bottle up my emotion. I stammered out thanks as best I could, stroking the sheath of the sword – 'My sword,' I thought – and grasping its leather lined hilt to draw it out. Its balance and its weight felt so natural in my hand. Thoughts of the great deeds I would accomplish with it flashed through my mind. I could not wait to try it out and hear its sharp blade whistle through the air. Godfrey saw my pleasure and excitement, and smiling indulgently gave me an affectionate slap on the back.

Later, when I was back at my desk, handling some last minute correspondence, my elation was punctured by an unwelcome visitor. Baldwin's Armenian slithered into my room, his narrow face painted with a poor simulacrum of a smile.

"Now I must address you as Sir Hugh. I am truly pleased to hear that you will accompany us all to the east. What a fitting reward for your loyal services."

I received Bagrat's ingratiating congratulations with as good a grace as I could muster.

"But do you not think that Duke Godfrey might have been a little more generous? Some monetary recompense perhaps? Some payment? I have always found my Lord Baldwin a most open-handed master."

I must have given him a cold look, for momentarily the strangely accented Latin stopped sliming through the Armenian's lips.

"Please. Please do not misunderstand me. Not for a moment would I wish you to desert the good Duke's service; quite the contrary. We would have you continue to serve him as assiduously as ever. It is just that we would ask you to serve Lord Baldwin as well. A little information from time to time would be so well-rewarded. And it would do no harm. Indeed, how could you better serve the Duke than by fostering good relations with his noble brother – by making sure that fraternal communications flow smoothly, with nothing being hidden from the one by the other. Who says that one cannot serve two masters?"

Bagrat simpered, revealing a mouthful of pointed teeth in his dark face. I raised myself behind my desk.

"Our Lord Jesus Christ himself says so – both the holy Evangelists Saint Matthew and Saint Luke give us his words: 'For either he will hate the one and love the other, or he will be devoted to the one and despise the other.'"

As I stepped from behind my desk and moved towards him I was pleased to see his disappointment turn to fear. He backed away from me towards the door.

"And I am devoted to my Lord Godfrey, for he has been good to me. Work out for yourself where that leaves your master."

And with that he turned and scuttled away.

At long last our mid-August departure day dawned. The city of tents that had mushroomed along the Semois valley had been struck, the packhorses were loaded and the army was ready. I puffed with pride as I galloped with Godfrey's close retinue to the front of the line. I hardly noticed the weight or the heat of my mail over my padded undershirt. Like all the men in the army, I wore a white surcoat with the red cross embroidered on its left shoulder. I had heard that some had been overcome by such religious zeal that they had suffered the pain of having the cross branded into their own flesh.

Godfrey rose in his stirrups in front of the host and bellowed, "We follow the road named for Charlemagne, my great ancestor, onwards to glory and salvation." The soldiers roared back their approbation and beat their weapons on their shields so that the valley echoed.

In spite of the long column of camp followers with their slow rumbling carts, in three weeks the army had reached the valley of the River Danube, the like of whose great smooth flood of water I had never seen before. By the end of the month of September we were close to the border of the Kingdom of Hungary. Our way was clearly mapped by the path of desolation carved by Hermit Peter's army. Most of the villages we passed were deserted. The roughly handled peasants must have seen in the distance the clouds of dust we kicked up and had not waited to see if this new army was more benevolent than the horde which had already passed. All the villages bore the scars of violence. Dwellings were burned and broken. The carcasses of dead animals lay where they had been butchered. On occasion human bodies rested unburied nearby, fallen perhaps in a rash defence of their poor possessions and livelihood. These first signs of violence spent by Crusader on Christian shocked me to the core. We were well provisioned, carrying with us corn and driving flocks of sheep and cattle. There was no need for us to pillage, and the Duke's professional military eye looked with scorn at the wasteful damage that had been done. I consoled myself with the thought that Blanche must have passed that way.

We reached the Hungarian border at the town of Oedenburg. As we approached the walls, the gates opened and half a dozen well-mounted men galloped towards us. They turned out to be messengers from King Coloman, courteous in manner, but stern and unsmiling. From their solemn expressions I guessed that their news was unlikely to be welcome. Their leader handed Godfrey a parchment scroll grandly sealed with the royal double-headed eagle. Godfrey passed this missive to me.

"Be so good as to read it out for us."

I lifted the red wax with my dagger. The writing inside was Latin.

"I, Coloman, by the Grace of God King of the Hungarians, offer greetings to Godfrey de Bouillon, Duke of Lower Lorraine. As a true Christian monarch, I am ready to grant you passage through my dominions and to provision your men in your holy cause, but I seek assurances that my subjects and my lands will be left unmolested. The army of Cowled Friar Peter turned to pillage and many of his followers paid a mortal price on the swords of my knights. Truly by visiting violence upon their fellow Christians they forfeited the succour of God, for we have now had news…"

My reading faltered. Under a sharp look from Godfrey I gathered myself and continued.

"…that the Saracen has massacred them to the last man outside Nicaea."

My voice tailed off again as the attention of Godfrey's lieutenants sharpened. I rested my hands on my horse's neck to stop them shaking, crumpling the scroll in my anxiety. I could not blame the air's crisp chill for my shivers. Blanche – what had happened to her? Had she been with the army? Pray God no. Pray God she had stayed safe in Constantinople. I saw degrees of my own anxious concern reflected on the faces of most of the Duke's council. In Godfrey's eye, though, there was a gleam of something like satisfaction that his prediction to Walter Sans Avoir had been fulfilled. Only Baldwin's pale face was free of all emotion, frozen in cold indifference.

I gathered back the tatters of my concentration and struggled to continue reading in a steady voice.

"As surety for your good behaviour, I request that you send forward your noble brother Lord Baldwin and his family, to be held by me as vouchors of your peaceful passage. They will naturally be treated with all honour and courtesy but I tell you plainly that no lesser guarantor will do. They will be returned to you once you have peacefully passed into the Byzantine Empire's province of Bulgaria."

Now the cold blank of Baldwin's face flushed full with proud anger.

"I'll not act as hostage for this foreign kinglet. You can go, or Eustace."

"Come, Baldwin, it won't be so bad. You will have a comfortable time at the court of the King with that lovely wife of yours while we roughen our arses on the saddles of our horses. Or would you rather leave Godehilde here with me?"

The icy look on Baldwin's face said that Godfrey had gone too far. I could tell all too easily that he had made a foolish mistake in letting slip the careful tone he habitually used with his younger brother, and especially in joking at his expense in front of others. Bagrat lurked behind his master, aping Baldwin's cold expression. Godfrey paused and for a moment I thought he was going to needle his brother further. Then better judgement gained the upper hand, and he changed his tone to solicitous flattery.

"Come, Baldwin. You know that you can rely on me to keep discipline. There will be no risk to your safety. The Hungarian King has doubtless heard of your fearsome reputation and of your high position in our councils. Your bruit and fame is what prompts his single-minded demand for you."

Under his breath, so quietly that only I could hear, he added, "Or perhaps he has heard of your wife's beauty and wants to eye her for himself."

Scowling, Baldwin still refused to go.

"Send Eustace. Or go yourself."

Now it was Godfrey's turn to flush angrily as the issue developed into a test of strength between the brothers. He changed his point of attack.

"I had not thought to see the day when my brother Baldwin was scared. Your time as a churchman obviously took a greater toll than I had thought."

The gathering was now tense and utterly silent. The two brothers glared at each other, reliving who knows what trial of strength from their childhood. Baldwin's horse fidgeted from side to side and he brutally pulled its reins, snarling.

"Very well. I will go, to answer the slur that you have dared to cast on my courage, but the day will come when you will regret treating me like this. You know I do not forget a slight so easily."

Baldwin and his family followed Coloman's messengers, with a small retinue including his dark Armenian shadow. Baldwin's brittle bearing as he left plainly expressed the high price in fraternal discord that had been paid for safe passage. Our journey continued, now in the company of a large escort of King Coloman's troops.

When we had crossed the broad Hungarian plain without incident, I almost regretted the good discipline that Godfrey enforced on his men, because Baldwin was safely restored, still angrily sulking that his brother had been willing to place him at risk. But either the event had passed from Godfrey's mind, or he relished taunting his brother and could not resist showing off to his sister-in-law. For he greeted the Lady Godehilde on her return with a deep bow and another over-familiar kiss on the hand. He was rewarded by a flash of warm admiration from beneath her long eyelashes. I could see that neither gesture escaped Baldwin's basilisk eyes.

But I had greater worries. Anxiously I fingered the ribboned hank of Blanche's hair as it nestled beneath my undershirt. I told myself that it was impossible that I would not see again the owner of those beautiful locks. God could not be so cruel. My anxiety fought my excitement, two days before the sacred feast of the Nativity, in the year of Our Lord 1096, when I saw for the first time the ramparts of Constantinople. Behind them, I hoped and fervently prayed, I would find Blanche safe and sound.

SAINT LAZARUS' COLLEGE

Back in the rooms which had been his home for nearly twenty years, the Modern Languages Tutor nursed a dry martini and a feeling of poisonous resentment towards the Master. The empty feeling in his stomach made him think bitterly to himself, "So this is how the Fisher King must have felt when he was wounded in the guts. If he'd given me that sword I'd have it out of its Venetian embroidered scabbard in a flash."

Two more dry martinis and the Modern Languages Tutor had been emboldened enough to reach a decision. The Master could not be allowed to get away with it. He knew what he had to do. He slipped out to the street and headed for the hardware store.

CHAPTER SIX

UNREAL CITY

*I came to Constantine's great city thinking only of
finding news of Walter Sans Avoir's retinue. But I
confess that, when I first saw that extraordinary
metropolis, my thoughts were diverted for a while
towards simple awe and amazement.*

At night around the camp fire I had listened to much talk
about Constantinople. None of those who talked had seen the
city, but I could believe them when they said that its
fortifications had never yet been breached. I could almost
believe their claim that it was greater than Rome herself, but
I found it harder to accept that its walls encompassed more
people than the whole of France. However, I did not dare to
contradict them. During the weary months of our journey I
had built Constantinople in my imagination. But when I
arrived I had to knock down the fantasy I had constructed,
so small and puny was it in comparison to the reality. As soon
as the city came into sight, I could immediately believe
everything that had been said.

Even in the distance the walls looked as if they had been
built by some race of ancient giants. Close to, I could

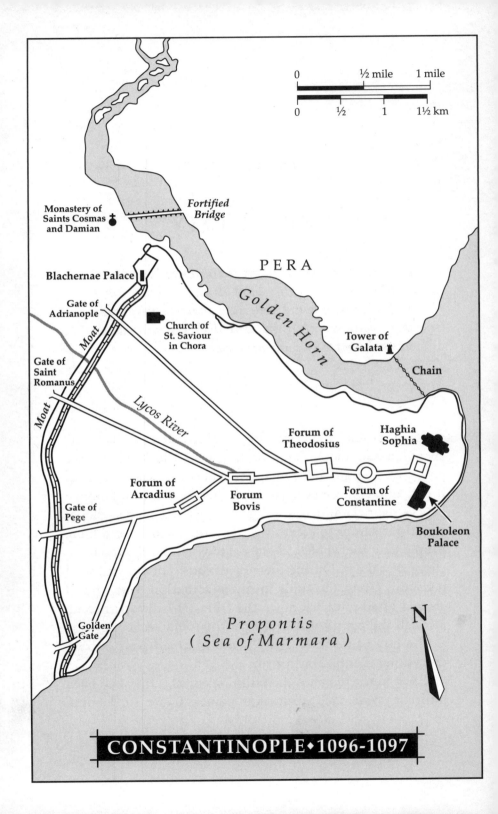

Monastery of
Saints Cosmas
and Damian

*Fortified
Bridge*

P E R A

Blachernae Palace

Golden Horn

Gate of
Adrianople

Moat

Church of
St. Saviour
in Chora

Tower of
Galata

Gate of
Saint
Romanus

Chain

Moat

Lycos River

Forum of
Theodosius

Haghia
Sophia

Forum of
Arcadius

Forum
Bovis

Forum of
Constantine

Gate of
Pege

Boukoleon
Palace

Golden
Gate

*Propontis
(Sea of Marmara)*

N

CONSTANTINOPLE ◆ 1096-1097

0   ½ mile   1 mile

0   ½   1   1½ km

Our guides – or guards – told us that we should be honoured by the place given to us to camp, for it lay just opposite the Emperor's own Palace of Blachernae, separated from it only by the tall city walls. There we settled down as best we could to celebrate the Feast of the Nativity. The weather had at last turned cold. A northern wind swept the exposed site, and many must have shared my wish that we were inside the shelter of the fortifications. My Lord Godfrey's tented pavilion, in the middle of the army, and those of the other barons, provided some shelter, but most of our men shivered in the open around their smoky campfires.

So I was well pleased when the Count de Vermandois, with three of his French followers and three of Alexios's men, rode into camp bearing the Emperor's invitation to Godfrey and his lieutenants to enter the city and take up more luxurious lodgings. Vermandois greeted the Duke with an embrace of affectionate condescension. I could see that Godfrey had been needled by the Count's patronising bearing when he stepped back, holding out his hands, and said, "My Lord Count, look at you and your fine raiment. You look quite the Greek in these rich silks. You put us simple soldiers to shame."

Indeed the sumptuous purple and red silk tunic and the fur-trimmed cloak worn by Vermandois set a sharp contrast to the dull travel-stained woollen garments worn by the rest of us. Otherwise, squat and round-faced, with a cold arrogant glint in his eyes as he tilted his head slightly upwards to answer, he made a poor comparison to the taller Godfrey. I wondered what justified his grand manner.

"We heard rumours that you had been shipwrecked on the Dalmatian shore and even ill-used by the Emperor's underlings. I am glad to see the falsehood of these reports."

"Indeed I was shipwrecked, my Lord Duke, but when the noble Emperor Alexios heard that the blood of the royal family of France runs in these veins of mine he became especially gracious and generous towards me."

I looked with renewed interest at the first person of royal blood that I had seen. I still could see no external justification for the respect the little man's pompous manner appeared to demand.

"He has heaped me with rich gifts, and in return I have taken an oath of fealty to acknowledge his imperial suzerainty and to agree to restore to him any territories that I conquer. I am here at his request to ask you to do the same."

Baldwin thrust forward into the surprised silence that followed these words, his black eyes flashing, and hissed, "I will take no such oath. I have not travelled all this way to wield my sword in the service of some foreign emperor and then to hand back all the conquests that I make."

Even Count Eustace's habitual stolidity was shaken, and he nodded his head as Godfrey blustered.

"My emperor is Henry the Fourth in Germany. I am with brother Baldwin. I'll not swear. Nor will Eustace. What is more, I do not trust this Alexios. I'll not venture into his city unprotected. Tell him to come here if he wishes to speak with me. He has only sent me a few heralds," gesturing rudely at the Count and the Byzantine officials who had accompanied him, "so I will send him back some of my own."

"You go too," he said to me quietly, "and listen carefully to what they say to each other in their own slippery tongue."

I grinned with delight before I remembered the gravity of the occasion and dressed my face with a suitably fierce military expression. The Count de Vermandois had been taken aback by the force of Godfrey's reaction, and I now clearly saw the weakness beneath his pompous kingly manner. He turned to look at his Byzantine companions, as if for instruction. Two of them wore splendid gold body chains, which reached over their shoulders and under their arms, to secure a pierced disc of gold at front and back. Their leader, grey-bearded, and clad in a silver studded leather cap with bizarre ear flaps which hung down far below his lobes, shook his head slightly. At this signal the Count turned back to Godfrey and began to remonstrate.

"My Lord Duke, you do not understand the power and prestige of this emperor. His lands stretch almost as far as you have travelled. The wealth and splendour of his court outdoes even my father's. As a king's son myself, I know how to treat an emperor such as Alexios. How can I expect you to fully understand royal sensibilities? But I do ask you to follow my advice in the interest of our great cause."

Angrily Godfrey cut him short.

"Go away, you pompous popinjay. You may be easily won with flattery and gifts but in the House of Boulogne we are made of stronger stuff, are we not, eh, Baldwin, Eustace?"

Despondent, the French Count turned and left the tent, followed by the rest of his party. Godfrey brusquely indicated to me and three others who happened to be standing by that we should now follow. Concern touched my delight as I reflected that I was being sent where my master had said he feared to tread. Godfrey's words about the Emperor's untrustworthiness echoed in my ears. Further displeasure came when I saw Bagrat forming up as a member of our party at Baldwin's command.

We rode back a league or so the way we had come on the previous day, down the length of the walls, before turning into the Golden Gate across a wide drawbridge over the city moat. The gate was topped by four huge bronze statues of exotic creatures unlike anything I had seen before. Their noses hung down almost to the ground between curved tusks at least twice as long as my sword, while wide flat ears framed each side of their wrinkled faces. These fearsome sentinels stood guard over sights beyond of which I could not even dream.

Once inside the walls I was struck first by the sheer numbers of people about their business in the street. Our embassy passed through great squares packed with many hued crowds, varying so much in form and dress that I knew they

94

must have come from all the corners of the earth. They swirled before my eyes, so that I caught brief impressions of different figures before my attention moved on. Behind the billowing purple cape of one proud citizen I saw two men with black faces – devils surely! That was my first reaction before I discerned slavery in their humble demeanour. The crowd opened respectfully before their master and they disappeared. Then I blushed under the curious gaze of a pretty olive skinned girl. Did I look as odd to these Greek citizens as they looked to me? Her strange dark ringlets were swallowed up in turn by the throng which was packed especially tightly around an open space where two bug-eyed dwarves were raising laughter and alms by tumbling and mumming. I dragged my attention away from this human theatre towards the slender pillar nearby. It was topped with a robed figure, utterly realistic except that it was two or three times life size. Similar graceful statues, and vast beasts fashioned of bronze and marble, occupied every public space. The streets and squares were lined with fine colonnaded buildings, their large windows, some even covered in precious glass, watching my passage as if to ask 'Have you ever seen such splendour and magnificence?' I affected nonchalance at all these sights, not wanting to show my Byzantine escorts how their city stirred and impressed me, lest I revealed how different it was to the crude and humble towns of my homeland. I was also conscious that Bagrat had seen all this splendour before. At no cost would I compare poorly with my rival.

But for all this affected calm, my head was spinning as I tried to absorb the sights, to breathe the exotic smells, to catch the foreign sounds of unfamiliar tongues and distant music. Then we reached the greatest square of all, in which a colossal bronze statue reared up of a mounted emperor – from his proud mien he could only have been an emperor, and I later learned that this was none other than the famed Justinian – holding in one hand a crossed orb, and raising the other as if in admonition to any enemies who dared to threaten his city. Behind the emperor crouched an enormous building, its corners rounded like the haunches of some mythical beast about to pounce. I could conceal my amazement no longer, and I felt my mask of impassivity cracking and falling apart. I fear that the knowing Byzantine at my side had watched my struggle with amusement beneath the gleaming cone of his helmet. Now he beamed in triumph and murmured through his beard in Greek.

"Our cathedral of Haghia Sophia. Isn't she magnificent?"

Then, in spite of myself, I started with surprise at one of twenty-four doors flying open on a great mechanical clock. Bagrat sneered openly at my naivety; at least the Byzantine had the decency to turn away to hide his smile.

"The clock tells that we have an hour before the time appointed for the audience with his Highest Majesty Emperor Alexios. I would be pleased to show you inside if you wish."

I understood that another opportunity was being taken to awe and cow me ahead of our imperial audience but I thought to score a diplomatic point of my own by comparing favourably the noble abbey church at Cluny with this bizarre, multi-domed structure. So I gratefully accepted the invitation. My hopes of outfacing the Byzantine began to fall before the splendour of the glittering gold tiles that decorated the vestibule's arched ceiling. Then they shattered on the marble floor of the huge body of the church as I saw that it could have comfortably swallowed Cluny whole. I could not stop myself gaping at the magnificence of its decoration, the pillars, capitals and panels of semiprecious stone, red jasper, orange cornelian, blue lapis lazuli, cream chalcedony and green heliotrope, yellow citrine and every other colour of quartz. My Byzantine guide told me proudly that each stone column had the power to cure a different disease if the sufferer rubbed his body against it. I had just enough presence of mind to reply that I was in perfect health, thank you. My guide pointed out the huge silver iconostasis that screened off the chancel, unnecessarily for it was the height of six or seven men, and crowded with pictures of unfamiliar saints. He spoke proudly of the relics kept there: the Holy Cross and the actual lance which pierced Christ's side, both brought from the Holy Land by Saint Helena, mother of the Emperor Constantine; the bones of Saint Anne, the mother of the Virgin Mary, and of many other saints.

"Our relics here are the genuine ones, not the copies and counterfeits so often seen elsewhere."

I would remember that assertion well in the times ahead.

In the round apse above the altar, where Cluny had Our Lord Jesus Christ supported by Saints Peter and Paul painted in mere coloured pigment, Haghia Sophia boasted a richly gilded mosaic of Mary the Virgin Mother of God, the Holy Christ Child nested in Her lap, supported on either side by the Archangels Gabriel and Michael. Above all this splendour a majestic dome seemed to hover without support. A second look showed me that it was held up by columns between two score arched windows, some glazed in jewelled colours of the type for which my abbot had longed for his church at Cluny. Others were plain, allowing light to fall in moted beams, to pierce the gloom of the vast chamber and illuminate the quiet movements of the worshipping throng below.

Speechless, I crossed myself and staggered back outside with the rest of my party. I was now utterly overawed as we turned towards our reception in the Emperor's old palace. In its entrance hall stood a life-size bronze of a lion savaging an ox. From this it took its name – the Boukoleon. When I had overcome my astonishment at the realism of this statue – the animals might simply have been frozen there in mid-fight – I could not help myself imagining the Emperor as the lion and its bovine prey as my master Godfrey. If Haghia Sophia spoke of incomparable religious power, this imperial palace, marbled, gilded, dressed in gorgeous silks and rich fabrics, told a tale of unparalleled secular might and wealth.

We passed through courtyards filled with fruiting shrubs and plants, exotic beyond compare with the simple herbs in Cluny's gardens. I longed to pause and taste them but we were hurried on to an imposing entrance. Fearsome figures stood on duty here – Varangian Guardsmen, the axe-armed Northmen who formed the Emperor's personal bodyguard. They could have provided more than a match in hand-to-hand combat for the best of our men. We entered an antechamber and I jumped with surprise, seeing what at first glance I took to be an internal window with a young man walking on the other side. Then I looked again and saw that I was looking at my own image in a polished silver disc held up by standards wrought with fruited vines. Involuntarily I lifted up my hand to touch my bearded cheek and saw my own hand moving there on the wall. Captivated like Narcissus, I drank in my own clear reflection for the first time. The brown colour of my hair I knew because the ends are sometimes long enough to catch out of the corner of my eye, and had sometimes been cut. I did not know that my eyes matched my hair, though, and I tried to make out their expression. Did they always contain that look of wonder or was that provoked by all the new spectacles that I had seen that day? My brow above was high and clear. The nose looked straight enough. My chin seemed firm under its beard, itself lighter than the hair on my head and flecked with red. Set against my companions I looked three or four fingers taller than I had expected – perhaps before I had measured the level of my eyes against the crown of their head. Self-consciously, and not displeased by what I saw, I straightened my back and squared my shoulders.

Then the great gilded doors swung wide to reveal the high-pillared rectangular throne room and its inexplicable splendour of Ionian white and gold. Arched windows stretched the length of the right-hand wall and were filled with glass of such fineness and transparency that they gave a clear view over the busy shipping entering the Bosphorus, the taxes from which flooded the imperial treasury. Beyond the crowd of courtiers, under a coffered ceiling, in a chair like a burnished throne, set on a dais higher than all around it, so that none save God should be above the Emperor, sat Alexios I Comnenos, dressed in cloth of gold – the master of this magnificence.

I bowed low with my companions. Then we hesitantly approached the throne. Behind on the wall I saw a row of crowns, which I supposed had sat on the heads of Alexios's predecessors and were perhaps intended to attest to his long lineage. The Count de Vermandois took the lead, and I filled with disgust at the sight of this arrogant son of a king making such easily bought obeisance to the Emperor. Watching this royal masquerade, I glimpsed from the corner of my eye Bagrat melting into the crowd, and registered surprise before thinking that he had perhaps noted an old acquaintance from days gone by. Then all my attention was absorbed as thwarted pride spoiled the urbanity of Alexios's face at the Count's report of the Boulognes' refusal to wait upon him. With a brusque gesture of his bejewelled hand the Emperor commanded silence. The thunderous anger now in that regard rekindled my fears for my own safety.

"Who are these unruly knights, believing in their arrogance that they can ignore our imperial summons? Do they think that I, Alexios, the Roman successor of Augustus, Justinian and Constantine, will allow them to cross my wide dominions without swearing the customary oath of allegiance?"

Then he turned to his advisers clustering around the throne. I strained to catch his quietly spoken words of Greek, realising that with Bagrat elsewhere only I could hope to understand this aside.

"We must move these ruffians on across the Bosphorus and away from our precious city, before the other turbulent Crusader bands catch up. We know Raymond of Provence and the one I fear most – my sworn Norman enemy Bohemond of Taranto – are close behind. Joined, they might even be a match for my armies."

Then Alexios raised his voice again in a tone intended to reverberate around the room.

"Very well. We shall see how you all enjoy the Feast of the Nativity with no provisions. When you have shown yourselves willing to act as worthy guests, we will welcome you again as generous hosts. Meanwhile you may celebrate Our Lord's birth with a holy fast."

My heart sank into the empty young stomach below, which had been eagerly anticipating Christmas rations more plentiful and varied than normal. Given to understand in no uncertain terms that the audience was over, we bowed and our guards began to reverse us away from the throne. It was just then that hope surged up in me, as a small figure emerged, revealed behind a line of taller courtiers. A white habit stood out against the backdrop of richly coloured garments, the only one of that colour in the room, for, as I later discovered, white was the colour of mourning to the Byzantines. Wasn't that the costume of a travelling friar? Surely such a garb could belong only to Peter the Hermit? I rapidly scanned the room for the bulk of Walter Sans Avoir. If one leader had survived, perhaps so had the other…and perhaps his retinue. Was it possible that the reports of the annihilation of the Crusade's first wave had been cruelly exaggerated? I longed to stop my relentless flow towards the door, and to question the figure whose white garment stood for sudden hope. But the escort penned me in and swept me inexorably back through the gilded doorway. Outside the palace I found myself being guided reluctantly back towards our windswept camp. There was nobody I could ask who would confirm or deny the identity of the man in the pale habit. My eagerness overcame even my distaste and without thinking I asked Bagrat, who had emerged furtively from the crowd in the audience chamber and was now riding alongside me, whether he had noticed the friar and whether he thought it might be Peter. I immediately regretted my words, for Bagrat's shrugged reply managed to combine ignorance and lack of interest with scornful derision. I completed the journey in silence, knowing only that I had to find some way to return inside the city walls to find and question the man in white.

Our camp's muddy squalor and cold discomfort provided a harsh contrast to the extraordinary splendour I had just witnessed. I found Godfrey in a black mood, uncomfortably closeted with Baldwin and Eustace.

"My Lord, I can scarcely find words to communicate the splendour of this city and the power of the emperor who rules it."

"Don't bother me then," he growled. Confused by this rebuff, I could recall only my reflection in the mirror, my glimpse of the white habit that I so hoped was Peter's, and my image of the ducal ox being savaged by the imperial lion. I faltered before pulling myself together to offer my more useful piece of information.

"But he knows his power is not invincible, my Lord. I heard him say in an aside to his advisers that he fears our strength if we combine with the armies of Count Raymond the Provençal and Bohemond the Norman. He will deny us provisions because he wants to force you to swear his oath and move you on across the sea before the others arrive. His scouts have plainly told him that they are not far behind."

Godfrey now looked up sharply.

"You see! What have I just been saying to you, Eustace? There is no need to swear the oath. With a little patience and persistence we will soon have this emperor where we want him. And you see, Baldwin – we do not have to rush to confront the Byzantines – we will not have long to wait for our allies to arrive."

I was delighted by the warm smile Godfrey bestowed on me, and cheered further by the sharp look that Baldwin turned on Bagrat with the angry unspoken question why he had not heard this intelligence.

"So that decides us. We will continue to refuse the Emperor's oath. We'll just wait as the approach of our allies increases the pressure upon him. He'll crack. You'll see."

"Very well," Baldwin hissed, "and if this slippery Greek will not give us provisions, we shall take what we want. Let's give our men a special gift to mark this Christmas feast. They should be at liberty to plunder these suburbs at will."

Baldwin's eyes glittered, betraying his preference to take with violence rather than to receive in peace. Godfrey shrugged in idle concurrence.

That Christmas was not a good time for the unfortunates who lived beneath the great walls of Constantinople. Once already they had suffered the violent depredations of soldiers who supposedly worshipped the same God as they, when Peter the Hermit's mob had swarmed through their homes. Now they suffered the organised cruelty of Baldwin's men. I stayed in the camp and prayed fervently that this savagery of Christian on Christian would cease, that this wicked behaviour would not turn God against our noble cause. I tried to close my eyes to the brutality around but I could not shut my ears to the heart-rending screams of the women dragged back to the camp to be used at will by the soldiery. What if Blanche had suffered a similar fate?

Just after sunset on the third day of this savagery I was writing in Godfrey's tent when I heard a commotion outside. I emerged to see three captives being hauled along by men of Baldwin's. The pointed helmet still worn by one marked them as Pechenegs. I knew them by now as the Emperor's policemen. They had been given the task of escorting us on our arrival and were now detailed to do what they could to contain our army's worst excesses. These three unfortunates had already plainly taken a beating for their pains. Two were young, scarcely my own age, and where their swarthy faces were not marked with blood and bruises they were pale with fear. The third was older, struggling to set an example for his younger colleagues by maintaining a firmer demeanour.

Baldwin himself approached, his eyes hard with anticipation.

"Bring me fire and tools," he ordered. Then he hissed to Bagrat, who stood as usual simpering close to his master's side, "Translate for me."

"So you are three. Yet I need only one messenger to take back to your imperial master the news of how we treat those who dare to thwart us. Should I kill two of you and release the third? That seems most unjust to me and I am nothing if not fair. So I will spare all your lives."

The terror in the two younger prisoners' faces turned momentarily to relief. The eldest of the three narrowed his eyes in surprise. Baldwin laughed malevolently.

"I'll leave one messenger able to see the way, one to open barriers, and one to speak the message."

When Bagrat had translated, the Pechenegs began to squirm with fear again. In unison the two younger men began to plead for mercy in their broken guttural Greek. As the two braziers were set on either side at Baldwin's command, the older man cracked too, gabbling prayers so fast that strings of spittle dribbled from his mouth. The terror in their squat faces was lit in high relief from below by the red light cast from the braziers. Torches held high by some of the soldiers completed the flickering illumination of this infernal scene. Baldwin gestured to the men holding the older prisoner. They pushed him forward and forced his arms out in front of him. Baldwin's sword swung twice, cutting through the back of each hand and severing fingers and thumb. For a moment the shock silenced his victim. Then high-pitched screams pulsed out in time with the blood from his wounds.

"Stop his bleeding before he soils my surcoat," Baldwin

ordered. His guards lifted their prisoner bodily to plunge his mutilated limbs into the nearest brazier, filling the air with the stench of burning flesh and ratcheting his screams to a climax. At Baldwin's gesture Bagrat passed over a short poker from the second brazier. Its red hot end disappeared sizzling into the unfortunate's eyes. The screams stopped, to be replaced by pitiful whimpering.

I felt disgust and horror, but somehow mixed with an awful fascination that would not let me tear my gaze away. They dragged the first of the younger men forward blubbering to lose his hands by Baldwin's sword. Then Bagrat forced open his jaws and grabbed his tongue with a pair of pincers, wrenching it forward for Baldwin's dagger. Blood bubbled from his mouth. Baldwin read the brutal gleam in Bagrat's eyes and handed the dagger over to his acolyte. I saw the Armenian shaking with excitement as he dragged out the third prisoner's tongue and sliced it off before exchanging pincers and dagger for poker and burning out his eyes too. Now I understood that Bagrat received more for his services than just the monetary recompense offered to me as a bribe at Bouillon. And the expression of arousal on the master's white face as he watched his henchman was awful to behold.

"Even the Emperor should understand this message," sneered Baldwin.

My hatred was swamped by my shame that I stood there as an impotent observer of this perverted scene. I turned into the darkness beside my tent to hide my tears of horror and retched violently.

At least this atrocity marked the end of this period of savagery, for three days after Christmas, Alexios heard the cries of his subjects – or the wiser counsel of his advisers – or perhaps he had just sated himself in his own Christmas revels and was prepared to turn his attention to the plight of his citizens. In any event, ambassadors arrived again in our camp. This time they introduced a consignment of provisions, and brought the offer to provide comfortable accommodation in the suburb of Pera. Godfrey was cheered by this small triumph.

"You see how the Emperor responds to a firm hand. Now we'll have a solid roof over our heads, and my troops will be sheltered out of this damned north wind."

So we struck camp. Our army filed past the ancient hospital monastery dedicated to the pharmacist brothers Saints Cosmos and Damian, across the fortified bridge over the Golden Horn. I was despondent, for I was determined to find a way inside the walls in search of the friar, and knew the geography of the city well enough now to understand that I would have to retrace my steps to do so. Then my heart sank further, for no sooner had we settled in our new lodgings than an imperial missive arrived to make it known in no uncertain terms that any of Godfrey's men found on the southern side of the Horn would be subject to summary execution. I read the message out to an indignant Duke's council, knowing myself that I would be one of the first transgressors to risk his neck. I would find news of Blanche or die trying.

SAINT LAZARUS' COLLEGE

The Modern Languages Tutor drew back his narrow shoulders in an attempt to look firm and unconcerned.

"I need some rat poison," he said to the assistant behind the counter. He did not often come into the hardware shop, but on the few occasions when he had cause to do so it was normally to buy a cigarette lighter. The old-fashioned shelves, stacked apparently at random behind a scarred wooden counter, had always rather appealed to him.

"Rat poison, sir? Oh dear. I am so sorry to hear that you have a problem in that department at Saint Lazarus'. What sort would you like?"

The Modern Languages Tutor had not considered the possibility that there might be more than one type on offer and was momentarily confused.

"Mmm...the strongest you have, I suppose."

"Well, that would be one of the modern warfarin derivatives. Now if we were in China you could get some tetramethylene disulfotetramine – it has been used regularly there for bumping off unwanted enemies but it is so lethal has been banned everywhere else in the world."

The shop assistant laughed loudly at his own joke, but seeing the sudden concern on the Modern Languages Tutor's face, he changed his tune and became serious again.

"Don't worry Professor, difethialone will do the job for you. You are not going to put it down in an area where pets might be? It'll kill pretty much anything, you know. And I don't suppose that the problem is just confined to your rooms. Normally these creatures range quite widely. Why don't you mention it to the College Steward and have him deal with it?"

"No, well, I thought I'd better sort it out myself. He is such a busy man, you know."

The Modern Languages Tutor essayed a smile of

reassurance but the shop assistant's slightly startled look told him that his lips were twisting unconvincingly. He dropped his gaze and fumbled in his coat pocket for a cigarette.

"I can put it on the College account, if you like, sir. Seeing as I know you so well. And because it is poisonous, I am obliged to enter the sale in my dangerous substance ledger here."

The Modern Languages Tutor began to stammer, so that the unlit cigarette now bobbed up and down on his lower lip. He decided to capitulate.

"Oh, don't worry. Maybe you are right. It should be one for the Steward. I'll report it to him. I expect he'll be in soon."

He turned abruptly and scampered out of the shop, leaving the assistant scratching his head and muttering about the eccentricities of university academics.

CHAPTER SEVEN

ENTERING THE WHIRLPOOL

Later I wondered whether I had tempted fate by preferring my own concerns amidst such barbarity and suffering. Would I have done better to bury my own emotions under my duty to others? After all, that was what I had been taught to do by mother and monk. Yet I was driven by an irresistible compulsion to find news of Blanche. Then nothing else mattered. Now perhaps I have paid the price for my selfishness.

I chose the Feast of the Epiphany in early January for my undertaking. I thought that the day when the Magi succeeded in their quest might also be auspicious for me. More practically, it was dark and gloomy, and a thick fog swirled off the black waters of the Golden Horn. I could not make use of the cover of night, because I would have to penetrate the walls before dusk, when the gates were locked until dawn. I saw no way to pass in daylight back across the single fortified bridge over the Horn. It was well guarded, and however cleverly I disguised myself, however fluent my Greek, I would surely be discovered as one of Godfrey's men by the garrison. They must have been given orders to keep careful watch for such as me.

Instead I would have to cross on the water. This filled me with trepidation. I was no waterman. I could not swim and had never handled a boat. So my courage was in shreds as I donned my old black habit. Trying to pull myself together, I made a silent prayer of thanks for the instinct that had made me decide not to discard it and to stow it in my pack. With dismay I realised that I would have to leave behind my precious sword and my mail. Without them, I felt bare and unprotected. I pulled my sword's scabbard off its belt, leaving just the dagger which hung opposite at my right side. This I strapped around my waist under my robe. I tested a couple of times how fast I could get the dagger out. It was slow because I had to hitch the skirt of my habit right up to get at the handle. I'd just hope to avoid using it. Nevertheless, feeling it through the material of my habit provided some reassurance. Then I set off down towards the shore. Godfrey's pickets stationed there posed no problems for me – they had no reason to doubt my story about embarking on a secret task for the Duke. Indeed they willingly helped me to find a boat. I expect their respect turned to hidden mirth behind me when they saw how I struggled to control the coracle I selected.

Every movement I made, every effort to paddle, threatened to upset the fragile craft. In the fog I could not see across to the further shore. Indeed I had little idea of how far away it was. A brisk swell rippled the shore. The noises were all unfamiliar – the harsh mewing of seabirds overhead, the sucking and slapping of the water. Rocking and wobbling, I came close to turning about but mastered my fear better than my boat. Eventually I made out the sea walls of the city through the murk and began to paddle against the current so that I could beach below the bridge but beyond the walls. To my alarm I found myself scarcely moving forward. When I stopped paddling for a moment to see what was wrong I was disconcerted to find myself moving rapidly in the wrong direction. I was being carried downstream. Realising the speed and Ovid so many centuries before, will show you instantaneously the distance of civilization's backward movement since the glorious era of Ancient Greece and Rome."

The combatants glared at each other across the table.

In the body of the hall the undergraduates had finished their lesser meal and trooped away noisily from their hard benches. The Master leant back in his comfortably armed chair, withdrawing before re-engaging his guest.

"Do have some port. In your honour I've had them dig out the last couple of bottles of the Taylor '45. I think you'll find it's still drinking exceptionally well. Of course, at the rate we are going, the whole cellar will have to be sold off to pay the College debts. That is unless an insolvency practitioner gets to it first. My predecessor allowed some truly terrible investment decisions. So we need help and I am talking to as many of our distinguished alumni as I can."

The Best-Selling Author had known that this moment would come and as his final fortification took a deeper draft of the old port than was quite decent. He sighed as the sweet-sharp warmth travelled down his throat. He avoided the steel of the Master's gaze by making a great play of appreciative concentration on the ruby glow refracting in the antique cut glass.

"Yes of course, I quite understand. I'd really like to help the old *alma mater*. The trouble is, I'm in a bit of a pickle myself. My divorce was painful, and came just after that fantastic film rights deal. You might have read about it in the tabloids. So the bloody wife got half of it. And frankly we creative types are not much good at looking after money either. It just seems to trickle away."

Now he leaned forward and injected a confidential tone into his voice.

"But to be honest, the real problem is that I haven't written anything new for quite a while. My last book goes back three, of the flow, I feared that I would be swept out into the open waters of the Bosphorus, adrift with the turning tide. I set to with vigour renewed by panic, and bit by bit, sweating in spite of the cold, muscles cracking from the unaccustomed motion of paddling, I pulled towards my goal. To my relief, the current weakened near the shore, and the stretch of bank seemed unguarded, so I was able to beach my little boat behind some bushes just beyond the water's edge. A rat crept softly through the vegetation dragging its slimy belly on the bank.

I paused to gain my breath and looked carefully round to confirm the absence of guards. Clearly no waterborne approach from Pera had been anticipated. Awkwardly I fished my dagger out from under my robe and cut a blaze on one of the stunted trees by the water's edge. That would help me find my boat again. Then I pulled my cowl over my head and struck out briskly through the fog in the direction that I estimated would bisect the road from the fortified bridge to the northernmost city gate. Reaching it, I slowed to a more monkish pace. The gradual approach of the gate grated on my impatience. Nevertheless, I forced myself to remain in character, my head humbly bowed, my hands folded across my chest and each thrust into the opposite sleeve. In this guise I attracted no attention from the small number of passers-by travelling the road in the hostile weather. The feverish activity in my brain made up for the slow pace of my feet, as I worked to construct a story to tell, should I be stopped and challenged. As the square gate towers loomed out of the gloom I mouthed a silent prayer of thanks that I had done so, for every traveller was being curtly asked his business by the guards. When it was my turn, I stepped up and made a Sign of the Cross in benediction. I forced myself not to grasp the dagger through my garment. The guard spat a question at me. At first I could not understand his guttural Greek. Frustration showed in his narrow eyes as he spoke again more slowly and I realised with relief that the language was as foreign to the Pecheneg as to me. I was not the only one who found him difficult to understand. Any strange tone in my own accent was likely to go unnoticed by him.

"I come from the Monastery of Saint Cosmos and Damian. I was sent there by my abbot to recover from a high fever."

The wheezy voice I affected and the news of my illness caused my questioner to draw back a little.

"I am now better, much better..." I burst into a fit of coughing "...so I have been sent to return to my own cloister."

Eager to remain clear of sickness, the guard waved me brusquely through. Lifted by the success of my subterfuge, I turned my mind to my next challenge – how to find the man I hoped to be Peter the Hermit.

'Monks lodge with other monks,' I said to myself. I remembered my sojourn with my abbot in Clermont and felt a rush of loneliness. 'So I will just make enquiry at the first ecclesiastical establishment I reach.'

A little further down the street, I came upon a small church and cloister. As I hammered on the door, my heart seemed to pound in my chest as hard as the heavy knocker against the wood. A peephole swung open to reveal a single eye that rotated disconcertingly in its socket, studying me cautiously before disappearing again. I was about to resume my hammering when a larger panel opened and the rest of a face appeared. The eye's owner was a monk with a wrinkled face of gentle simplicity. His expression was so childlike and kindly that I felt myself smiling in return in spite of my nervousness.

"Brother, greetings on this Holy Day. I seek the French Friar Peter, known as the Hermit. Have you heard of him? He came here at the head of a Christian army. I am an old acquaintance of his with news from his homeland. I was told that he was lodged in this part of the city."

The old monk's artless expression turned to deep sorrow as he shook his head softly.

"Sadly Friar Peter does not lodge with us. Our establishment here is too small and humble..."

My heart sank. Then his previous beatific expression returned.

"...but he will be staying at Saint Saviour in Chora just down the street. It lies just beside the Emperor's Palace of Blachernae..."

Here he crossed himself in respect.

"...so that is where his important ecclesiastical guests are housed."

I was cheered by the goodness that radiated from my informant. My faith in human nature temporarily restored, I turned away with a lighter step. The monastery of Saint Saviour in Chora was scarcely a hundred paces further on, and was indeed far grander, so that its arched doorway might have passed for the entrance of some nobleman's palace. Its gatekeeper was equally grand and lacked the holy humility of the old monk. He eyed my tattered habit with some distaste before summoning one of his fellows to take me to Peter. Prayers of thanks were still on my lips when I was ushered into the Friar's chamber. I filled with optimism, sure that God would not have brought me safely to Friar Peter to receive other than positive news. The room more luxurious by far than any of the cells at Cluny. I glanced at a sacred picture of a strange saint hanging on the wall. My appreciation turned to unease at the large limpid eyes which bored me through, following me around the room wherever I moved, at the long straight nose, and the narrow lips pursed in apparent disapproval.

The Hermit's eyes were more alarming still. They would not stay still in his close-cropped head, but widened and narrowed, darting from place to place as if expecting danger from any direction. A tick in one cheek completed the impression that this little man, scarcely larger than a child, was a bundle of uncontrolled nerves or even close to insanity. Unsettled, I bowed to introduce myself.

"Friar Peter, I am honoured to find you here. I was once a novice at Cluny, and had the privilege to act as secretary to the holy Abbot Hugh."

At the word Cluny, Peter grimaced in disgust and spat. His glutinous spittle made a small slug on the floor. Shaken, I hurried on with my explanation.

"I am now fortunate enough to perform the same function for Lord Godfrey of Bouillon, Duke of Lower Lorraine."

It seemed that Peter had no more respect for my secular master, for two more slimy gobbets landed on the flagstones. I struggled hesitantly on.

"Before he joined you, Brother Peter, Walter Sans Avoir lodged with my master Duke Godfrey at Bouillon. They became fast friends. That's why I have been sent to you to ascertain his whereabouts on the Duke's behalf."

Peter the Hermit now twitched and jiggled.

"Sans Avoir," he quavered, "Sans Avoir was meant to answer to me. He ignored my orders. There were hordes of them. Arrows brought down his horse. They had to stick him over and over before that vast body would be still. Over and over.... He should have obeyed my orders."

The Friar's eyes widened as he looked directly at me, perhaps because I was now shaking almost as much he.

"And his retinue, what about them? What about his family, his womenfolk?"

"All gone, all gone, all lost. No more."

The Hermit curled up on his bed, turned his face to the wall, and would not speak another word. I stepped forward and shook his shoulder in desperation.

"Please. I must know what happened. He has...had...a ward...tall, slender, blonde. Look, her hair was this colour."

I pulled the precious lock from under my garment. Roughly I dragged the Hermit's little body round and brandished Blanche's keepsake under his nose.

"Look, damn you."

113

But his eyes were blank and glassy, his expression frozen. I raised my free hand to strike him, but when my movement produced not the slightest sign of awareness I let it fall again in resignation. Helpless I stood there, under the mocking gaze of the icon. The saint's fingers pointed at me in accusation. Then I could stand it no longer and I turned and fled.

I wandered miserably through the streets, careless where they led me, until I noticed that the murk was thickening. I remembered that I had to get back out of the city before the gates closed at dusk. Quickly I pulled myself together and made my way back to the Adrianople Gate. I arrived just as it was closing. I hurried through the gate unchallenged, but followed by strange looks, for the traffic was all now in the opposite direction, made up of citizens and visitors eager to gain the shelter of the city walls before they closed for the night. Nobody other than I was venturing into the falling night outside. Forgetting to dissemble, I hurried onwards at a pace more military than monastic. Once at a safe distance from the thicket of poor dwellings and hovels outside, and now enveloped in the dark, I turned off the road towards the place where I had hidden my boat. Already I dreaded the watery crossing back to camp. This time I had no hope left to sustain me. I made the shore, close I was sure to the right spot. I found the scraggy bushes where I had concealed the coracle. But my craft was not there. My first thought was that I was in the wrong place – but no, the blaze that I had cut was clear. Then I feared that it must have been discovered. I froze still, knowing that whoever had found the boat must be lying in ambush for its owner. I stayed there motionless in the mist, expecting to hear at any moment hostile cries raising the alarm, and to be seized by the Emperor's guards. I peered into the murk, straining my eyes and ears, but could hear nothing except the slow slurping of the water.

Then I realised that the water had risen up beyond the mooring place on the bank. I had forgotten about the tide.

My boat must have floated off. I cursed myself as a useless landsman as it dawned on me that I was stuck on the wrong side of the Horn. I had no alternative but to try the bridge when its gates opened in the morning. Freezing, miserable, hungry, for I had been unfed all day, I huddled down in a wretched heap to rest as best I could. I fingered the precious lock of Blanche's hair which tickled inside my tunic. Was that all of her that was left? Was it all of her that I would ever touch? I urgently told myself that Peter had not actually witnessed the fate of de Boissy's retinue. Perhaps she had survived; perhaps she had just been taken into captivity. Then I thought that maybe she would be better dead than enslaved, dishonoured, pressed into some Turk's harem. I remembered the treatment given by Baldwin's troops – yes, and Godfrey's – to the poor women dragged back to camp. Eventually some sort of half-sleep took pity on me but its mercy did not last for long. Soon I was fully conscious again, woken by my own shivering. The cold gripping me both inside and out reached such depths that I stood and walked down to the edge of the bank. I looked into those Stygian waters. I imagined them closing over my head and bringing me relief. I think that I might have thrown myself in then, if I had not seen the first light of dawn touching the horizon bringing with it some sort of hope. Stiffly I turned and staggered off in the direction of the fortified bridge, scarcely bothered whether or not I was able to pass the guards there. What was there left to live for? The quick release of summary execution might be the best solution to my anguish.

Perhaps my indifference to my fate gave my manner confidence. Or perhaps the guards on the bridge were just sleepy and bored after a night of duty. Looking back on it, I suppose their orders were to prevent any Franks from crossing the bridge from north to south. None had done so. What reason would they have to suspect a Greek-speaking monk coming from the south? I span them the same story that had gained me access to the city, of a monk who had been nursed back to health at the monastery of Saint Cosmos and Damian, except that I was now returning to my cloister north of the Horn. The day before I had been delighted at the success of my artifice; now, when I found myself walking towards the suburb of Pera, my triumph seemed utterly hollow.

A few of the houses in Pera were built of stone, but more were of wood, poor in contrast to the magnificence of the city south of the Horn. The streets between them wound narrowly along the contours of the slope up from the water. Now, before it was fully light, they were empty and deserted, for there was little to occupy the troops in our idle stalemate with the Emperor and their routine had been allowed to slacken. I hurried towards the lodging I occupied with Godfrey and the rest of his retinue, in one of the grander stone buildings of the suburb, constructed recently by some rich merchant who had been unceremoniously ejected from his home to make room for the Duke. Then I saw another shape emerging quietly from a nearby house. I realised that this was the building occupied by Baldwin. Fearing detection, I pulled back quickly into the shadow of a doorway. The figure looked as anxious as I to avoid being seen. Its cloak was pulled up over its head, and it glanced furtively from side to side down the street. With mounting surprise, as it looked in my direction, I made out Godfrey's blond-bearded features. What business could he have at such an early hour with his brother? Why would he be visiting and leaving again in secrecy? Then the realisation broke upon me that Godfrey must have been with a different relative, not one of blood, but one of marriage – Godehilde. Temporarily all my own troubles and sorrows were wiped away by my master's brazen impunity. My shock mixed with something close to admiration – even jealousy – that the Duke could be so bold as to cuckold his dangerous brother under his own roof.

When Godfrey had satisfied himself that the coast was

clear, he strode out briskly. He scarcely bothered to keep to the shadows at the side of the alleyway, and again I felt something akin to reverence for his audacity. My admiration melted away quickly when I saw a different form dark-wrapped in the shelter of another doorway, spying on Godfrey's receding back. I could not make out its shape under its voluminous cloak but its presence boded ill. Then, as the figure turned to enter the door through which Godfrey had left, the mean features of Bagrat showed, twisted with a type of satisfaction very different to Godfrey's – a satisfaction fashioned from pure malevolence. In a cold rush I wondered how Bagrat would use the information that Godfrey and Godehilde were lovers. Would he tell Baldwin immediately, or bide his time for when he could cause more mischief? And how would Baldwin react?

With Bagrat safely out of sight, I slipped from my own place of concealment and hurried in the same direction as my master. I stepped forward automatically, turning the complexities of the position over in my head. To tell Godfrey that his clandestine departure from his sister-in-law's bed had been noticed could provoke a violent rage. There was also the small matter of explaining why I was abroad at that early hour, lurking surreptitiously outside Baldwin and Godehilde's lodging. Nevertheless, I fast decided that I had to be open with my duke, whatever the consequences. I owed him that and more. And it would be best to get the confrontation over with as soon as possible, so I made my way directly to his chamber. The Duke looked too satisfied and sleepy to show much surprise at my sudden appearance. Before the drowsy expression on his face could turn to anger, I spoke out quickly.

"My Lord, your exit from the place where you spent the night was spotted..." Godfrey was now looking at me sharply, all signs of sleep driven from his face..."spotted by your brother's servant Bagrat. I was returning here when I saw you emerging from…" I faltered "…and saw Bagrat watching you nearby. You need to guard your back against your brother's vengeance."

Godfrey frowned, opened his mouth as if about angrily to deny my insolent assumption, and then closed it again. His irritation drained away and he looked quizzically at me, and even showed a touch of embarrassment. I returned a level and steady gaze. Then he burst out laughing and I found myself grinning back at him.

"By God it was worth it! What a night that was! That woman is wasted on my cold brother! She needs a man of real passion to satisfy her." He balled his hand into a fist and shook it with excitement. "Yes!" Then he laughed again.

"So from what tryst were you returning, young Hugh? Stuck here at the damned Emperor's pleasure it seems we all must seek nocturnal adventure and excitement."

Godfrey's eyes widened as I told of how I had entered the city and sought out Peter the Hermit. My voice broke when I told of the fate of Walter Sans Avoir and I could not go on. The Duke stood and gripped my shoulder in sympathy.

"I remember the shine you took to that young ward of his. I would not have minded her myself…" Godfrey broke off his sentence at my hurt look. "Godehilde is more my sort. I'm sorry. But do not give up hope. Your little friend may be held a comfortable captive for a rich ransom. Why would a captor damage such a pretty, valuable item, eh?"

I thought bitterly that Godfrey did not really believe what he said.

"And Baldwin…well. I don't think he will act openly against me. His pride will never allow him to admit to the world that his beautiful wife is less than loving and faithful. He will not admit that she turns to his brother for the satisfaction that he cannot give. And if he attacks me without reason he will forfeit the others' support."

"Maybe, my Lord. But he will be plotting some secret assault. Bagrat will wield the weapon. Or maybe some other henchman."

"It is your job, Hugh, to keep your eye on that Armenian. But I still think I am safe for the time being. Even as a boy Baldwin was cold enough to be patient when scheming to get his way against Eustace and me. Now he benefits from a show of unity as much as I do if we are to reach the Asian shore untrammelled by Alexios's damned oath of fealty."

"So you think he will wait until we are on the other side?"

"I'll bet my life on it." And Godfrey roared with laughter.

The next weeks showed that this judgement of his brother was accurate. However, his appraisal of the Emperor was optimistic. My master may have understood Baldwin's machinations but he was as confused as the rest of us by Byzantine diplomacy. One week we would be tempted by rich gifts wrapped in honeyed words, and offered grand titles whose names we could scarcely understand. Sometimes these would be for all; on other occasions they were pointed just at Baldwin, or Godfrey, or Eustace, to threaten our unity. Veiled threats might accompany this largesse, or might follow. Eventually the Emperor must have realised that his subtlety was wasted on us, for he resorted to a show of overwhelming force. On that saddest of holy days, Good Friday itself, he faced down a large group of our men who had rashly surged across the forbidden bridge over the Golden Horn. The fearsome Varangian Guard massacred many of them in a brisk skirmish outside the Adrianople Gate. I heard the fighting from my writing desk in camp where I was preparing despatches for the armies of Bohemond of Taranto and Raymond of Toulouse. In spite of these allies' approach, when faced by the Emperor's full might, Godfrey judged that the risk of rout and ruin from delaying his oath was too great.

So, on Easter Sunday itself, I rode a second time through the great Golden Gate, this time in the company of Duke

Godfrey, Baldwin, Count Eustace and their senior lieutenants, and with a close escort of Byzantine cavalry front and back. The Greek lances were poised at the ready beside long pointed green shields to make sure that nobody would be tempted to step out of line. I could tell that under their affected nonchalance the Boulogne brothers were as deeply impressed as I had been when I first passed that way. Arriving once more in the great Augousteion square, I noted that with spring a colony of herons had built nests on the head of Emperor Justinian's huge statue, and down the back of his horse. The dark bronze was now streaked with white guano. I smiled when I heard Godfrey joking pugnaciously to Eustace beside him.

"That's one fine emperor covered in shit."

Then we entered the Boukoleon, where the current incumbent of Justinian's throne had laid out all the pomp at his disposal, even outdoing the splendour that I had witnessed there before. Intricately patterned silk carpets now swirled in motifs of red and blue down all the paths and corridors. Exotically uniformed soldiers lined every hallway, announcing the wide extent of Alexios's domains; among them stood the tall Varangian Guardsmen, but there were many others that I did not recognise. I passed great black men, their cheeks gleaming like polished purple grapes, in white turbans whose soft fluffy feathers contrasted with their sharp curved swords. Further on, narrow eyes peered from sallow faces under helmets like lobster tails, their owners holding spears and shields grounded by their sides. The throne room was packed with richly cloaked attendants, and through the great arched windows all the ships and galleys at the Emperor's disposal were on display. The Count de Vermandois, his bobbed brown hair freshly dressed with some oily pomade, stood below Emperor Alexios's high throne with a smug expression on his weak royal face. Although Godfrey, Baldwin and Eustace had used all the means at their disposal to smarten themselves for this occasion, they looked mere poor rough soldiers in that room of riches. And nobody paid attention to me, but for all that I was uncomfortably self-conscious of the stains and mended tears in my own homespun cloak. A quiet murmur of foreign voices spread round the room as we advanced. Then absolute silence fell as Alexios, wearing a cloak with long jewelled tassels, spoke down from his throne.

"It pleases us to greet thee, great nobles, allies from the West. Much have we heard about your martial prowess."

Did I detect irony in his voice that these great soldiers' troops had been faced down just two days previously? I saw that Baldwin at least shared my thought, for a flash of anger passed over his proud face.

"I welcome you to Constantinople, capital of my Holy Roman Empire, truly the greatest city the world has seen, and to our imperial service. We will reward you with many honours and precious gifts, as we have those who have already sworn fealty to us." He turned and smiled graciously at Vermandois. "So, with no more ado, let us bring forward the oath."

A functionary stepped up, the square of his beard matching his flat black hat. His arms shook under the weight as he held out a large Holy Bible. I remembered the punishment I had suffered at Cluny and thought that I could do better than he, before being dragged back to the present when Godfrey was instructed to rest his hand on the book and intone:

"I, Godfrey de Bouillon, by the grace of God Duke of Lower Lorraine, acknowledge the overlordship of his Highest Majesty, the purple-born Emperor Alexios I Comnenos. I swear fealty to him, and in return will receive help and succour in my holy quest to relieve the Holy Land from its infidel yoke. I further swear that I will restore to my overlord Emperor Alexios any lands or territories which I wrest from the infidel and conquer by the strength of my arm, and which were previously possessions of his great Roman Empire."

A loud "Amen" echoed around the room. Godfrey's

reluctant vow was followed by Baldwin, gabbling the oath with little enthusiasm and less sincerity, and then Eustace and their lieutenants. Four scarlet-clad trumpeters blasted out a fanfare at the end of this solemn ceremony. Four bearers inserted velvet-covered poles through Alexios's throne and carried him to celebrate Easter Mass in Haghia Sophia. I trailed in his wake with the rest of the court.

Over the next three days, the Emperor's galleys plied back and forth across the Bosphorus, ferrying our army to its first camp on the continent of Asia. No sooner were we installed, than we received news that Bohemond of Taranto had arrived with his Normans at Constantinople. He was said to be closely followed by the Provençals of Raymond of Toulouse. Emperor Alexios had only narrowly achieved his object of preventing the joining of the three Crusader armies, and I wondered how differently things might have turned out if Godfrey had held his nerve a little longer.

Like Godfrey and Baldwin before them, Bohemond and Raymond were taken aback by the request of the Emperor that they should swear oaths of fealty. This time Godfrey and Baldwin performed the role that they felt had been so pusillanimously fulfilled by the Count de Vermandois, and acted themselves as the Emperor's advocates. For it was sure that they did not want to lose face in front of their fellow Crusader leaders, nor to be placed at a disadvantage when it came to treating with the Emperor. With the weight of the brothers Boulogne added to the argument, Bohemond and Raymond took less time to reach the same conclusion. They swore the oath before the month of April was out, so that our noble army of the Cross could soon be united on the eastern side of the straits.

SAINT LAZARUS' COLLEGE

The Master sat in the same chair from which he had delivered his crushing decision to the Modern Languages Tutor. Now it was the turn of the Best-Selling Author to sit nervously under that steely gaze. He was already wrought up because he had had to drive himself up to town. Cash was now so short that it had been a choice between his driver and the Maserati, and as there was no point having a driver without a car, the driver had had to go. But the Best-Selling Author's driving frightened even himself.

"You promised me an adventure about the Holy Grail. But we must be a third of the way through and we have had no mention of it yet. At the moment we seem to be caught in a Byzantine labyrinth of eleventh century politics. It that really what your readers want? Where are the Templars? Are you sure that you have not lost your touch?"

The Best-Selling Author shifted uncomfortably.

"I can't bring in the Templars because they were not founded until 1119, well after the First Crusade. The History Don is adamant about that. But don't worry, Master. The grail stuff is coming. I've worked in the love interest, and we've already had quite a bit of sex and some juicy violence. And I am pleased with some of the characters. I must say that I feel a particular rapport with Godfrey. Don't you think? Just be patient."

But under this bluster the Best-Selling Author did have some concerns. The History Don had placed him under intense pressure to stick closer to the real events than would have been his norm. And the Professor of English had insisted on providing his chapter headings, as well polishing his prose to make it more literary. In some places he had even inserted whole new sentences. The Best-Selling Author had to acknowledge that some of these included very nice turns of phrase. Some sounded almost poetic. But one or two were eerily familiar and he wondered whether some private joke was not being made at his expense.

Chapter Eight

THE RATTLE OF BONES

I knew my God was not cruel. Blanche had done no harm. She could deserve no punishment. I was sure to find news of her when we passed the place where mad Peter's army had scattered. Only if I doubted my God's goodness would I be punished through Blanche's suffering. So I prayed piously and clung to my hopes.

At daybreak in our previous camp, I could watch the sun rising behind the city and silhouetting its splendour darkly against the dawn sky. Now, when I woke, I looked out in the opposite direction over the water to see the sun's rays gilding the ancient sea walls and polishing the roofs of Haghia Sophia and the other great churches. I could even make out the arched windows of the Emperor's throne room, and I imagined the sun streaming through the precious glass to light and warm the grand interior where I had just been.

In between, the water sparkled blue like lapis under the sunlight's dapple. Even at that early hour it was already busy with craft of all shapes and sizes: imperial galleys beating the waves with their banked oars, fast feluccas hung with white triangles of sail, and heavy cargo vessels struggling along low in the water, their holds weighted with precious freight. On still days, vapour smoked from the surface in wispy tendrils, and the whole rich scene shimmered in the sun. Overhead, flocks of seabirds wheeled and dived with raucous cries. Some were all white and grey; others had neat black heads and made me smile because they looked as if I had dipped them up to the neck in my inkpot. Busy as I was, assisting Godfrey with the many preparations for the campaign ahead, I returned again and again to the beguiling sight of the Bosphorus. It was fortunate for my master that I was still young and romantic enough to allow my attention to be drawn by those famous straits.

Many mornings, just as dawn was beginning to touch the sky, I walked down to the strand to watch the sun varnishing the walls of the city across the water. My favourite vantage point was a broken tower overlooking a small jetty. Supplies for the army were occasionally unloaded there but I liked it because at that early hour it was always empty and peaceful. One morning, a fortnight after landing on the eastern shore, I climbed the short flight of steps up the tower and was surprised to see one of the fast lateen sailed craft docked at the jetty. A hurried transaction was underway, money passing from the hand of a cloaked figure, and a small flagon being given in return. The Smyrna merchant on the boat then quickly turned away, looked nervously from side to side and gave the order to cast off. It was clear that he did not want to be found there in the daylight. As the purchaser turned, his silhouette was cut sharp against the water, now silvered like a mirror by the rising sun. I saw that it was Bagrat and ducked behind the tower's flaking walls. I waited as Baldwin's creature passed by on the path below, a sneer of satisfaction twisting his face. Allowing a safe distance between, I slipped quietly down to the path to follow him back towards the camp.

Bagrat seemed in a hurry, perhaps not wishing the break of day to strip him of the cloak of darkness. As he approached the camp, instead of turning left as I expected towards Baldwin's quarters, he bore right, in the direction that I would have followed myself to return to my small tent alongside Godfrey's grand pavilion. Now I had to hang further back to remain unseen, for here the path levelled out. Between the tents Bagrat disappeared from sight, and I had a moment of panic before glimpsing him again, now heading back the way I had first expected him to take. He looked less furtive, as if his purpose had been fulfilled. With surprise I saw that he no longer carried the newly purchased flagon that he had handled with such care. My puzzlement turned to awful suspicion and I ran in alarm to my master's tent.

I knew that Godfrey was wont to break his fast with a draft of wine and water. I threw aside the flap covering his tent's entrance and saw him sitting up on the new couch provided for his ease by the Emperor. To my horror he was raising the customary goblet to his lips. He turned his head angrily at my sudden intrusion, giving me just enough time to dash the cup from his hand before he drank. The wine splashed across a new rug, and he erupted with fury.

"My God, have you taken leave of your senses? What in Hell's name do you think you are doing? See what you have done to the carpet. Fine silk given me by the Emperor, damn it."

"Poison, my Lord," I gasped, and we both turned our gaze to the mess that one of Godfrey's favourite greyhounds was now lapping fastidiously. The dog whined plaintively as its thin legs trembled, crumpled and gave way. It rolled onto its side and twitched spasmodically in its death throes. Godfrey's angry amazement gave way to relief as I stammered out what I had just seen.

"So Baldwin has made the move we expected," concluded Godfrey when I had finished. "Yet I cannot openly accuse my brother. He has too many admirers in our ranks. It's too dangerous for me to risk a public rift. And he'll be well-prepared in case we attempt to repay him in his own coin. I'll take more precautions. I'll have tasters try my food, and lay plans so that Baldwin will know that we are on his track. I'll be safer if he sees that he will not benefit from my demise."

Godfrey gripped my shoulder.

"Thank you Hugh. Once again you have served me well."

I glowed with pride.

Baldwin was summoned to Godfrey's tent on the pretext of discussing the army's plans. I fancied I saw surprise and disappointment well-veiled in his black eyes at the Duke's good health. In a great show of bonhomie, Godfrey sat his brother down, and with an earnest expression offered him a goblet of wine. Frostily Baldwin replied that he had decided to abstain until he had reached the Holy City.

"I'll hold you to that," laughed Godfrey, and Baldwin's expression froze colder still. In that look I clearly read that Godfrey would not be secure whilst Baldwin could safely harm him without suffering disadvantage from his brother's death.

Four days after this excitement, on the third Sunday after Easter, a great council of war was to be held. Godfrey dictated to me a letter for Bohemond of Taranto.

'My Lord Bohemond, it would give me great pleasure if you would do me the honour of joining me in my camp two days before the council. When we met at the ceremony of your oath before the Emperor, I saw at once that you stand with me head and shoulders in body and in spirit above the other noble leaders of our crusade. It behoves us to work together for mutual success and to that end I would spend time in discussion and relaxation with you before our meeting with the other princes.'

Bohemond responded eagerly to Godfrey's overture. On the appointed day he was ferried across the strait to the same jetty that had witnessed Bagrat's treacherous transaction. There he was greeted with loud fanfare by Godfrey, Eustace and a smartly turned out guard. I felt proud that my presence at Godfrey's side was now taken for granted. Baldwin, uninvited, remained sulking in his tent.

Bohemond was half a head taller even than Godfrey. Their encounter reminded me of the meeting between my abbot and Holy Father Pope Urban a short year and a half before. Then the great new abbey church at Cluny had provided a fitting backcloth for those two towering pillars of the Church; now the exotic setting of the Bosphorus made an equally appropriate stage for these two tall warriors on whom the success of our campaign rested. I was surprised to see how similar the two men were. I could almost imagine them as twins. Like Godfrey's mane, Bohemond's hair was blonde, but straight and cut short just below his ears. Bohemond was clean-shaven but shared Godfrey's blue eyes and the expression that spoke of boldness and ambition. Godfrey looked broader and more deeply muscled, but when I studied the two of them more closely I saw that Bohemond's impression of relative slenderness was just given by his greater height. With all the charm at his disposal, Godfrey reached forward and grasped Bohemond's right hand in both of his.

"My brother-in-arms," he said, and I wished that black Baldwin had been standing by to wince at those words.

"It is not often that I have to look up to one of my fellow men, but in the case of Bohemond of Taranto, I am honoured to do so."

The Norman laughed with pleasure at this flattery.

"You know that my real name is Mark, after the holy Evangelist? But as I grew my father nicknamed me for the giant of legend. So I have been known as Bohemond ever since."

Turning, Godfrey reached his arm around his new friend's shoulders and walked him towards the pavilion, the guard of honour marching behind. He beckoned me to follow but made it clear that the others were to stay outside. I warmed with pleasure at my inclusion, feeling that this confidence was the just reward for saving my master's life. Bohemond's expression of surprise at my company deflated me again, but Godfrey explained that I was his cousin-scribe and would be asked to document part of the conversation.

"My Lord Bohemond, you and I are similar men of similar ambition. I am not here to further the aims of the Church, and certainly not to recover lands for the Greek Emperor. I am here to carve out a dominion for myself. If, thanks to our Holy Father's dispensation, such an action earns me a place in Paradise, then I'll not argue."

Godfrey laughed. I flinched at such frank irreverence.

"We are the only two men who can lead this army to success, and we should support each other to win through to our objectives. Two great cities lie ahead of us around which fine fiefdoms can be built to fulfil our desires – Antioch, and Jerusalem itself. I propose that you should take Antioch for your own. I will support you in that goal, and in return Jerusalem will be mine with your acquiescence. We'll swear an oath of loyalty to each other, written and witnessed by friend Hugh here. It will provide that if either of us should fall on the way the other's vassals and knights should acknowledge the leadership of the survivor."

Bohemond's brow furrowed as he considered Godfrey's bold proposal. Godfrey continued.

"Let me be open with you, my friend. I mistrust my brother Baldwin. He has already made one attempt on my life. I wish to remove any temptation towards another, and if he fears that he would have the fierce Bohemond of Taranto to contend with when I am gone he will leave me in peace. It is well-known that my elder brother Eustace plans to return home after reaching Jerusalem, and he is too easy-going by far to provide any counterweight to Baldwin."

I smiled at Godfrey's audacious cunning. I saw Bohemond thinking hard, and recognised, strong soldier though the

Norman might be, that Godfrey was the more accomplished diplomatist and plotter. Then Bohemond's brow smoothed again and his handsome face relaxed into a smile.

"I asked Emperor Alexios to appoint me Grand Domestic of the East. That's the title he gives the commander of all his Asian armies. He denied my request. Maybe he remembered the campaigns I fought against him in the Balkans under my father's command! He hinted that the title might be mine after I had proved my loyalty in battle. But he did not offer me Antioch. Once it was the second city of his empire. I'll freely say I like your offer. And the way it is made, my Lord Duke Godfrey!"

Godfrey turned towards me, and I saw triumph in his eyes.

"Come on Hugh, write out what we need." And turning back to Bohemond, "Now my friend, let's celebrate. I'll have some wine brought, with some delicacies to savour. We need some warm flesh – both living and dead." His deep laugh rang out, thickened with gluttony and lust.

I went back to my own tent to sharpen my quills and polish my parchment, trying to close my ears and concentrate on writing as the sound of drunken carousing rose in the nearby tent and women's giggles turned to sounds of pleasure.

For the council two days later, Godfrey had a grand pavilion erected. It was decked out with his carpets and silks and all the other gifts he had received from the Emperor. I thought it a fine display – not the Boukoleon perhaps, but impressive none the less. Godfrey stood together with Bohemond at the entrance to welcome the other Crusader leaders. Baldwin, banished to a subsidiary role, watched in bitter chagrin.

First came Raymond of Toulouse, scented and pomaded by oils from the fragrant shrubs for which his Provençal homeland was famous. Raymond was older than the others, approaching his sixtieth year, and his once black hair was grizzled grey. His empty left eye socket bore testimony to his valour against the Moor in Spain. Beside Bohemond and

Godfrey he lacked physical stature; to make up for it he adopted an air of gravitas and urbanity. Accompanying Raymond hobbled the representative of the Holy See, Adhemar, the Bishop of le Puy. I remembered this grey, measured and respectable Bishop for the uncharacteristically impetuous enthusiasm with which he had flung himself forward when inspired by Pope Urban's great speech at Clermont eighteen months before. I wondered why he now limped, and later heard that he was still recovering from the wounds inflicted by the Emperor's troops when they set on him overzealously after he strayed from the path followed by the rest of Raymond's army.

Godfrey courteously showed his guests to a round table at which eight tall chairs were set. Godfrey and Bohemond sat side by side with Raymond and Adhemar to their right, and Eustace and Baldwin to their left. The number was made up by two Byzantine generals. I observed them carefully from my place behind my duke's chair. The one called Tatikios in particular cut a striking figure. He was mocked behind his back by the Frankish leaders, for after the bizarre custom of the Byzantine court he was a eunuch, as his corpulence and high voice confirmed. For all this lack of manhood, however, his dark round face, mutilated like Count Raymond's, attested to his bravery in battle. In combat he had lost his nose, and now wore a golden replica in its place, behind which his breath whistled gently.

"So," said Godfrey with a great show of geniality, "Here we have our council of princes. We will not attempt to appoint one commander for how could any one of us in all conscience defer to another? But I would have you all know one thing. To seal our alliance, I have appointed Lord Bohemond as my heir and successor to my command, and he me, should either of us fall in battle."

Godfrey beckoned me to hand him the document that I had prepared. Nervous at feeling all eyes on me, I placed it before him. With an extravagant flourish he made his mark upon it, passing it over to Bohemond to do the same. The company looked most surprised at this dramatic gesture. I was pleased to see Baldwin's bloodless face turn paler still as he realised that for the time being his ambitions had been thwarted. Overawed though I felt by the solemn occasion, it was a struggle for me to keep triumphant glee from my own face, and I knew from Godfrey's choked expression that it was costing him a similar effort. I caught a slight tremor of victorious amusement in his voice as he continued.

"I think we are all agreed that our first objective must be the city of Nicaea, are we not? We must recapture the place where our Credo was composed and free its Christian population from near twenty years of Turkish tyranny. That will be sweet revenge for the death of Hermit Peter's followers."

"Yes," Bohemond answered with military pragmatism, "and will secure our line of communications southwards."

"Ni," agreed one-eyed Raymond in his nasal Provençal accent. The other knights nodded their assent.

A few days later our frenzied preparations came to an end and we started. Perhaps those early days of the journey were coloured by my eagerness. In any case, I remember thinking that the green hills on the way to Nicaea were delightful, sprinkled in that early spring by yellow cup-like flowers of a type I had not seen before and studded with straight cypresses and bent pines. In front of the pass that split the hills, a forest of these trees had been razed and dead wood scattered over the ground. I began to think with pleasure of the blazing camp fires that we would light that evening to drive away the April chill. But as I came closer, I recoiled in horror. No forest had been cut down here. This was where an army had been chopped to pieces. Here it must have been that Peter the Hermit's rabble had been caught by the Turks and massacred. Here was the place where dead men lost their bones. I was gripped by the hideous thought that Blanche might have met her end here too. In anguish I wandered amongst the bleached skeletons as the shadows lengthened, making ghosts of the broken shapes. I prayed as I had never prayed before. Surely her beauty could not have met its end here. To some of the hollow skulls there still clung sad wisps of hair, useless to the beasts which had picked the bones clean of flesh. Nowhere could I see any that matched the fine golden silk that I carried next to my skin. The carcasses of some baggage carts remained on the battlefield, their wheels and frames too battered to be carried off by the victors. Thinking that the camp followers would have been gathered here, I searched hardest nearby but found few human remains. Perhaps most had been taken alive, spared death at least for the ransom they might bring, or for the slave price they might command. My stomach churned as I wondered again whether to wish this fate on Blanche, or a quicker death. I tried not to give up hope. I tried to tell myself that in Nicaea I would hear word. But anger and despair burrowed into me like the insects that had bored into the slaughtered bodies all around, devouring my faith and my optimism.

My mood remained grim as I witnessed my first siege. Nicaea was encircled. A relief force sent by Sultan Kilij Arslan was beaten back. I had no action to calm my turmoil, as Count Raymond's Provençals bore the brunt of this sharp engagement. Further round the line, I had to wait with the Lotharingian contingent, watching lest the garrison took the opportunity to sortie. Then began the efforts of the army of the Holy Cross to spread terror and disease amongst the civilian population of the city. The siege catapults provided for us by the Emperor were put to macabre use pelting the severed heads of the dead over the city walls. Christian soldiers roughly hacked the heads from all the Moslem corpses they could find, sniggering at their dark foreign faces while they worked their blades between their vertebrae. At least this was work for men-at-arms and not for knights. To strike even greater terror into the unfortunate citizens we held penned inside Nicaea, wounded prisoners were strapped alive to the catapults, and flung through the air alongside the decapitated heads of their fellows. I was appalled at the ghoulish amusement taken by the red-crossed soldiers of Christ from the thin screams released by these living human missiles as they flew through the air, and nauseated when they were punctuated by the sound of the bodies breaking against the ramparts.

Otherwise the catapults and mangonels were not much use against the double ring of stout walls girdling the city. Impatient, our leaders instead decided on a dawn assault with ladders. I was excited by my first prospect of battle, but scared too, so my feelings were mixed when I woke from a restless sleep to the surprising sight of imperial banners flying over Nicaea's walls. Emperor Alexios's subtle diplomacy had achieved the city's surrender during the night. I felt pleasure and mouthed a silent prayer of thanks that our objective had been achieved without bloodshed or harm, but I hid my feelings from my comrades. They were furious at being denied the opportunity to loot and pillage. Some salve was provided by the Emperor in the form of further presents – food for all the common soldiers, and more gold and jewels for Godfrey and our other leaders.

However, I soon discovered the insincerity of these gifts, and the Emperor's real feelings towards us, his supposed allies, when I tried to enter Nicaea to find news of Blanche. All the gates into the city bar one were closed to us. Even then the imperial guards had orders to admit no more than ten men at once. Maybe, given what I later saw, they were right to fear the uncontrollable behaviour of a larger group, but their price was a rise in anti-Byzantine feeling. Most of my comrades lacked the patience to wait their turn at the gate. Their hope for a bit of fun in the city was less urgent than my need to find news of Blanche. So most of them returned grumbling to camp. Nevertheless, I had to wait the best part of a day for my turn. When at last I was allowed through, I had only three hours before the curfew. Search and question as I might, I could find no trace of any of Peter the Hermit's followers. I was forced to accept that any who might have been captured had not been taken to Nicaea. I tried hard not to lose faith but inside I feared more and more that I would never see Blanche again. In bitterness and sorrow I assisted the preparations for the march south, all the while trying to regain purpose from the thought that I would soon be moving on towards the Holy City.

After some discussion it was agreed that the army would have to divide into two. Tatikios had advised that each division should have to march at least a day apart so that the supply of water along the way in the small streams would be adequate. Bohemond, now joined by his flame-haired nephew Tancred, seemed determined to have the honour of leading our advance.

"You know what they say about redheads, Hugh!" Godfrey exclaimed to me with glee. "Just as hot-headed inside as out. I'm sure Tancred has worked on his uncle. That's why he insisted on taking the vanguard. He can't be a day older than you. His inexperience shows. He is welcome to it. The Sultan is still out there somewhere. Any blow he strikes will fall first on the Normans. And they will have the pleasure of old gold nose's company. Tatikios may claim to be a useful guide but we know what he is really about. He just wants to poke his prosthesis into our affairs for the Emperor's intelligence."

I could not share Godfrey's good spirits and rode morose and subdued nearby. Behind us came those Provençals under Count Raymond and Bishop Adhemar who were fit enough to travel after their fierce encounter with Sultan Kilij Arslan outside Nicaea. We moved at a stately pace, not wanting to tire our warhorses, the camp followers and baggage sandwiched between bodies of fighting men. I found my mail and helmet uncomfortable under the hammering sun which was beginning to bake the countryside into shades of brown.

Three hours after sunrise on the fourth day, I saw a cloud of dust ahead. Two riders emerged from it, galloping back down the path trodden by the forward army the day before. They pulled their panting horses to an abrupt halt and gasped out their news to Godfrey.

"My Lord Duke, help us. Hurry. We are under attack. The Sultan's army came over the hill at our camp in the plain of Dorylaeum just after sunrise. They took us by surprise. There are thousands of the devils. By now we will be encircled. Lord Bohemond urges you to come to his aid as fast as you can. He will not be able to hold out for long."

Godfrey looked at me with a grim smile of satisfaction that he had been right. Then he sprang into action, sending messengers back to Raymond and Adhemar to bring their troops forward past the camp followers. Orders were passed among his knights to ready themselves to ride into battle.

"Don't look so worried, Hugh. Stay close to me with the rest of my bodyguard. You will be fine. When we charge we'll be in the middle, three ranks back from the front. You won't have to do anything. You'll just be carried forward by the momentum. You'll see."

I felt ashamed that I had allowed my fright to show and I composed myself. But I could not conceal my nervous energy from my horse beneath, which shied and reared so that I was grateful for the high-backed saddle which held me in place.

Then the trumpets blew. In response spurs goaded horses forward. Pennants flew out in the wind behind us, revealing the orange cross of Lorraine and the three balls of Boulogne. As we galloped, my mouth dried. I told myself that it was from heat, dust and exertion, not fear. At last we crested the hills that looked down over Dorylaeum and pulled our horses to a halt. In the plain below a desperate scene played out. Bohemond's soldiers and knights, all on foot, had formed a wide circle three or four deep around a green patch of grass that contained a spring. In some places they had used baggage carts to form crude barricades. In the middle huddled the horses and livestock, neighing and lowing plaintively, with the stores and the non-combatants. Some of the women and children passed to and fro carrying water to the thirsty fighters. All around the rim of this circle, the Sultan's men wheeled in their thousands on swift horses, screaming like demons, one wave firing arrows, then retiring to be replaced by the next, again and again, so that a constant downpour of deadly missiles rained upon the defenders. The riders threw up clouds of orange dust, through which the sunlight glittered on swords, lances and armour. Many of the Normans returned crossbow fire, to some effect judging from the Turkish men and horses lying dead or wounded on the ground. But I could see that the defenders' casualties were far worse. Battle cries rang out – "Bohemond" – "Tancred" – "Deus le volt" – "the Holy Cross" – amidst the guttural alien shouts of the Turks.

Hurriedly, my training overcoming my nerves, I took my place near Godfrey in the battle order. At his signal, in two groups, tightly packed knee to knee, lances at the ready, each some fifty abreast and three times fifty deep, our force poured down the shallow slope. With the noise of thunder we picked up speed to a full gallop. As Godfrey had said, squeezed together with the other knights I was carried forward and could not have turned from side to side had I wanted to. Jammed in my saddle I felt a rising panic-infused thrill. The dust, the speed, and the closely bunched horses made it hard to catch breath. I thought momentarily what would happen if my horse stumbled and fell. With grim instinct I gripped my saddle still more tightly with my knees and pressed down harder on my stirrups. I felt war cries – "Bouillon and Boulogne – the Cross, the Cross" – erupting from my throat and joining a deafening roar from the others as the furious flood tide of our charge poured down the slope into the plain.

We took the Sultan's horsemen by complete surprise – they must have thought that they had surrounded the whole of the Crusader army. Our charge punched into their side. The ground quaked under the impact as our momentum ploughed us deep into the enemy's ranks, knocking over horses and riders which were then trampled under the heavy hooves of our destriers. Wedged between comrades on either side, I had no time, no room to use lance or sword. More lightly armed, and mounted on smaller, swifter horses, the Turks span away, guiding their mounts with their knees and turning in their saddles to fire back. Their light arrows made little impact on our mail but some horses fell, to be trampled in turn, for there was no time or space to avoid riding over our own.

A great cheer rose from the Normans and French as we newcomers joined them and turned together to face the enemy line. Now we became an easier target for the Turkish arrows. The horse archers' manoeuvrability made it hard to come to grips with them. More of our horses went down. I muttered thanks to God not to be in the front rank and then was immediately ashamed of my fear. As if in admonition, a black feathered dart thumped my shoulder with a bruising blow and hung there by its barb in my mail. I was startled and shocked but realised it had scarcely penetrated my flesh. It vexed me, flapping up and down there with the movement of my mount. I saw that some others around suffered the same irritation, like me with no hands free to tear the missile away. The enemy started to waver as Bohemond's knights remounted and began to join us in the charge. The Saracens turned to flight. Excited cheers rang around me. Then I saw the reason; the group of Provençals led by Bishop Adhemar had come over the hills by a different route and taken the enemy in the rear. Caught a second time by surprise and doubtless fearful of being trapped between two attacks, the Turks scattered. Godfrey waved his revitalised force forward in hot pursuit, urging them to make short work of enemy stragglers. He beckoned me with his bodyguard towards Bohemond's post. By mid-afternoon the victory was won.

But it came at a heavy cost. Over the next three days we buried more than four thousand of our comrades. Most of these were from Bohemond and Tancred's contingent, which had lost at least a fifth of its strength, helpless victims of the furious hail of arrows poured down by the Turkish horse archers. In places the ground was so stuck with darts that it looked like a sinister field of black corn. Some dead horses had so many arrows in them that they resembled giant hedgehogs or porcupines. And the barbs made them harder to butcher for the feast after the victory. If knights had been killed or injured, it was only when their horses had been brought down, hurting them in the fall, and leaving them to be crushed on the ground by their own comrades. I remembered how Peter the Hermit had described Walter Sans Avoir's end. The men-at-arms, many dressed in leather jerkins rather than iron or steel, had suffered far worse from arrow wounds than the fully mailed mounted knights. But even more of the dead were camp followers, soft targets unprotected by mail or armour. When I saw the damage done to them I thought of Blanche and turned away.

Throbbing emptiness was my main emotion in the aftermath of the battle. The exhilaration of the charge was followed by numb exhaustion. The groaning agonies of the wounded and the dying released in me a tired feeling of relief at being unhurt. My pride at having taken part in the great charge down the hill was tempered by frustration that I had not blooded my own sword or lance, and that packed into the middle of the charge I had been unable to distinguish myself. But I also felt relief that I had not had to kill a fellow human being face to face. Unjustified vainglory swelled my chest when I joined in the great Mass of celebration and thanksgiving led by Bishop Adhemar the morning after the battle, the Te Deum echoing forth from thousands of throats, reminding me that

I had fought in the name of God and had been given victory by His grace.

But confusion tumbled after that sensation. My monkish upbringing should have made me glory in the triumph of Christ. But I wondered if perhaps it had also made me too sensitive to the horrors after battle. Few of my comrades seemed to pay attention to the ghastly wounds that their neighbours had suffered, the severed limbs, the disfigured faces. Unaffected, the soldiers set to with gusto, bloodying themselves further as they dismembered the dead horses for their next meal. They did not seem to mind the vultures which soared from leagues away, spiralling down on black-fingered wings to settle on any dead body, human or animal, where they could find a safe space. Then they would tear into the exposed flesh with their hooked beaks, burrowing their bald white heads deep into the innards until they were painted grotesquely red down to the neck. Boldly they fought each other for the choicest pieces of carrion, squawking harshly, and were scared away only if a man came within striking distance. Then they flew up in a flock to settle down on the next corpse a little further off. With a shudder I remembered the damage done by the ravens and the crows to the sightless dead bodies of my father and brothers all those years before; but they were no match for these vultures. I shot one or two with my crossbow until Godfrey laughed and told me not to waste quarrels.

And I watched with disquiet as soldiers greedily stripped the corpses of Moslem foe and Christian friend alike in the selfish search for better equipment. Their squabbles with each other over the choicest bit of mail or weaponry were little different to the vultures' fights over the tastiest piece of lung or liver. Once stripped of useful accoutrements, the Christian dead were unceremoniously buried. The Moslem corpses were just heaped aside. Within two days in the hot Turkish sun, the choking stench of rotting bodies became unbearable. They attracted cloud upon cloud of iridescent blue-black and black-green flies. The army moved on south to camp away from the smell and the memories.

Godfrey seemed oblivious to this misery. His high spirits were boosted by the extreme booty from the battle. What the common soldiers had been able to pilfer from the rotting, scavenger-ravaged corpses were poor pickings compared to the treasures found in the Turkish camp over the crest of the hill from which the attack had fallen on the Norman vanguard. Then I was ignorant of the habits of the Seljuk people, but from the contents of their Sultan's camp it was clear that this was a race that carried along its most precious possessions wherever it went. It seemed that the Sultan even carried his treasury along with him, for in his tent we discovered stout wooden chests full of coins minted in gold and silver. Some of these were Byzantine, bearing the Greek markings familiar already from the Emperor's gifts; others were dinars bearing the Turks' own looping script. I was eager to learn this language, and in return for promises of merciful treatment I sought lessons from an educated prisoner, and found out that the marking on these gold coins which now lined Christian pockets were verses from the Koran, the Moslem holy book.

Supplies near Dorylaeum were scarce, especially of water, for many of the streams and springs were now clogged and poisoned by rotting corpses or trampled into mud by the horses. Coupled with the smell, the flies, the vultures, and the fear of plague, this forced the decision to move on rapidly. But within days I remembered that foetid field of battle as a paradise on earth; for now began far the worst suffering that I had yet undergone.

SAINT LAZARUS' COLLEGE

The Chaplain came into the Senior Common Room wearing a more serious expression on his solemn face than usual.

"I'm afraid I've got bad news. There has been an accident. The Porter's just taken a call to say that our friend crashed his Maserati on the way back to London. Apparently he just ploughed straight across a roundabout without stopping. No, I don't know how badly he is hurt. They cut him out of the wreckage and took him off to hospital so I assume that he was alive at that point at least."

Thunder clouds gathered across the Master's brow.

"Oh, for God's sake. What the hell are we going to do now? I'll see what I can find out. Don't wait for me; I'll have some food brought to my rooms later."

He stalked out.

"What rotten luck. Do you remember him telling us all that he was going to have to get rid of his driver? He was obviously out of practice," said the Classics Fellow.

"Terrible news. Terrible." His eyes full of alarm behind his thick glasses, the Modern Languages Tutor tried to inject as much compassion into his voice as possible. He must tell the Steward about the "rats" in his room before any unfortunate conclusions about his murderous intentions could be drawn.

"He was such a nice chap, too," added the Professor of English. "I had really got to like him. He was so receptive to the suggestions I made. Fortunately we talked a lot about the rest of the book, so I will definitely be able to finish it off."

"Come, come," said the History Don, as always a stickler for facts, "let's not leap to conclusions. The poor fellow isn't dead yet."

CHAPTER NINE

WHERE THE SUN BEATS

I was assailed by doubts during that hellish journey. Perhaps I had been wrong. Perhaps after all my God was no less cruel than his servants. Then I blamed myself for bringing suffering down on my comrades with such wicked thoughts, and prayed for the return of my untroubled beliefs. But instead my doubts redoubled, for I could still not see why those around me should be punished so bitterly just for my heretical wavering. In more lucid moments during my ordeal I began to fear that the false motives of my leaders and the brutality of their men were to blame for turning God's face away from us and leaving us to the mercy of Satan.

Now it was high summer. How much better it would have been to go south in the winter. As our advance moved onwards, the landscape became barer, browner, rougher. To our right rose a range of mountains, shallow at first and then steepening, their grey upper slopes deeply scarred by long dead streams, the lower parts dotted with scrubby thorn bushes. To the left stretched a desert wasteland as far as the eye could see. It was unvarying, unbroken, save by occasional salt pans where perhaps there had once been water. Water! Supplies ran out within days and then our march became desperate. Tatikios had promised water along the side of the road in storage tanks built for travellers by earlier Byzantine Emperors, but in the long years of Turkish occupation these had been allowed to fall into disrepair. All we met were empty cisterns and exhausted wells. Perhaps some had been deliberately destroyed by the fleeing enemy; certainly the few small villages through which we passed had suffered that fate and were ruined and empty. Across the desert in the direction of the rising sun, in cruel mockery, shimmered occasional lakes and limpid pools, but I quickly learned that these were just visions, mirages. From time to time thirst-maddened men would crack and run towards them, burning their last reserves of energy before collapsing flat and motionless on the ground.

I could almost accept that it was just for the sinful soldiers of God to suffer, as His Son had suffered and died for us. The shreds of my faith helped me through my own misery, but I witnessed innocents suffering so hellishly that I could not understand. At first, with the rest of Godfrey's close retinue, I was better off than many, and felt almost guilty for it, for the Duke had the foresight to fill a covered wagon with barrels of water for our use. We were rationed to two small cups a day but this was relative largesse. More was set aside for our horses. On the third day, I heard a pregnant camp follower screaming in labour by the side of the road as the tattered army staggered heedlessly by. I ran to fill a cup from the water wagon and took it to her. She gulped it down and as if in response to the drink immediately gave still birth to a shrivelled desiccated creature that might have come from hell itself. She pulled back down her skirts, and struggled back to her feet, leaving the diabolical object where it lay. She staggered on for a few more paces before collapsing herself and lying still.

Sickened, I turned back towards the wagon, to see the Duke watching me with a face of fury.

"What are you doing, you halfwit? What do you think will happen if they all realise that we have a supply of water here? As like as not we'll have an outright mutiny on our hands. If you go near that wagon again I'll have you strung up. And see – your monkish charity has achieved nothing. Nothing."

Godfrey gestured roughly at the prostrate figure of the women before turning and climbing back onto his horse. After that, helpless, I watched hundreds of other women, children and sick men reach the end of their endurance and just drop as they marched. Perversely, I felt almost relieved when our own water ran out the following day.

Then, every two or three days, if God deigned to answer our prayers, we might cross a small stream oozing out of the dry hills. Each was quickly trampled to mud by desperate men, all now fending only for themselves, so that those behind had to stumble a distance to either side of the main trail to find a place to drink. I lay down with the others to try to wet my cracked and darkened tongue, desperate to slake my thirst and to refill my skin bottles even with that sandy brown liquid. When the water had run out I followed the example of others and cut twigs from the thorn bushes that were the only vegetation for miles around, chewing them to extract a little bitter moisture. Then I turned to drinking my own urine. Ashamed at first, I stood aside from the line of march, trying to fill my water skin with a few spurts from my parched body. Surreptitiously, I poured the filthy liquid back down my throat, gagging on the sour salty taste which became more acrid still as my body dried up. Then I had no piss left.

The heat of the July sun was so intense that I found my helmet and mail too hot to touch. Only the night gave any respite from the heat. I threw myself to the ground where I stood, exhausted, when the sun dipped behind the hills to my right, to rest for what seemed like only a short time before that merciless orb rose again over the desert to start its cruel cycle. Soon, Godfrey gave the order to march at night and to rest by day. Then I lay dozing in the terrible heat, half dead in whatever shade I could create by spreading my cloak over the thorn bushes.

When we halted at dawn after a night's march, Bishop Adhemar led the army in prayer, and on the Lord's Day he inspired us by celebrating Mass and delivering a rousing sermon. He reminded us how Our Lord spent forty days and forty nights in the desert alone with Satan's temptations, and told us how honoured we should be to be sharing His privations. I might have cried with confused emotion if I had had any moisture left in my body.

The suffering of our poor horses was truly terrible to behold. Before long they were all too weak to carry their riders. Knights had to dismount and walk along leading their animals behind. Many horses just collapsed and died by the road. When that happened they were quickly butchered, even before they were quite dead, and their meat fought over by desperate men whose discipline had long since snapped. Those lucky enough to win a morsel moved a safe distance away to chew it raw, not so much to stave off the pangs of hunger as to provide their parched bodies with some precious moisture. I saw other knights whose horses were still alive bleeding them and drinking their blood. I swore that I would not do that to the fine steed which had carried me so far, but I cracked after another day under the burning sun. Just before setting out at nightfall I had a groom hold my mount's head while I slit a vein in his neck. He rolled his eyes and whinnied feebly in fear and reproach. With a mixture of greed and revulsion I gulped down about a pint of the glutinous liquid, retching at its salt-sweet taste and thick consistency, but forcing it into my shrunken stomach. The following afternoon my poor beast could go no further, however hard I tugged on his leading rein, and he lay down and died. I turned away, unable to bear the sight of him being dismembered, and I could not bring myself to fight my fellows for a handful of his scrawny flesh. Without a horse, I felt that I was no longer a knight, and staggered sorrowfully forward no better than a common footsoldier. The creatures which best survived this march were the sheep and the goats. Like the horses, most of the mules and donkeys died, so these lesser animals – even dogs – were hitched in their stead to the baggage carts and laboured along. If they had been unable to perform this task they would have been slaughtered quickly for the blood in their veins.

Lest I made things worse, I tried to put the anger I felt at God out of my mind and prayed instead for deliverance. And at last I could acknowledge that my prayers were answered. Gradually the landscape became greener and less barren. In the distance a city or town could be made out. A ragged cheer rose from the van of the army. This, at long last, was our goal, the ancient Roman town of Iconium. Godfrey dispatched scouts who rode gingerly towards the city walls on such horses as remained; our men were in no shape to attempt to storm the fortifications and I prayed that we might enter unimpeded. The scouts returned, reporting that the city was deserted. It seemed that the entire population had fled with all their moveable possessions. However, the fugitives could not take with them the River Meram and the delightful orchards on its banks. Here at last was water, fresh and sweet. The discipline which had begun to crack during the march now broke completely as men threw themselves into the shallows and drank greedily. I stripped off with the rest of them and let the cool water wash over my wasted body.

Water and rest rapidly restored our health and morale, and we were able to take stock. Our greatest concern was the lack of horses, for barely half our knights still had mounts. When a few horses were found, they were traded at exorbitant prices. At least Godfrey had money enough from his share of the spoils of Dorylaeum to ensure that his close retinue were remounted, and, a knight once more, my spirits began to rise. I tried to put behind me all that I had seen, and to stop searching for reasons for all that I had witnessed. A few days after reaching Iconium I felt cheerful enough to be pleased when Godfrey proposed some sport.

"We could do with some more fresh meat, Hugh. I am sick of stringy goat. Let's ride up into the hills over there and see what game we can find. Do you remember that first hunt we had together? You speared my boar. This time I will show you how to do it."

With half a dozen fellow huntsmen, we equipped ourselves with lances and short bows and rounded up a small pack of powerful hounds from the dogs which had survived the desert. The most promising direction appeared to be to the East, towards the thick woods covering the base of the two dead volcanoes named for the Holy Apostle Saint Philip and Thecla, the chaste virgin disciple of Saint Paul. I felt exhilarated to be riding unencumbered for once by mail, the breeze blowing through my unhelmeted hair, and the sun pleasantly warm though my clothes instead of boiling me in the cooking pot of my metal skin. A gentle wind blew in our faces down the river valley, and the hounds soon picked up a scent. As they gave tongue, I put spurs to my horse. For the first time since the downhill ride at Dorylaeum, I filled with youthful exhilaration and excitement.

A few minutes' hard gallop and we came up on a herd of deer, bounding in front. They were slighter than the harts I was used to from home, and their ruddy backs were scattered with white spots. Black-striped white tails bounced up and down as the scattered animals sprang over the undergrowth to escape the hounds. The slowest, a doe, was caught and pulled down. Two huntsmen leapt from their horses to stop the dogs tearing their prey to pieces. Able to shoot now without risking the hounds, I loosed off at the escaping herd and to my great satisfaction saw one of the small stags fall, my arrow quivering in its shoulder.

Godfrey was delighted and gave orders for two of the

huntsmen to strap the deer to one of the spare horses. "A good start, eh Hugh? Look at these pretty little spotted creatures. That was no mean shot of yours. I wonder what we'll come upon next?"

Then we rode on. As the ground rose slowly into the foothills of the conical mountains, it became rougher and rockier. The hounds found another scent, and bounded forward out of sight, for the steeper ground now made it harder for the horses to keep up. This time their growls gave away that the game was something bigger.

Indeed, as I came galloping up I saw that the hounds held a bear at bay at the base of a rocky cliff. The beast had reared up on its hind legs. The hounds leapt at it, trying to sink their teeth into its thick throat. It swatted them away with round swipes of its clawed arms. One was already down on the ground, gasping its last as blood bubbled through a rent in its neck.

Spear at the ready, Godfrey spurred his horse forward. On that first hunt with me his mount had stumbled as he was leaning forward to strike. Luck was still not with him, for now the girth of his saddle suddenly snapped. This time Godfrey's spear found a mark, not in the bear's heart as he had aimed, but in its upper arm. Godfrey rolled helpless to the ground right at its feet as his horse galloped away, free of the weight of rider and saddle. Ignoring now the dogs, with roars of pain the bear swiped at this new and seemingly more dangerous enemy. I leapt down but before I could drive it back, it had torn at Godfrey. Even with three men threatening it with spears, the bear proved a good match. It parried my angry feints with the practice of a skilled swordsman. The first time I penetrated its guard I failed to drive the spear through its tough hide, just pricking it so that it bellowed more furiously. Finally I managed a low thrust under its rib cage into its vitals and my companions were then able to finish the creature off.

I quickly turned my attention to my stricken master, the

exhilaration of the chase and the fight rapidly ebbing away. Blood poured from a deep wound in Godfrey's loins where the four razor claws on the bear's right hand had torn through clothing and into the flesh below. Under his blond beard and moustache, his face was still white with shock but the pain was hitting him and he began to moan in agony. With my dagger I cut strips of cloth from my cloak and used them as bandages to stop as much of the bleeding as I could. More strips of cloth then served to tie together some boughs, fashioning a rude litter.

I gathered up Godfrey's saddle to see if it could be repaired to hold one end of the litter. It was my turn to go pale. Surely that girth had not just snapped of its own accord? The break was too straight and clean. I could see that the leather strap had been deliberately two-thirds severed by some sharp instrument. At the moment of greatest pressure, when Godfrey was leaning forward to kill the bear, it had been unable to hold his weight, and had broken. My suspicion immediately turned towards Baldwin and Bagrat. They must have committed this act of sabotage themselves, or bribed some groom to do so. Their plot could scarcely have worked out better. My mind began to race. Automatically I played my part slinging the litter between two horses. We lifted Godfrey onto the litter as gently as we could, nevertheless struggling with his weight and provoking awful curses and groans of pain. Our mournful cortege then plodded its way back to camp, in low spirits and in utter contrast to the excitement of the outward chase.

Godfrey was popular with his men and the news of his wound spread despondency through the camp. His broken body was taken to his tent and laid down on a mattress. He was given wine to drink to numb the pain and help him to sleep. The surgeon then pulled back the rough bandages that I had used in his attempt to staunch the flow of blood, causing Godfrey to cry out in pain. I gasped too when I saw the depth and rough edges of the wounds across both his upper thighs.

On one side, his flesh was cut back to his white leg bone. And in between, his testicles hung half severed. The surgeon shook his head grimly and crossed himself.

"My God, it is bad. And bear's claws carry poison. He'll be lucky to live. For sure he'll not sire any children now."

He poured wine across the wound, making Godfrey scream again. I held down my master's shoulders while the surgeon sewed the edges of the wound together with fine silk thread, provoking more moans and pleas for the pain to stop.

"We may need to bleed him later. I expect yellow bile to pour from the wounds and we'll need to reduce his moist humours to balance it."

Mercifully, Godfrey passed into unconsciousness. I sat up beside him, occasionally wiping sweat from his brow, trying to sooth the tossing and turning of his unsettled sleep. He had treated me well and I felt affection for him. His flashes of anger and bad temper were always rapidly erased by his innate geniality and zest for life. I wondered what would happen to me if, God forbid, he were to breathe his last. Perhaps Godfrey's alliance with Bohemond would hold, and I could pass into the Norman's service. But perhaps instead I would fall into Baldwin's power, and I shuddered to think what might happen then at the hands of the loathsome Bagrat. So I sat and tended Godfrey, keeping a weapon close to hand against any attempt to complete the job, and prayed.

Godfrey was not the only one suffering in the camp that night. The beautiful Godehilde had survived the desert but was now in the grip of a terrible fever, and the doctors despaired of her. Their usual remedy of bleeding had failed to rid her of her bad humours and she was becoming weaker and weaker. At first it struck me as a strange symmetry that the woman whose voluptuous looks had been the root cause of the rift between the brothers now lay in mortal danger at the same time as her improper lover. Then I wondered whether her state was really a coincidence, or whether Baldwin had taken his revenge simultaneously on his wife and her lover. Perhaps Bagrat's supply of poison had not after all been exhausted in Godfrey's wine.

It was as part of a sorry party that I travelled forward, this time not proudly in the van of the army, but with the sick and the wounded just ahead of the rearguard. I rode watchfully beside Godfrey's litter, which was covered by a canopy to protect him from the sun but open at the sides. The Duke tossed and turned, passing in and out of consciousness, muttering in his delirium about his home, the green lands of Bouillon, the fresh fish-filled River Semois winding between its hills. His crazed nostalgia made me ache too for the verdant woods and fertile fields of my homeland, and to long that I could somehow turn time backwards. Thankfully, at least, this part of the journey was easier than the terrible march through the desert. We now passed almost due east, through land that was somewhat less arid, and we had anyway taken care to well provision ourselves with water from the River Meram. The surviving horses and pack animals were freshened by five days of rest with plenty of fodder and drink, so we made good time.

Early in September, after five or six days on the march, scouts brought back menacing news of another Turkish army massing at the town of Heraclea. In spite of this alarm I had time to wonder for which of the Greek hero's deeds the town was named, remembering with longing my reading of the demigod's exploits at Cluny. In battle order the vanguard moved forward, now led again by Bohemond and his Normans, only for the word to come back that the enemy had fled without engaging in battle. A cheer of relief rang through the army, and suddenly a great comet rushed through the sky, which many read as a sign from God of His favour. The council of war thus gathered the next day under better auspices. Godfrey showed some signs of recovery. The flow of yellow bile from his wound had subsided and it appeared to be knitting. His fever and delirium were less frequent. But he was still far too weak to stand and underneath his golden beard, now streaked with grey, his eyes were dulled and his face gaunt. He was propped up on cushions in his litter, the canopy removed, to participate in the discussion. Lady Godehilde had been less fortunate, and had perished twisting in agony where she had once writhed in lust. Cold Baldwin looked untouched, his face expressionless and his eyes adamantine. His lack of emotion added fuel to my suspicions of his hand in his wife's demise. Bohemond, the hero of the hour, entered the council tent, his rude health now a sorry contrast to the weakness of my master, where once they had been so similar. And in spite of their shared birth year, Bohemond now seemed a good ten years younger.

"So the Danishmend Emir had no stomach for a fight," he boomed, "I hoped for hand-to-hand combat when I charged forward to seek him out, but no such luck. He turned tail with his so-called men and ran like a woman."

When we had all heard enough of Bohemond's boasts, the discussion turned to the main business – by which route should the army travel forward to the City of Antioch? General Tatikios explained that there were two possible roads. The army could turn south and climb the Taurus mountains up to the high pass of the Cilician Gates, the route followed by the Great Alexander on his way to his glorious conquest of Persia, or it could circle back northwards to skirt round the mountains by the towns of Caesarea and Mara to enter the plain of Antioch further east. The Byzantine general argued that the pass was too narrow and too steep and could be easily held by a small group of men against an army. Now that the Danishmends had turned to flight, he urged the longer and easier route. This was supported by Bohemond, cautious in spite of his victory. Godfrey, Count Raymond, who was also litter-bound by illness, Bishop Adhemar and the other Frenchmen all concurred. Tancred, though, dissented, boiling over with resentment harboured towards the Emperor and his men since they had thwarted the sack of Nicaea.

"We listened to you before," he growled, "and suffered most terribly in that desert as a result. You just wanted to weaken our force and reduce our knights to foot soldiers. Then we could pose no threat to your imperial master. Well, I have heard that there are rich pickings to be had the other way – in the city of Tarsus. I am not going to make the same mistake twice. That is the way I will lead my men. If it was good enough for Alexander, it is good enough for me."

And he stormed out of the tent. I heard Baldwin hiss to Bagrat, "I'll not let that ginger Norman seize all the booty in Saint Paul's city. He'll have with him only three hundred men; I'll take five hundred of our knights and follow him over the pass. I have nothing to keep me here any longer."

In his enfeebled state Godfrey could do nothing to prevent his brother having his way. Perhaps too he thought that Baldwin's enmity could do him less harm from afar. Troubled and petulant, he curtly beckoned me. His voice was so weak that I had to strain my ears to catch the quiet words intended only for me.

"Hugh, I want you to go with Baldwin. Someone's got to watch him for me. Someone I trust. I'll not have him using my men to carve out a kingdom for himself without sharing the spoils with me."

It was on my lips to tell Godfrey that I would not go, that it was too dangerous, that I feared Baldwin and Bagrat too much. They might not know all my role in foiling their plot to poison Godfrey, or my suspicions about the hunting accident. But about my loyalty to the Duke they could have no doubt. My welcome from them would scarcely be warm. I would be in grave peril. My hesitation must have showed, for Godfrey added querulously, "You failed to protect me from that bear – I don't want any arguments. You can damn well go."

I knew then that any protest I made would be ignored and

would only cause fruitless disfavour. Instead, many questions bubbled up in my head...when should I return?...how should I send messages back?...what should I do if...? – but I did not want to show my weakness and anyway there was no time to ask. Godfrey fell back exhausted on his pillows, and after a short interval I followed Baldwin out of the tent.

SAINT LAZARUS' COLLEGE

"It's a strange thing, but the Police have told me that they believe the hydraulic brake lines were deliberately severed. I know I have made some enemies along the way, but I don't think even my ex-wife would stoop to such depths. Or would she...?"

The Best-Selling Author was once again the centre of attention, in the most comfortable armchair with the cast on his broken leg stretched out in front of him and a neck brace holding his head stiffly upright. The Members of the Senior Common Room clustered round him in various attitudes of commiseration and concern.

"Thank God for airbags and seatbelts, that's all I can say. And good old Genoese engineering – or is Maserati Milan? I can never remember. It's very kind of you, Master, to organise a car and driver for these trips. I know my little accident has caused a few weeks delay but I'll now be able to get cracking again. I can hardly move from my desk unaided, so I'll have no choice but to keep hard at it." He forced a laugh, cut short by the uncomfortable constriction of the neck brace.

"And what about the Police inquiry?" asked the History Don. "Is it really true that they want to interview all of us here?"

"Well, we were the last group of people to see the victim before the accident," reasoned the Classics Fellow.

"Too much like an Agatha Christie for my taste," said the Professor of English.

The Modern Languages Tutor burst into a choking fit caused by taking a nervous drag on his cigarette before he had swallowed his mouthful of gin. This attracted unwelcome attention and he waved his solicitous colleagues away. What would happen if his attempt to buy rat poison were discovered? What if it was somehow construed as murderous intent?

He pulled himself back together to answer the Best-Selling Author's question of whether he saw the parallels between Duke Godfrey and the Fisher King.

"There is that awful wound in the loins, after all. And what about the questions that Hugh wants to ask but doesn't?"

But before he could respond, the injured man had continued.

"I could hardly bring myself to make poor Godfrey suffer so. He has turned into such a sympathetic chap. I don't often feel such a close rapport with my characters."

Chapter Ten

AGONY IN STONY PLACES

*It saddened me to part from my duke still more than
leaving my abbot two years earlier. Both had been almost
fathers to me. Once of my own free will I had exchanged
my dull monastic existence for an exciting secular life
and the new hopes it contained. Those hopes now seemed
increasingly forlorn. But at least then I had replaced one
protector with another. Now, at my duke's order, I had
to strike out entirely alone, hoping that I was hardened
enough to withstand unassisted his enemies and mine.*

With a heavy heart I watched five hundred of the toughest
and most brutal of the Lotharingian knights flock to Baldwin's
banner. With them came perhaps four times that number of
men-at-arms. I joined the throng, wearing the same garb as
the knights around me, making myself as inconspicuous as
possible. I congratulated myself on my success in joining the
column unnoticed. It was only later that I realised how
misplaced my confidence had been.

From my discreet position in the middle of the column I
watched Baldwin and Bagrat carefully. With some jealousy
I saw Bagrat coming into his own as a guide as he neared his

homeland. I assumed that Baldwin did not want Tancred to know that he was on his heels. That seemed the likely reason for the easterly course on which Bagrat led us for a day before turning south toward the mountains. Even in the September heat the highest peaks were patched in snow and cloud. Baldwin had decided to travel light, taking with him no carts, just a few score baggage mules, carrying food and most important of all skins full of water. His men rode in silence, grim, intense, focussed only on their goal. This was not what I was used to. My duke had been affable, remarking on the features of the road, pointing out thickets nearby which might harbour game, and joking with those around him. His good humour had been infectious. I missed this easy camaraderie, but in a way the silence now suited me well, for I had no wish to remind anyone of my presence.

As the road rose into the mountains I saw that for all Tancred's ranting the much maligned Tatikios had in fact provided sound advice. The steep rocky track soon narrowed so that only two horses could ride abreast. Far below foamed the waters of some fast flowing river. Occasionally hooves dislodged a stone which then cascaded down into the gorge, a reminder of the fate awaiting anyone who lost his footing. Certainly this path would have been impassable for the army's baggage carts. As we neared the top of the pass, a narrow defile thirty paces across between tall walls of grey rock, the way moved from the river valley and became easier. Then the road began to descend. The barren scree gave way to scrub. A long way below I saw a fertile plain and even made out a silver sliver of sea glimmering in the far distance.

Before the sea, astride the Cydnos River, stood the city which gave the world the great Saint Paul. A force of armed men was drawn up in the plain before it. I could not be sure from that distance but I assumed that these were Tancred's Normans, as yet denied access by a Turkish garrison. Our column emerged into the plain in the late afternoon. To

Baldwin's frustration it became too dark to march further and he was forced to make camp. He ordered the start at first light, and his seasoned force moved as fast as possible towards the distant walls, through rich orchards and cornfields whose harvest had already been gathered.

The situation had changed overnight. Tancred's men were now nowhere to be seen, and the ever-suspicious Baldwin sent scouts forward to test for an ambush. As we approached, I saw banners flying the Apulian emblem – a chequer board in green and gold – over the city walls. Unusually, Baldwin lost his composure and fired off a string of curses, so loud that I could hear them from my place in the column.

"May those damnable Normans burn in eternal hellfire! It is Nicaea all over again. Once again our supposed allies steal a march on me and snatch the prize from under my nose. This time I'll not allow them to get away with it."

After a whispered conference with Bagrat, which I noted but could not follow, Baldwin waved his men forward to advance towards the main gates of the city. As we approached, the drawbridge swung down over the moat and the young Norman rode out with a small retinue. Smiling, he greeted Baldwin.

"Thank you, my friend. When you appeared yesterday evening from the mountains, the Turkish garrison must have realised that they were outnumbered by far. Anyway, they left the city under cover of darkness. I had already sent back for reinforcements to my uncle. I thought I'd have to wait for them to get here. But instead you did the work for me. At dawn this morning the good Christian citizens of Tarsus flung the gates open for us. Now the city is mine."

"I think you are being a little hasty, young Tancred," hissed Baldwin, half a dozen of his henchmen closing round. "As you have just acknowledged, my force is five times the size of yours. What is more I now have your person in my power."

Before Tancred could react, Bagrat's dagger was at his throat.

"If I were you, I'd instruct your men to file quietly out of the city and move on to find pickings elsewhere. Otherwise they will be looking for another leader."

Tancred's face turned as red as his hair, and then pale again, as he realised how his impetuosity had lured him into a trap and cost him his conquest. The fox had been outwitted by the snake. Snarling, he gave the order to his men to turn Tarsus over to Baldwin. When Tancred's small force had issued forlornly from the city, Baldwin moved his troops gradually inside, taking care that his numbers facing the Normans in the plain remained superior.

"Come, friend Tancred, come with me and have one last look inside the city that might have been yours. When my men are all safely behind the fortifications I'll set you free."

"How do I know that you will keep your promise, you traitor?"

"You have my word of honour as a knight of Christ," sneered Baldwin. Tancred had no choice, and on this occasion Baldwin did keep his word. He had nothing to gain from incurring the greater enmity of Bohemond by butchering his helpless nephew.

Baldwin rapped out orders for his men to take up positions on the city's fortifications. On pain of death we were told to refrain from any pillaging which would alienate the Armenian population on whose goodwill Baldwin depended. I joined a group which took a vantage point above the main gate. From there I watched as the Norman force galloped off forlornly into the distance. They turned rapidly into a cloud of dust and then puffed from view, doubtless anxious to put a good distance before nightfall between themselves and the city whose former garrison might be lurking nearby waiting for an opportunity to extract revenge for their loss.

Tancred had disappeared from view for just two hours, and it was late afternoon. From my position above the gate I saw another force of men approaching from the direction in which we had come just that morning. As they came near I counted about three hundred men and guessed that these must be the Norman reinforcements sent for by Tancred when he was held at bay before the walls. A messenger ran for Baldwin, who mounted the battlements. I shrank away, taking care to remain unnoticed, fearful of what would happen if I were spotted. The Norman captain approached and shouted up to the walls.

"My Lord Baldwin of Boulogne, your banners there make a noble sight indeed. We have come as reinforcements at Count Tancred's request. I hope he did not receive an injury in the fight for the town? Why is he not at your side? Lower your drawbridge, I pray you, so that my men may take shelter within the city walls. Our scouts have just brushed with a large body of Turks and I would like to be inside before nightfall."

Baldwin yelled back from the battlements.

"You want Tancred? Then follow him." He pointed eastwards. "I'll not open the gates for you. This town belongs to me and it is going to stay that way."

Deaf to the desperate pleas of the Norman, Baldwin turned away, giving fierce orders to the officer of the guard not to open the gate under any circumstances. I saw some measure of my own horror reflected in the captain's face, for to turn fellow Crusaders away from safe shelter was a heinous crime indeed. But the captain was not brave enough to question Baldwin's orders.

In despair at Crusader threatening Crusader, in brazen betrayal of our holy cause, I could not sleep. Instead I remained on watch at the gate through the night. The climate was close and steamy, and mist rose from the marshes around, filtering the light of the moon, while clouds of biting insects tormented me. It must have been around midnight that I heard the sound of clashing weapons and desperate shouts of alarm through the mist from the direction of the Norman camp. My own dismay I saw again reflected in the faces of those around. I turned to the captain of the guard.

"Surely we must open the gate and give our fellows shelter? Unless we help them they will be massacred to the last man."

"You heard Lord Baldwin. You heard his orders," he growled back behind a shame-faced expression, "It's more than my life is worth to disobey."

I was gripped by despair. I could not wait and do nothing while fellow Christians perished on Saracen steel a stone's throw away. But nor was it safe to expose myself to Baldwin, doubtless adding wrath to enmity if I begged him to rescue the lives of the Normans outside. I suffered a short agony of indecision before my conscience won the day. I abandoned my post, ran down the steps to the street and set off to seek Baldwin. I found him still carousing at a rich banquet provided by the leading citizens of the town, Bagrat lounging as ever at his side. From the surprise in my enemies' eyes I could tell that they were astonished to see me in Tarsus. Before the anger rising in Baldwin's face could form into words, I told him breathlessly that our Norman comrades were under attack.

"My Lord, the Turks must have fallen on them through the mist. You must give the order to open the gate and let in any that survive. We must make a sortie to drive away the enemy."

Baldwin was already flushed drunk from his feast, so I could detect no blush on his face. With fleeting amusement I marked to myself the evidence of the breach of the vow of abstention he had vouchsafed to Godfrey. But where I had expected only anger I thought that I could almost detect shame touching that sibilant voice. All the same, Baldwin stubbornly refused to open the gate.

"It's too late. Anyway I'll not put the town and its citizens at risk," and he gestured at the scared and startled new friends with whom he had just broken bread. Bagrat vigorously nodded his agreement at his side and spoke words in his native tongue to those around which met with apparent approval. Now I completely forgot myself and my fear of this man.

"My Lord, this is treachery. You cannot leave our fellow Christians. They are dying on heretic steel. Think...think what your brother would have done."

Baldwin rose unsteadily to his feet, pushing back his chair, and struck me furiously across the face with the back of his hand. We stared at each other coldly. I turned before anything could be done to stop me and hurried from the room.

Dolefully back at the gate I found that an ominous silence had fallen outside the walls. The guards' ashen faces were washed whiter still by the mist-filtered moonlight. As night gave way to a grim dawn, I made out a terrible scene of death and destruction. Nothing alive was left in the Norman camp. Broken spears and lances stuck from the ground, itself stained dark with the blood from piles of Christian bodies, betrayed and forsaken by their allies. Their horses lay dead too, those that had not been stolen away by their nocturnal Turkish assailants.

That could have been the end for Baldwin, for with the sun rose anger, and his soldiers' blood was warmed from shame to rage. But the luck of the man held – or was it the luck of the devil? – for from the far side of town came a cry that a fleet was sailing up the River Cydnos from the sea. From mourning the dead and blaming the man whose orders had caused the slaughter, the mood of the living turned to concern for their own self-preservation. For that they looked to the same leader for guidance. No friendly fleet was known in these Turkish waters, so they could only be Saracens or pirates. The order came to move men from the main land gate to combat this threat from the sea. Scared and disconsolate, I tramped with my detachment round the city walls.

Three ships were making their way up the river. These were neither the galleys with their banks of oars, nor the triangular sailed ships which I had seen in numbers in the waters around Constantinople. These ships bore white square-rigged sails emblazoned with the Cross, and pennants fluttered from their mastheads bearing the three red balls on a gold field that I knew all too well from Baldwin's own coat of arms. 'If Baldwin had a fleet at his disposal,' I thought to myself, 'he has kept it pretty quiet.' I watched from the fortifications while the ships, too large to dock at the town quayside, dropped anchor in the broad estuary. A longboat was unloaded and landed a small group under a white flag. Nervously they approached the riverside gate. Shouting up to Baldwin on the battlements, they received a more favourable response than the unfortunate Normans the day before, for the gate was opened and they were welcomed inside.

Rapidly an excited rumour spread through our ranks. Pirates they were indeed, led by one Guynemer of Boulogne. Reckoning that the Crusaders could use a fleet and would reward him well for good services, he had gathered some of his fellow cutthroats who for years had plagued the coasts of the North Sea. They set sail from the Low Countries in spring, down the English Channel, hugging the coast of France and Iberia before passing through the Pillars of Hercules. Reaching Turkish waters, and hearing rumours that there was an army nearby, led by none other than the brother of the Count of his home town, Guynemer led his fleet up the river to offer his services. To Baldwin's pleasure, he now knelt and swore homage.

For all Baldwin's brutality he was a subtle judge of the morale of his men. He was able to judge the strength of feeling against him after his cruel act of treachery towards the Norman contingent. Loathe him though I did, I could not but feel some respect for the rapid and decisive way in which he set about turning his men back to his side. First he made generous distributions to the leading knights from the tribute paid him by the elders of Tarsus. Next he moved quickly to remove the evidence of the massacre, ordering some of his most loyal troops to bury the dead. Then he announced that the army would move on from Tarsus in two days' time, and that

Guynemer would furnish a garrison from his ships and hold the town as his lieutenant.

"This place is too warm and too damp for our European blood – and it's plagued by insects. If we stay here, we risk fever and plague. Our friends, arrived over the sea by the grace of God just at the time when we needed them, will hold this city secure in our rear. My friend Bagrat tells me of the riches in his Armenian homeland to the east. There we will be welcomed by fellow Christians who will freely share their wealth with us."

Since revealing myself to Baldwin, I trembled in trepidation at the vengeance that would doubtless be visited on me. At any moment I expected a summons, or to be clapped into irons without warning and led away to execution. I scarcely dared to sleep at night for fear of Bagrat's dagger between my ribs. When nothing happened, I reflected that I must owe my survival to Baldwin's same subtle appraisal of his men's mood. I doubted whether they would have stomached the execution of one of their number for no reason other than that he had pleaded with Baldwin to do what all knew was right. It was also known that I was close to Godfrey, and many of those who now answered to Baldwin's command had once been Godfrey's men. Nevertheless I knew that I was now closely watched. What I did not know was that Baldwin had other plans in store for me.

The evidence buried of the heinous crime in which all felt complicit and which all thus wanted to forget, and before his appeal to their base instincts of fear and greed had faded, Baldwin led his troops out of the city of Tarsus towards the east. We were unavoidably following in the footsteps of Tancred, now our sworn enemy. The depth of the enmity between the two erstwhile allies soon became clear. The first town on the march east across the fertile Cilician plain was Adana, on the River Seyhan. Tancred had passed through, leaving Welf, a Burgundian knight, in control with a small

Norman garrison. Paying him back in his own coin, Welf stoutly refused to open the gates to Baldwin. With some difficulty we found a crossing over the river and passed on.

We discovered Tancred himself two days' march further on, in the city of Mamistra, also on a river running south into the sea. The city itself lay on the eastern bank of the river, with one ford of sorts to its north. A local tale told that the town had been founded by Mopsos, the legendary seer, son of Apollo and Manto, herself blind Tiresias' daughter, when he fled from Troy. But I hardly needed powers of second sight to foresee the reaction that Baldwin would get from Tancred to any request for safe passage or entry into the town.

Now came the summons from Baldwin that I had been dreading. My nemesis Bagrat appeared with four men-at-arms and an expression of glee which sat awkwardly on his weasel's face. He ordered me curtly to accompany him to Baldwin's tent. Hastily I counted off my options. I could not run; I was too closely watched. I could scarcely refuse to attend Baldwin and call on my companions' sense of fairness and their residual affection for their former commander, for the order I had been given was unexceptionable. I had no choice but to comply. Bagrat watched me with cunning understanding as if he could read my thoughts. My heart was cold with fear but I tried to present as calm an exterior as I could manage as I followed the Armenian. The guard formed up closely behind me.

Baldwin sneered when I appeared.

"So, Godfrey's little monk, you thought you were being brave when you showed yourself to us at Tarsus, didn't you. But no. We have been watching you all along. Ever since your duke had his unfortunate accident."

Bagrat snickered and I marked that as a confession that he had cut Godfrey's saddle girth. I swore to myself that I would extract revenge for my friend and patron.

"But you did surprise me. I didn't think you had the guts to show yourself openly at Tarsus. It made no difference. I have been keeping you because I thought that you might come in useful. I need someone to cross the river to beg Tancred's indulgence. Someone to request a safe passage across the ford. Yet for reasons that I struggle to understand," here Bagrat sniggered again at his master's sarcasm, "no-one appears very keen to accept this mission. After those unfortunate events at Tarsus they seem to fear what Tancred might do to a messenger from me. They seem to think that he has a temper to match his red head. Ah well. I am sure you will be able to persuade him in one of the many tongues at your disposal. If you receive an arrow in the guts for your pains before you reach the walls, or a slower and more painful death in a Norman torture chamber, at least I will not have lost a real fighting man. The only loss will be my dear brother's – of the report on me that you are doubtless readying for him."

Fear of Tancred's vengeful rage now washed through me, followed by hope that the embassy might offer a chance of escape. Perhaps I could ride away before even reaching the walls. Or perhaps Tancred might be persuaded of my true feelings for Baldwin. Perhaps I could persuade him to offer me shelter. Baldwin and Bagrat regarded me silently like black cats playing with their prey. Then Baldwin continued.

"Thinking of a daring escape, are you? Know that you will go to Tancred in plain woollen garb, like the feeble monk that you are. My men will escort you to the edge of the river. After that, should you deviate, it will be an easy matter for them to pick you off with their crossbows, unarmoured as you will be. And just in case your silver tongue persuades Tancred to accept you as his guest, know that five of Godfrey's old soldiers will die in your place if you fail to return."

Bagrat walked to the entrance flap of the tent and at his curt gesture Baldwin's guards pushed in five chained veterans. I recognized them behind their bemused expressions as decent Lorrainers who had survived the long journey from Bouillon. With a start I saw that one was none other than Stephen, the sergeant who had taught me to fight, and who now gazed forward with a silent plea on his face, his scarred eyelid drooping more mournfully than ever. What on earth had possessed him to ride with Baldwin, I asked myself?

"What did they do, Bagrat? Ah yes, disobeyed my orders. Found looting perhaps, or was it fornicating? Dreadful breach of discipline. Anyway, we can decide later, if we have to put them to death. But I am sure that will be unnecessary. Brother Hugh here is an honourable man. He would not wish to have the deaths of innocent men on his delicate conscience."

Baldwin's sneering jibe showed me the hopelessness of my predicament. I was determined to show no fear in front of this monster. As commanded, I took off my mail, thinking it better to do so myself with a modicum of dignity than to be stripped by force. Bagrat went through my belongings and sniggered when he found my old black habit still in my pack.

"Put it on – little monk."

He thrust it scornfully at me and then led me with his escort to the river. There he stopped, safe from Tancred's men, and told me to go on. I rode slowly through the stream. On the far bank my horse shivered off some of the water. I echoed his motion with a shudder of my own, cold in body under my thin garment, and cold in heart at what awaited me. Then I rode on, acutely aware of the crossbowmen's quarrels pointing at my back. I hoped that they had kept on their safety catches; I knew how light those crossbow triggers could be. At the gate I told the captain of the guard that I had a message for his commander. With a new escort I passed through the town to the fine house that Tancred had made his residence, dismounted and went inside. I looked up at the sky above the narrow street, thinking that I might not see it again. Admitted to Tancred's presence I bowed low, in spite of the fact that the Norman was no older than me, hoping with good manners and flattery to deflect his rage.

"My Lord Tancred, Hugh de Verdon, of the household of Lord Godfrey de Bouillon, at your service."

"How is Lord Godfrey?" answered Tancred, "Has he yet recovered from his wound? And tell me your news of my uncle Bohemond and the rest of the army. Have they secured their safe passage round the mountains?"

"Nay, my Lord," I stammered, "I'm sorry. I come from the opposite direction. At my master's command I went with his brother. Baldwin has now sent me to you, to crave your pardon and indulgence for his sins toward you at Tarsus. He wants you to give him safe passage across the river and on towards the East."

Tancred coloured as he rose from his seat. His voice rose in a furious crescendo.

"I admire your courage. But I question your wisdom. How dare you come to me with a message from that fiend? His trickery was bad enough. But do you think I don't know how he caused the cowardly slaughter of my Norman cousins?"

The room burned with hostility stoked by these words. Tancred reached for the dagger in his belt and stepped forward.

"Why shouldn't I slay you on the spot, or at least cut out your tongue or put out your eyes?"

I remembered with acute clarity Baldwin's maiming of the Pechenegs who had been sent back as broken messengers to their emperor. Trying hard to hold Tancred's gaze and to show no sign of weakness in case it precipitated violence, I answered quickly in a level voice.

"My Lord, I was only chosen as messenger to you because Baldwin hates me."

Tancred's angry eyes widened a little.

"He is as cold as he is cunning. If I do not return, or if I return harmed, he will see the anger that you feel for him. Then he will be forewarned to battle his way across the river. He still has many more men than you. As they are complicit in his crime at Tarsus they will fight hard for him."

171

Tancred moved towards me, his dagger levelled.

"Wait, please. If you harm me, Baldwin will have won. He'll have driven a wedge between you and Godfrey, and thus between Godfrey and your uncle Lord Bohemond. Godfrey loves me well, for I have served him well."

Tancred now paused.

"I am a little like Uriah the Hittite, you see. David set him in the front rank of his army to be struck down to serve his own purposes."

I managed to wring out a weak smile.

"Not that I wish to compare the great King David with the unholy Baldwin of Boulogne. But I must go back, for he holds hostages against my return. He will kill them if I seek refuge with you."

The flame still burned in Tancred's eyes. He looked round the room to see how his comrades had reacted to my words. A couple looked sceptical but more seemed impressed. To my relief Tancred was a little calmer when he turned back to me.

"I count Godfrey as a friend. He is my uncle's ally. I see perhaps why he values your service. You may be young but you seem no fool."

I still had enough of my wits about me to see the humour in this comment. After all, I had seen this contemporary of mine fall for a simple trick and lose a city.

"Go back to your camp. Tell Baldwin that he may pass unmolested on his way. Tell him that I have enough troops to man these walls but too few to sortie against him. Tell him that I seem to have heard nothing of the slaughter outside the walls of Tarsus. Let him think that no survivors were left to tell of it. And tell him that I am man enough to chuckle at the trick he played on me, now that I am master of a richer city. Tell him even if you like that I am now a wiser and less trusting knight and grateful to him for his lesson."

Trying to contain my relief, I bowed deeply and turned to go. Tancred grasped my arm, pulled me round, and brought his pale freckled face up close to mine. I smelt sour wine on his breath.

"And if you play me false, next time we meet I'll not be so merciful."

I have no memory of how I got back to the street, nor how I passed through the gates, but once riding back towards my escort across the river I started to shake. I longed to return to the relative safety of Tancred's walls, but could not bring myself to leave Stephen and the four soldiers to their fate. Nor did I wish to expose to Tancred my cowardice. So I struggled back across the ford, and in silence rejoined the escort, now without Bagrat, who had not deigned to wait for my return. They led me back to Baldwin's tent.

"So…what treachery is this?" he hissed as I entered, his sibilants lengthening as always when he was angered, making him seem more reptilian than ever. "What price did you pay to escape the rage of that ginger-headed fool?"

I tried to hold Baldwin's eyes in mine as I gave an honest enough account of my interview with Tancred.

"He wants you to believe that he is too weak to attack you, but your men should stand ready for an attack at any time. Forewarned, you will have no difficulty fighting off his inferior Norman force. When you have driven them back behind their walls, you will then be able to cross the ford unmolested. There, that is what you wanted. Now get it over with. Make an end of it."

I felt weary, exhausted as though I had come to the end of a hard journey. I saw the plea glinting unspoken in Bagrat's hard eyes, and expected Baldwin to hand me over as a toy for his henchman's cruelty. Indeed I was so tired and drained, that a strange half-feeling of disappointment pricked me when instead I was returned to the charge of my escort. As if from a distance, I heard the order to bind and watch me carefully, and a separate order given to double the guard on the camp in expectation of an attack at any time. I hoped that Tancred would attribute this watchfulness to Baldwin's natural suspicion, and not to a warning given by me. If I survived, the last thing I wanted was a second dangerous enemy.

Things did happen as I had predicted. Tancred's men fell angrily on the camp just after dawn the next day. Baldwin's men were prepared and easily held the Normans off, and then pushed them back with their superior force. Bound and guarded, I was well back from the fight. I was gladdened by that at least. I had seen too much of Crusader at the throat of Crusader. Tarsus had been betrayal enough but here Christians were spilling Christian blood with their own weapons. This was a sin of commission to follow one of omission. After a rough struggle that left a few dead and wounded on either side, Tancred's men withdrew to the other side of the river and took refuge behind Mamistra's walls. Baldwin then gave the command to strike the camp and move on eastwards.

I still expected to discover my ultimate fate at any time, but instead remained a prisoner, tied to my horse during the now noticeably shorter days. Through mid-October we marched straight into the morning sun and watched it set in the direction from which we had come. When evening came my numbed legs were untied and I flopped unceremoniously to the ground, unable to stand until the blood had flowed painfully back into my limbs. I could only speculate that Baldwin thought I might be useful again and kept me alive for some such eventuality. I remembered Lord Godfrey's comment about Baldwin's almost inhuman patience, and the memory made me long to be back at his side.

The Christian Armenians through whose towns and villages we passed welcomed Baldwin's force with open arms as liberators and protectors from the Saracens. I felt pity towards them. Soon they would discover the real nature of the man. Their land was rich and the harvest had been plentiful, and the Armenians gave freely of their provisions.

Baldwin was anxious to move forward without delay, and was glad to receive supplies rather than forage for them. So in spite of the pleasure he took in pillage and cruelty, he had given a strict command that the inhabitants were not to be molested in any way. Tight discipline was maintained, and any soldier foolish enough to transgress the order paid a dear price, usually discharged at the end of a rope hanging from a wayside tree. I came close to envying them their quick death, expecting that when my own time came, Bagrat's ingenuity would fashion something lingering and altogether more unpleasant. Meanwhile I struggled with my captors' knots, which were retied the same way every day, until I dared to hope that I had their measure and, given the opportunity, might be able to release myself.

We crossed the great River Euphrates and passed into Mesopotamia. We reached a small town, peaceful, surrounded by orchards. Neat houses of wood and stone clustered around an ancient domed church. My captors camped a little way outside in an idyllic grove amongst almonds and peach trees. Fine rows of vines, now relieved of their juicy purple burdens, rose up the shallow slopes on either side of a small stream that ran down from the gentle hills beyond. I was put in mind of the Garden of Eden before the Fall.

Darkness fell. Perhaps some slight was given in the town, or imagined, or manufactured. Perhaps the inhabitants sought to hide some of their crops; perhaps they tried to protect the choicest barrels of freshly pressed wine. Maybe Baldwin simply wanted to loose his dogs and exercise their brutality before tightening the leash of discipline once more for the final advance towards Edessa. I was left tied to a tree on the edge of the camp, which was itself almost deserted. Most of the troops went to collect supplies in the town and only a skeleton guard remained behind. From the direction of the town came the sound of men shouting, women screaming, and I saw the orange flicker of rising flames. The few soldiers nearby looked quickly at each other, perhaps wondering if they were under attack, or if they were missing some entertainment. They grabbed their weapons and raced through the darkness towards the commotion.

Now was my chance. I struggled with the tight knots behind my back, whose familiar contours I had mapped out so carefully on those painful daily rides. Bit by bit the rope began to give a little and loosen. I swore under my breath as a fingernail broke but then my wrists came free. In triumph I pulled my arms from behind my back only to gasp with pain as blood and feeling poured back into my hands. I had to wait a few frustrating moments before my fingers would obey my command to undo the ropes around my ankles. Then, cautiously looking about, I pulled myself upright.

I had earlier marked that all my belongings were carried on a packhorse led behind my guards. Perhaps none of them had felt strong enough to claim them for their own; probably Baldwin had ordered it thus. Anyway, I was able quickly to re-equip myself, slipping into the weight of my mail coat, and strapping back the precious sword given to me by Godfrey. Accoutred as a knight once more, I should have taken horses and supplies and fled. But instead some strange force of fate drove me stealthily towards the noise and flames rising in the town. I was curious. I wanted to see what had drawn all Baldwin's men. Maybe they really were under attack and I could witness their destruction or even join in. Before making good my escape I also told myself that I needed to know what pursuit to expect, and whether I had to contend with a new enemy. So I slipped through the shadows to the edge of the main square.

On the far side a scene from Hell unfolded. It reminded me of the paintings on the wall of my old abbey's church showing the awful fate awaiting sinners after the Last Judgement. Now those moral pictures were cruelly perverted, for the devils here were visiting their atrocities on the innocent.

Against a background of leaping flames the black silhouettes of Baldwin's frenzied troops ran amok. Already a twisted pile of bodies lay heaped on the ground in front of the church. More townsmen shouted desperately for mercy as their assailants dragged them from their homes. Their pleas went unheard. Baldwin's fiends hacked them to pieces. A dark pool of lifeblood spread viscous across the packed earth. Groups of soldiers held down screaming women, ripping the clothes from their bodies, and taking turns to violate them. When the soldiers, their red sullen faces sneering and snarling, had their fill, they threw the objects of their brutal lust to one side to visit on them the same fate as their men. Staved-in wine barrels rolled empty on their sides, giving a clue to one of the fuels for this depravity. I stood frozen for a moment by the horror of this scene. Then I found my sword suddenly in my hand, without knowing what I was going to do with it.

My attention was caught by a woman running in my direction. She mothered a small girl in front of her. Terror etched itself across her face as she panted to escape the two soldiers pursuing her. She mouthed some words in my direction. I could not hear over the crackling flames and the animal roars from all around, but I imagined 'Please.... Please.' At least I could do something to save her. I jumped forward but was too far away to stop the dogs catching their quarry. One wrenched the girl away and struck her head from her small body, which folded to the ground like a puppet whose strings are cut. Blood pumped from her severed neck, spraying up to soak her mother's dress. As I ran closer I now saw that the woman was heavy with child. Her tormentors, perhaps angry at being cheated of rape, slashed open her round belly and reached forward as if to pull her unborn child out before her dying eyes. It cannot have taken more than a few seconds for me to come up with them but my feet felt like lead and would not move fast enough. I slashed at the nearest man, catching him a vicious blow up through the base of the nose

177

so that his face split across into a second, red, grinning mouth. His companion turned in alarm towards me and I recognised Bagrat. His alarm became angry recognition and then fear again. I thrust my sword through my enemy's belly with such force that the point pushed out through his back. Agony now chased surprise across Bagrat's face as I pushed him back with my left hand on his chest and wrenched my weapon out of his guts. He toppled slowly backwards. I felt purged. For a moment I watched him writhing there on the ground, and venomously mouthed the words "May you die slowly."

So far nobody else had noticed me in the mêlée. What should I do now? What else could I do? I could not take on all of them. I had to escape. I turned and ran from the inferno into the outer darkness, stumbling in the murk, my only thought to get away. Back in the camp, I found a half groomed horse, and with what little presence of mind was left to me I grabbed the leading reins of a pack mule, before riding off into the night. I moved as fast as the moon and starlight allowed, desperate to put as much distance as possible between myself and those diabolical scenes. I had no idea in which direction I headed. I just rode, until dawn began to streak with pink the sky in front. Then I knew that I must have travelled east. My horse and mule could go no further. I tottered into a small wood at the base of a hill, from which ran a stream, and tied them nearby so that they were able to drink. I fished some rye bread from my mule's pannier. Noticing that it was mouldy, I grimaced but ate it nevertheless, before collapsing unconscious to the ground.

The next days were a dream. I do not know how far or how long I travelled, nor scarcely whether I woke or slept. Hordes of monsters chased each other through my head: black hissing serpents, fire-breathing demons with leering red faces, great bears which suddenly grew human heads, satanic figures with empty eye sockets seeping blood, sometimes dressed in a Benedictine's black habit. The one thing that I knew in my delirium was that I must keep moving, ever moving. I had to escape.

But escape from what? My conscious mind said that Baldwin was far behind and could no longer catch me and punish me for killing his friend, even if my act of retribution had been seen. I was just running from my dreams, from my conscience and the images that kept forming in my head. I saw strange villages of mud-cracked houses shaped like tall round beehives but kept away from them and whatever creatures lived there. I could not imagine facing a human being again.

I had killed for the first time. I had sinned by putting to death two Christian soldiers unshriven and in a state of mortal sin. Evil men perhaps they were, but my act had condemned them to burn in hell for eternity. Hatred and the deadly sin of anger had fuelled my wrongful deed. I had sinned by failing to protect those innocent villagers, by failing to prevent the unholy crimes visited upon them by the so-called soldiers of the Cross. I had sinned by joining a Holy War which had been twisted into a campaign of evil. I had surely sinned by leaving the Abbey of Cluny and my life of prayer and by ignoring the wise advice of my abbot. But worst of all I had sinned because I had felt a tingle of gross excitement from the scenes in the square; a thrill at the memory of my sword crunching through flesh and bone; a rush of pleasure at the pain and shock in Bagrat's glazing eyes.

Then I filled instead with anger – rage that man could visit such suffering on fellow man, woman and child – fury that God could allow such evil – wrath that I should have been dragged into such an abyss. Why had He taken from me the girl I loved? Why had He laid low the duke I served? Then my anger became self-pity, feeble tears, and then fear again as I sank down into the turbulent violence of my lurid dreams.

At first I wandered at night and slept by day, feeling cloaked in the darkness and safer from the eyes of man and God alike.

The stars and the moon provided just enough ghostly light for my horse and mule to find their footing. Once I passed through a boggy marsh, where the way was lit by wispy green flickering lights, dancing in the distance as if luring me on. There, my mount stumbled, throwing me off in my reverie. I found myself looking down into a noisome pool of water from which a dead white face stared back up. Terrified, I scrambled back onto my horse before I realised that I had seen my own reflection. But I travelled more by day thereafter, to avoid other ghostly apparitions.

I remember two visions of lucidity and peace from those days in the wilderness. Once, I happened upon a tiny church, half ruined, high up a hillside. I tied up my long-suffering mounts and went inside. Damp had grown patches of dark mould on the ceiling. But still, the frescoed figure of Our Lord looked down from the little semi-circular apse. His gentle almond eyes gazed out with infinite pity, and His hand was raised in the sign of benediction. I touched my forehead to the cool floor and prayed for forgiveness and understanding. That moment of peace quietened my turmoil for a while and gave me enough strength to go on.

In my next vision I sat beside the shore of a vast lake, so vast that I could not see its other side. I thought I might have come back to the sea until I tasted the sweet water. Out on an island stood a chapel, a cross topping its small dome, a symbol of suffering, peace, and reconciliation. I sat there and wept. My heart was heavy that the narrow stretch of water cut me off from this holy place of prayer; my head told me it was just that one in a state of sin should be denied its solace. I filled my water skins from that unkind lake, and drinking found that I was as hungry as if I had not eaten for days. I took from my mule's saddle pouch a tough morsel of salted meat and some hardened flatbread, which I softened in the limpid water. The sustenance restored me and returned some clarity to my thoughts. I was completely lost, utterly alone. I had no idea of whence I had come, of how far I had travelled, nor of where to go. I just moved on in the same direction, possessed by the belief that I might find some goal to end my quest.

The landscape was now rougher and more mountainous. The weather turned cold and the sky changed from blue to grey. The wind rose, blowing hard into my face, and driving snow at me so that I could scarcely see my way. I could go no further and stopped, dismounting and taking shelter as best I could behind my shivering mounts. For two, three, four hours or more we remained motionless in the storm, unable to see anything beyond a blank expanse of whiteness. Then at last the storm died down, and I was able to move forward again, chilled, now across a frozen landscape. Some way on, at the bottom of a rough slope of scree, powdered with snow, I saw the body of a man beside a dead horse. It looked as if the unfortunate animal had lost its footing on the loose rocks at the top of the slope and had tumbled down. Either it had broken its neck in the process or, unable to get up after its fall, had just frozen to death in the blizzard. I could see too that its rider was dead or badly hurt. One leg bent at an unnatural angle as if the bone were snapped.

As I came closer, the turban and robes, and the swarthy complexion, told me that a Moslem lay there defenceless. I stood over him; I had the man in my power. I could do what I liked and no-one would see. This was the heathen enemy which I had come so far to kill. But some human instinct, some feeling of compassion stayed my hand in that frozen waste. My head cleared, and I just saw a fellow human being lying there in distress and in need of succour. I bent down to straighten the broken leg. I tied the shaft of my lance to it as best I could as a makeshift splint. I struggled to lift the unconscious body, as gently as possible, over the saddle of my pack mule. Fearing lest my new companion die from the cold, I took Saint Martin's example and covered him with my own cloak. Then I shivered onwards.

To my relief the track now began to wind downhill, and the snow became thinner, although the blizzard had clearly blown hard over a wide area. Rounding a blind corner, I saw to my consternation a group of riders galloping at me. The sound of their hooves had been muffled by the snow, otherwise I might have had warning of their approach. Wearily I pulled my horse to a halt. I was too tired to turn and run even if my mount had had it in him. I abandoned myself to my fate. The riders were six in all, dressed after the same custom as their supine compatriot, and fiercely armed with curved swords and spears at the ready. They surrounded me in a threatening circle. One dismounted to check what I carried on my pack mule. He rolled back the cloak. What he saw beneath provoked an excited gabble to his comrades in a guttural tongue which sounded to me like another dialect of the language that I had begun to learn after Dorylaeum. Fortunately, the man I had rescued began to stir and raised himself painfully to a sitting position with help from his fellow-countryman.

A harsh debate began. I gathered that my life hung in the balance. One of the Saracens showed angrily the red cross on the shoulder of my white cloak, exclaiming, *"Al-franj, Al-franj."* They obviously knew this as the mark of their Christian enemies and they shook their spears and turned dark looks upon me. One made a cutting gesture across his throat and raised his guttural voice, arguing for my death. To my disappointment the man whose life I had saved nodded his head up and down, clicking with his tongue, as vigorously as his weakened state would permit. My death sentence was sealed. His robes, and the curved gold-embroidered dagger sheath that he wore round his waist, were finer and more elaborate than his colleagues'. He must be their leader. Surely his word would prevail.

"So my reward for mercy is to have my throat slit like a sheep," I thought and mouthed some silent prayers to commend my soul to God. Nevertheless, I felt no sense of unfairness, for I knew that were the roles reversed, and were I a captured Moslem, I would die on a Christian blade. The angriest one, the one who had been arguing hardest for my death, inclined his head forward slightly, touching his extended fingers to his brow in what I took to be a gesture of respectful obedience. Completely drained, I sat on my horse trying not to flinch or show fear, hoping that the blow which would send me to my Maker would be quick and true. The executioner dismounted, and roughly lashed my feet together under the belly of my steed, who hung his head, soft nostrils steaming in the cold air. Then my hands were tied behind my back. I tried to hold the eyes of my imminent assassin, but the man turned away and remounted. The whole troop wheeled and rode off the way they had come, with me surrounded in their midst. I sagged like a sack, expecting the riders to stop at any time to effect my execution.

It was only later, when I was familiar with their language and their customs, that I learnt that when a Persian nods he means no. It was a shake of my captor's head that I should have dreaded as confirmation of the sentence of death.

South we now rode through mountains dusted with snow, lower but no less rough than before. Then we began to climb again, and from time to time to the left I caught glimpses of another great lake or sea. Riding with hands and feet tied I suffered torments again. My ankles were chafed by the rope, my body was jolted by the horse's movement and my muscles protested as I struggled to hold myself upright in the saddle. At the end of the day, untied, I could neither dismount nor stand, and like Baldwin's men my captors derived some amusement from watching me flop to the ground like a fish gasping for breath on dry land. But their treatment of me was otherwise kinder. They shared their food – mostly flat bread and some spicy paste. It was clear that they were rushed and anxious to reach their journey's end, for they rode as long and as hard as our harsh road would permit.

On my third day with these new companions, we entered a defile from which no path appeared to lead, a dead mountain mouth of carious teeth. But at its end a track led up a narrow crack in the rock to a long valley. Perched on a great rock above, I saw a fortress, impregnable, an eagle's eyrie. The slopes were scattered with great stones, like tumbled graves about a chapel. A thin path spiralled round the rock, and as they made for it I guessed correctly that we had reached our destination. But the fate that awaited me there I could not have possibly predicted.

SAINT LAZARUS' COLLEGE

"Well, if you ask me I think our writer has taken too many painkillers."

A fierce argument was raging about the merits of the latest chapter, which the Professor of English found too melodramatic and psychologically unconvincing.

"Actually you do him a bit of an injustice." The History Don was feeling rather smug. "All that stuff at Tarsus did really happen – and the subsequent struggle at Mamistra between Baldwin and Tancred. It may be hard to believe that the Crusaders fought between themselves and betrayed each other like that but it is all clearly documented in the Chronicles. Just wait until we get on to the siege of Antioch – what went on there was stranger still. And I find Hugh's hallucinations really interesting – I wonder how those were described in the original manuscript. It is an area where I have been doing a bit of work. You see, the mould that grows on rye bread secretes lysergic acid…LSD to you and me. Medieval man ate a lot of that, and other wild materials like poppies, hemp and darnel, especially when they were short of food. Some old documents refer to 'crazy bread', which must have been some sort of ancient hash cake. I am thinking of writing a short paper about hallucinogenic drugs and their unpredictable impact on crowd behaviour at important medieval events."

The Chaplain spluttered. "That really is a bit far-fetched. I don't see any problems with Hugh's crisis being purely spiritual. After all, the poor fellow had been under a prolonged period of acute stress. He has just seen some horrific violence and broken one of his main taboos – if you ask me, it is not surprising that he went into a bit of a tailspin. After all, how would you feel if you had killed for the first time?"

This last remark was addressed to the Chaplain's neighbour, who unfortunately happened to be the Modern

Languages Tutor. His eyes bulged behind his thick glasses and he stood up and rushed from the room without saying a word. The other Fellows looked at each other in surprise.

"He seems to be becoming more and more eccentric."

"Perhaps like a medieval peasant he is on something else in addition to all that alcohol and nicotine."

"If you ask me, it's a jolly good thing he is leaving us at the end of the year."

CHAPTER ELEVEN

LA TOUR ABOLIE

I had escaped from the clutches of one set of enemies only to fall into the hands of another. The first at least I knew and understood; the second was foreign and strange. I will leave it to you to judge whether my position had become better or worse, and to guess whose hands were pulling the strings of my fate.

Unseen eyes must have watched us wind up that spiral path, or some magic was at work, for as our winded horses reached the top the gate swung wide. We passed under a pointed arch topped by fine stonework. I noted a delicately carved inscription in the Arab script. Was it a warning, a spell, an imprecation, a prayer? I was momentarily angry with myself for my lack of understanding. Then I was enclosed by the high walls of a long narrow courtyard. Behind, strong square towers guarded the only gate. In front stood the tall keep. The shape of its windows was unfamiliar to me, the round arches sharply pinched in below each shoulder. Their size, larger than was the custom in the West, said that the owner here feared no assault, protected by the remote location, the impossible approach, and the power of the place. Nothing moved. A singular aura of arcane authority hung in the chill air.

The rush of guards shattered the stillness. My hands and feet were untied. I was pulled down to the ground where I struggled to hold myself upright as the blood pumped painfully back into my extremities. My arrival obviously provoked excitement and consternation, for a heated gesture-laden conversation took place between the broken-legged leader and the watch. Then I was led into that silent keep, through an empty hall, and up a spiral staircase to a small stone room. There I found a platter of fresh flatbread and the spiced paste that I had eaten before, fat grapes, an ewer of water with a goblet and a bowl, and a clean set of clothes. The ewer and bowl, in fine white-glazed earthenware scratched with brown patterns of flowers, stood beside the food on a little wooden table intricately inlaid with bone. The clothes lay on a low couch, which doubled as a bed.

My room was set in the outside wall. The slit window was much too narrow to allow a man to pass, but gave a fine view down into the valley. In the distance behind, sharp snow-covered mountain ranges sliced the sky. I was impressed by the comfort of my prison; it was more civilised by far than the dank oubliettes beneath the castle at Bouillon, but prison it surely was, for I had heard a bolt slide home, and shake the door as I might there was no give at all. Famished, I tore the bread and wiped it in the paste, gulping it down with draughts of water. The dark grapes were sweet and juicy. I then tasted a small lump of some waxy perfumed sweetmeat, only to recoil, finding that it stung my tongue and dried my mouth. Fearing poison, I took some more water to rinse my mouth and noticed that it foamed, a little like the liquid soap I had seen the Abbot use to wash his hands at Cluny on special occasions when he allowed himself small luxuries. I stripped, grateful at last to shed the heavy mail coat that had chafed my skin for so long, and tested the scented waxy soap on my skin with a little water.

The smell and the sensation were good and I vigorously rubbed myself over, creating a white foam on my body, which I wiped off with a cloth. The garments left for me were robes in Arab style, fine white cotton, loose and flowing. I donned them tentatively but found them very comfortable after my rough undershirt. Thus restored and reinvigorated, intrigued by the sophisticated civilisation of my prison, I lay down on the couch to wait.

I was not kept for long. The bolt grated back, the door swung open, and four dark gaolers stood there indicating that I should follow them. Two in front, two behind, all well-armed with short spears fashioned from a strange white wood, they escorted me back down the little stairway, and through a wide doorway on the far side of the hall. I supposed my fate was about to be decided, but for all that I felt strangely calm as I followed along winding passageways, up twisting stairs and then down again. I lost my sense of direction utterly in that labyrinth, spending my attention instead on the outlandish nature of the decorations and furnishings. At last a wide corridor led to a closed wooden door, covered in the finest carvings the castle had to offer. In the middle gleamed a bronze knocker shaped like a hand, hinged at the wrist. The first guard swung it three times so that the tips of the fingers tapped on a brass plate beneath. From inside, a dark voice gave the guttural command to enter. The guard opened the door with nervous respect and gestured to me that I should go forward.

I found myself in a narrow space, the walls on either side lined with precious books. I moved on into the perfect proportions of an oval room. On all sides were shelves, packed with volumes whose leather gilt-stamped spines gleamed gently. This spectacular library was interrupted only by a massive stone fireplace, which reached right up to the dark vaults of the cedarwood ceiling. The floor was laid with fine carpets patterned with medallions and arcane symbols whose meaning was obscure to me. Four lamps set on beaten copper

189

tables spread pools of warm light, but most illumination was provided by a window at the far end of the room, of four arches, pinched at the shoulder in the same way I had seen before, held up on three slender columns. Silhouetted against the light, gazing out at the same mountains visible from my chamber, stood a tall figure, robed and turbaned. This ominous form turned slowly round. His white robes hung down behind like the wings of some vast snowy owl. A cruel hooked nose beaked from his face between two hooded black eyes. I faltered and then continued my approach. I was chilled to see that the black centre of each eye was ringed by a bizarre yellow circle inside the iris, accentuating the whole impression of some great bird of prey.

"Welcome to Alamut, the nest of the eagle."

I started, for the harsh voice had spoken a Latin that was passable, if strangely accented.

"I," he continued, after a pause as if for effect, "am Hasan-i Sabbah, Grand Master of the Nizaris, Lord of the Assassins, known by some as the Old Man of the Mountains."

I bowed low. Determined not to be outdone in the matter of languages, I replied with words that I had picked up on my journey, "*Salaam Aleikoom*. I am Sir Hugh de Verdon, knight of the Cross, at your service."

Hasan-i Sabbah's eyes glinted. "*Wa Aleikoom Salaam*. I see you are more cultivated than some of your kind. Most of you appear to think that we are ignorant barbarians simply because we do not share your religious beliefs. As you can see," and he gestured at the great shelves of his library, "some of us have just a little learning. Are you one who knows only how to ravage, pillage and kill, or can you read too?" he continued with harsh mockery in his voice.

"My lord, I have had the honour of being a novice at the great monastery of Cluny. I have studied Latin, as you can tell," for my lack of Arab vocabulary now forced me to revert to this familiar tongue, "but also Greek. At Cluny we had a

190

famous library which is perhaps..." I was about to use the words 'even greater' but another glance round the room revised my choice, "almost as great as this."

Hasan's strange eyes now drilled into me with an almost physical force. "So you read Greek, do you?" he said with sudden sharp interest. He stroked his neat pointed beard pensively.

"I hear you spared the life of my son. Maybe you even saved him. For that reason alone you have been spared in turn and brought here. You are the first *Franj* soldier ever to see the inside of Alamut. I had not planned that you should live to tell others about it. But now perhaps...perhaps Allah has brought you here for other reasons too. Great is His wisdom. I could perhaps use you, my Greek-reading Crusader knight, to further my plans."

"My lord, I am hardly a Crusader knight any more. I am an outcast from my own people. I killed two fellow Christians in a vain attempt to save the lives of foreign women and children. I ran from my fellows. I can never return. At Cluny I failed to complete my novitiate. I never became a full monk. Now I have also failed my test as a Knight of the Holy Cross."

Hasan smiled sardonically again. "What do you mean – Knight of the Holy Cross? How is it possible? If I understand your Bible correctly, your god teaches that all killing is wrong. He teaches that you should turn the other cheek when your enemy strikes you. Your Saint Augustine worked hard against that creed to justify your wars in the name of God. But personally I find the writings of Saint Basil so much more convincing, with his arguments that even for a soldier to kill is a sin. Perhaps this accounts for the greater civilisation of the eastern church."

I understood the mockery behind this erudite display of knowledge of my own culture, but my desire to interrupt was quelled by Hasan's fierce gaze and I could only listen quietly as he continued.

191

"Why, after all, we Moslems revere Jesus the Christ as a prophet. All we challenge is your absurd belief that he is the Son of God – for what father would be so cruel as to condemn his only son to agonising death when that son is loyal and obedient? And when it is within his power to prevent it? And as for his death and resurrection. Well, perhaps there is some truth in that part of the story. My religion, you see, is the true Islamic faith. We too believe in resurrection. For Nizar, the rightful Imam, will be reborn. They killed him treacherously in his prison in Alexandria. But he will return. He will return as the Mahdi. To accomplish his return is my life's work, for then even the most fanatical Sunni will have to acknowledge the true Shi'a faith, and all the Shi'ites will be united with us Nizaris.

"From the days of my boyhood I have felt love for all branches of learning. I have always been a seeker and searcher for knowledge, always on a quest for truth. It was thanks to my learning that I won control of this castle. Have you read your Virgil? The Roman poet tells us how poor Queen Dido struck a bargain to buy all the land that could be fitted inside an ox's skin. They laughed at her but she cut the hide thinly round and round into a great rope to enclose the site of her city. As if to Carthage then I came, I struck the same bargain for Alamut. I bound this castle round with strips of hide from one buffalo. I even went one better than Aeneas's queen, for the three thousand dinars of my bargain were paid for me by another. He was too scared to resist my command. Thus I won control of this castle.

"Since I became its master, I have not once left this room. Here I stay, surrounded by my books and my knowledge. I sleep little, for why waste time that can be used for study? I eat and drink only what I need to stay alive. What do I care for worldly treasures? What do I care for silver or gold? All that matters is wisdom, knowledge, and the power that they bring.

"If I need something done in the world outside, I send my *da'is*, my Assassins, to complete my mission. My *da'is* give me absolute obedience. They will die for me without question. They can bring me anything I require. Indeed, the group which you encountered were entrusted with such a task. How important their mission, you can judge from the fact that it was led by my own son Mohammed. As I said, it is to your good fortune in saving him that you owe your own life."

While we had been talking, the sky outside had grown dark, and now the only light in the room shone from the four lamp-lit tables. Hasan moved towards one of these and lifted an ancient volume bound in tattered hide. The lamp lit his aquiline features from below, casting deep shadows up his sinister face. A shudder ran up my spine, as if a breath of cold air picked my bones in whispers.

"This is what they brought me. This is what they brought me back from Georgia, the ancient land of Colchis. I first heard of this book many years ago on my travels to the north. At first, I thought it mythical, but then I had word that a copy lay in a hermitage at Nokalakevi on the Black Sea. My *da'is* had to get there before Georgia's new King David won his land back from the heretic Seljuks and made such journeys as good as impossible for my people. They achieved their end only just in time; those feeble Turks have now been crushed there just as at the other end of Asia Minor by your comrades."

But my attention had been caught by the book which had previously been covered by the old volume in Hasan's hand and now lay revealed on the table. As I read the title – '*P. Ovidi Nasonis – Metamorphoses*' – a sharp flash of painful memory shot through the scars left by those thirty-six lashes across my buttocks, transporting me back to my punishment and humiliation at Cluny. Hasan's sharp eyes, shadowed black from below in their deep sockets, fixed me and read my expression.

"I see you know that book. Just as Virgil's tale of Dido

helped me to win Alamut, so there is truth behind some of the old legends retold by other ancient poets. Not of course in Ovid's silly tales of girls raped and transformed into nightingales and swallows, but in the stories he tells of ancient lore and medicine, yes."

Hasan began to recite in his strange Latin, and the rhythm of those well-remembered lines made my heart beat faster:

"Interea validum posito medicamen aeno
fervet et exsultat spumisque tumentibus albet.
illic Haemonia radices valle resectas
seminaque floresque et sucos incoquit atros;
adicit extremo lapides Oriente petitos
et quas Oceani refluum mare lavit harenas;
addit et exceptas luna pernocte pruinas
et strigis infamis ipsis cum carnibus alas
inque virum soliti vultus mutare ferinos
ambigui prosecta lupi; nec defuit illis
squamea Cinyphii tenuis membrana chelydri
vivacisque iecur cervi; quibus insuper addit
ova caputque novem cornicis saecula passae.
his et mille aliis postquam sine nomine rebus
propositum instruxit mortali barbara maius,
arenti ramo iampridem mitis olivae
omnia confudit summisque inmiscuit ima.
ecce vetus calido versatus stipes aeno
fit viridis primo nec longo tempore frondes
induit et subito gravidis oneratur olivis:
at quacumque cavo spumas eiecit aeno
ignis et in terram guttae cecidere calentes,
vernat humus, floresque et mollia pabula surgunt.
quae simul ac vidit, stricto Medea recludit
ense senis iugulum veteremque exire cruorem
passa replet sucis; quos postquam conbibit Aeson

aut ore acceptos aut vulnere, barba comaeque
canitie posita nigrum rapuere colorem,
pulsa fugit macies, abeunt pallorque situsque,
adiectoque cavae supplentur corpore rugae,
membraque luxuriant:"

"And so the caldron with the potion in
boils furiously and foams about the brim.
In it she cooks a potent brew of flowers;
juices with magical, mysterious powers;
roots dug up in the vales of Thessaly;
Orient stones; and sands washed by the sea,
its ebbing tide; frosts gathered by the light
of a full moon; wings now bereft of flight
once a fell screech-owl's, and its carcass too;
the entrails of a dubious werewolf, who
is able to transform his aspect grim
into a man's; she adds the scaly skin
of a Cyniphian water-snake; also
the liver of a long-lived stag; a crow
nine generations old bestows its head
and eggs. When these, and others left unsaid,
countless in number, all were in the pot
to form the Eastern witch's magic plot,
she took an olive branch, withered and dry
and stirred and stirred the mixture thoroughly.
And as the dry stick stirred the steaming brew
first it turned green, then quickly from it grew
green leaves, and in a another trice it bore
a load of bulging olives. Furthermore
wherever from the fiercely boiling pot
froth was flung upwards, on whichever spot
the hot drops landed, there the ground turned green
and blooming flowers suddenly were seen
amid fresh grass all soft and lush with life.

On seeing this Medea took her knife
and in the old man's throat she made a slit
letting the blood out and replacing it
with potion. And as Aeson took it in
through mouth and wound, his hair, so white and thin
before, turned thick and black, as did his beard
while all his former leanness disappeared
and with it, too, his bloodless, pale aspect
and general demeanour of neglect;
his wrinkles vanished and his flesh became
quite firm and full, his frail limbs strong again."

"...Aeson miratur et olim
ante quater denos hunc se reminiscitur annos,"

I completed,

"He looked on wonderingly and seemed to know
himself when young, full forty years ago."

Hasan-i Sabbah's eyes flashed with wild excitement.

"For you see, in my hand here I hold...I hold the recipe
used by Medea to give Jason's father Aeson new life and vigour.
A dangerous procedure indeed, for we know Pelias's subsequent
sad fate. But now Allah has sent me the perfect subject on
which to test this experiment. Tomorrow we shall try Medea's
medicine out on you."

Aghast, I struggled for words.

"But you must be mad. Quite mad. How can you believe
that such pagan magic could possibly work? Anyway I am not
old."

Hasan cackled with laughter.

"I see you do not understand what this magic can do. I am
searching for knowledge. Medicinal treatises I have in number,
for my race is learned in that science." Hasan gestured towards

one section of his shelves. "I wish to know whether this book," – he shook the slender volume in his right hand – "whether this book should be added to the section of my library on medicine, or shelved over there amongst my ancient myths and legends."

He gave another bitter, cruel laugh.

"You will need a good night's sleep. You will need all your strength for tomorrow. I want my subject to be as fit as possible to withstand the treatment."

I was speechless in amazement and horror as I tried to absorb what was going to happen to me. Hasan must have given some secret sign, for the doors opened and I was marched back down the labyrinthine corridors to my little wall-bound space. More food and drink had been left and I did it such justice as I could manage before lying down in an effort to sleep. I spent half the night contemplating my fate, trying to pray, passing through my mind the events of my life, unable to think of anything stranger than the interview I had just experienced. Soon at least I would be sent to join Blanche. Eventually I fell into a troubled, restless dream-filled sleep.

Did I wake from those dreams? Or did I fall deeper down into them? The door of my chamber – my cell – opened, and the impassive guards led me away, their white spears at the ready. They fell in behind two more guards carrying great gold candleholders worked with enamel, each holding at least ten candles, and followed through the dark labyrinth to Hasan's library. Again they tapped the brass fingers on the carved wooden door and again I passed fearfully inside.

A vast bronze cauldron was now set before the library's great fireplace. It must have recently been taken from the fire, for fumes seethed from it and filled the room with strange synthetic perfumes. The heady scent made me drowsy and weakened my knees. Unstoppered vials of ivory and coloured glass were laid out on a table whose top was so finely fashioned that it looked to be one single piece of bone held up by legs

197

of hard black wood. But above all, my attention was drawn to the great golden dish, a shallow grail, set upon that table.

Hasan was busy adding ingredients to the cauldron, watched with fearful respect by four white-robed attendants. He turned and I saw malice and great excitement contained in his yellow-ringed hooded eyes.

"So do you have any questions to ask about the procedure, Crusader monk?"

I had many questions but my tongue was tied by fear, and by fear of showing fear.

"First we must make room in your veins for Medea's potion, by bleeding you dry into this golden dish. I believe that your blood's reaction with the metal is important, for then we add it to this cauldron. When mixed, we plunge you in the cauldron itself. We hope your heart still beats enough to suck the potion through your veins. So very simple. But the mixing of the potion is less easy; if the quantities are wrong, or of insufficient strength, it seems that the liquid will not pass into your veins, or brings death, not life. That is why I want to try it out on you."

Now the full horror of what was about to pass broke over me, and I struggled briefly, muttering desperate prayers as the robe was stripped from my back. Naked before the table I found bizarre pleasure in the fire's warmth, the heat and fear mixing to stir my loins. Both my arms were firmly gripped by Hasan's assistants and held out above the grail dish. Hasan pulled a dagger from his belt. It was so sharp that I scarcely felt the deep incision made in either wrist, but I could not stifle the cry in my throat as my lifeblood pumped into the dish. The red and gold began to spin as the strength ebbed from me. Had I not been pinioned in that firm grasp I must have fallen to the floor. My glazing-over eyes saw the pumping flow of my blood become a trickle. The grail was taken and its contents emptied into the brew. Too weak to fight, swooning, I felt myself being lifted up and two more cuts made in my ankles. Then they folded my knees and plunged me into the cauldron up to my neck.

Never before had I felt such pain. The liquid in the cauldron was hot but the heat that I felt upon my skin was as nothing to the flames inside my veins. A long way off I seemed to hear a ghastly scream and somehow recognised it as my own. My head hammered like a tightened drum and my whole body pulsed as if about to burst. The room span so that Hasan seemed to rush round me, his arms pointing wildly to the sky.

"Now!" he cried.

Lifted from that deadly pot, I felt a stabbing pain in my side and saw a whitened spear piercing through my ribs. Suddenly the pressure faded, the pain erased, and mercifully all went black.

"No, no, no. I really must protest." Nobody could remember having seen the Classics Fellow so angry before. "You cannot take Ovid's wonderful legend of Medea and pollute it with all that grail nonsense. It is a sacrilege. I bet there was nothing about Ovid in Hugh's original manuscript."

After two stiff gin and tonics, the Modern Languages Tutor's memories of his difficulties had been numbed enough to eliminate his diffidence. A bilious sense of bad temper remained at the injustices of life. Now he exploded, his wizened jowls shaking with irritation, and his eyes blazing behind their thick glasses.

"It is completely the other way round. Completely. You are talking utter nonsense. This is Chrétien's description of the grail castle to a 'T' – it is unmistakable – the white lances, the ivory ebony-legged table, the candelabra…it is all there. That is what has been polluted by Ovid, not the other way round."

The Professor of English, delighted to see his two colleagues at each other's throats, begged to differ.

"Gentlemen, gentlemen. Calm down for heaven's sake. Actually, you are both completely missing the point. This is the most interesting part so far. You see, all these legends have the same roots. Medea's restoration of Aeson is just one fertility legend which then re-emerges with the Fisher King in the Grail stories. A central element of Eliot's genius was to understand all that – helped a little by James Frazer and then Jessie Weston, of course – and to blend it all together in *The Waste Land*. That is how the poem achieves its universality, how Tiresias can be the central bisexual figure representing all humanity."

The Best-Selling Author laughed as freely as his neck brace would allow.

"I would not read too much into it if I were you. I just think it makes a jolly good yarn. At least we have got to the grail bit, and I have worked the Assassins into the mix; I think that more than makes up for the lack of Templars."

But the Master, ever-demanding, was not wholly satisfied.

"I do not pretend to know your audience as well as you do, but surely we need some more love interest?"

The Best-Selling Author smiled knowingly.

CHAPTER TWELVE

STAY WITH ME

*Often I have looked back and asked myself whether it
all really happened, or whether it was a dream. Perhaps
I am still in the dream, perhaps I will wake soon and
find release. Or perhaps I do not want to wake from it.*

I woke in Paradise. I lay in a room of glowing white, softly
pillowed in a smooth-linened bed. Light flowed through two
pinch-arched doors from a garden beyond. And beside my bed
sat a white-robed angel. In my surprise at seeing Blanche
beside my bed I tried to raise myself but fell feebly back on
my pillow. Now I knew that I had died and gone to heaven,
but the sweet music of her voice seemed to tell me another
story.

"What a sleep you have had, so long and deep. For days
and nights you have scarcely stirred. At times I thought
perhaps you would never stir again."

The Blanche-angel spooned me some warm gruel.
Confused, bewildered and weak, I sank back into my
cushioned sleep, clear only about one thing – my hope that
if I woke again the angel would still be there and would still
be Blanche.

I slept, I woke. And whenever I woke I did see that the angel sat there still. She gave me more to drink. Each time I slept again I knew more surely that the angel would still be there when next I woke. Each time I woke my strength had grown a little more. Soon I could sit up though it tired me fast, and I began to stay awake for longer. I saw that the angel's long hair of gold did truly belong to Blanche and I smiled in wonder. I could also see that her blue eyes now held far in their depths all the sorrows of the world.

I said her name – feeling foolish for so doing. She smiled gently. "Yes, yes, I really am the Blanche you knew." Behind her smile I saw a sadness I did not understand. I smiled shyly back and sank again to sleep. When I woke I was stronger still. With Blanche's help I stood. Now I noticed the bandages binding my wrists, ankles and side. Resting on her shoulder I walked slowly round the room and out through the arches to the garden. The sky was pale, the sunlight thin, the air cool. In the garden one yellow jasmine bloomed, one white, and softly scented the breeze. I knew it must be spring. Then I was drained again and Blanche led me back to bed.

When I next walked in the garden I saw small green shoots. Some hyacinths flowered. Hesitantly, I asked Blanche to tell her story. Pain crossed her face and she turned away from my gaze. I wished I had not asked. Still looking away, unable to hold my gaze, she began to talk.

"I had little love for Walter de Boissy. He was not of my blood. But you know that. I was a cousin somehow of his wife …quite distant. I felt sorry for Mathilde but had little cause to love her either. They took me in, when my parents died, that's true, but for my inheritance. Then they treated me no better than a servant." She sighed. "But neither of them deserved to die like that. I did not see him fall, but I heard that his horse came down pierced by more arrows than could be counted. And then… . Well, you are a soldier, you know better than I what happens to knights laid low on the field of battle. Mathilde…she died in my arms. The men were all slaughtered, their throats cut like goats. We thought that we might die the same way, after…" Blanche shuddered. "But we two women of better birth were taken, I suppose for the ransom we might command. Mathilde was too weak. She could not cope with the journey…and the usage she received."

Blanche now raised her eyes to mine, with a surprising look of defiance, and hurried on with her story before I could interrupt. "It was the day after she died that my captors were attacked in their turn. They were taken by surprise, but they had far greater numbers and were still no match for these people here. These ones seem to have no fear. Their ferocity, their fanaticism…" She shivered again. "It was almost as if they seek out death. I could not understand why one set of infidels wanted to attack another. But since then I've learnt that these people are very different – almost like monks. Except they showed no mercy – again blood was everywhere. Then we rode for weeks and came here. I suppose they wanted me for ransom too. Little do they know that I have nobody to pay for me."

I heard something close to bitterness in the harsh laugh she gave and moved towards her, wanting to provide comfort, but she started and stepped back.

"And their leader, the one with the ringed eyes…" she shuddered again and looked momentarily terrified. "They took me to him briefly when they brought me here. I knew him at once as a man to fear, a man to obey. He has such power. Be careful of him. He speaks in Latin to me when occasionally I am summoned to…to receive his orders. "

Then her soft smile returned.

"He told me you are very important to him. My orders are to take great care of you, to nurse you carefully back to health and strength. I am so glad it was you and not some other."

I filled with joy at her words. There was much more that

I wanted to ask but now she turned in firm silence to her duty, leading me back into the room. She removed my bandages and gently traced the scars where I had been cut.

As little white flowers pushed through the ground and opened in our garden, my strength returned. Soon I could walk unaided, although I still pretended that I needed Blanche's help so that I could put my arm around her waist and lean on her. Then Blanche slipped gently into bed beside me. She stroked my hair, my beard; I stroked her downy cheek and touched her lips with my fingertips.

We kissed, softly at first, then with hunger and greed as passion rose. I felt her form through her robe, and she felt mine. I touched her hard budded breasts through the cotton and she murmured quietly. My cock's stalk grew tall and stiff, and I lifted her robe and pushed her onto her back. I entered her as gently as my greedy passion allowed, and she gasped, gripping me between her thighs. I thrust harder, faster, deep inside her. Her gasps came faster too and turned to little mewing cries. Her hands were on my back, her eyes were closed. Mine closed too as I erupted as never before and lay spent inside her.

We slept, mine now at last a healthy sleep, in each other's arms, and woke together. Now we stripped off our robes and felt each other skin to skin. Her skin was so soft, like the finest velvet, as I stroked her back, and she laughed as the twists of hair on my chest tickled her nostrils. My cock rose hard again, and again I entered her, now so slippery from my seed. This time she pushed over and straddled me, her hair hanging like a fine curtain as she took her pleasure. Her nipples brushed my chest and I cupped her breasts, now hanging softly down, and took the point of one between my lips. Again she gasped and moaned, while I gripped her buttocks and pumped out a second time. She lay on top, my arms around her, and again we slept.

So now I knew I was not in Paradise, except a paradise of

205

an earthly sort. I quietly said to Blanche that I loved her. She put her finger to my lips to still them and said she loved me too. I felt so happy, proud at last to be a proper man. I realised how lonely I had felt, how empty, and now I felt whole and full. Puppy-like I wanted to play. Blanche laughed and rolled away, demure no longer in her nakedness. Then turning sad, she told me not to be such a boy, saying that I should dress against the cold before I fell ill again, and donned her own robe. We walked out into our little garden, a small walled world all our own, keeping out the others and closing us in. I said, "We must marry", and Blanche asked "What are you thinking of?" and began to weep. A knock came at the door, which opened. Food and drink was passed in. I heard a whispered conversation. Now famished, we ate and drank. I feared the next knock at the door, lest it spell the end of my paradise. And then I heard it. The door swung wide and my white-speared guards stood there to take me to their master.

"Stay with me," Blanche said, "My nerves are bad. Stay with me." But I could not. I was led back through the castle's twisting corridors to its master's lair.

Hasan-i Sabbah stood at his window as before, gazing out over the sharp snow-dusted peaks in the distance. I passed through the narrow opening to the room into the wide womb of the oval library. With relief I saw this time that no apparatus awaited. The cauldron, the white black-legged table, and the great golden grail dish had been long since cleared away. Hasan turned and looked at me through his eagle's eyes with sharp interest.

"Well, a bit gaunt as one might expect for one who has slept for forty days and forty nights, but otherwise no great outward sign of change. You look no younger, as Ovid would have us believe Aeson did. But perhaps you look more a man. That is just what I would have expected from the Colchean witch's treatise."

A look of sardonic amusement passed over his face.

"I trust that the lovely Blanche tended you well."

I felt the blood rising in my face, part blush of embarrassment, part flush of anger at the slur I perceived on Blanche's honour. I remembered her ominous fear of this man's power.

"We will be married," I said, raising my head proudly.

"Married?" Hasan raised an eyebrow. "By what rite?"

"We have the right if we love each other," I said hotly.

Hasan laughed harshly. "By what priest, you fool? You seem to forget that you are my prisoners. You are wholly in my power. Unless I permit, you will never see your Blanche again."

Boiling then with hatred, I watched him stroke his beard pensively in the characteristic gesture that I now knew spelled menace. Hasan seemed to read my passion with deep satisfaction.

"Perhaps if you perform a small service faithfully for me...perhaps then I could permit you to have Blanche. Perhaps then I could set you free and you might take her with you as wife..."

Watching me closely under his hooded eyes, he continued, "I have heard of another book I want. It is a gnostic gospel, known as that of Lazarus. They say it is hidden in Antioch, in the ancient Cave Church of your Saint Peter. I cannot send my own men. In these times of siege and turmoil they would have no chance of penetrating the city, let alone coming away again. And besides, to identify the book I need one who can read Greek."

"That I can do," I said with rising eagerness.

"Yes. So you will return to your Crusader army. According to my da'is it is still encamped around the walls of Antioch. The city is surely fated to fall. When it does, you will go to the Cave Church, find the book, and bring it back to me. Do you understand?"

I heard with distant excitement the news that my comrades

had reached their next objective, but felt a little disappointed that it was not yet in their hands. Most of all, though, my reaction was of uneasy curiosity. Hasan was not a man who acted from whim or without purpose.

"What does this book contain? Why is it so important to you? Where in the church can I find it? And how do you know it is still there?"

"If I knew its contents for sure, you young fool, I would not need the book. I have just heard rumours of ancient truths. I want the book to satisfy my curiosity of them. And how do I know exactly where it is hidden? Pray to your god and perhaps you will find it. Now go and get ready. You will leave immediately."

I felt as if he had struck me and I wanted to strike back.

"No, old man, before I run your errand for you, before I fetch your precious book, you must grant me one last night with Blanche. I will not leave without bidding her a proper farewell."

"How dare you gainsay Hasan-i Sabbah?" His eyes blazed.

"I dare because you have no hold on me, old man." I suddenly felt strong, tall, vigorous. "You need me to go. You say yourself that you have no-one else. If you kill me you will have no book. If you harm Blanche I will not go. You have no choice. You must grant my wish."

I saw anger, desiring my doom, and greed, longing for the book, battling each other across Hasan's harsh face. I realised that never since he became master of Alamut had he been challenged thus. I determined to press home my advantage and continued.

"I once believed that the service of God was the whole point of my life. But now I have seen Him allow too many atrocious crimes in His name. Either He is cruel, or He is weak. Either way, He deserves little praise from me. Now I have felt the elemental force of love. I do not know what vile substance you have put in my veins. But whatever my heart now pumps, it can feel love as it never could before. Perhaps I should be grateful to you for that. I doubt it was the outcome you intended."

"You may have learnt one good lesson," Hasan flashed back, "if you have begun to question your so-called god. But not for love. Love could not matter less. Knowledge is all that counts, for the power that it brings. Your god threw humankind out of the Garden of Eden because Adam and Eve ate fruit from his forbidden tree of knowledge. He feared that knowledge would make them gods too. He feared that knowledge would make them able to challenge his authority. Allah, my god, dictated knowledge to His prophet Mohammed to be written in the Holy Koran. But He only dictated such knowledge as He wished to share. Much is not written there. I will find all the knowledge that is not written in the Holy Book," with both arms wide he gestured wildly round the room at his shelves, "and then I can be as great as Allah."

His arms fell back and he shrugged his shoulders. The crazy fire in his eyes went out, leaving only ashes of dark malice.

"Go then. Have your night with the woman. You will learn soon enough that love is not all it seems. You will leave tomorrow at dawn. My son Mohammed will lead your escort."

As Hasan made the secret sign that caused his guards to open his chamber's door, I felt like a fine general who has won his greatest victory. But I could not relish my adversary's expression of defeat, for Hasan had turned away to gaze once more out of the window at the mountains.

The steady march of the guards through the labyrinthine corridors filled me with frustration. I boiled to see my lover; I wanted to see her face fill with surprise and delight. And indeed when I re-entered our love chamber, surprise was in her sad blue eyes, mixed with alarm, as if she feared what Hasan might have said to me. The door safely closed, she threw her arms around my neck and kissed me gently. The room was lit red by the setting sun.

"I did not expect to see you again," she said, gentle tears rolling down her cheeks.

I kissed her greedily back and she pulled away, turning her back sadly to me to look out at the garden, bloodstained by the last dying rays.

"Tell me what the old man said. What do you have to do?"

Eagerly I told her how I would go to Antioch, win the book, and return to collect her to be my bride. Proudly I told how I had stood up to the old man and forced him to grant us one last night together. As she turned to meet my gaze, I saw deep sorrow in her eyes mixed with wisdom that far outdid all the knowledge sought by Hasan-i Sabbah. How right I was to choose love when it came joined with wisdom too. She gently took my hand and led me back to the bed. We sat like friends and helped each other slowly out of our clothes, savouring the time it took to bare our flesh. Her long blond hair hung down, covering up her breasts. I reached to move it away and by accident brushed a nipple with my hand. She jumped and giggled softly, escaping back beneath the covers.

"You are not safe from me there," I laughed, and stalked round the bed, my cock showing her that my words were true. She circled it in her small neat hand and pulled me towards her. "I do not want to be safe from you," she breathed into my ear, guiding me inside. "Love me slowly now." For as long as I could, I obeyed her wish, moving slowly and gently above her, watching her expressions change. On her face I saw passion rising to match my own. She gasped, closed her eyes and bit her lips, pushing up her chin, showing the sinews of her straining neck. I pressed down tightly on her, my arms around her back, and thrust hard until I heard her cry and then let myself gush out.

Through that long night we writhed and twisted like Tiresias' mating snakes, so closely entwined that a watcher could have hardly told male from female. So we remained, when sated we lay still, and slept a dreamless sleep.

A hammering on the door woke us and broke us apart. A pale dawn now chilled the room. The garments I had worn on my arrival were brought and brusquely I was ordered to rise. One last kiss, one last gentle stroke, and I stood up from the bed to pull on my undergarments and boots. With a heavy heart, I lifted the weighty mail coat, the leather beneath moulded by sweat to my shape and still smelling of sour fear and exertion. I placed it over my head and stood there in the grim aspect of war. Now truly a man, truly a soldier and a knight, I kissed Blanche a gentle goodbye, careful lest she bruise her tender skin on my rough metal carapace. I swore to return as fast as I could. I swore to be faithful and true. She swore that she would not lose hope, that she would wait patiently for my return. Then she turned her face to her pillow to hide her tears. I set my own face hard to show no sign of weak emotion to Hasan's men, cast my cloak round my shoulders, gathered up my helm, and left the room.

Outside, they brought me my horse. I was glad to see that he had been well fed and cared for, and enjoyed his whinny of welcome. Mohammed waited there, mounted already, with two companions. Spare horses carried weapons and provisions. As I left Alamut, and my beloved, I saw something white fluttering like a captive dove at one of the narrow windows. I thought perhaps that it was Blanche waving goodbye.

SAINT LAZARUS' COLLEGE

The Oxford Detective's pleasure at being offered a drink was diluted by his annoyance at not being asked to stay for dinner. They really were a snooty lot. Still, at least he had got through his interviews, and begun the difficult process of sorting truth from falsehood. None of them had satisfactory alibis; after all the vehicle had been parked for most of the day in the multi-storey car park. Anyone could have got at it; the CCTV cameras had been broken again. It would not really be reasonable to expect them to account for their whereabouts during that whole period. Indeed, if one of them had been able to, that would have aroused his suspicions more than anything.

He looked around the room at his suspects over the rim of his glass. He could not understand what the motive had been. Several of them were pretty poisonous about the writer chappie, but in his experience these profs always were bitter and twisted. They didn't really have anything proper to do all day except squabble with each other. He'd have said that the little fellow with the narrow shoulders, the thick glasses and awful greasy hair had something to hide. But after his subtle interrogation it was clear that that one had no idea whatsoever about the workings of the automobile. There was no way he could have cut the hydraulic brake lines, and then somehow disabled the sensors, especially on a complicated machine like that Maserati. He'd learnt from the Master about the termination of his appointment – now that could be a motive, but surely only for bumping off the top man.

Ah well. It was much more likely to be the ex-wife. *Chercher la femme*, as they said. Or maybe some other woman – none of these literary types could keep their trousers on for long. Even so, it might be a good idea just to check through the records to see if any of them had ever worked in a garage. Unlikely, but you never knew. Leave no stone unturned...

CHAPTER THIRTEEN

HOODED HORDES

Some things you lose and never find. But when you lose something precious and do find it again, you take more than double care not to lose it a second time. I had torn myself away from Blanche, but I was utterly resolved and determined to return. Nothing would stand in my way. Nothing was more important. Nothing.

When I first came to Alamut, the castle had towered above a cold, bare, barren valley. Now the change wrought by the seasons matched the change wrought in me. We rode down through fertile fields of green, watered lush from deep dug wells. My escort followed byways which were familiar to them but little known to others, and for the weeks of our journey we saw no-one on our way. I felt regret as distance stretched thin the invisible, unbreakable bond that tied me to Alamut, but at least I was riding with stern purpose. I told myself that this mission was not for Hasan but for Blanche. The object of my quest was not to bring Hasan what he wanted, but, by doing so, to deliver Blanche from her captivity. I was newly confident in my power and my strength, riding for my lady. Gone was all my adolescent diffidence, all my youthful insecurity. I regretted but did not rescind the angry words about my God that my passion had torn from me in that conversation with Hasan. I tried to pray for forgiveness and understanding, and to be granted success. Somehow though, my expectations of the power of prayer were weaker than they once had been.

Mohammed had greeted me with warmth. Shyly, he had stammered a couple of words of greeting in Latin. I understood that he bore me good will for the favour of saving and sparing his life. I looked at him with renewed interest. There was no doubt that he was his father's son, but slighter and more graceful than the Old Man of the Mountains. If Hasan was an eagle, Mohammed was a hawk, proud and beaky. I returned his greeting as best I could in his own language and we smiled at each other. Here was a fellow of my own age. I realised how little opportunity I had had for such friendships. I determined to cross the divide of language and culture, and pointed to him.

"Mohammed," I pronounced, "Mohammed-i Sabbah," and pointed back at myself. "Hugh, Hugh de Verdon."

"Mohammed-i Hasan-i Sabbah, Mohammed the son of Hasan the son of Sabbah," he corrected me.

We both laughed. He pulled his horse's head round and trotted out under the gate. I kicked my mount and followed. We rode hard through the morning, stopping briefly at midday to water the horses and change mounts. Mohammed and his two colleagues knelt down, touched their foreheads to the ground, and prayed.

"Mohammed Saracenus infidele est. Miles fidele Christi sum. Mohammed is a heathen Saracen. I am a faithful soldier of Christ," I said with a grin, as he handed me a piece of flatbread after he had got back to his feet. He grinned back and nodded in the Persian manner which made me laugh because what he meant as a denial was to me a gesture of agreement. I stopped laughing as I remembered the terror I

215

had felt at our first meeting, when I thought that his nod was condemning me to death.

In his halting Latin he said, "Miles fidele Dei veri sum. Hugo infidele Christianus est. I am a soldier of the true God. Hugh is an infidel Christian."

Then he repeated the sentences in his own language. I spoke his words back to him, causing him to roar with laughter in his turn, for now it was as if I agreed with him. After that we rode side by side, pointing out features of the landscape to each other in Latin and Persian, and repeating the words, laughing loudly at each other's mistakes. We halted again at twilight to camp and to eat a meagre meal. Our two companions were mostly silent, listening to our double-tongued banter, suspicious of the *Franj* and a little in awe of their master's son.

That evening our broken conversation taught me that our journey would last six or eight weeks, that Mohammed was his father's only surviving son, that his mother was dead, and that we did indeed share the age of twenty. This information he first proffered in Latin, but then he gave it in Persian which I carefully repeated. I found that this language came to me with the same facility as Greek back in the abbey, and as each day went by more and more of our conversation took place in Mohammed's native tongue.

The next morning Mohammed woke me just before sunrise. He offered me his water bottle and told me that I should wash my face.

"No, no," he said as I made to dry off the water that I had splashed over it. "The sun must dry it." He turned towards the East, and I followed his example. The horizon broke as the bright edge of the sun cut through it, driving away the darkness and bringing our surroundings back to life. As the rays warmed my face I felt the water drying.

"You see, the sun needs water too." Mohammed smiled. "If you offer him a few drops from your face in the morning, he will be kinder to you in the cruel hour of noon." Then he faced south, fell to his knees and prayed with his comrades.

Our haste allowed no time to stop and hunt – my escort only halted to rest the horses and to pray – so most days we supped on a poor meal of hard bread and dried meat. Normally my companions – for increasingly I thought of them thus – did not bother to light a fire. Nights were mostly warm and gathering fuel would have required an earlier halt, or perhaps they feared attracting attention to themselves even in that wilderness. But occasionally we would happen across game, normally small deer, on our path or close by, and then they would take the opportunity to supplement our poor diet. I could not join in the chase, because I was allowed no weapons, mine being carried on one of the spare horses led by the Nizaris. I think that Mohammed might have trusted me but the other two were still watchful, and one always stayed to guard me. One evening when they had been lucky, Mohammed gave the order to stop before the sun had sunk.

"We are making good time," he said with the smile that I now found infectious, "I think we can indulge ourselves a little."

So they lit a fire and spitted the deer. Soon I saw my hunger reflected in their eager expressions as the smell of roasting meat sharpened our appetites. Sated, more comfortable than usual, Mohammed and I lay back. From habit I murmured words of thanks.

"To Jesus Christ, my most Holy Lord and Saviour, I give thanks for this meal."

"You know that in my religion, your Jesus is a prophet too, a wise and holy man," mused Mohammed.

"Yes, so your father told me," I replied.

"We just do not believe that he is the Son of God. For if he were why did his father allow his suffering and death?"

"Your father also said that to me. But he exposes you to danger, and the risk of death. How is that different?"

Mohammed shifted with discomfort. "My father is powerful, yes, but he is not God. There is no god save Allah, and Mohammed is His prophet, a holy man indeed, but not his son."

I looked into the fire in silence for a few moments.

"So what were these prophecies made by your holy namesake, then?"

Mohammed moved again, looking into the fire and choosing his words with care. "To Mohammed was given the honour of recording the very words of God. He wrote them down in our holy book, in our Koran. They tell us what to believe, and how to lead our lives." He looked at me, the fire now lighting the profile of his beaky face. "My father told me once that you have not one holy book, written by one prophet, but many. That the story of your Jesus' life is told by many writers who do not even agree with each other. Can that be true?"

Now it was my turn to shift uneasily. "There are four Gospels, yes, it is true, but they are all the word of God. In places, perhaps, they are not quite the same..." My voice faltered as I remembered the disquiet that I had felt in my studies at Cluny for this very reason, and as I struggled for the Persian words to explain these complexities.

Mohammed pressed home his advantage. "So tell me why there are just four Gospels? Is this book that my father sends you to fetch not a gospel too? Why is that not part of your holy book? If they tell you different things, how do you decide what is right and what is wrong? How do you decide how to lead your life?"

"We have ten commandments, given by God to Moses."

"To Moses?" Mohammed looked surprised. "Yes, we know him too. But he was an Israelite, a Jew – why were the most important commands for Christians given to him?"

"Our First Commandment is like your words before – 'I am the Lord thy God and thou shalt have no other gods before me.' But our second is different – unlike you we are told not to worship idols or graven images." I remembered Pope Urban's stirring speech at Clermont, and his castigation of Moslem idolatry.

Mohammed looked shocked. "No, no, you are wrong. It says in our book that 'Thy Lord hath decreed that ye worship none but Him'? We are strictly instructed to 'avoid filthy rites associated with idols'."

Now it was my turn to look surprised. I tried to frame a response but again struggled for the Persian words.

"And what of war?" Mohammed continued. "We are told that we can fight only in self-defence, that we can only kill transgressors. You are here, attacking my people's lands in the name of religion. Your rules must permit violence and aggression."

I felt the same discomfort given me by Hasan on this point. Worse, my old abbot's voice rang through my head, expressing his concern about the morality of our Crusade. Hesitantly, I began to render Augustine's argument into Mohammed's language.

"Our Sixth Commandment is 'Thou shalt not kill', yes. And Jesus tells us to love thy neighbour as thyself."

Mohammed interrupted with a grin. "So you love me then? I am your neighbour now, yet I am a Moslem, one of your unbelievers."

I felt angry, frustrated that I could not express my views as clearly as I would like, but also fearful that if I had expressed them they might have sounded weak and flimsy.

"But you fight amongst yourselves. You kill your Moslem brethren. In the Christian world only evil men do that. I know from Blanche that your men slaughtered her first captors. Why was that?"

Now the grin faded from Mohammed's face and it was his turn to look uneasy. "We are Nizaris. We are the true Moslems. We follow the Prophet's proper heir and believe that the true

Imam will return from the dead to lead us. Your Blanche was captured by Seljuks. They are Sunnis. To us they are heretics." Seeing the scepticism on my face he shrugged. "I cannot explain. It is what I was taught. It is what I was told to believe."

It took me a long time to fall asleep that night. I lay wondering whether my Christian God and Mohammed's Allah could be the same, and then, fearful of retribution, I banished the thought from my mind. Eventually I fell into a troubled sleep.

After six weeks of hard riding we forded the great River Euphrates. In front, wheeling squadrons of vultures warned of death and destruction. In another hour or so we came upon the path of a great army. The feet of thousands of men and beasts had trampled out a broad track. Here and there by the way lay the carcasses of animals which had dropped from exhaustion or illness. This was the bait which had brought the vultures circling down. A quick consultation took place between the three *da'is*, after which Mohammed turned to me.

"This must be the path of Emir Kerbogha, Atabeg of Mosul, who marches to raise the siege of Antioch. We will leave you here, for your way is now clearly marked. And Kerbogha, Sunni servant of the Caliph of Baghdad, is no friend of ours."

Mohammed showed no response to my triumphant smile at this practical admission of the Moslem schisms we had discussed.

"You must overtake his army, for once the hosts meet, you will be unable to rejoin your Christian friends. May Allah be with you and protect you on your way."

We looked at each other with affection and respect across our religious divide. Mohammed did me the honour of placing his fingers to his brow and bowing his head. I returned this salute in the same style, pulled my mount's head towards the southwest, and kicked my spurs. Mohammed called after me, "And remember to complete fast and faithfully the task my father has set you, if you would see your Lady Blanche again. We will always be watching."

I knew that overtaking the army's sorry trail would be no light task. Even changing my crossed Crusader cloak for the Moslem overgarment in my pack would not enable me to ride straight past without challenge. There were sure to be many careful scouts posted in the rear and at the sides. Nevertheless, I determined to approach the Turkish host as closely as possible, for any information that I could gather would be valuable to the Crusader cause. I was uncertain of the reception I would get if I reached Antioch. Godfrey might be long since dead from his bear wound, leaving me with no patron in the Christian camp. Perhaps Godfrey's alliance with Bohemond would provide me shelter under the Norman's wing. But Tancred might be suspicious of my actions at Mamistra, and might poison uncle Bohemond's ear. Most of all, though, I feared Baldwin, who would be hungry to sate his antipathy towards his former captive. He might even suspect my hand in his friend Bagrat's death. I felt very alone in that wilderness, and daunted by even the first step of my task. Then I angrily reminded myself of my objective. I would rescue Blanche or die in the attempt. Good information of the enemy's size and order could win me a warmer welcome in Antioch and maybe provide some protection against the malice of my enemies. So that information I would get. I studied the trail of debris. From the state of the carcasses along the way, I estimated that the body of the slow moving army had passed by three days before. Riding hard, travelling light as I was, I hoped to catch them up within a day. I thought then to circle around them, with luck finding a path through the rough hilly country to one side of the valley road. Once beyond the army, I could ride in open speed to carry news to the Crusader troops around Antioch, or God willing, by now safely inside the city walls.

And for sure, another half day's riding brought me within sight of the great cloud of dust thrown up by the Turkish army.

As dusk fell, I moved off the path to camp in a patch of rock-strewn ground, protected from sight by some large boulders. I rose with the sun and cautiously picked out a path behind a rough escarpment which I judged ran parallel to the army's path. From the manner of the marches in which I had taken part, I thought that Kerbogha's men would rise at dawn but would then take a couple of hours to get underway. That would give me time to circle into a position from which I could observe their passage. So I rode until the sun was two hours higher in the sky, then dismounted and hobbled my horse in some thin grazing watered by a small stream. On foot I climbed to the top of the escarpment and to my satisfaction found myself looking down from behind a screen of rocks upon the bottom of the valley which must form the army's route half a mile below. The sight that came into view gave me cause to tremble for the Crusaders at Antioch, and for the success of my quest.

The Atabeg of Mosul had assembled a vast host. As it passed by in the valley beneath, the sun rose to its zenith and sank again, so that the army must have taken fully eight hours to pass. The main column was preceded by a screen of lightly armed scouts, mounted on fast horses with fine small heads, tightly reined in by their riders. Their white robes and rope-bound head-dresses flowed out behind them as they rode. Then followed thousands of cavalry, drawn from many different tribes, to judge by their diverse styles. Some wore pointed metal caps, some turbans, and others helmets wound about with cloth. Many carried the curved bows which had so harried Bohemond's followers at Dorylaeum; others were armed with lances or javelins, and most carried curved or straight swords at their sides. The sun glinting on their helmets reminded me to make sure that mine was well covered by my hooded cloak, lest a reflection warn of my presence and bring riders swarming upon me. Many were cloaked in white, others in rough brown, a few in the green which I now knew from

Mohammed to be the sacred colour of Islam. Light round shields of hide or metal hung from their shoulders, some covered in alien devices. Each company or regiment followed its own emir and his banner, often embroidered brightly in Arab or Persian script.

I estimated the cavalry alone at some twelve thousands. Behind them plodded doggedly the infantry. Companies of archers and spearmen were intermixed with baggage carts and pack animals. Amongst these lurched disjointed animals with long curved necks and humps on their backs. Later I discovered that these creatures – camels by name – could carry a heavy load for days without food or drink. I thought how it might have been to have had some on the desperate dry march after Dorylaeum. At the rear followed another strong mounted force. In all, Atabeg Kerbogha must have gathered a force of forty-five or fifty thousand fighting men.

When the troops had passed by, I slipped carefully down from my vantage point back to my horse. Thirsty from watching in the hot sun, I drank from the stream and refilled my water skins, before riding cautiously forward once more. Again I was able to move ahead of the Saracen army and camped discreetly for the night. Under the black velvet star-spangled sky I almost began to enjoy my second sojourn alone in the wilderness. Before, I had been frightened, aimless, sorrowing, tormented by my sinful slaughter of Bagrat. Now, I felt confident, purposeful, determined in my quest, anxious only to succeed and to return to claim Blanche. This time, no black, turbulent dreams disturbed my sound sleep, but instead happy memories of my woman.

Daybreak woke me again and I at once set off, thinking by now to be safely ahead of the army. However, I had reckoned without Kerbogha's white-robed scouts. Returning towards the main valley road, hoping to make good time across the level plain, I saw three of them fanned out in front. For an instant I thought to melt away into the cover of the rough ground, but they were too close. They saw me and wheeled in my direction. I soon knew that I could not outrun them. Their horses were faster and carried lighter burdens. I would have to fight. For the first time I would face an enemy soldier hand to hand. With this realisation came a sudden rush of excitement. I fumbled my lance from its sling. Its weight momentarily unbalanced me, before I settled back in my saddle, pressing down on my stirrups and spurring forward. Taken by surprise, the leading Arab was too slow to evade this sudden charge. My lance crunched against his chest. His eyes widened, his face contorted in a silent scream. The force of the blow thrust me backwards in my saddle. To keep my seat I had to allow my weapon to twist sideways from my grasp. It had gone so deep into my victim's unprotected body that I could not wrest it out. As his horse ran past, he twisted off stone dead to the ground, my lance quivering in his centre.

I scarcely had time to take in my success, because the other two horsemen were upon me. For an instant I thought I would not get my sword out in time. Then I felt its long blade loosen and heard it come rasping from its scabbard. I was too late to dodge and had to ride straight between them, answering their harsh war cries with an inarticulate roar. Two curved swords blurred down from either side. I parried to the right and heard steel ring true on steel. To the left I swung my shield. A heavy blow, only part blocked, struck my shoulder. But then I was through.

Gripping with my knees, I wheeled my horse. The force of the blade on my shoulder as yet caused no pain, and I prayed that it had not cut my mail coat. Now I could manoeuvre. I addressed the right-hand rider, spinning away from the left. My ferocious blow knocked his raised scimitar down to one side. With a trick remembered from those lessons at Bouillon, I swung my sword back in a reverse thrust. The sharp blade bit deep into the base of my adversary's neck. He tumbled from his horse, the side of his white cloak soaking with blood. I kicked forward again, feeling the wind from a savage swipe brush my face. With the excited thought that it was now one-on-one, I turned back to my remaining adversary. Fear and panic rose in the last Arab's face, as he pulled his horse round to flee. But he was too slow to avoid my sword thrust into his unarmoured torso, so that he too dropped to the ground with an awful cry.

I did not pause to retrieve my lance, for fear of other horsemen lurking nearby. Breathing heavily I sheathed my blooded sword and galloped on. I now felt the aching pain of the blow to my shoulder, as the joint began to stiffen. I shook uncontrollably as my excitement subsided. In its place rose a feeling of empty regret. For the first time I had killed infidel enemies. It had been a fair fight, but I remembered that they were husbands or lovers, loved-ones like me. Perhaps the only difference was that they had more family to mourn them. Angrily I asked myself why they had tried to stand in my way, why they had forced me to take their lives. But then I had no time for further reflection; over my throbbing shoulder I saw another group of horsemen some two hundred paces away.

The plain in front sloped down to a distant river, spanned by a stone bridge guarded by stout gated towers at either end. Suddenly I recognised that I might be trapped. I had not thought that there might be a river to cross in front of me. If the bridge was held by the enemy I would be finished. I looked to either side for another place to cross, but the waters were wide and the current strong. Then I realised that if the river could be forded no bridge would have been built there. A volley of arrows rushed past me, well wide, for at that range and at a gallop even the most skilled horse archers would struggle to hit a fast-moving target. Even so, they were near enough to remind me what would happen to my horse if they came closer. My mount was tiring beneath me, beginning to stumble where the ground was uneven, and I dug him hard with my spurs to drive him over the remaining half mile toward the river. I would have to trust to luck. Then, as I hurtled closer I spotted with relief the familiar red-crossed standard flying above the nearer tower. But the Arabs on my tail were gaining fast, eager to avenge their comrades, their horses fresh. The skin on the back of my neck prickled, expecting to feel a barbed missile at any moment. Another volley whistled over my head and I leant lower over my horse's nape. Then I realised that it came from the friendly battlements in front. A quick glance over my shoulder showed me that it had warned my pursuers off. Thwarted, they wheeled away. The gate in front of me creaked wide and I hurtled safely through.

The garrison that greeted me presented a sorry sight. They were gaunt and thin, clearly underfed for many months on end. They were nervous and suspicious too, for before I had had time to draw breath one man-at-arms had grabbed my horse's bridle, and the others had surrounded me with their spears raised.

"Can't you see that I am one of you?" I exclaimed in some irritation. Nevertheless, as I dismounted one of them pulled rudely at my hurt shoulder. I turned in pain and in anger and was about to strike him for his insolence when their haggard commander bustled up.

"Thank you for opening your gates," I smiled, "and thank you chasing those Arabs off my tail with your volley. I am Sir Hugh de Verdon. I was once in the household of Duke Godfrey de Bouillon. I left the Duke wounded some nine months back and went with his brother Baldwin to Tarsus and Mamistra. Then I was captured by the Saracens. I have been held a prisoner in a castle far to the East. I managed to escape and have followed the footsteps of a great Turkish army. It is now less than two days' march from here. Tell me, though, is Lord Godfrey alive? And what of his brother Baldwin? Have we won Antioch?"

The captain of the gate listened to my speech with his mouth half open under his scruffy beard. He seemed almost too tired to speak.

"Duke Godfrey is alive. He walks with a limp, but he lives. They say that his brother Baldwin has made himself Count of Edessa, a rich city somewhere over the mountains to the north there. Messengers came from him some time back, bringing a few horses and provisions. That was weeks before we took the city. Praise God, it fell just two days ago. We have the great Lord Bohemond of Taranto to thank for that. He found a traitor and brought – or bought – him to our side. This traitor commanded a tower in the southern wall. He gave our men entry at the dead of night. The fight was fierce but the city is ours. Otherwise we'd still be out there on that damned godforsaken plain."

"Praise be to God and thanks to Lord Bohemond indeed," I answered. I found myself grinning at this news, and at my expression of glee even the captain's exhausted face lifted a little. My first reaction was excitement that I could now get to the Cave Church and fulfil my quest. My second was relief that Baldwin was far away and could do me no harm. Then I thought of the news I carried and put on a sombre expression.

"I fear that the victors will shortly become the besieged. The army behind me is at least fifty thousand strong. I have tracked their passage and counted their numbers. They are just days behind me. You cannot hold them here. Fall back with your men to the city, before the enemy's full strength falls on you. Fall back – even their vanguard will be far too strong for you."

The captain said with proud resignation that he had his orders to hold the bridge for as long as he could. "This is the only road by which the enemy can pass. Every extra hour that we can win gives another hour to prepare the defences of Antioch itself. They call this the Iron Bridge, and my

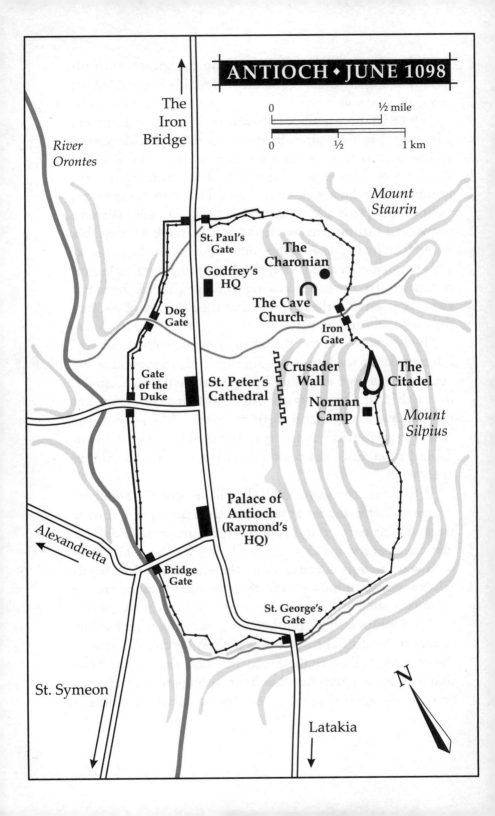

men and I will earn it its name by the strength of our defence."

I did not see the same resolution on the faces of the men nearby. I clasped the captain's hand. "God be with you then," I said and climbed back into my saddle, taking the reins from the nervous soldier at my horse's head. "Good luck."

I kicked my long-suffering mount into a clattering trot over the bridge and through the second tower to carry my news on to the city. On my right now ran the broad River Orontes, curving southwards from the bridge. In the distance to the left of the river a mountain shimmered blue-grey through the dusty haze off the plain. The plain itself was utterly desolate, dusty, brown and bare, wasted by the ravages of the battles which had raged for months back and forth across it. I understood what the captain had meant. Once there must have been rich fields and orchards; now only broken trees and trampled ground remained. The walls of Antioch stretched from the river to the foot of the mountain and then scrambled steeply up its flank to run along its ridge, enclosing the city. The saw-toothed battlements gave them the ominous look of the jaws of some giant mantrap hinged at the base of the hill. Like Constantinople, Antioch's walls were built of brick-banded stone by long-dead Romans. Those emperors might have honoured the fortifications of their eastern capital with more breadth and height, but they had drawn on deeper reserves of skill to plant the walls of Byzantium's second city up that precipitous slope.

Closer to, I passed earthworks doubtless thrown up for the siege, and these looked crude and puny in the city's shadow. The contrast between ancient might and modern weakness became sharper still when I rode beneath the nearest of the towering gates. I answered the challenge of the guard and a postern opened to admit me into the city where I remembered Saint Peter held his first see and the disciples were for the first time called Christians. I asked eagerly where I might find

229

Duke Godfrey, and followed the directions down the main street which led arrow straight from the gate.

On all sides Antioch bore the scars of combat. Dead bodies of men and women – and the sad small shapes of children too – lay in the streets and alleyways, swelling and stinking in the heat, feeding clouds of buzzing flies. Some feeble efforts were being made to drag corpses away to burial or cremation, and the air was choked with the sick smell of charring human flesh so redolent of war. Dried blood darkened the square Roman stones of the street and in places had splashed high on the walls. I had never before seen the gruesome aftermath of a battle for a city's heart. As I looked around, I shuddered and wished that I could turn back the way I had come. The only creatures which looked comfortable and well fed were the dogs which slunk around, or lay lazily in shady corners, sated on corpses. All the human creatures looked famished and wild-eyed. The storm of the city had plainly not yielded the provisions for which the victors had hoped. As I watched, one of the dogs fell victim to an arrow from a hungry soldier's bow, and the others ran off yelping in sharp indignation at this interruption to their repose. The siege must have lasted so long that the former defenders had left no supplies of food for the victors. My horse attracted glares of jealous hunger. I resolved to keep a close eye on him.

Those mournful streets infected me so that my high spirits had sunk low by the time I reached the building pointed out as Godfrey's headquarters. It had once been a fine palace but now was battered and ransacked. I explained my business to the guards and rode into a small courtyard. Dismounting tiredly, I winced now at the pain burning my shoulder. I tied up my horse and gave strict instructions for him to be guarded closely, backed up by threats of awful vengeance. To my pleasure, the men showed more respect than I had been used to before, as if I now exuded greater authority and power.

I found Godfrey seated in a large chair at one end of a long table, looking disconsolately at a platter containing a small rat-shaped piece of meat, grumbling to his attendants that there was not even any wine left to wash it down. His once-blond hair and beard were grizzled and his face was thinner and etched with lines. The Duke started as if he had seen a ghost and broke off his complaints.

"What apparition is this? It can't be. It looks like my Hugh. Surely that cannot be?"

He raised himself from the table, and, limping slightly, came forward with an embrace.

"You are no spectre. You feel like flesh and blood."

I flinched and gasped at the pressure on my hurt shoulder.

"Are you wounded, my friend?" asked Godfrey.

I smiled. In fact the pain had now subsided somewhat, in spite of the force of the Arab's blow. "Compared to the wound with which I left you, my Lord, it is nothing."

Godfrey grimaced at the memory.

"Yes, that was bad. But as you can see I am better. I limp, it is true, but I can ride a horse without much discomfort. Most important of all, I can ride a woman too."

He guffawed, and then his face darkened again.

"Although they tell me I'll never now sire an heir.... But tell me of your adventures. I had word from Baldwin of his seizure of Edessa. If he wanted to make me jealous with his tale of the rich fiefdom he had won, he succeeded. And to poison the chalice further still, he told me that you were lost, dead in some skirmish on the way. He had the nerve to say that I would receive no spy's report from you. I thought he'd murdered you. I feared that from my sickbed I had sent you to your death. So by what miracle can it be that you are now standing before me?"

Godfrey sat down again to his meal, lowering himself heavily. I told him of my treatment at Baldwin's hands, and of the vengeance I had wreaked on Bagrat. Godfrey's eyes regained some of their old sparkle. But I did not speak of my true purpose in Antioch. I did not want to suffer the lewd jibes that Godfrey would make about Blanche. Nor did I want to have to explain everything that had happened at Alamut. I did not wholly understand myself. And Godfrey would not wish me to leave again with Hasan-i Sabbah's book. So I simply related that after my escape from Baldwin I had been captured by a wandering group of Turks, to be held prisoner for months in a remote stronghold until a gaoler's careless oversight had allowed my escape.

"It strikes me that your captors minded you well," said Godfrey. "You look to me fitter and stronger than I remember. Or perhaps it is just the sad contrast with the rest of us after the hardships we have suffered."

I then told how I had observed the Turkish army, of my skirmish with the Arab riders, and of the headlong gallop to the Iron Bridge. Godfrey grinned with delight.

"I knew you would turn out more warrior than monk, Hugh. We must take your news to Bohemond when he returns from his battle at the citadel, for he is our general now. He took the city, you see."

"Yes, so I heard. I was told that Bohemond found a turncoat inside the walls and had him let down ladders to his Normans."

"Another Armenian, he was. They're all like Bagrat – cannot be trusted. The only one who does not acknowledge Bohemond's leadership is Count Raymond. His Provençals hold a section of the city by the Bridge Gate and he sulks there in the best palace in Antioch. That single eye of his watches Bohemond with careful suspicion. Anyway we all shared in the plunder of the city."

Godfrey pointed to an untidy pile of treasures stacked in a corner of the room.

"But we cannot eat gold and silver, nor even silk and wool. There's no food left; our blockade was too tight and no provisions were left in the city when we took it. Now we are suffering from our own prowess. This skinny rodent," he gestured at his plate with disgust, "cost me two silver shillings."

"It'll get worse still when Kerbogha's army shuts us in," I said as Godfrey took another bite. "Do our knights have any horses left to ride? Mine was eyed in the street greedily for its meat."

Godfrey mumbled through his stringy mouthful. "When we won the city scarcely more than seven score stallions were left to the whole army; perhaps four hundreds were found inside but most of those can scarcely stand for want of fodder. Half of those have probably now been eaten. But that's not the worst of it. The Turks still hold the citadel up the mountain. It commands the lower town and they can sally forth at will to harass us." He shook his head and picked his teeth. "If Bohemond can find a way to keep this city, good luck to him. I've stood by my pact to help him win Antioch. I hope he'll leave me Jerusalem if I last that long. What a time you have chosen to rejoin us! Few would be bold enough to enter these walls at a time like this. More have fled to safety – some ran away even before we won the siege. So, Hugh, you are a brave man but I'll wager that you'll soon wish you'd stayed away. But I'll not pretend to be other than pleased to see you."

With a woeful expression on his hungry face Godfrey turned his attention back to his roasted rat.

"My Lord, I am just glad to be back with you. I swore that if I won through to rejoin you I would give prayers of thanks in the ancient Cave Church of Saint Peter. I'd heard it is the holiest place in the city. I want to fulfil my vow as soon as I can. Then I'll lend my help to the city's defence. Can someone direct me that way?"

I thought that if I could find the Lazarus Gospel and take it from the church I could be away before Atabeg Kerbogha's noose tightened around Antioch's neck. But Godfrey laughed bitterly.

"You've chosen the wrong place for your prayers, my friend! Old Adhemar also wanted to say his prayers of thanks in Saint Peter's holy cave, but found that it is set upon the hillside under the citadel. You'd be brought down by arrows before you reached it, or cut to pieces whilst you were on your knees inside. Either say your prayers somewhere else or wait until we have dislodged the Turkish garrison."

So I learned that after all I would have to stay while Kerbogha besieged the city. The image of Antioch as a giant trap was unpleasantly real. All that was left for me to do was to fight as best I could to dislodge the citadel's garrison.

As soon as his poor meal was over, Godfrey took me to deliver my news to Bohemond. The Norman had just returned from leading the fighting at the citadel. I saw that privation had taken its toll on him as well. His broad form had been thinned by a meagre diet and the responsibility of command. His blue eyes were reddened and bloodshot from lack of sleep and the dust of battle. His shoulder-length hair was uncharacteristically unkempt and his smooth face was for once roughened with stubble. To my concern Tancred was with his uncle. I quickly thought back to my last encounter with him at Mamistra. Both Normans heard my tale of capture and escape with sceptical expressions. Bohemond leaned sideways to allow Tancred to whisper up into his ear, and then turned fiercely back.

"Turkish walls and dungeons are more solid than this man pretends. Your story does not ring true. My nephew tells me that you were with bloody Baldwin at Tarsus. That was where he shamefully betrayed our Norman kin and locked them out of the town to be slaughtered. Then he was at Mamistra when Baldwin came to blows with our men. Why do you come here now of all times? Is this part of some plot hatched by your crafty brother, Godfrey?"

Godfrey protested that I had travelled with Baldwin at his direct command. I remembered how flattery had soothed Tancred's anger once before and bowed deeply.

"My Lord Tancred, when we last met I told you that I was with Baldwin at my Lord Duke's request. I told you that Baldwin hated me. I said he had chosen me as a messenger to you to put me in harm's way. I had no love for Baldwin – I was his prisoner. Remember that I gave him no warning of your intent, for when you fell on his camp with your men, seeking just revenge for Tarsus, you found he had made no special preparations."

"His camp was well guarded, but no better that I would have expected of one of his distrustful cast of mind," Tancred acknowledged grudgingly, and I breathed a quiet sigh of relief. The Normans' suspicion soothed, I rushed on to tell Bohemond of the disposition of Kerbogha's army, hoping to confirm his trust with good information.

"You will find that his army is numerous. But it is made up of many different tribes each under their own emirs. Maybe it can be fragmented by a stout and single-minded force under your command, Lord Bohemond."

Bohemond soon learned that my appraisal of Kerbogha's army was correct, for over the next few days disparate thousands arrived and surrounded the city, taking up their positions in the same earthworks that had recently been held by our men. So the besiegers did indeed become the besieged. Gone now was any chance for me to reach Saint Peter's Cave Church and escape before the siege began. Bohemond and his Normans had fought valiantly to dislodge the Turks from the citadel whose towers brooded over the city from the top of Mount Silpius. But the approach to the fort was too steep, the walls that faced the city too strong, and the defenders too determined. Foiled, the Normans had established a camp to the south of the stronghold, and were readied to launch a flank attack from there should the Turks attempt to charge down the slope into the town. But it was essential to build fortifications at the foot of the mountain to meet the force of such a charge. This task was given to Godfrey and his

Lorrainers. Here with other desperate men I laboured, my shoulder now quickly and fully healed. I hoped from here that I could throw the enemy back and fight through to the Cave Church and its precious secret. High above on the hillside, brooding over the same valley, a great statue had been cut in ancient times into the rock of the mountain. It showed the head and shoulders of a man, ominously veiled. The Antiochenes called him the Charonian. His shrouded gaze threatened me as I worked. I wondered if I would be among the many whom he would row across to Hades in the days to come.

My feeling of foreboding rose until I lived in fear. But that was no shame. I think every man, however brave, if he were honest, was scared. Neither wine nor ale was left in the city, and nothing could dull the dread we all felt, of pain, suffering, disfigurement or death in the fight to come. We knew what had happened to the garrison at the Iron Gate, for Kerbogha had ordered their heads to be impaled upon lances and mounted within sight of our walls, the brave captain's in the middle on a pole somewhat longer than his unfortunate men's. The Normans in their improvised camp on the flank of the mountain could only watch in helpless apprehension as the citadel filled with the freshest and strongest of Kerbogha's troops through its outer gate. We all quaked in expectation of their attack. Nerves were stretched to breaking point and petty squabbles broke out frequently between comrades. Bohemond had ordered the houses near the ramparts to be burned, to create more space for his soldiers to manoeuvre if the outer walls or gates were breached, and to make it harder for deserters to climb out unseen. At dawn on my third day in the besieged city, rough smog from the fires still billowed through the streets. The guards peered into the thin grey light with eyes red-rimmed by smoke and lack of sleep. Suddenly one man, his watch sharpened by fear, screamed the alert.

"They're coming; oh God in Heaven, they are coming."

Desperate men gripped their weapons as enemy wave after enemy wave poured down the slope in a tide of vengeance. They seemed unstoppable. Their war cry *"Allahu Akbar"* was answered by ragged roars from dry Christian throats. I felt a rush of relief brought by the start of combat. At last the waiting was over.

Those defenders who had their crossbows to hand had just enough time to let one salvo fly. A few Saracens in the front line tumbled, knocked back by the force of the quarrels at short range and tripping others behind. Another roar came from the right, "The Cross, the Cross, Bohemond, Tancred, Deus le volt", as the Normans sallied from their camp and crashed into the attackers' flank. The weight of their charge squeezed the Saracen ranks together and forced some to turn to defend themselves. It slowed the attack just enough to prevent us on our rudimentary walls at the bottom of the slope from being swept away. Nevertheless, the tide broke over us with terrible force.

A few Saracens were carried to the top of the wall by the momentum of their downhill charge. We threw them back and then we held the enemy off with spears, thrusting down at them from the top of our makeshift wall. The Turkish archers behind could not fire now for fear of hitting their own men. I was in the thick of the fighting. My conscious mind was torn between keeping safe for Blanche and my own sake and straining every muscle to drive the enemy away so that I could win through to my goal. But in truth I had no choice but to fight; I was caught up in a furious tornado. Some of the Saracens hurled missiles, and in my eagerness to stab down at the enemy I showed too much of a target and received a great blow in my ribs. I fell backwards, for a javelin had torn through my coat of mail and cut a long gash in my side. I staggered from the fight to staunch the flow of blood.

My wound bound up, and slightly refreshed by a draught of vile brackish water, I returned to the fray. The enemy numbers were beginning to tell. Baying soldiers had climbed the defences and were dropping over the wall. Rallying a group of men, I rushed at the foe, hewing and hacking with my sword until its blade streamed with blood. The swordsman at my left fell, his face cut open by a scimitar. I turned to face the killer, who now swung ferociously at me. I sidestepped but not quite far enough, and felt a line of fire burn down my left cheek. The enemy's defence lowered, I swung back and struck a great blow at the side of his head. The half-severed neck pumped blood out in a scarlet fountain which sprayed over my surcoat. Elated, I turned to find my next adversary, but saw that the other Saracens who had climbed the defensive wall had been dealt with and were dead or dying. Those outside the wall turned and ran back to regroup, before flooding back in wave after wave again and again.

That battle at the base of Mount Silpius raged until night fell and the dark delivered some respite. My shield was battered and dented by countless blows; my arms and shoulders ached from the effort of wielding my weapons and fending off the enemy. The wound in my ribs throbbed with pain, and the deep cut down my cheek stung and burned. My body was a mass of bruises. I staggered back exhausted to Godfrey's lodging and collapsed fully clothed on the pile of squalid straw that passed for my bed.

I woke at dawn, reinvigorated, to the sound of the trumpets announcing the renewal of conflict. I stripped off my sweat-stinking mail to inspect the wound under the bloody dressing on my side. To my surprised relief it was already healing well and most of the pain had passed, although it itched madly. I found the same when I gingerly fingered the deep cut on my cheek. Breakfast was some tough cold camel meat that Godfrey's steward had found, the scrawny carcass of which had cost no fewer than fifteen marks of silver, or so he had said with disgust the day before. Picking morsels of the stringy flesh from between my teeth, I returned to my station at the wall, knowing that my poor breakfast had been better by far than most of the other men had enjoyed.

Another wave of attackers poured down the slope. Again I was in the thick of the fight. My energy and skill began to attract admiring glances and inspired by example those who watched me. We drove them back and in bold enthusiasm I leapt to the top of the wall, yelling defiance and challenging the Saracens to take me on. None dared face me sword to sword but a determined Turkish spearman lurking wounded at the foot of the wall thrust his weapon upwards. It flashed under my mail coat deep into my right thigh. A scream of pain burst from my throat. Leaning down, I split the spearman's head with my sword but tottered backwards. As I weakened, I shouted for a leather thong to be brought and tied in a tourniquet round my upper thigh to staunch the flow of blood. This time the wound was bad enough to lay me in the hospital, a grim and ghastly building full of grey-faced men bound with dirty bandages. Less than one in three left those rooms alive. An overworked surgeon grimaced and pursed his lips when he saw the damage the spear had done.

I passed the rest of that day and the night in that dank and dreadful place among men with stumps where limbs had been, surrounded by groans and animal whimpers forced by relentless agony. I too was tormented by pain but feared most the look on the surgeon's face, where I read that the amputation saw might soon be sharpened for me too. Nearby, through the stench of gore and excrement, I could detect the rotten smell of someone's gangrened flesh.

Kind sleep took these thoughts away, only for them to return with morning's cold light. I reached down to my damaged thigh and found I could bend my knee and hip joints. They were a little stiff, yes, but the muscles seemed to work. The wound could not have been as bad as I feared. But how it itched! Cautiously I rose to my feet. I was able to stand, albeit a little unsteadily. The surgeon stared at me with sharp astonishment, and shrugged his shoulders as his patient limped slowly away.

Godfrey was no less surprised and showed his delight by thumping me on the back.

"Hugh, my friend, I was worried about you. I thought you had had it this time. Since you came back you seem to be indestructible. Perhaps it is your youth that heals you so fast."

For three more days the fighting continued on Mount Silpius, broken only by the hours of darkness. I returned again and again to fight in the front rank, earning praise and respect from all those who saw me. I learned more in those desperate days about how to handle arms in battle than in all the months of effort in the training lists. My growing experience and skill gave protection from further injury, whilst I exacted a terrible toll on the enemy, despatching many unfortunate souls to their next world. Battle-hardened, I now scarcely thought of the damage I did, or of the pain I inflicted.

On the night after the third day of the fighting, a star with a great tail flashed across the sky, disappearing over the horizon behind the Saracen camp. Many took this as a portent of God's favour. Perhaps the Moslems took it as an evil omen, for on the fourth day of the struggle, they decided that they had had enough and stayed inside the citadel. A great cheer went up from our crude wall. Those of us who remained standing felt that we had won a great victory. The slopes were littered with dead Saracen bodies which we left to the vultures and the jackals. Our Christian dead numbered hundreds too. Although exhausted, we collected our broken comrades and buried them as best we could. Many bodies were unrecognisable, either dismembered by enemy swords, torn by birds and beasts, or already stinking, swollen and blown with maggots.

But victory was by no means won. Kerbogha had simply changed his strategy. Now he would starve us into submission, or perhaps wait until we were too much weakened by hunger and the disease that stalked with it to hold out against another assault. I filled with despair. At least when under attack I fought with hot blood flowing. Now, penned into the festering city, surrounded on all sides by putrefaction, all I could do was await my fate. And worst of all, the citadel was still held by the Turks so I could no more reach the Cave Church than walk on water.

"I knew it. I knew it. I saw it coming. I said so. I knew we were going to get all that nonsense about how Islam was better than Christianity."

The Chaplain spluttered in a distinctly unchristian rage and the Best-Selling Author looked uncharacteristically alarmed by his outburst.

"Look old chap, it is just two young men in a book talking to each other. You should not take it to heart so much. And if you read it again more carefully, I think you will see that neither Hugh nor Mohammed is able to provide a full justification for their beliefs. Honours are pretty equal."

The History Don watched this exchange with glee. "Just wait for what is coming. I am sure I know what happens in the next chapter. The Christian chronicles are fascinating about the Battle of Antioch, but they were all too closely involved – like Raymond d'Aguilers – or had too much of a vested interest for their accounts to be trusted. Only the Moslem historians – Ibn al-Athir in particular – give a credible explanation of what must have happened. You won't be pleased by the Christian chicanery and deceit that went on!"

The Best-Selling Author now looked at the History Don with some annoyance. What writer likes his reader to anticipate his plot?

Chapter Fourteen

A WICKED PACK OF CARDS

*If I had known, when I left Cluny, full of idealism for
Pope Urban's holy war, that I would have fraudulently
used religious belief to attain my ends, I might have
chosen to stay in my dull life of prayer. Why did my God
not warn me? Why did He not make me stay a monk?*

As the state of our army – if it could still be called an army
– became worse, the squabbling princes called a council.
Around a table in the Palace of Antioch occupied by Count
Raymond sat a group of desperate men: Bohemond, stooped
and weary from his valiant efforts in the van of the fighting;
Godfrey grumbling hungrily; Bishop Adhemar, the image of
a calm churchman with resignation in his face; Raymond
himself, his single eye glinting dully beside his hollow socket.
Even Tancred's red fires were burning low, though the day
before he had quietly sortied with ten comrades and returned
bearing six Moslems' severed heads, which now adorned a row
of spears in front of his lodgings. The men who stood like me
behind the high backs of their princes' chairs looked no better.
I could only imagine that I looked the same.

"We cannot leave the shelter of these walls and give battle

in the plain," said Bohemond. "Our men are too weak, their morale is too low. Kerbogha's host is too strong. We have no horses for our knights. They are reduced to common footsoldiers. We would just be cut to pieces."

"So you'd have us stay here and starve," growled Godfrey, "Why only yesterday my steward gave three marks of silver for a nanny goat old enough to be my mother. For all I know it is the last goat to be had in this whole city. Now our men poison themselves by digging up any roots they can find and boiling them up with old leather."

Raymond glared across at Bohemond. "Ni! I'll not leave this part of the city. My Provençals won it. I'd rather die here than hand it back to anyone, whether Moslem or Norman."

Bishop Adhemar quickly intervened, "My Lords, we must not argue amongst ourselves. Remember that our cause is just. We have the Lord Our God on our side. He will show us a way, as He has done before. We must make penance and pray, and He will answer our prayers."

For all the Bishop's wise words, the council of war broke up in recrimination and disagreement. With Bohemond and Godfrey, allies still, I left the Palace to walk back north towards our respective lodgings.

"Our arms are too weak," complained Godfrey. "If only we could find a powerful weapon to rout the Moslems."

"Perhaps the pious Bishop is right," said Bohemond, "Perhaps it will take a miracle to save us from this mess. The pact we swore will be wasted – Antioch will be a grave for us both, no fiefdom for me, and you will never see Jerusalem, much less rule there."

The two princes' words coalesced in my head in a flash of inspiration.

"My Lords, if a powerful weapon and a miracle are what we need, could we not mix them together? If we were to find a great holy relic...a sign that victory would be ours...could morale not be raised to put fighting spirit back into our men for all their weakness? Perhaps a martial relic..."

I thought back to Alamut and the white spears carried by Hasan-i Sabbah's guard, and further back to the treasures of Haghia Sophia.

"...like the lance used by Longinus to pierce Our Lord Jesus' side on the Cross? Accompanied by a vision telling that those who followed it into battle could not be defeated? Given credence by Raymond and the other princes, this sign could reinvigorate the army and give us all renewed hope."

Bohemond's mouth opened but, before my idea could be dismissed out of hand, Godfrey intervened.

"And then perhaps a sortie would stand some chance, if we could fragment Kerbogha's diverse force. Hugh, what genius! But to convince the others, especially Raymond, the lance will have to be discovered by one he trusts. Is there anyone amongst his Provençals whom we can enlist to our cause...?" Godfrey mused for a few moments. "I think perhaps I do know a man, greedy and resourceful, one Peter Bartholomew. He sells me some of the sorry meat I have been eating. He seems to have a knack at nosing out supplies, and little loyalty to his own lord. Instead of bearing what passes for food to Raymond he brings it here, knowing that I will pay him better. He is no fool and he bargains well."

Plainly Peter Bartholomew had worked out that Godfrey was his best market, for he was waiting in our courtyard to purvey a brace of rats which he held concealed under his worn brown cloak. He was an unprepossessing and bedraggled little man with a pointed face not unlike the features of the rodents he had for sale. His head was scabby and roughly shaven. His concave chest hunched and twisted his narrow shoulders. His mean eyes glinted with self-pity and resigned alarm when Godfrey imperiously gestured that he should follow me and Bohemond into his chamber.

Godfrey sat down behind his table. Bohemond, his

handsome soldier's face bearing a confused expression, was beside him. Peter Bartholomew bowed and scraped nervously in front of these two great lords, whilst I stayed at the door to make sure nobody entered.

"I'll do your Worship a special deal on the rats," the Provençal stammered in his nasal twang, pulling the rodents from under his cloak, holding them up by their tails, before placing them on the table in front of the two Princes.

"There's one for each of you."

He glanced from one grim face to the other.

"They're nice and plump."

He reached forward to demonstrate by squeezing them, but jumped back in alarm as Godfrey roared at him. I chuckled quietly.

"Silence. You know the penalty for racketeering at a time of siege, you scum. I could have you strung up for attempting to profit from the starvation of your comrades. Or perhaps that would be too quick a death. Maybe I should slice open your navel and pull your miserable guts slowly out through the hole to show the rest what happens to rascals who leave their friends with empty stomachs."

Peter Bartholomew's face went as white as a cloud as he bobbed and bowed in front of Godfrey, rubbing his hands together and pleading.

"My Lord Duke, your Worship, your Highness, I only bring such poor food as I am able to find, to you before others, because I know the importance of your great leadership to the whole army. I have my comrades' best interests at heart."

Godfrey struggled to keep his face straight and stern. Bohemond's bluff indignation came to his rescue.

"Call the guard. Have him taken away and put to a slow death to encourage the others."

Now Peter Bartholomew was shaking with fear.

"Wait. Is it true you are one of Count Raymond's men?" asked Godfrey.

"I am sir, I am. He trusts me. He trusts me well."

"Well, we would not want to harm one of our friend's trusted men, would we?" pondered Godfrey. "Perhaps …perhaps if you were to perform a small service I could show you some mercy. Indeed I am so merciful that I might even pay you well if you faithfully fulfil the task. Otherwise," his voice now rose again into a growl of menace, "you will surely suffer a slow and most painful death."

Godfrey explained his plot while Bohemond looked on, his bemusement gradually clearing.

"You will join one of the details cleaning the filth left by the infidels in the Cathedral. You will find a way of burying a rusty old lance head before the altar. You will then go to your master and inform him of your visions. You will say that Saints have told you that the Holy Lance, the lance used by the Centurion Longinus to pierce Christ's side on the Cross, is buried in that very cathedral. You will say that the lance must be found, for you have been told that whoever carries it into battle will be invincible. Is that clear?"

A cunning grin crept over Peter's face. He bowed and backed away, promising to carry out Godfrey's request, and turned quickly to rush from the room. Bohemond turned to Godfrey in amazement.

"How do we know he will do as you ask? What if he goes straight to Raymond with the story of our plan?"

Godfrey shrugged his shoulders.

"I'd wager that the combination of fear and greed will keep him on the straight and narrow. Even if he does go to Raymond, what harm can he do us? Nobody will believe such a fantastic story from a rascal like him."

With satisfaction Godfrey observed, "And he has left his rats behind – for free this time."

Two more days of hunger passed. Once, our planned deceit perpetrated in religion's name would have shocked me to the core; now I was excited to be one of the arch-plotters of the hypocrisy. My only thought, my only desire, was to drive the infidel from Antioch, to open the way to the Cave Church and its treasure. Then I could complete my quest. Then I could claim Blanche. With no assaults on the walls to defend against, I languished in an undernourished torpor, from which I was shaken only when a messenger rushed from the Count of Toulouse calling Godfrey to a council in his palace.

We hurried through the streets and entered the chamber we had left two days before. Raymond sat at his round table, a beatific expression on his sallow face. Bishop Adhemar gazed sternly down at his hands. In the expressions of their retinues I read eagerness, expectancy. I saw through the unconcern affected by Bohemond when a nervous glance flashed between him and Godfrey. Tancred sat impatient, wondering what the other leaders knew that he did not. Raymond's single eye scanned the room portentously.

"Bishop Adhemar and I have heard some news from a loyal Provençal in the service of my knight William of Cunhlat."

He gestured to the guards by the door.

"Bring in the man."

A fearful Peter Bartholomew entered the room and halted in front of the princes' table. He took care to avoid the eyes of Godfrey and Bohemond as he bowed deeply to Count Raymond and murmured, "My Lord…"

"Repeat to these noble princes the tale you told to me and my Lord Bishop," oozed Raymond.

Peter Bartholomew cleared his throat.

"My noble lords, I am but a poor servant of one of the knights of the most worshipful Count of Toulouse, but I have been chosen as the humble vessel for a holy message. I have been frightened and nervous about bringing this message before you. Please, I beg your indulgence."

His voice shook and broke, allowing the room to fill with silence. Raymond indicated with a nod that he should continue.

"For some months now, I have seen strange visions. The first came to me shortly after the holy Feast of the Nativity. In all my visions I am visited by two holy men clad in shining raiment. One, the elder, has red hair sprinkled honourably with white, and a thick grey bushy beard. The other, the younger, has a countenance fair beyond all comparison with mortal men. The elder tells me he is Saint Andrew," here Peter piously made the Sign of the Cross with a shaking hand, "and says that his companion is none other than Our Lord Jesus Christ Himself."

A gasp spread through the room, shared by all except Adhemar, who sat awkward and austere.

"I knew Him from the wound in His side. In my vision Saint Andrew points to Our Lord's wound. He tells me that the sacred weapon which made it lies buried before the altar of the cathedral here in Antioch. When he first visited me, before we won this city, he flew me in my nightshirt over the walls and past the Moslem guards, to show me where the Holy Lance is hidden. Then he tells me that any Christian army which carries the lance into battle will sweep all its enemies away. Since then, until my last vision just this morning, Saint Andrew has scolded me more and more for not revealing his message to you, our leaders. I was frightened and overawed. I hope I have done no wrong. But now, in this dark hour, I overcame my fear and stand here before you."

He bowed his narrow shoulders and hung his head.

A fine performance indeed, I thought to myself, wondering how much of his display of nerves had been real. Triumphantly, Raymond looked around the room, letting this extraordinary news sink in.

"Surely this is the sign from God for which I have prayed. Let us dig up the lance, and carry it into battle to smite down our foes. I am honoured that a man of my own nation should be trusted with such a message from on high."

And he smiled on Peter Bartholomew with a benignity at odds with his one-eyed face. To him, our shifty purveyor of deceit was a messenger from God. Adhemar though made a sign of dissent.

"I know that the Holy Lance lies in Haghia Sophia in Constantinople. It was taken there by Emperor Constantine's mother Saint Helena. I have seen it there with my own eyes. There cannot be two Holy Lances. Of all people, I understand the power of the holy relics. As you all know, I carry with me a portion of the True Cross, also brought by gracious Saint Helena from the Holy Land to Constantine's city. But we must beware lest a rash belief in a false relic breaks the Second Commandment and brings down the wrath of God upon our heads."

Godfrey, fearing the failure of his carefully laid plan, growled, "It may well be that the relic held by the Emperor is false and the one revealed to this holy man," gesturing at the rascal who two days before had tried to sell him a pair of rats at an outrageous price, "is real. Will he swear an oath that what he says is true?"

Solemnly a great Bible was brought and Peter laid his right hand upon it. He looked at Count Raymond with a masterly combination of awe and assurance. The man had an unexpected gift for theatre.

"I solemnly swear upon this most holy of books that the account of my visions as related to these noble princes is wholly true. If I have told a falsehood may my body be broken on the wheel and may my soul burn in the everlasting fires of Hell."

Godfrey breathed a sigh of relief. Now it was Bohemond's turn.

"Surely we have nothing to lose by searching for this relic in the cathedral where this man directs?"

Universal assent greeted this simple suggestion, and the room emptied. A procession formed behind Peter and Raymond and grew in numbers as it went, spreading palpable excitement through the city. By the time it reached the square before the cathedral, a great throng had gathered expectantly behind. Raymond gave orders for the church doors to be closed and guarded to prevent the crowd from breaking in and hampering the work. Peter Bartholomew pointed to a spot on the beaten earth floor before the altar and a dozen men set to eagerly with picks and spades. They even included some priests, among them the Count's own chaplain-chronicler, Raymond d'Aguilers. They dug in relays. After two hours nothing had been found.

"The fool has buried it too well, or not at all," growled Godfrey uneasily in my ear. The nobles in the basilica were starting to get restless. Raymond looked nervous, Adhemar quietly satisfied, Tancred impatient and Bohemond more confused than ever. But they had all reckoned without the theatricality which was now consuming Peter Bartholomew. As another group of diggers flagged, he stripped off his outer garments. Urging prayer, he took a spade and leaped into the trench in his undershirt. A few moments more and with a cry of triumph he pointed to a rusty lance head protruding from the earth at the side of the hole. Raymond d'Aguilers knelt down and devoutly kissed the point. A gasp went up from the watchers. Carefully the chaplain extracted the lance head from the ground and passed it reverentially to Count Raymond, who bowed his head and in turn ardently placed his dry lips on the old metal. Raymond's nervousness hardened into confidence; Adhemar's satisfaction melted into dismay. The Count marched through the body of the ancient round-arched basilica, signalled for the west doors to be flung open, and raised the false relic above his head on the steps outside. His nasal voice carried loudly round the square.

"Ni! Behold the Holy Lance, which Centurion Longinus used to pierce the side of Our Holy Saviour on the Cross. Know that an army which rides to battle behind this sacred weapon cannot be defeated and will carry all before it."

A resounding cheer rang out, so loud that it must have

echoed outside the walls and struck the besiegers with fear and wonder.

"Deus le volt, Deus le volt! Hail Count Raymond of Toulouse!"

Bohemond watched the scene with disfavour and turned to Godfrey, grunting, "Perhaps your scheme works a bit too well. You have built Raymond into a heroic leader."

Ecstatic religious fervour, the like of which I had not seen since the council at Clermont, gripped the sorry denizens of the city, soldier and civilian alike. The light-headedness of hunger fed fanaticism as siege-famished crowds knelt in the streets, giving praise to God at the top of their voices.

Godfrey and Bohemond returned to their headquarters to plan and prepare for the assault on Kerbogha's lines. But then the oracle we had created out of the rat vendor spoke again, demanding that every inhabitant of the city give five alms – one for each of Jesus' wounds – and that three days' fasting and prayer take place to cleanse the army from its impurity and sin.

"What is this monster that you have unleashed?" demanded Bohemond of Godfrey. "Not only is that one-eyed merchant Raymond made our leader and the hero of the hour, but now we are forced to fill his coffers to overflowing with alms."

"And what is the madness in making folk fast who already have nothing to eat?" replied Godfrey with gloom. Bohemond stalked off in fury.

Luck then intervened, for Raymond, an older man than the other princes and never in the best health, fell ill and was forced to take to his bed. At least that was the news that spread through the city. I wondered whether Bohemond had played a part in Raymond's sudden indisposition. He certainly looked satisfied enough with the outcome. But probably if he had been able to strike with poison he would have made sure that his rival did not rise again from his sickbed. Anyway, it was the Norman who made the plan for battle and led the council of war. Fortunate it was too for our cause, for he was by far our finest general.

"We must deploy our troops through the Bridge Gate onto the left side of the river as rapidly as we can. Kerbogha has fewer men on that bank and will take some time to get his main force to a position where it can confront us. We'll divide our force into four main regiments. First a squadron of lightly armed archers will rush out of the gate and drive the Moslems back from the bridge. Then three regiments will deploy across the bridge in the plain beyond; the first shall be the Northern French, the second you, Duke Godfrey, with your Lotharingians, and third Bishop Adhemar with the Provençals, carrying the lance. With Tancred, I will hold my Normans in reserve to sweep down on any Moslem counterattack. Sick Raymond will remain in the city with a small force of two hundred men to counter any attack from the citadel. Each regiment must stay tightly packed. If we can rout the first waves that come against us and put them to flight, Kerbogha's main force will be thrown into disarray by his own fleeing troops and may fracture and turn tail."

All agreed that this was the best plan, but Godfrey turned to me and said *sotto voce*, "We are still outnumbered by at least five men to one. The lance will help us for sure, but we need some more supernatural help. I have another plan for you, Hugh. Your horse is a grey. Gather all those that are left to us of the same colour, and if need be douse some piebalds with whitewash. Twenty mounted men are all you will need. Fashion twenty great banners – one for each man – from the finest samite, white save for a plain red cross. As the main army issues from the Gate of the Bridge, ride out through the Iron Gate on the mountain on the other side of the city. Climb to the top of Mount Silpius and show yourselves charging down its slope towards Kerbogha's flank. I'll put a rumour round the army that Saint George, Saint Demetrius and all the other soldier saints are riding down from heaven to our aid. With our troops in this crazy fervent mood they'll believe anything they're told and will fight all the harder for it."

Before my exploits at the wall, I might have doubted my own ability to gather and lead a troop of men on the task set me by Godfrey. Now my stature amongst my fellows was such that I could have found ten times the number I needed, all eager to follow me. With care I spoke individually to the twenty that I judged most discreet and swore each of them to secrecy, but without sharing the purpose of the mission. Two I posted on guard at the gate to the small courtyard behind Godfrey's quarters, and the rest, furnished with ample funds by the Duke, I ordered to set about assembling the necessary horses and materials.

The day of battle dawned greyly for the end of June, and as the troops took up their stations a gentle drizzle fell down on them. I heard them praising God for this refreshment and the energy it gave to weary man and horse alike. The streets murmured with the prayers of priests. At the head of my little white-horsed troop, our banners furled discreetly, I wound my way in the opposite direction up the steep ravine beneath the Charonian. I hoped for now to avoid the unwelcome attention of the Moslems in the citadel. I made sure to present a calm exterior to my men but underneath I trembled with excitement. Not only was this my first command but also the closest I had yet come to the Cave Church.

Once through the narrow gate across a deep ravine, I understood the challenge set me by Godfrey, for the slope was steep and of treacherous scree. Above to the right I saw a black flag rising above the Moslem-held citadel. My heart stopped for a moment, in case it was a signal that my troop had been spotted. Then I realised that it was just a warning to Kerbogha's army of the main sally now taking place from the Bridge Gate. The garrison was too preoccupied with that to pay any attention to my small detachment. I raised my hand to signal the halt. My men looked nervous, expectant.

start his career, help to get me my...I mean help us to overcome our little financial difficulties."

The Taylor '45 had clearly also assuaged the fellows' awe of their Master, for now a hubbub rose round the table.

"We must check the facts and make sure it is historically correct and tallies with the sources."

"It must be religiously sound. It should deal appropriately with the clash between Christianity and Islam."

"The old French must be translated correctly."

"Not to mention the Greek and the Latin."

With a gesture that had once struck terror into Whitehall committees and brooked no disagreement, the Master demanded silence.

"You seem to forget who is Master here. I shall retain full editorial control. You may be permitted to contribute some ideas, and perhaps a bibliography. But nothing, nothing at all, must be allowed to interfere with the readability, the popularity of the book." The Best-Selling Author nodded with grave surprise. "Our objective here is purely commercial. We need a bestseller."

This time the Professor of English managed the last word.

"But we must have a good literary title at least. What about *The Waste Land*?"

I summoned a grin. "Don't worry. We are not going to charge the citadel by ourselves. We are heading the other way. Straight up that hill." I pointed to the right behind me. "When we reach the top, on my command, unfurl your banners and charge as fast as you can down towards the valley. Make as much noise, draw as much attention to yourselves as you can."

They looked surprised, relieved at their task, and one or two even murmured to their neighbours as they relaxed. I raised my voice. "Don't think it will be easy. Look at that slope, how steep it is, and the loose scree. It will be just as bad on the far side going down. Saints do not fall. Yes, that's what you are, fighting saints, riding to the aid of the army. Our soldiers will see you and fight all the harder because God's holy knights are riding to join them. But if you fall, they'll take it as a sign that they'll be defeated and then they'll turn tail and run. The outcome of the whole battle depends on your horsemanship." I glared at them. "And when it is over, not a word of this must be breathed. Death will be the punishment for indiscretion, and I will personally make it a slow one."

I then turned to spur my steed up to Mount Silpius's left -hand peak. Hearing my men slipping and sliding behind me, I worried that we might reach the top too late. I turned and urged them on. It seemed to take hours to reach the summit, as we crested ridge after ridge, thinking that each was the last but finding another beyond. But then, finally, we were there.

The mountain commanded a wide panorama. Relieved and excited, I could see the battle unfolding below. We were not too late. And things seemed to be going according to Bohemond's plan. Down to the left our troops were deployed in tight formation on the plain. The rearguard was under great pressure from Saracens who had moved round from their blockade of the city's southern gates, but was still holding. Our disciplined soldiers, famished maybe, had been toughened by months of hardship. Now they were enflamed by religious fervour, spurred on to make ground against the loose vanguard

255

of Kerbogha's vast host. In untidy clusters which made a stark contrast to our tight Crusader formations, the patchwork of the Atabeg's diverse force made haste to reinforce their front line.

"Hurry up, please, it's time."

I gave the sign to my troop to unfurl their banners and loosed my own. In a biblical gesture, the clouds chose that moment to part. A bright shaft of sunlight splashed the side of the mountain. I bellowed the order to charge, and hurtled down the precipitous slope, my men close behind. Our shiny banners streamed out behind, over the dust thrown up by our horses' hooves. The sun's rays caught the glistening samite and sparkled on the white flags. I imagined an excited roar from the soldiers on the plain below, even above the war cries and the clashing weapons. Exhilaration filled me at my headlong slip-sliding downhill rush, elation erasing fear of a terrible fall and the catastrophe it would bring.

Now, in the valley below, the Moslem line broke in one place as their men turned to run, and then in another and another, like a wave curling back when its force is spent upon the shore. Kerbogha's front line was now in full retreat, and rushed back into the wave behind, carrying that away too in a fast ebbing tide. The whole mighty Saracen army was now on the turn and began to run, pursued by bloodthirsty Crusaders.

On the gentle lower slopes of the mountain I relaxed and reined in my horse. I gave the order for my unit to drop their banners and disperse. In the fiercest possible tones I again warned of the consequences if any of them told tales of our part in the battle. Godfrey's stratagem must not be known through the army. The troop needed no urging to draw out their weapons and join the chase. They could see their comrades pursuing the broken enemy back towards the Iron Bridge, and itched to join them in that merciless pursuit.

I felt drained. I'd had enough of blood-letting. I took pride that my part in the battle had reduced the slaughter by contributing to the rapid turning of the Moslem tide. I had no bloodlust left to slake on the unfortunate foe, for they no longer blocked my way to my goal. I knew from my journey with Mohammed that they were ordinary men, who believed in their god, just as we Christians believed in ours. Instead I turned to seek out Godfrey. I found him in Kerbogha's main camp.

The Duke was directing a group of his followers to load up half a dozen ox carts with some of the choicest spoils. Others were rounding up sheep and goats, as well as mules, precious horses and some of the strange-looking camels. Seeing them close to for the first time, I burst out laughing at their wrinkled noses and puckered lips, and the lashes of absurd length fringing their moist protruding eyes. It felt like the first time I had laughed freely since the siege of Antioch began. Godfrey was in equally high spirits.

"Well, if it isn't Saint George," he muttered in an undertone. "Our little plan worked rather well. You cut a fine figure glittering up there on the mountain. Our men were just beginning to meet stout resistance from those Turks. You gave them the courage and determination they needed. I'll laugh when I hear how the chroniclers describe the miracle – and also when we learn what they have to say about the Holy Lance! They are all monks, so they will most likely record these miraculous events with a pious absence of doubt!

"Now, look at these victuals – we'll not be eating rat for a while – nor drinking stale water."

I saw that one cart was piled high with kegs of wine, sacks of flour and other provisions.

"I tell you, this Kerbogha's taste is far from poor. Try some of this."

He offered me a goblet brimming with dark wine, which I gulped thirstily. Godfrey's expansive manner showed that he was several draughts in front of me.

"And look in here, Hugh."

Godfrey led the way to one of the larger tents, and in the gloom inside I made out the scared dark almond eyes of some Saracen's veiled harem.

"It would be a shame not to use them for pleasure before some fanatic comes and spears them all to death."

The unfortunate women in their exotic robes shrunk away before Godfrey's unmistakeable gesture. I thought of Blanche and tried to ignore the stirring in my loins.

"My lord," I said hurriedly, "I will make sure that these carts and animals get safely back to our camp."

Remounting, I gave the signal to the men-at-arms to drive the wagons forward. Godfrey grinned at me and turned unsteadily back towards the tent.

I picked my way across the battle plain towards the city. Men and birds stole back and forth taking their different spoils from the dead. Here and there half-alive Saracens met their end at Crusader hands. Some groaned and pleaded for a rapid finish to their pain; others, perhaps less hurt, begged for mercy. All their pleas were shown the same face of Christian stone. A spear or sword flashed, a broken body slumped limply back, its earthly torment over. The executioner then stripped anything of use from the corpse, before casting it away, the revealed whiteness of death scarred by livid red wounds. Whose will was now being done?

But even this thought could not wholly destroy my good humour. I had my own concerns and all that mattered to me now was that nothing blocked me from the precious book in the Cave Church.

SAINT LAZARUS' COLLEGE

The Master groaned. What on earth could he have eaten to make him feel so awful? His agonising stomach cramps injected even more testiness than usual into his voice.

"If you ask me our writer friend has been watching too many 'B' movies – isn't that what they call them?"

This question was directed at the History Don. The Master had summoned him to give his views about whether the Best-Selling Author's account of the Siege of Antioch was too overblown to be credible.

"You'd be surprised," the History Don replied. "Fact is stranger than fiction, as they say. That is one reason why I love my subject. So much more interesting than the literature that some of our colleagues set so much store by, and true into the bargain."

The Master sighed. These academics never missed an opportunity to run down their rivals.

"And the defeat of Kerbogha at Antioch was one of the most extraordinary military events of the age. Even allowing for the exaggeration of the chroniclers, the Crusaders were outnumbered four or five to one. They had no cavalry to speak of, and were exhausted and half-starved. Bohemond handled skilfully the forces at his disposal but there is no way they could have won unless their morale was boosted by their genuine belief in divine intervention. The chronicles speak of the discovery of the lance, and of the military saints appearing just when they were needed. The only way to explain those events to modern minds is in terms of some sort of plot behind the scenes; even the Chaplain would not believe that it really happened as it is written. It's probably a bit like some of the things your committee got up to when you were in Whitehall."

The Master scowled.

✳

Chapter Fifteen

WILL IT BLOOM THIS YEAR?

*Perhaps I did deserve to be punished for my part in the
schemes that gave us victory. My motives were selfish,
not pure, and my methods those of deceit and calumny.*

The day of the famous battle for Antioch was followed by the
feast of Saint Peter and Saint Paul, the twin patrons of my
old abbey. As I took part in the victory procession through
the streets to the cathedral, my thoughts cast me back to the
calm solemnity of the annual celebrations in Cluny's church.
I remembered then how I had risen before dawn to chant in
my sincere faith the praises of the guardian saints of the
foundation. The thanksgiving for victory over Kerbogha was an
utterly different affair. Cluny's pacific congregation of tonsured
monks, uniform in their black habits, eyes modestly downcast,
would have shied away in fear and horror from the savage
variety of the band in the cathedral, whose only common
feature was their lean, battle-hardened aspect. And from those
hard faces stared eyes which would have made any monk quake
– eyes which had seen every form of human suffering, and whose
owners had borne and perpetrated many of them. As I gazed
around at my fellows I wondered if I was similarly marked.

The cathedral was packed, and a great crowd had overspilled in the square outside. Nearest the altar, the princes were arrayed in finery looted from Kerbogha's camp. Godfrey swaggered in a cloak of heavy gold Damascene silk. Bohemond towered beside him in a scarlet cape embroidered with gold thread. By Godfrey's generosity, I was decked out in a mantle of deep purple whose unaccustomed splendour made me self-conscious. The congregation's bright colours were spotted here and there by the plain black, brown or white of the clerics in the nave. Part of me wished that I could once more make myself one of them.

Bishop Adhemar, who led the service, was clothed as much as prince as priest, in gleaming vestments of white and gold, a mitre tall on his head. Instead of his bishop's crook, he bore the Holy Lance, now fastened to a fine shaft of white wood. The earth before the altar showed the refilled scars of the trench dug to reveal the sacred relic. I tried to fill my mind with gratitude to God for sending this great victory. But as the *Te Deums* and the prayers echoed under the barrel-vaulted roof, I could not suppress a feeling of guilty cynicism. I was unable to drive from my head the irony that this holy victory was founded on fraud and falsehood. Was it just in my imagination that Bishop Adhemar looked uneasy holding the lance and relieved when he passed it on to one of the other priests officiating at the ceremony?

Looking sideways, I could discern no such doubts in the features of Godfrey and Bohemond. Each had filled his face with martial satisfaction. And the rest of the congregation, with no reason to believe that the lance was anything other than it was meant to be, raptly gazed at it and at the altar in bovine devotion. They genuinely believed that God had brought them this miraculous victory because of the justice of their cause. Bishop Adhemar raised the host and then the chalice, intoning, "*Hoc est enim Corpus Meum* – This is My Body" and then "*Hic est enim Calix Sanguinis Mei* –This is the

261

Chalice of My Blood." On their knees the fierce congregation lowered in reverence the heads that the Moslem hordes had been unable to bow. I bowed my head too, and a feeling of shame, sadness and uncertainty chased away my last vestiges of pride. Surely God would punish me for what I had done? I gazed up in confusion at the great fresco of Our Lord Jesus Christ behind the altar, which some said had been miraculously protected from desecration by the Turks during their long occupation of Antioch. The first infidel who climbed up to deface it had fallen to his death and then none had dared to follow. No miracle, I thought to myself, just a coincidence, fortunate or unfortunate depending on your perspective. In future I would leave such superstitious conjectures to others.

In this disturbed state, I itched for the service of thanksgiving to be over so that I could climb the hill at long last up to the Cave Church. At last the echo of the final chant rang around the arched roof and died. I filed out with the crowd. I turned to Godfrey and said that I now planned to fulfil my vow to breathe a private prayer of gratitude in the location I had promised. Godfrey smiled at my piety.

"What a holy monk you still are, Hugh, to climb that rough shaley hill in this heat. I suppose you will be doing it pilgrim style in bare feet and hair shirt!"

Uncomfortable in my hypocrisy, I still managed a smile of my own in reply.

"No, my Lord, I will ride up there like the true knight that I now am!"

And so I pressed my horse, reluctant in the midday heat, up the same track I had ridden with my troop of false saints on the previous day. From time to time I found myself glancing uneasily up from the rocky path at the stone-veiled face of the Charonian, brooding with menace above me. At length my way turned off uphill, too steep to ride. I had to leave my horse tethered gratefully in the small pool of shade spread by a boulder. On foot I scrambled up in the direction of the statue of the Stygian boatman. My nerves jangled like the stones I dislodged in my anxious clamber up the hill. Where was the church? I could see no building, no holy structure at all.

Then, as I crested a fold in the hillside, a dark mouth opened in welcome. It had been invisible from the path below. Almost on all fours now, I scrambled up to the narrow platform in front of the cave – for cave this was, much more than church. Was this truly the place where Saint Peter had prayed? My heart pounded with the exertion of the steep slope, but also driven hard by excitement at reaching my goal and by fear that this might not after all be the right place. I went in. The chamber was cool and larger than the entrance suggested. The grey walls and roof were mottled green by mould and black by ancient candle smoke. In the gloom an altar, cut roughly from the back wall, gave some reassurance that this humble spot was indeed the object of my quest.

It was very different from my expectation. I had anticipated a church, a building, a library or at least a room where documents might be stored, perhaps even a priest who could show me what I sought. How foolish I had been. Now I realised that this simple space was of course where men would have gone to pray in those early days of the Church, hidden away from prying eyes and persecution. To the left of the altar a passageway led off, a tunnel perhaps for escape if the main entrance were threatened. I bent to enter it, cursing my lack of foresight at bringing neither candle nor torch. I stumbled my way into the deeper darkness with arms outstretched but after a few steps found nothing more than a fall of rock. I turned back out and knelt before the altar. I saw nowhere that could conceal a book and in despair more than expectation I murmured a prayer to Saint Peter.

"Oh Holy Saint, first venerable pontiff from whom all others descend, co-patron of my old abbey, you are the rock on which Our Lord built His Church, now show me, I pray, where in this rocky place my treasure is hidden."

The only other object in the cave was a crude font to the right of the altar, also carved from the solid rock. I rose to inspect it and half saw, half felt an inscription around its edge. Perhaps this would guide me to what I sought.

NIΨONANOMHMATAMHMONANOΨIN

'NIPSON ANOMEMATA ME MONAN OPSIN'

My attention was sharpened when I saw the inscription was palindromic, reading the same both ways. Unconsciously I rolled the Greek around my tongue, translating it in my head as 'wash the sin as well as the face'. I could not see how this advice could help me but in spite of my disappointment I smiled at its gentle humour. I walked around the cave again, carefully inspecting the walls, and went back into the dark tunnel where I scrabbled at the fallen rocks. After a hour of hard work all I had achieved was to bloody my fingers and discover that the rock fall concealed nothing more than a dead end. Exhausted in body and in spirit, I leant back against the old font, my hands behind me on the rim, and looked out through the cave's mouth into the bright light outside. It made a dazzling contrast to the internal gloom.

My hands rested on the ancient deep-chiselled letters, and I felt their hard clean outline with pleasure. Which disciple had chipped them out all those years before, I wondered. Perhaps even Saint Peter himself? I spread my hands out to trace the 'N' at either end of the inscription, then brought them in to the 'I', then the 'Ψ', and the 'O'. Then, with a start of surprise, I went back to the 'Ψ'. Yes, I was right. The 'N's', the 'I's' and the 'O's' were all identical, perfect twins. But the stonemason had slipped up on the third letter. The first 'Ψ' was carved as I would have expected, with a rounded bowl –

shaped a little like the font itself, I thought. But the last one, the letter third from the end, was different. It had a sharp point, like an arrow. Pointing down.

In sudden excitement I turned round; could this be a hidden message? I bent down and scrutinized the old font. I pushed at it but it seemed firm. I pulled out the dagger I wore at my waist and scratched around the base. I became more agitated as I discovered that unlike the altar the font was not carved from the rock as I had first thought. The material at the join was softer than the surrounding stone. My dagger marked it more easily. The font was fixed in place with mortar which with age had become indistinguishable from the stone that it held together. Careless of my blade, I chipped away, periodically stopping my work to heave against the rim. Eventually a grating sound told me that my work was not in vain. The muscles in my arms and back cracked as I pushed at the heavy stone, but bit by bit it shifted far enough to reveal a dark hollow at its base. Eagerly, panting from excited exertion, I reached in. My hand was too big. Cursing, I bent my shoulder to its work again and heaved the font backwards another inch. Now I could squeeze my hand through the gap. Something brushed against my fingers, soft, and hairy. I snatched my hand away, thinking that I had pushed it into the lair of some insect, or some poisonous spider. I remembered the agony suffered by one of Godfrey's men when he had pulled on his boots without the precaution of checking what might have been inside. A scorpion had stung him and his foot had swelled up to almost twice its normal size. But I had no choice. Gritting my teeth, I made myself push my hand back inside again. I found that I had involuntarily shut my eyes, and angry at my own timidity, I forced them back open. Again, something tickled the back of my hand but the sting that I feared did not come. Now I gingerly stretched out the tips of my shaking fingers. At the bottom, I felt a thin cylinder. I picked it up between my index and middle fingers. It seemed to be wrapped in something. As I brought it up towards the hole it snagged and slipped out of my grasp. I pinched my fingers together more firmly and lifted it a second time. It was too long to fit through the hole I had made. I tried a third time. Now I held it at one end, allowing it to hang vertically as I lifted it. This time I withdrew it in triumph. With my prize I rushed out into the light at the front of the cave.

In my hands I held a wooden tube the thickness of a fat finger and a hand's span in length. It was wrapped in frayed material, and I laughed out loud when I saw that I had been tickled and scared by a piece of harmless cotton. Both ends of the tube were plugged with wax. Impatiently I offered it to the sun to soften it and dug at with my dagger, whose once bright blade was now dulled and scratched by its valiant work on the mortar of the font. My triumph began to fade as my head told me that the tube was too small to hold a document as substantial as a gospel; my heart hoped beyond hope that this was the secret writing so desired by Hasan, Blanche's deed of release. I levered out the wax plug. Then I flooded with disappointment as I gently eased one single papyrus sheet from the tube and unrolled it. It was still strong and surprisingly supple after its long sojourn behind the seal. But it was completely blank. I slumped down in the bright sunlight at the cave's mouth. I could have wept. What use was this?

My despair turned to anger – anger against Hasan who had given me this task, anger against the long dead owner-hider of the papyrus, anger against God who had so unfairly tricked me, anger against myself for my foolishness and gullibility, anger against the physical manifestation of my failure, the papyrus itself. I felt a compulsion to tear it to pieces, to scrumple it up and hurl it far down the slopes of the valley. I looked at it again with hatred. But some remnant of monkish respect for a writer's material, for the documents that I had tended at Cluny, caused me to stay my hand. I let the papyrus curl itself up again and stowed it away in its tube, then thrusting it inside my tunic next to the pouch which held Blanche's precious lock of hair.

The sun was now low in the sky, the shadows long, but before returning to the city below, I determined to search though the Cave Church one more time. I had little hope and this time at least my expectation was correct. The secret chamber beneath the font was void and had given up all that it contained. For no reason other than some strange wish to leave things as I had found them, I dragged the heavy stone back into position. The altar was solid rock. The cave walls were virgin and unhewn. There could be nothing more here to find. Nevertheless, I resolved to return the next day with torch and candles to explore more thoroughly.

I slithered back down to my horse, which carried me down the hill far more willingly than on the upward journey. Indeed, it was as if we had exchanged our moods for the return, and I had swapped my outward enthusiasm for my steed's outward reluctance. I returned to Godfrey's quarters and found him preparing to go to the Palace of Antioch and Raymond's round-tabled council chamber.

"So one more vow fulfilled now, Hugh. And thanks given for your safe return to my side. How did you find your cave church?"

I mouthed words to cover my bitter disappointment.

"Not good, my Lord. That holy space is forlorn and open to the elements. Wild animals and beasts are free to make their homes there – in the sacred place where our first pontiff prayed. It is a sacrilege. It should be walled in. Whoever takes on the task of restoring it will earn favour in heaven."

At the council, Bohemond began by proudly staking his claim to the city of Antioch.

"It is thanks to me that we occupied this city. I found the Armenian Firouz. I persuaded him to let my men up into the tower he guarded. Otherwise the city would never have fallen. And if I had I not shown you the way, and led you into the city, you would all have been massacred miserably in the plain outside by Kerbogha's forces. Then it was me who laid the battle plan which gave us victory. Under my command it was executed successfully. My supremacy was recognised by the enemy. After all, the Emir who commanded the citadel would surrender it only to me. Some others tried to grab it but no. He insisted on waiting for my return from the field of battle. And now he and his men have accepted my command, and converted to the true faith. So my Normans now hold the citadel. My flag flies from its tower, just as mine was the first flag to fly over the city itself. We all know that the citadel commands the city; I hold Antioch by right of conquest."

Raymond quavered weakly from his litter.

"Ni, by right of conquest I hold this palace, the Bridge Gate, and this quarter of the city in which it lies. By rights the citadel should have surrendered to me; it was only thanks to some devious plot of yours that the Emir refused to hoist the famous blue and silver flag of Provence. Wasn't I here, commanding the town and defending it against a possible sortie from the fortress above?"

"Yes, and protecting your feeble carcass from the dangers of battle," muttered Bohemond.

Raymond coldly ignored the interruption.

"And remember that it was the Holy Lance which gave us victory, not mere mortal efforts. Remember who found the lance – the Lord chose to reveal it to one of my Provençals and to give it to me."

Bohemond snorted and scowled, but he could not reveal the truth about the rascal Peter Bartholomew. Raymond continued.

"Without the Holy Lance, the silver saints would not have come to the army's aid at the crucial moment and turned the battle."

Here Godfrey caught my eye. In spite of my gloom I had a struggle to prevent myself laughing at the Duke's expression and our shared secret. Raymond looked sententiously round the table.

"Lord Bohemond wants Antioch to keep; I do not want Antioch for myself. We have sworn oaths to return it to the Emperor. I will do so. Christian knights do not break their oaths; to do so would be to bring God's wrath upon our expedition. Besides, we would be fools to make an enemy out of Alexios, whose help we will surely need again."

"Again? Again?" raged Bohemond, hammering on the table in fury. "Where was the Emperor when we needed him? His eunuch Tatikios took his gold nose out of our business months ago. He and the rest of his effete soldiery fled as soon as the going here got tough. The Greek Emperor'll not have Antioch freely from me and I'll wager he's got no more balls than his eunuch to fight me for it."

Bohemond sat seething, looking belligerently around the table. Godfrey and Tancred spoke in favour of his cause but the Count of Toulouse, with Bishop Adhemar's support, was adamant that Antioch would not be delivered to the Norman. In deadlock, the princes were able only to agree on inaction – that the armies should not move south until November at the earliest, the excuse being that their men needed rest after the privations they had suffered. The council broke up in vile temper.

That night I tossed in restless sleep on the palliasse in my first floor chamber. Disturbed dreams troubled me, of an eagle soaring high, diving on a white dove and clutching it viciously in its talons. The eagle's face turned into Hasan-i Sabbah's cruelly beaked aspect, and the dove became Blanche, a look of terror etched on her soft features, her blue eyes wide with fear and sorrow. In the shadows behind, half-human, half-animal shapes circled, lions, bears, some bearded, others one-eyed, others still red-headed. Malevolently they wrestled with each other, snarling, as a huge black serpent slithered behind them spraying out hisses. They all watched the struggle between eagle and dove, doing nothing to intervene, gleeful that the bird of peace was about to be torn to shreds in the raptor's claws.

I jerked awake from this nightmare to feel a dagger's blade cold on the sweat at my throat. It was Mohammed.

"Don't think that you are unobserved," he whispered. "I warned you we would be watching. Your journey to the Cave Church was remarked. Have you found the book my father desires? Are you ready to return with me to Alamut? My father will fast become restless and your Lady Blanche will be at risk."

Angry, I pushed his weapon away.

"You do not frighten me, my friend," I whispered back. "If you kill me your father will not get what he wants. You are a fool to sneak in here. You are risking discovery and all my hopes. But I suppose at least that I can tell you what happened up there."

Mohammed tacitly acknowledged that there was no point keeping his knife at my throat and slipped it away into its curved sheath. His attitude seemed respectful and even a little touched with awe. He listened quietly and with some sympathy to my account.

"Can I see it?" he asked. I fumbled for my tinder box and for one of the stock of candles on the table I used for writing. When I had a flame I gave the candle to Mohammed, felt inside my tunic and pulled out the tube. Carefully I extracted the papyrus, unrolled it and brought it into the light.

"You see, it is blank, useless." I turned it over to show him both sides. Anger seized me again. "The Devil take it. I'm going to burn the damned thing." And I moved it towards Mohammed's candle. Anxious, he moved his hand away, but not before the warmth of the flame had touched the papyrus.

"Wait. See. There is something there."

The excitement in his voice brought me to a halt. I looked

again and saw indeed that some faint marks had appeared in one corner.

"Give me the candle. No, I won't burn it. I just want to warm it a little."

Mohammed moved the candle nearer and I passed the papyrus through the heat rising from the flame. Now, as if by magic, letters began to appear, to cover it. They were the colour of dried blood. I made them out to be the same script as round the Cave Church font, the Greek for the knowledge of which Hasan had despatched me on my noxious quest. I spelt the words out and found the same sentence written out over and again:

ΠΡΟΣΤΗΝΔΥΣΗΝΠΕΠΟΡΕΥΜΑΙ
ΜΕΤΑΤΟΥΒΙΒΛΙΟΥΟΦΟΒΕΙΣΘΕ
ΤΟΑΛΛΟΕΝΤΗΙΑΓΙΑΠΟΛΕΙ
ΑΣΦΑΛΩΣΚΕΚΡΥΜΜΕΝΟΝ'

'PROS TEN DUSEN PEPOREGMAI
META TOU BIBLIOU HO PHOBEISTHE
TO ALLO EN TEI HAGIA POLEI
ASPHALOS KEKRUMMENON'

'I have travelled to the West with the book you fear.
The other is hidden safe in the Holy City'

As I translated for Mohammed my hope and excitement faded away again. What did this mean? What could have possessed the writer of the papyrus to set down repeatedly the same words? Was he somehow taunting the person to whom it was addressed? Could the author be the owner of the Gospel of Lazarus – perhaps even Lazarus himself? Why was it in the cave if not addressed to its occupant – could it be a message for Saint Peter or one of his early acolytes? Could it be that the book it mentioned was actually the gospel that I sought?

But if so, how could I possibly find it somewhere undefined in the great metropolis of Jerusalem, for that was what I supposed the 'Holy City' to be? Mohammed and I looked at each other.

"What does it mean? Have you ever seen such a thing before?"

Mohammed's question stirred some distant reminiscence. Surely somewhere, long ago, I had seen something like it, that same script, that same red-brown colour on a papyrus of similar fashion. I felt the material between my fingers and thumbs. Then suddenly the memory came pouring out. Of course, it had been at Cluny, in the library, dropping from inside the parchment leaves of that fatal volume of Saint Victorinus. That was where I had seen such a papyrus before. In some way the two documents must be twins. In some way they must each unlock the other's secret. The answer to the riddle must be at Cluny. There I must return.

I stared back at Mohammed. I scarcely knew whether to laugh or to cry. I would now have to undo my whole journey. I would have to return to my beginnings. Could I again face my former mentor confessor Abbot Hugh? Would the book still be in the old library? Would I be able to find it once more? Would Hasan be patient or would he vent his enmity and frustration on poor Blanche? All these thoughts churned through me. But in my heart I knew that I had no alternative. My fate led me back to Cluny.

My expression had given Mohammed the answer to his question, but now I spelt it out in words. "Yes, I have seen such a thing before. I think I have. In my abbey, in the place where I started my journey. In the library there I have seen a document with this same writing, in ink of this same colour, written on this same material. I am sure of it. So you see, I'll have to return to Cluny."

Mohammed looked at me with scepticism, and, I thought, some alarm.

"My friend, it is the only chance we have. It's the only way I can find the key to unlock the Lazarus Gospel's hiding place in the Holy City. Only at Cluny will I discover the answer your father wants. I cannot search all Jerusalem, can I?"

"But I have orders from my father not to let you out of my sight. If I let you go, I cannot answer for what he might do to Blanche. I cannot even be sure what he will do to me." He sighed. "I had a brother once, you know. Ustad Hussain. He was six years older than me. My father suspected him of treachery, of murdering another *da'i*. He was put to death. Later the real murderer came forward. He was innocent."

"And how would it be if we go back to Alamut and tell him we know where his answer lies but have not dared to fetch it? How would he react then? Only I can find the matching document. I could not take you with me even if I wanted to. You would be discovered and slaughtered for an infidel before we even left Antioch. Anyway, I will only go back to France if I know you have taken this news back to your father, only if you have made sure that Blanche is safe. Mohammed, you must trust me. I give you my word, my solemn promise. We must trust each other. You know that whatever I find, I will return for my love of Blanche. I depend on you to persuade him of that."

Mohammed gave a sigh of regret. "All right. I will carry your message back. I will do my best. But I cannot answer for how your Lady Blanche might be treated. I just do not know how my father will react. He has little understanding of the power of the love that holds you to your course. I think I do trust you, but my father may think me a fool, or worse. Hurry. And be careful."

As he turned away I clutched his arm. "I saved your life once, Mohammed. I am relying on you to tell Blanche that I have not forsaken her. Tell her that I love her faithfully. Say that whilst there is breath in my body I will return to free her.

For pity's sake tell her that I will be back, however long it takes. Ask her to wait for me."

I scanned the Assassin's dark eyes for sympathy. Before I could wholly understand what I read there, the black-robed figure had turned and slipped away towards the arched window. Mohammed looked to left and right before climbing silently through. I rushed to the opening and watched my friend melt into the shadows and disappear down the narrow street.

Plague now broke out in Antioch and men began to drop like flies. The first symptom was a deep lassitude and tiredness, then a raging fever, accompanied by vomiting and diarrhoea. Then a sinister rash painted the skin in blotches of pale pink. The victims were force-fed to maintain their strength, but they could not keep down their food. Even bleeding had no beneficial effect. Once this terrible disease had its grip, death's release usually came within a week. Bishop Adhemar was one of the first to succumb, taking his doubts about the Holy Lance with him to his grave. I hoped that he would not be too shocked by the truth when he reached the other side. Everyone who could planned to leave the city. Godfrey intended to lead a foraging party towards the North East. I resolved to desert him. The exodus of souls and bodies from Antioch provoked by the plague gave me the opportunity. It meant that there were many more boats now sailing west from the nearby port of Latakia. In the confusion bred of illness I was able to slip quietly from the city, sell my horse and take passage on a Phoenician ship captained by one Phlebas, sailing for Cyprus.

"Is the Master not coming to dinner, then? Should we start without him?"

The Chaplain's solicitousness was partly prompted by his pleasure at the opportunity to take the head of high table in the Master's absence.

"I don't think he will," replied the History Don. "He really looked quite ill to me. Kept rubbing his stomach and complaining of dreadful cramps. It wasn't quite the plague, but it did look to me as if it could be food poisoning."

"Oh dear," said the Professor of English. "We've all been eating the same things, so if that is what it is, we'll probably go down one by one. I've been saying for ages that we need to modernise the kitchens, but there is never enough budget."

The Modern Languages Tutor's alarmed appearance could have been attributed to his fear of suffering the same disorder as the Master as much as to a guilty conscience. But, if so, the excessive nature of his agitation would have forced the conclusion that his dislike of an upset stomach was far greater than the norm.

The Classics Fellow, on the other hand, was positively glowing with pleasure, as if he had no fear of food poisoning whatsoever.

"Thank you, my friend, thank you," he murmured to the Best-Selling Author as they sat down side by side. "I loved those Greek word games of yours. They definitely raise the tone!"

✳

Chapter Sixteen

LOOK TO WINDWARD

There was a time when the prospect of a sea voyage, across that element so strange and unfamiliar, would have filled me with excitement. But now the sea was a mere irritation, another barrier to be surmounted. And beyond that barrier I would have to face a more daunting obstacle still – my former abbot.

The Phoenician crew, expert with sail and oar, sped me to Cyprus. There I re-embarked on a Genoese ship destined for her home port. In Genoa I soon found a small vessel bound in easy stages along the short length of coast to Provence, and so it was at the beginning of December that I found myself disembarking in the port of Marseille under the brown fog of a winter dawn. All around, over the cries of gulls, I heard accents that brought the now distant Provençals Count Raymond and Peter Bartholomew closely to mind.

I was still just monk enough to feel it meet and proper to give thanks in church for my safe voyage. And as the Basilica of Saint Victor was right on the quayside it was there that I went. The church looked new, built less than fifty years before, and boasted those modern pointed arches eschewed by my abbot for his edifice at Cluny. But when I entered, I saw that the new structure encased the skeleton of a building more ancient by far. Perhaps it had been partly destroyed in one of those Saracen raids, vengeance for which had started Count Raymond on his career as a warrior in the name of religion. I ventured to the venerable heart of the building, the deep undercroft, and fell to my knees in front of the altar. Above was set a silver reliquary from which grinned a toothy brown skull, wisps of hair still glued to parchment skin above its empty eye sockets. Putting my doubts about my faith aside, I managed to offer up sincere prayers of thanks. Then I turned to quit the low candlelit chapel. As I made to leave, I inquired politely of a priest standing by the door:

"Father, tell me, please. Before whose saintly relic have I just had the honour to pray?"

The priest looked at me with scorn for my out-of-town ignorance.

"You see before you the head of the friend of Our Lord Jesus Christ – Saint Lazarus himself."

He must have taken my wide-eyed surprise for devotion, for he softened his tone, crossed himself and continued.

"This church was built by Saint Cassian many centuries ago – on the very site where Saint Lazarus was martyred. On this very spot, the ungrateful heathen whose souls he wanted to save struck the head clean from his body. But the church and its monastery were dedicated to Saint Victor, for he too suffered martyrdom here. Saint Victor was ground between two millstones before being beheaded. That's why he is called the patron of all millers as well as of the sailors of Marseille. But this ancient house of God might as well have been named for Saint Lazarus, his sister Saint Martha of Bethany, or even Saint Mary Magdalene. You see, it was close to here that they made landfall after the Jews set them cruelly adrift from the Holy Land. So many saints have passed through our port city, or been martyred here, that it is hard to honour them all. They even say that the famous library here was started with documents brought from the Holy Land by Saint Lazarus and his party."

I quivered with excitement. It was on the tip of my tongue to ask if I could see this library. But before I could phrase my request the priest had continued.

"Some time ago now – before my time here – the most ancient texts were taken for safer keeping to our Benedictine mother foundation at Cluny."

The stunned expression that passed over my face must have been taken for another sign of stupidity by my interlocutor, whose tone reverted to the scorn with which he had begun.

"Surely you have heard of the great monastery of Cluny, even if you are from foreign parts?"

I did not answer. I imagine that my sudden and silent departure added to the smug priest's poor opinion of me.

In the square outside the Basilica, I was accosted by a hawker selling little cakes crudely baked in the pointed shape of a ship. I was minded to brush him aside until I made sense of his thick Languedoc accent and understood that these boats were baked in a tradition to commemorate Saint Lazarus' voyage. Thereupon I fished in the purse under my cloak for a small coin and tasted one of the cakes for luck.

Perhaps my purchase really did bring me good fortune, for shortly afterwards I fell in with a group of pilgrims making the trip northward through the Provençal hills towards Cluny. They welcomed the addition of a well-armed fighting man to their number, especially one, their leader said, whom they could tell was a hardened veteran of the great battles in the East. They hoped to hear exciting tales of the war against the infidel, but were disappointed by my reserve. Denied entertainment, they were nevertheless willing to accept the additional protection of my presence. I certainly had no wish to satisfy their curiosity and their thirst for fancy tales of the Crusade. I had seen too many horrors and too much cruelty to curry popularity by relating those terrible events. And I was too tense, too wrought up, to give blandly the easy banter and stories that they desired. I struggled instead to plan out what to tell the Abbot when I arrived back at my former home. Then I turned cold at the thought that the Abbot might be absent on one of his diplomatic missions. I knew that any delay might prove fatal for Blanche, languishing helpless in her distant prison. And perhaps Lazarus had not after all brought a copy of his book with him to Marseille; maybe it was too much to hope that it was one of the documents founding Saint Victor's library and taken from there to a safer home further inland at Cluny. Perhaps the strange irony that had brought my journey around in a great circle was no more than a bitter joke by fate at my expense. What if my memory was playing cruel tricks? What if the papyrus that I remembered seeing inside Saint Victorinus's Commentary was after all no twin of the one that I now wore so carefully pouched around my neck?

How those pilgrims complained at the hard road over the hills behind Marseille, at the cold and the biting wind! To me this journey of a few days seemed a nothing; my endurance had been forged in a hotter flame out east. We reached Avignon, where the party planned to recuperate from their exertions for a while, but I disdained the idea of rest and immediately attached myself to another group travelling up the easy main road alongside the River Rhone. My former companions had become tired of my sullen silences and my monosyllabic replies to their eager questions. I could tell that they were far from sorry to see me hurry on whilst they lingered.

As I approached the abbey through the grey-trunked beeches, I filled with memories of my first arrival with my mother a decade before. Then spring had brightened the forest, and little shoots of green had announced the renewal of life. Sun shafts had reached down to gild the thick carpet of brown leaves on the ground. Now everything was dead in the grim grasp of winter. Snow dusted the forest floor, but its whiteness did not sparkle; it merely stole the warmth from the fallen leaves and greyed them in dirty monochrome. The trees themselves seemed smaller, punier than I remembered, robbed of their splendour by the dull light and belittled in my eyes by the passage of time.

I emerged into the clearing around the abbey itself and shivered for the monks working outside in their black habits. There, unchanged, loomed the double-doored gate through which I had passed as a boy, and the squat guardhouse crouching beside it. There above the doors was the Cluniac coat of arms – those keys crossed over the raised sword. I remembered the message it had spelt to me that first time – that here I would be locked away from the knightly life I so desired. But that sword I now proudly wielded. For a moment my spirits rose. I had conquered Cluny once before; now perhaps its keys would unlock the mystery I needed to solve. But when I entered the bare room where I had parted from my mother, I shrivelled inside. I became just a frightened little boy again. My gaze was forced to the crucifix, still there on the wall. Once I had seen an expression of pity in Jesus' face; now all I saw was pain and blank helplessness.

A monk entered the gatehouse to ask the travellers' business. I recognised Brother William, a former contemporary in the novitiate. My face was well hidden beneath my hood as I asked for an audience with the Abbot. William assessed me with an arrogant sneer, taking in my worn and patched cloak, the proud red cross on its left shoulder all but erased by many soakings and its long sojourn in the bleaching sun.

"Our noble and saintly Abbot Hugh does not make himself available to greet common travellers. He consorts with bishops and princes and talks with God."

I stepped closer and threw back my hood, exposing the mail cowl underneath. I watched with pleasure as the arrogance drained from the monk's eyes to be replaced by nervous recognition.

"Hugh de Verdon..." He crossed himself urgently.

"Sir Hugh to you," came my brusque interruption. "I see that you have forgotten your vow of humility. I hope for your sake that you are not quite so careless of your vow of obedience."

I pointedly loosened the long sword in my scabbard.

"If I were you, I'd hurry to tell my Father Abbot that I am here, and that I beg him for an audience."

I chuckled at the cowed figure who scurried from the room to do my bidding. A wave of relief had washed over me to learn that the Abbot was indeed in residence, only to subside again, leaving trepidation at the confrontation ahead.

The chastened monk soon returned and respectfully beckoned me through the gate that led into the abbey proper. Now Brother William added silence to his rediscovered vows of humility and obedience as he politely ushered me into the Abbot's presence.

"Hugh, my son, what pleasure it gives an old man to see you."

That spiritual voice, at once firm and gentle, soothed the worries I had harboured about my reception.

"You have been in my prayers recently. But I never thought that Our Lord would show me such favour as to actually bring you here before me."

Now his voice shook. To my surprise, and for the first time I could remember, I saw his eyes brimming with tears. My own now also filled with reciprocal emotion. Partly to hide this weakness I went down on one knee and made to kiss the Abbot's ring. But he would have none of it; instead he lifted me to my feet. He embraced me warmly, his head over my shoulder and mine over his, for long enough to get his emotions back under control. Then he stepped back to regard me.

"So you are no ghost, but definitely flesh and blood. You

return like the prodigal son; I should find a fatted calf to kill in your honour."

I immediately felt uncomfortable once more under the silent inquisition of those grey eyes, clear again, staring out full of wisdom beneath the shaggy eyebrows, which were surely whiter than before. I saw pity and regret flit across the Abbot's face as he took in my appearance. Had I altered so much? Could he really see so much change wrought in me by time and war? Then he reassumed his normal calm expression.

"How you have filled out and strengthened! I am sure that when you left me you were at least two fingers' breadth shorter than me. Look at you now. You are fully a man. But I see in your face sorrows and sadnesses. Your innocence has been wounded by the weapon of war. I hope not mortally so. But I am sorry, my excitement makes me forget my manners; you have travelled far; take a goblet of wine – you will surely remember our flavoursome vintage; sit, tell me why you are here. Do you want to return to the abbey? Renew your vows? Embrace a life of prayer again?"

At the warmth of this greeting, and this effusion of radiant love, I filled with guilt. I forced out a wan smile.

"My Lord Abbot, you have been more than a father to me. I would have been wiser to follow your advice and stay here. But I cannot come back. I have seen too many things in the world outside…I have done too many things. I couldn't now return to my previous life."

The Abbot sighed. "Remember the sacramental power of the confessional. Remember how Our Lord Jesus Christ took all the sins of the world upon His own shoulders. When He died on the Cross and rose again He conquered death and all that is evil. Perhaps you have come to seek absolution? Would you like me to hear your confession? It will help to restore your inner peace."

Instead of peace I felt horror at the thought of exposing my sins to my former Father Confessor. In my eagerness to avoid the subject I moved hastily – perhaps too hastily – to broach the purpose of my visit.

"My Lord Abbot, let me tell you why I have come. I am on a quest. In a far off land a prisoner languishes. To secure that prisoner's release I must find a rare and valuable book and take it back to her gaoler. Then perhaps she will be set free."

The Abbot's eyebrows rose at my involuntary announcement of Blanche's sex.

"I believe that only two copies of that book were ever made. One of them, I think, lies in the library here. The book I seek is an ancient Greek text. It is known as the Gospel of Lazarus."

As I spoke these words, the Abbot raised his hand in a peremptory gesture, commanding me to stop. He no longer looked at me with warmth. A wintry cloud gathered across his brow. Sorrowfully he shook his head.

"Hugh, Hugh, if you knew what that book contained, you would not wish to read it – nor to take it back as ransom for any prisoner. I read the book many years ago. It was sent here from our daughter foundation at Saint Victor in Marseille. I read it, yes indeed. And when I had read it I burned it...I burned it under that very chimney there," he pointed to the fireplace in his room, "so that none might read it after me. Then I scattered its ashes."

My disappointment erupted in anger. "What gives you the right to read such a book and then to deny its knowledge to others? How dare you play God? Whatever was written in that book has done you no harm; why should it harm me?"

I remembered the crazy virulence with which Hasan-i Sabbah had claimed that all divinities, Christian and Moslem alike, sought to keep knowledge from humankind. Here was the proof. I also remembered Hasan's rage when I had gainsaid his authority. For a moment the same anger flashed in the Abbot's eyes. Like the Nizari, the Christian was unaccustomed to defiance. And to the Abbot perhaps my boldness was sharpened by the sometime obedience that it replaced. But where Hasan had ranted at me, the Abbot controlled his emotion. He extinguished the dangerous spark, leaving only the familiar expression of patient wisdom.

"Hugh, Hugh, my son, you forget yourself. Calm down. My faith is strong. Nothing could shake it, certainly not something I read. But, as I remember telling you once before, some books contain falsehoods so convincing that they can be damaging to those of lesser certitude. Had you read the lies contained in that false Gospel, I could not answer for the effect it might have had on the future of your eternal soul. Knowledge of the truth is wholly good and is to be found in the Holy Bible and the books of the saintly commentators. But there is also falsehood and mendacity, the Devil's own works. They can be taken for truth. They pave the way to the everlasting fires of hell. Remember, after all, the impact your own reading had on you in the impressionable days of your youth."

My own anger had also now subsided. I controlled the temptation to ask why the Abbot knew that the writings of Matthew, Mark, Luke and John were truthful but that the work of Lazarus was false. The book was gone; nothing could bring it back. Now I would have to gain access to the library and find the tattered papyrus again. With luck it might provide the answer to my riddle. If I further angered the library's master, he might deny me access. So I bowed my head in simulated submission and begged pardon for my impetuosity. The Abbot smiled gracious forgiveness and stood to indicate that the interview was over. As I moved towards the door, I turned back as if an afterthought had occurred to me.

"My Lord Abbot, you mentioned truthful books. I have had no opportunity for such reading on my travels. There are some works which I would be keen to revisit in order to refresh my memory of their wisdom. Would you grant me permission

284

to spend some time over the next few days reading once more in the library?"

The Abbot smiled at this apparent confirmation that I had accepted his rebuke. He summoned a young monk who had taken on my former position as secretary.

"It may seem unusual, I know. But Hugh here was once a valued and learned member of our community. I would be grateful if you would ask Brother Gerard to place a desk in the library at his disposal for the rest of his stay."

And so I found myself back in the dark quiet room where I had learnt so much. Little had changed. The same musty smell of parchment scented the air. The silence was still broken only by the scratching of the scriptorium quills, so regular that after a short while one noticed it no more. I remembered Brother Gerard faintly as a young assistant librarian, thin, pale and non-descript, but a much more welcome sight than the purpled jowls of Brother Anselm which still sometimes entered my dreams wobbling in indignation at my reading of Ovid. I inquired by sign after his predecessor's well-being and was not too sorry to learn that he had suffered a fatal apoplexy two years before.

Respectfully, Brother Gerard gave me a piece of parchment and showed me that I should write down the titles with which I wished to reacquaint myself. I offered a list of some of the commentaries on the Holy Scripture, particularly Saint Jerome, Saint Gregory, and Saint Victorinus. I then sat as still as I could at the desk I had been given, quaking lest they had disposed of the damaged volume that I had once used to conceal my forbidden poetry. Relief poured through me when Brother Gerard laid the familiar volume down with a smile. The dust on the cover showed that there was still not much demand for this recondite work.

I felt the eyes of many curious monks surreptitiously scrutinising me. I imagined they must wonder why a stranger to the community had been allowed into their inner sanctum.

Others perhaps half recognised me through the veil woven by time and tribulation, and tried to recollect when and where they had seen me before. So it was a while before I could turn my attention to the volume I really wanted to examine. Saints Jerome and Gregory severely tested my patience as I scanned their learned pages and their words danced without meaning before my unfocussed eyes. At last I judged that the monks had lost interest, and that I had merged far enough into the background. I placed Saint Victorinus in front of me. I shook with excitement so hard that I attracted attention again and a solicitous question from Brother Jerome. I responded that it was nothing, a mild recurrent ague picked up in the East, and calmed my shaking hands. Holding my breath, I opened the esoteric volume and exhaled in near ecstasy as I saw the square fragment of papyrus lying there inside the cover. It was a simple matter for me to secrete the single sheet up a sleeve. After all, I had succeeded in surreptitiously removing whole books from that library. But it was far less easy to sit there calmly until the time came to leave.

At last it was the hour for Vespers and I was able to make my way without remark to the quarters for passing guests of the abbey. These were much more comfortable than the long bare dormitory in which I had slept as a member of the community. More importantly for my current purpose, they were much more private, being divided into separate cells.

With infinite care lest in my excitement I did the fragile item some harm, I took the tattered page from my sleeve and placed it on the blankets folded at the end of my mattress. There were the brown letters like dried blood. At some point, I assumed, it must have been warmed to reveal its secret ink. Then I lifted the wooden tube from the pouch that gave shelter to it beside Blanche's lock of hair. I removed the wax lid and slid out the document inside. My heart pounded as I laid it gently down. They were twins indeed, those two documents, in dimension and in colour. The form, the size and shape of the writing were the same. I exhaled in relief. Then I looked from one to the other, and my triumph was replaced by desperate disappointment. The writing was all too identical – the papyrus from Saint Victorinus bore the very same doggerel. Those mocking characters danced over and over again in front of me:

ʽΠ Ρ Ο Σ Τ Η Ν Δ Υ Σ Η Ν Π Ε Π Ο Ρ Ε Υ Μ Α Ι
Μ Ε Τ Α Τ Ο Υ Β Ι Β Λ Ι Ο Υ Ο Φ Ο Β Ε Ι Σ Θ Ε
Τ Ο Α Λ Λ Ο Ε Ν Τ Η Ι Α Γ Ι Α Π Ο Λ Ε Ι
Α Σ Φ Α Λ Ω Σ Κ Ε Κ Ρ Υ Μ Μ ΕΝ Ο Ν’

'PROS TEN DUSEN PEPOREGMAI
META TOU BIBLIOU HO PHOBEISTHE
TO ALLO EN TEI HAGIA POLEI
ASPHALOS KEKRUMMENON'

'I have travelled to the West with the book you fear.
The other is hidden safe in the Holy City'

Far from unlocking the secret of the parchment I already had, this new possession merely repeated it. What good were two identical documents, one in perfect condition from the protection afforded by its wax-sealed tube, the other tattered with holes from the harsher treatment it had suffered? Maybe it had been burnt with holes when it was warmed to reveal its secret. If, as was surely the case, the papyrus referred to the Gospel of Lazarus, all I had now discovered was that one copy had found its way to Cluny, only to suffer destruction in the Abbot's fire. Its secrets were lost forever. The other had been hidden somewhere in Jerusalem and if it still existed would remain impossible to find.

As before at the Cave Church, I was on the point of taking impetuous revenge on the fragile sheet which had given me such frustration and dismay. I nearly tore it to shreds and destroyed it forever. But just as in Antioch, my hand was stayed by some impulse, perhaps some respect for the written word. Perhaps it could be useful somehow. So instead I placed the new sheet carefully on top of the old, lining it up edge to edge in preparation for rolling them together and slipping the reunited twins back into the tube. As I did so I idly ran my eye from top to bottom. And then I did so again with rising elation, again, and yet again. I could hardly believe what I saw, for a coherent phrase appeared, formed by the letters on the lower document as they came into view through the holes in its ragged twin:

ΠΡΟΣΤΗΝΔΥΣΗΝΠΕΠΟΡΕΥΜΑ
ΙΜΕΤΑΤΟΥΒΙΒΛΙΟΥΟΦΟΒΕΙΣΘ
ΕΤΟΑΛΛΟ**ΕΝΤΗΙ**ΑΓΙΑΠ**Ο**ΛΕΙΑ
ΣΦΑΛΩΣΚΕ**Κ**ΡΥΜΜΕΝΟΝΠΡΟΣ
ΤΗΝΔΥΣΗΝΠΕΠΟΡΕΥΜΑ**Ι**ΜΕΤ
ΑΤΟΥΒΙΒΛΙΟΥΟΦΟΒΕΙΣΘΕΤΟΑ
ΛΛΟΕΝ**ΤΗ**ΙΑΓΙΑΠΟΛΕΙΑ**Σ**ΦΑΛ
ΩΣΚΕΚΡΥΜ**Μ**ΕΝΟΝΠΡΟΣΤ**Η**ΝΔ
ΥΣΗΝΠΕΠΟΡΕΥΜΑΙΜΕΤΑ**Τ**ΟΥ
ΒΙΒΛΙΟΥΟΦΟΒΕΙΣΘΕΤΟΑΛΛΟΕ
ΝΤΗΙΑΓΙΑΠΟΛΕΙΑΣΦΑΛΩΣΚΕ
ΚΡΥΜΜΕΝΟΝΠ**ΡΟΣΤΗΝΔΥΣΗΝ**
ΠΕΠΟΡΕΥ**ΜΑ**ΙΜΕΤΑΤΟΥΒΙΒΛΙ
ΟΥΟΦΟΒΕΙΣΘΕΤΟΑΛΛΟΕΝΤΗΙ
ΑΓΙΑΠΟΛΕΙΑΣΦΑΛΩΣΚΕΚ**Ρ**ΥΜ
ΜΕΝΟΝΠΡΟΣΤΗΝΔΥΣΗΝΠΕΠΟ
ΡΕΥΜΑΙΜΕΤΑΤΟΥΒΙΒΛΙΟΥΟΦ
ΟΒΕΙΣΘΕΤΟΑΛΛΟΕΝΤΗΙΑΓΙΑΠ
ΟΛΕ**ΙΑΣ**ΦΑΛΩΣΚΕΚΡΥΜΜΕΝΟΝ

ʻΕΝΤΗΙΟΙΚΙΑΙΤΗΣΜΗΤΡΟΣΤΗΣ ΜΑΡΙΑΣʼ

ʻΕΝ ΤΕΙ ΟΙΚΙΑΙ ΤΕΣ ΜΕΤΡΟΣ ΤΕΣ ΜΑΡΙΑΣʼ

'In the house of Mary's mother'

I slid the documents apart again. Like Doubting Thomas I fingered the holes. They were perhaps too even, too carefully made, their edges too smooth, to be caused by wear and tear. Again I placed the holey twin upon its whole companion, cackling like a lunatic as in triumph I saw again the same sentence shining through.

ʻΕΝΤΗΙΟΙΚΙΑΙΤΗΣΜΗΤΡΟΣΤΗΣ ΜΑΡΙΑΣʼ

ʻΕΝ ΤΕΙ ΟΙΚΙΑΙ ΤΕΣ ΜΕΤΡΟΣ ΤΕΣ ΜΑΡΙΑΣʼ

'In the house of Mary's mother'

There could be no mistake. I wanted to leap round the room for relief. Gradually my euphoria subsided. I began to think of the hurdles and challenges I still had to overcome – which Mary, who was her mother, where was her house? – let alone making my long way back to Jerusalem. In Antioch, my fate and Blanche's had seemed inextricably wound up with the success of the Crusade. Until the battle of Antioch was won, the Cave Church had been closed and its treasure denied. Now it appeared that I could not enjoy my love until the Cross had won back Jerusalem itself. I felt like a man climbing a great mountain, like I had felt on Mount Silpius climbing up with my troop of false saints. From below, each ridge seemed the last. Then, when that ridge was crested, another appeared beyond, and the real summit rose still further in the distance. Nevertheless, the wellspring of my optimism bubbled up again. After all, I had reached the summit of Mount Silpius. Now I had made a great stride forward and could clearly make out my route to my metaphorical goal.

The Abbot detected my changed mood when the next day I came to take my leave. As a novice, I would have been unable to deflect my Father Confessor's sensitive perception, and might have revealed my secret. Now, as a soldier, I could wield the shield I needed to deflect that keen gaze away from my spirit.

"My Lord Abbot, I came here troubled and unsettled. I was uncertain and confused. Now I am once more at peace. The ragged edges of my soul have been smoothed by the reading I have been able to do at your indulgence in the library, and soothed by my prayers in the holy church of which I have such fond memories. I have prayed hard for guidance. Now I know that I must return to the Holy Land. I have my Crusader's vow to fulfil. What I have relearned here will truly help me on my quest."

I gazed steadily into my old confessor's eyes, confident that none of my words was literally untruthful. Let my wise abbot interpret them as he wished. I felt victorious; I had won. I would have the book he had denied me. But as the Abbot gave the blessing with serene compassion before fondly embracing me farewell, I felt like Saint Peter at the third cock crow. The Abbot seemed to me to own the moral victory still.

SAINT LAZARUS' COLLEGE

The Modern Languages Tutor lay in bed in his old-fashioned night shirt. He had drunk a couple more glasses than usual at dinner that night in order to calm his nerves. He was sure that the news of the Master's stomach upset would set off the Oxford Detective's suspicions. Once thoughts of poison had entered the policeman's mind, it was inevitable that an investigation would take place which would reveal his own foolish sally to the hardware store. Then the charge of attempted murder would follow, and his ejection from the college would come even sooner than the Master planned. Misery would be accompanied by disgrace.

The Modern Languages Tutor reached for the whisky glass brimming beside his bed and took a deep swallow. Then he reached for the cigarette packet – only three left, he noted – and lit up. He nodded off – or passed out – before the cigarette was quite finished, so that it rolled out of his scrawny fingers onto the counterpane.

It was the Chaplain, on his way back from a quick prayer in the chapel, who saw the smoke pouring into the Quad. He raised the alarm, and the Fire Brigade made it to the college within five minutes. When they got the Modern Languages Tutor out, he was unconscious, badly burned, but still just alive.

Chapter Seventeen

TOLLING REMINISCENT BELLS

Now, surely, I had left Cluny for the last time. But it had not left me. I had achieved what I hoped, but somehow the Abbot had hollowed my victory.

A group of pilgrims had spent enough time at Cluny and was now ready to move on southward. So, as on the outward journey from Marseille, for my return I was easily able to find travelling companions. The tumult in my soul had been stirred up in the abbey by conflicting emotions and memories. At the inn which provided shelter for the first night, I turned to an alternative salve for my troubled spirit, and matched my fellow travellers wine flagon for wine flagon. I surprised myself by becoming better company, regaling the party with tales of the splendours of Constantinople and of the famous battle of Antioch. I related the miraculous discovery of the Holy Lance. I told how, with the aid of that sacred relic and an army of military saints all dressed in white, a few hundred of the faithful had scattered many thousands of infidels to the four winds. It was a new experience for me to be the centre of attention, the focus of the group, and I found I enjoyed embroidering these stories. Yet in my core I despised my companions for their foolish gullibility; I was sure that they would still have believed me if I had said that the Saracen army had been washed away by a second great flood, and that the Crusaders had all been rescued by Noah himself reappearing in his Ark. I woke with a headache, full of self-disgust for my willingness to curry favour by pandering to their credulity. But this time, when I reached Marseille, my travelling companions were rather sorry to see me go down to the docks in search of a coaster to take me back the way I had come.

Towards the end of January I was back in Genoa looking for a ship that could give me passage towards the Holy Land. I soon found getting to Genoa was an easier task than leaving again. The port was busier than Constantinople, even though the Italian harbour was far smaller than the Greek. In the taverns round the quays where I sought a passage, I learned that the eager espousal of the Crusade by the Genoese merchants and sailors had made their city the main port of embarkation for the Holy Land. Some of the seamen with whom I talked acknowledged the irony of this when the original mercantile power of their port was built on trade across the Mediterranean with the Moslems. I spent all my time in the docks, watching with interest the unfamiliar maritime activity. I even saw new ships taking shape in the yards, floated part complete before having their masts and superstructure fitted. Nevertheless, above all my enforced sojourn filled me with frustration. All the ships were full, and even the largest of the Genoese armed merchant galleys could accommodate no more than seven or eight score. Some of the many Moslems sold as slaves on the quayside ended up at the oars of these galleys, but also many of the rowers were free men, hoping to win their fortune by taking a small share in the profits of their ship.

My money was running short, but anyway the town was so full that I could find no quarters even if I had had the funds to afford them. I was forced to sleep in the open, shivering in the wind that whipped off the cold sea, frustrated at being rejected by captain after captain. Eventually I found two brothers by the name of Embriaco who were willing to take me on as an oarsman in one of their two galleys, on the understanding that I would take no share in any profits of their voyage.

"You may be a landlubber," laughed Brother Guillermo, "but you look strong and fit enough. As you come free we'll just feed you to the fishes if I find you cannot pull an oar. Perhaps you will be useful to us when we reach Palestine and find your former comrades in arms."

I smiled. "I'll do my best. Have you had any news from the Holy Land?"

"The word I hear is that your army has still not reached Jerusalem. Some remain in Antioch; some have begun the journey south but stop to invest and sack infidel towns and strongholds on the way."

Here his friendly weathered face darkened. "I have also heard tales of barbarity that goes far beyond the normal rules of war, of cannibalism, of helpless captives cooked and eaten."

Full of gloom at the report of these atrocities, I rowed south in his galley, which carried a cargo of dried food, weaponry, and the wherewithal for constructing siege engines. All this the Embriaco brothers hoped to sell to the Crusader army at a high profit. My hands blistered, broke and then, itching like mad, quickly hardened again with calluses, as the wintry weather warmed into spring. We hugged the Italian coast before passing through the turbulent currents and forbidding rocks of the Straits of Messina. All the while I mulled over the import of my twin papyruses and puzzled anxiously about where the 'House of Mary's Mother' might be in Jerusalem. I had attracted some ribaldry from my fellow rowers at the pouch that I wore round my neck and refused to take off, even when the weather was so warm that all were stripped to the waist at the oars. "A love token then, is it?" they laughed, and

I assented to that. But I curtly refused their demands for a lurid description of the object of my affections.

I racked my brain for any reference to the name of a 'Mother of Mary' in the Scriptures. I could not remember a single verse which spoke of the parents of the Virgin Mother of Jesus. Joseph, of course, was said to be of the House of David, but Mary's lineage was obscure. Nor could I recall any reference to the parentage of Mary and Martha of Bethany, the sisters of Lazarus, and for that reason perhaps the most likely subject of the riddle. And the Magdalene similarly lacked family. I cursed my ignorance. My worries about how to solve the riddle rose like the seas around.

For after the Straits of Messina, our course led into the open, rougher waters beyond the heel of Italy. The tension amongst the crew rose. The height of the waves made it far harder to row and with our fear of foundering came the anxiety that out of sight of land we were more likely to encounter hostile shipping – pirates or Fatimids perhaps. A few years before, any Fatimid vessel from Egypt would have as like as not been friendly towards their Genoese trading partners; now I imagined they would do their utmost to prevent supplies from reaching their Crusader enemies.

Beside me on the rowing bench, pulling on the same oar, sat an excitable Greek by the name of Adelphos. He swore and prayed as the ship heaved in the swell, and his imprecations became louder the higher the sea rose. A week or so out from land, we encountered a squall of particular violence, and Adelphos began to declaim to every saint he could remember.

"Haghios Nicholaios, patron saint of seafarers, protect me! Haghia Thecla, they threw you in the sea to drown but you refused to sink. Grant your servant Adelphos the same buoyancy! Haghia Barbara, I have lit many candles to you. Now fulfil your promise that I should die a natural death! Haghios Christophoros, patron saint of travellers, you carried

Our Lord Jesus across the water, so carry me. Haghia Sophia, patron of widows, do not destroy my poor old mother's hopes; see me safely through this storm! Then like you I will give away all my worldly possessions."

The words 'Haghia Sophia' and 'my poor old mother' caused me to miss my stroke, so that Adelphos broke off from his prayers for a moment and used his deep voice instead to heap me with insults. But I had been carried back momentarily to that great church in Constantinople. I remembered the boastful servant of Emperor Alexios showing me the relics in the cathedral. I remembered him telling me of the bones of Saint Anne, described as the mother of the Holy Virgin Mary. Now at least I had a name to go by. Perhaps inside Jerusalem there was a house, or a church, of Saint Anne.

The high seas subsided, and land came in sight at last. Adelphos loudly attributed his salvation to his devout invocations. I preferred to credit plain good Genoese seamanship. Captain Embriaco made for the nearest harbour of Jaffa. Whilst the town looked drab and down-at-heel, the harbour which gave it purpose was large and well-protected by a long mole. Four English ships, square-sailed like those that had alarmed Baldwin's men at Tarsus, already sheltered in the haven, unloading on the quayside. The Genoese came alongside them and I shakily disembarked with the rest, to my surprise now feeling the land rocking beneath my feet as unsteadily as the sea. The experienced sailors around laughed as I tottered on the land; but it was not for several days that I wholly regained my balance.

I wondered how my former comrades had fared in the time I had been at sea. Perhaps Jerusalem was already taken. I hoped so. My shipmates did not share this wish, for their prosperity depended on the war being incomplete so that they could sell their materiel at an extortionate price. We set to unloading the cargo, unmolested for the town had been deserted by its Moslem inhabitants, perhaps scared away by the arrival of the

English ships. My war-seasoned eye saw that the abandoned fortress that overlooked the harbour would anyway not have held out against assault for long, furnished as it was with just one broken tower.

Nevertheless, the Embriaco brothers were canny and experienced enough to post look-outs at the top of their galleys' masts. After I had struggled in the heat through noon until the mid-afternoon heaving the cargo onto the dockside, I heard a warning cry from above. One of the mast-top watchers had spotted a cloud of dust rising behind the town, probably thrown up by the hasty arrival of a body of men. Orders were given to prepare for a fight. I hurried to don my mail and to strap on my sword. I felt some satisfaction at being dressed as a knight again after my long spell as a humble seaman, for all the weight and discomfort of the tight garments in the heat.

I relaxed again as the first soldiers spilled out from Jaffa's narrow alleys onto the foreshore, for they wore the familiar cloaks with crosses at their shoulder, and the banners they carried proclaimed them as Christian friends. Amongst them I saw with pleasure the double armed cross of Lorraine. I hurried forward to make myself known and to learn the news of my comrades.

It was Geldemar Carpenel who led the small troop of Lotharingians – no more than twenty knights and fifty foot soldiers in all. I knew him from Antioch, and my gladness at seeing a familiar face after so long overcame the dislike I had felt then for his dumb soldierly arrogance. I approached with a friendly greeting.

"Good God, I know you. It's Hugh de Verdon, isn't it?" Carpenel responded, grasping my hand and slapping my shoulder. "Where in blazes have you sprung from? When our Duke found you gone from Antioch he took you for dead in the terrible plague that raged there. He was even sorry to have lost you – for a couple of days that is."

He brayed with laughter, showing splayed teeth over his

undershot jaw. Without making room for an answer to his question, he rushed on: "We had a close call on the way here, by Heaven. My little band rode right into a vast Moslem army. We were almost through them when a band of Provençals came up behind us led by that ass Raymond Pilet – there he is, that's him with the face like a donkey over there – they are now saying that without their help we'd have been wiped out. Just like them – we do all the work and they try to take all the glory. But they've got their comeuppance now that all the other nobles follow good Duke Godfrey. They've shown that one-eyed lavender bag Count Raymond where he can stuff himself."

He brayed again in delight at his own wit.

"By God though we are famished…haven't eaten properly in days…or drunk. Do your Genoese friends have any provisions for us? I'd say a feast of celebration is called for."

Guillermo Embriaco had anticipated Geldemar's wish, for, good businessman that he was, he knew that it would be in his interests to give his customers a warm welcome before trying to fleece them by demanding outrageous prices for his precious supplies. And it did not need one as astute as Guillermo to see that the little Crusader band would welcome a square meal, for they looked as lean and mangy as any pack of hungry wolves. So the Genoese set about giving the Lorrainers and the Provençals a feast of greeting. They improvised long trestle tables on the quayside, and started fires to cook the fish that would anyway not last in the heat on the march to Jerusalem. They brought out loaves of bread, hard and stale from the long sea journey but edible by hungry men especially when dunked in the rich Italian wine, keg after keg of which they rolled out from the capacious holds of the galleys.

I stuck by Geldemar and his companions, eager to learn news of events since my departure from Antioch. Before the Genoese alcohol rendered them completely incoherent, I heard how finally Bohemond had achieved his ambition and thrown the Provençals out of Antioch, proudly assuming the title of Prince of that ancient city. Here there was much glancing and sneering in the direction of Raymond's men further down the shore. The shameful rumours that I had heard in Genoa of cannibalistic savagery were confirmed – the outrage had taken place in a sad town called Marrat al-Numan – where the Provençals and some of Bohemond's Normans, after brutally sacking it, had run amok.

"D'you remember how starved we were in Antioch? Boiling those roots and old leather to keep going. But we drew the line at human flesh, by God. In Marrat they did it for fun. They didn't just eat the dead. God knows that'd have been bad enough. But they cooked the poor bastards alive, like bloody lobsters. The old people, that is. They thought otherwise their flesh'd be too tough. The children – well – they were tender enough to be spitted and grilled."

"It's nice to see you eating fish instead of babies," brayed Geldemar in the direction of the Southerners.

I saw my emotions of sorrow and horror reflected in the eyes of some of Geldemar's more intelligent companions. At least a few of them were still human enough to feel regret that part of our so-called Christian army could have acted in such a shameful way.

"And what did Count Raymond do to make up for it? He took his bloody boots off for a couple of days and walked a barefoot penance at the front of the army. We stayed with Duke Godfrey in Antioch. Thought we might as well leave the hard work to them. Then Raymond got stuck at the great fortress of Arqa. He begged us to come and join him. He was scared shitless…right out of his pomaded head about some great Arab army coming and raising the siege," snorted Geldemar, whose words were slurring more and more under the influence of the Genoese wine. "We'd helped Bohemond to heave the last of Raymond's men out of Antioch by then, so why not?"

I asked about the fate of Peter Bartholomew, and felt some pity at the news that he had submitted to an ordeal by fire at Arqa to prove the authenticity of the Holy Lance.

"He was so badly burned, you see, that he died a week later. So the lance was a fake, a fake, all that time."

Geldemar turned his glazed eyes towards me wide open in astonishment.

"How about that! Now we all follow good Godfrey's golden cross…"

He took a last deep draught, breathed a great sigh and rested his head on his hands on the makeshift table in front of him. I heard him muttering, "It was a fake. A fake. All the time. Golden cross…" until rasping drunken snores took the place of his mumbles.

I moved away from the carousal to find a quieter place to sleep the night, hoping that the Provençals and the Lorrainers would not come to blows before morning. I thought this was happening when I heard cries of alarm and opened my eyes to see that it was dawn. Then I heard someone shouting over and over, "Enemy ships, enemy ships."

I ran down to the water's edge and saw beyond the mole a dozen galleys flying the Fatimid flag, plain green in honour of their Prophet. One of the English ships whose crew had been more alert than the others had taken advantage of a favourable wind to slip out of the harbour before the blockade was tightened, but the rest of the little fleet could now not hope to escape. Four of the Fatimid vessels were larger than the others, and fitted in the bows with mangonels. These now began to fire, crashing heavy missiles down into the harbour, interspersed by barrels of burning pitch. One trapped galley was already alight.

Ever the pragmatist, Guillermo Embriaco decided to cut his losses and to leave his ships in the harbour. We'd unloaded most of the cargo the day before, and certainly the more valuable items. So the Genoese piled it as fast as possible onto the few baggage carts and divided the rest into loads for the soldiers to carry. We fled the town, many in our little band cursing and swearing at their rude awakening and at their sore heads from the night before. I prayed that the Moslem army scattered by Raymond Pilet's men had not regrouped to block our way back to Jerusalem, but we took a different route for the return journey and so avoided molestation.

On the eastward march, heavily laden through the summer heat, my excitement at nearing the Holy City lightened my load and gave energy to my steps. At last my long journey was nearing its end. My goal was within reach. The optimism of youth said that I would not suffer the same disappointment as in Antioch, that I would win through to Jerusalem. There I would find the House of Saint Anne, and return to Alamut to free Blanche from her prison. The realism of experience tempered my optimism when I breasted the final rise and saw the puny and ragged band around the walls of the Holy City. Scarcely fifteen thousands remained, perhaps a tenth part of the great armies that had reached Constantinople.

The Genoese sailors divided into two groups, some going with Raymond Pilet to join the Provençals to the South of the city to sell their provisions there, and others marching up to the north to join the bulk of the army where, according to Geldemar, Godfrey was now acknowledged as the supreme commander. As we approached the camp, I could indeed see the tall golden cross of which Geldemar had babbled in his cups, set up as a holy standard outside Godfrey's tent. I had worried how to explain my long absence to the Duke, but now Geldemar's beef-brained bonhomie came to my rescue.

"See what I have brought you, my Lord Duke," he boomed as Godfrey issued from his tent at our approach. "Hugh de Verdon wasn't dead of the plague in the fever-pot of Antioch after all. He took off to Latakia for the fresh sea air, only to be press-ganged into the galleys. After many adventures, sailing to Italy and God knows where else, he's guided some well-provisioned ships to our shores. Now here we are with nails, ropes and tools for building siege engines, supplies. There's even some wine which I can warmly recommend from my personal experience."

I gave thanks for the simplicity of Geldemar's bluff soldier's brain, and went down on one knee in respect before Godfrey. The Duke raised me to my feet.

"Let me see. Look at me. It can't be."

I was delighted by the warmth of his embrace.

"Hugh, Hugh, I thought I had finally lost you. And now here you are again, with valuable provisions, in the nick of time to join in the last great assault of our campaign. How many more times are you going to come back from the dead?"

For the first time I was Godfrey's equal in stature. The ten months that had passed since Antioch had stooped and grizzled the Duke further. He had still not shaken off the limp from his bear wound and the lines on his face formed deep canyons round his features. But some vigour and enthusiasm still remained, and these were now turned to directing the construction of the machines of war that were needed to reduce great walls. Hot-headed Tancred had already led one ill-prepared attack. This had come to grief for want of siege ladders, and had almost cost him his life.

First the supplies of wood had to be found on which the naval carpenters could work their skill. Anxious to redeem himself for his failed assault, Tancred welcomed the chance to set off with a caravan of camels which returned laden with timber. Now construction could begin. The carpenters' saws and hammers were sped by the news that a huge army was on its way from Egypt to relieve Jerusalem. If they attacked us in the open before the city was taken their numbers would annihilate our meagre force. It was Antioch all over again.

SAINT LAZARUS' COLLEGE

"Well, sir, I am very sorry to say that I have just had news that your colleague died this morning. For the week that he was in hospital they really did everything humanly possible, but in the end eighty percent burns for a man his age was just too much."

"Especially for someone who had abused his own body for so long."

The Master could not help insinuating that if the Modern Languages Tutor had smoked and drunk less he might have pulled through. He was only just over his appalling bout of food poisoning and still unusually choleric as a result.

"And in the end, smoking in bed..." The Master shook his head in disapproval. "I suppose we are lucky that the whole College didn't burn down. We have the Chaplain's piety to thank for that. One should not underestimate the power of prayer. Perhaps we should have another look at some of the passages in our book which are more critical of religion."

The Best-Selling Author shifted uncomfortably and exchanged glances with the History Don and the Professor of English, looking for support. But before the argument could progress the Oxford Detective cleared his voice.

"Actually, sir, I think that there may be more to this death than meets the eye. As far as I am concerned we have a murder investigation on our hands. We already had one definite case of attempted murder. It is too much of a coincidence that we have now had a death in the College. And I would not eliminate the possibility that your recent stomach troubles were due to something other than natural causes. If it was something wrong with the food, or a bug for that matter, isn't it rather strange that you were the only one to suffer? I would not discount poison and foul play. I am sorry, but I am going to have to ask you all not to leave town until I have cleared this up. I shall want to interview you all again."

The Oxford Detective looked sternly round the room, meaning to include everyone in this statement. Nor did he ignore the Research Assistant.

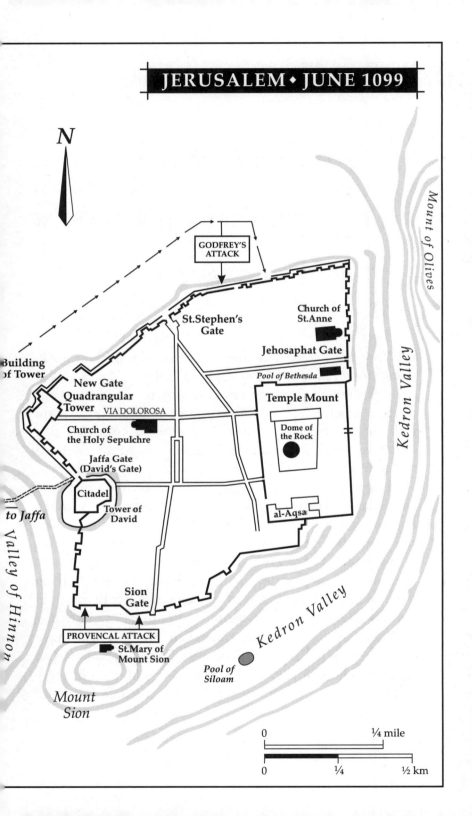

CHAPTER EIGHTEEN

FALLING TOWERS – JERUSALEM

O daughters of Jerusalem...

Godfrey and I stood watching the carpenters at their work. A battering ram was beginning to take shape. We needed it to break through the curtain wall. Nearby, the frame of a siege tower was being laid out, tall enough to surmount the main walls of the Holy City. But they were so high that this structure would use up all the remaining wood that Tancred had found.

"I don't like it, Hugh, I don't like it at all. We won't have any element of surprise. They will know exactly which stretch of wall we plan to attack. They'll only have to divide their strength in two, facing our tower up here and Raymond's down in the south. They have more than enough mangonels and heavy bows to pour a devastating fire onto our assault. Even if we had more wood, I haven't enough men left to attack in two places at once. The siege tower has to be so tall that it will be even more cumbersome than usual. It will move desperately slowly, however many men I have pushing it. And look how uneven the ground is. We can't build it in one place and then move it under cover of darkness because we would never get it far enough to make a difference. Under the concentrated barrage we'll face, it will stand little chance of reaching the main wall at all."

I remembered what I had seen in the shipyards in Genoa.

"My Lord, when they build ships they do not nail all the parts together before the launch. The masts and other parts of the superstructure may be fitted in dry dock but then are often taken down again so that the hull can be floated more easily. Perhaps our carpenters could employ the same technique here. What if they build the ram and the tower in sections which can be taken apart, transported, and put together again?"

Godfrey's eyes lit up, and he turned to Gaston de Bearn, who was in charge of the carpenters.

"You heard what Sir Hugh had to say. Could do it like that?"

The engineer sucked his teeth and thought for a moment. "Won't be easy. But could be done."

"Hugh, Hugh," Godfrey said with a broad smile that made him look his old self, "Yet again you prove your worth. Make sure you stay close by my side until we have taken the city."

Whilst the carpenters hammered away, the spiritual preparations for the assault were not neglected. A great procession was decreed around the city walls to the Mount of Olives, where a Mass was to be said on the very site of Christ's Ascension into Heaven. I prayed that, thus blessed, the assault on the Holy City could be as merciful as possible. But I had seen enough of a siege's aftermath at Antioch and heard enough of Marrat to know that brutal massacre and bloody slaughter in the name of the God of Peace would mark Jerusalem's fall.

The hot south wind blew incessantly. Grit, dust and sand were everywhere – in the rationed food, in the poor supplies of water, for what had been brought from the ships was soon exhausted, in the tents and scratching inside clothes and mail. The day prescribed for the procession dawned under a cruel clear sky in the second week of July. All the knights and soldiers, save a skeleton guard on the earthworks and around the near-complete siege machines, formed a column behind Godfrey's gilded cross, and marched barefoot around the ancient walls. With loud psalms and chants we drowned out the jeering of the Saracens from the battlements. But we were unable to ignore the wooden crosses set up there and could only watch helplessly as our enemies desecrated them with spittle, urine and excrement. I wondered what this taunt was meant to achieve – except to incense the Christians so that, when it came, our attack would be more furious than ever.

At one point the procession had to pass within bowshot of the walls, for the valley at their feet was too narrow. A flurry of Moslem arrows wounded some of the unmailed priests and monks at the head of our procession. Further enraged by this cowardly abuse of our few men of peace, we reached the summit of the holy Mount of Olives and looked down over the towers and spires of the city. Able for the first time to see inside the walls, I wondered where Saint Anne's house might be. The ancient city looked a confusing maze. In distraction I scarcely listened to the Mass, and only took in the end of the stirring sermon at its conclusion.

"Worthy soldiers of Christ, you now stand gazing over the Holy City of Jerusalem, the navel of the world. Many moons ago, you vowed not to rest until the faithless Saracens were driven from it. Now, thanks to the grace of God, you stand on its threshold. One last battle, one last assault, and your solemn oaths will be fulfilled. You will be purified; all your sins will be forgiven, and your place in Heaven will be assured. If we fall, we will join all our brothers who have perished along this hard way, only to be installed in glory among the Saints in Heaven."

A great 'Amen' answered these stirring words, followed by cheers. We all returned to our stations for the final preparations, and a fast was ordered. I concluded with weary cynicism that supplies were again running short.

Our siege tower was now ready, menacing the Quadrangular Tower at the north-west corner of the city. Its three tiers reached just higher than the main walls. Its wooden structure was clad in hides which could be soaked in water to protect against incendiaries and flaming arrows. Wicker panels were fixed to the front and sides to deflect missiles. Beside it, like some malevolent tortoise, squatted the new battering ram, the head of its huge iron-capped trunk emerging beneath a stout wattle roof. New mangonels were set along the perimeter of the city and were already busy at work throwing rocks, and occasionally the broken bodies of tortured captives, at and over the walls.

Geldemar Carpenel had not exaggerated the jealous rivalry between the two sections of the army. Most of the contact we had with Raymond's men now came from his supporters flocking to join us, fed up with their leader's overweening arrogance. From some of these new recruits we learnt that the Count only retained his force through bribery; even the common soldiers at work filling the ditch near the south wall had to be paid a penny for every three stones they threw into it. Nevertheless, even Tancred had enough sense to acknowledge the need to co-operate enough to press the attack simultaneously at north and south. So a date for the final assault was agreed.

All day we had rushed feverishly with our final preparations. As night fell, the stratagem I had suggested to Godfrey was put into action. The carpenters swarmed over the great siege tower, breaking it into its component parts, some of which they loaded on to camels, and carried to the north-eastern corner where we actually planned to attack. Complaining teams of soldiers manhandled the rest. The great battering ram received the same laborious treatment. We also moved our three best mangonels. Carpenters raced against time to rebuild the siege tower just outside the range of the enemy catapults. I prayed that they would do their work thoroughly, for my station was to be in the top tier of the tower with Duke Godfrey and Count Eustace.

As the first light of dawn touched the sky on that fateful day, the mangonels shuddered awake and began to release their payloads, bombarding the top of the curtain wall and the higher ramparts behind. Under this cover the battering ram inched forward, parties of men pulling on ropes fastened to its front, and pushing from behind and at the beams inside.

At first, the defenders made little response, for our tactics had had the desired effect and this corner of the wall was thinly garrisoned. I could almost feel the panic and consternation among the enemy soldiers opposite, as they rushed hither and thither and called frantically for reinforcements. As more men arrived, the fire raining down upon the battering ram intensified, and the Saracen archers began to take a heavy toll on the unprotected men pulling the ram forward. Soon Godfrey gave the order for them to run back with their ropes to shelter behind the engine, and its forward momentum slowed as the burden fell solely on those pushing underneath the wattles. Nevertheless, watching from a slight rise beside the siege tower, the Duke was well pleased with progress.

"See Hugh, they have no catapults in this corner. It will take them time to bring them up. They will have to set them on the towers there," he pointed right and left, "The streets behind must be too narrow and the walls too high for them to throw up missiles from below. For the moment we have the advantage. The ram will be safe until it is right under the walls. Then they will be able to hurl stones and incendiaries straight down on it."

All the same I thought the movement of the ram painfully slow. I watched at Godfrey's side, scarcely able to stand still, fidgeting with tension, willing them forward, listening to the regular shouts of 'Heave' as the sergeants urged on their teams.

I involuntarily tensed my own muscles at each cry of command. The sun was past its zenith before the ram reached the base of the curtain wall. It had now turned from woodlouse to hedgehog, its rounded back bristling with Saracen arrows. Battle was joined in earnest as the reinforced enemy heaved down boulders, boiling oil and the fearsome incendiary Greek fire. Our mangonels continued to pound the walls, an occasional direct hit on the ramparts raising cheers from our lines and shrieks from the Moslems who were crushed or toppled down. Companies of archers exchanged fire like the barbs of a religious argument, but the defenders enjoyed the advantage high behind their battlements.

The hammer blows of the ram were now drumming in a regular rhythm against the wall, which shook and vibrated at every blow like a stone tabor. I counted a score of these great blows, and then another score. Then with a thunderous crash the wall cracked and tumbled. The momentum of the ram was so great that the whole vehicle was hurled forward through the breach. It hurtled across the narrow space beyond the curtain wall and slammed to a rest at the bottom of the main rampart. I cheered with the others, only to fall silent as incendiaries poured down from the battlements and the protective wattle caught fire. The soldiers who had driven the ram forward scattered from inside and scuttled for safety.

Men had set great flagons of water beside the siege tower in preparation for drenching it against the same threat to which the battering ram now succumbed. Teams now ran these forward, and doused the flames at a heavy cost in dead and wounded. Too late came the realisation that the broken shell of the ram was now wedged in the breach through which the siege tower had to penetrate. It should have been left to burn. Godfrey cursed such stupidity and ordered teams forward to set fire to the ram again. Now, in a bizarre reversal of roles, the defenders poured down water to put out the flames instead of incendiaries to set them ablaze. At last, though, the bones of the ram caught irresistibly, and flared away through the dusk. Then Godfrey gave the order to withdraw out of bowshot, so that our men could eat, drink and rest, and gather their shredded strength for the final assault on the morrow.

Soon after dark, Godfrey received humbled messengers from Count Raymond. The fight to the south of the city had not gone well. The Saracens were well-prepared, for they knew exactly where the Provençal attack would land, and they had been able to concentrate their mangonels and heavy bows at that point. So as the southern siege tower approached, they had subjected it to a murderous crossfire. They set alight wooden nail-studded mallets, covered in tarry pitch, and threw them against the sides of the tower, where they stuck and burned and could not be put out by water. In lucky desperation a Provençal sprayed one in vinegary wine and discovered that this was an effective antidote. Godfrey thanked the messengers for this intelligence and immediately gave orders for skins full of vinegar to be stashed at the top of our tower.

"We'd have faced the same stern resistance if we had attacked where we were expected," said Godfrey with satisfaction. "So far, Hugh, the plan you seeded has worked but they will be readier for us tomorrow and we must be at our best. I will turn in."

I did not share Godfrey's sang-froid, and all my attempts to sleep were in vain. I soon gave up and instead paced about the lines, listening to the excited murmurings of the troops. Bursts of exuberant and drunken song punctuated the groans of the wounded and dying. Tired of such callousness, I walked into the darkness away from the camp, where occasionally the eerie churring of a nightjar sounded above the chorus of cicadas. Moving towards these peaceful noises, away from the damaged walls and the smell of smoke, death and charred flesh, I breathed the dry odour of the land, so different to the moist scents of my home. Memories of those smells carried me back to the beginning of my journey just three years before. With bitter nostalgia I longed for the absolute certainties of my boyhood. At Cluny I had known right from wrong. Now I had fulfilled my childhood ambition to see Jerusalem. But on the next day I would join in a violent battle, fight, maim and kill in order to achieve my own end. How was that right? In my mind's eye I saw Abbot Hugh, quizzical sorrow in his expression, and I knew the answer. Angrily, I shut the Abbot out and replaced him with an image of Blanche, picturing her smile lighting up at my return and the melancholy chasing from her blue eyes.

That happy thought was jerked from my mind by a sudden shadowy movement, half seen, half felt behind me. The hairs prickled on the back of my neck but before I could react, a firm hand was over my mouth and a sharp blade at my throat. A familiar voice whispered in the Persian tongue. It was Mohammed.

"Greetings, Hugh. I seized you because I did not want you to cry out and give the alarm before you knew who I was. Now I am going to loose you; just keep quiet. You will gain no benefit from betraying me.

"You see, my Christian friend, we are well informed. I knew of your return from a *da'i* watching in Jaffa. We have comrades in all the ports along the coast. Word reached me in Damascus, but this is the first chance I have had of speaking with you. What did you find on your journey to the West?"

"How is my Blanche?" I countered, scanning Mohammed's face for news, but the darkness foiled me.

"I haven't been at Alamut for many months," he replied, "My father has kept me busily employed elsewhere. I returned there briefly after our last encounter at Antioch, and then I saw her in good health."

"And looking forward to my return? Did you give her my message?" I imagined sympathy gleaming from his eyes in the dark.

"I gave her your message as best I could, my friend," he

313

replied, and I breathed a sigh of relief. "But come, to business, where is the book?"

Wearily I gave a brief account of my trip back to Cluny and my frustrating discovery that the Abbot had possessed one copy of the book but destroyed it. I told of my elation at my rediscovery of the second papyrus, and my unravelling of its riddle.

"Tomorrow, or maybe the next day, Jerusalem will fall. I will find the 'House of Mary's Mother'. Then the book will be mine. As soon as I have it, I will ride north to Alamut."

I filled my words with outward confidence but I shrivelled inwardly at the enormity of the challenge.

"As ever, I will be watching. *Ensha'allah*, God willing, you will be successful. God be with you."

As he melted away back into the darkness he touched his forehead with his fingers. I returned his salute.

I walked back to the Duke's tent in the dark hour before dawn. The sliver of reassurance provided by Mohammed's news of Blanche was negated by the apprehension of battle. Godfrey was dressed and ready. He gave me a kindly greeting.

"So you could not sleep, Hugh? When I was your age I was the same. I too would spend a sleepless night before a fight. Now...well." He shrugged his shoulders. "We old men need our rest."

He passed me an earthenware flagon. "Here, have a swig of this. It'll warm you up in the cool morning air."

I poured a large shot of the strong wine down my throat. I coughed and spluttered and Godfrey laughed. It certainly helped to fill the hollow feeling in my stomach. I passed the bottle back, and the Duke took a deep draught.

"Time to take our positions."

Briskly I followed him towards the dark looming mass of the tower. Inside it was foetid with the smell of nervous bodies. The men whose task was to push the tower forward were already there in position. I fumbled in the dark for the ladder.

I clambered up and emerged into the freshness of the open air at the top. A quiet chorus of greeting sounded from the shadowy figures already gathered behind the wooden chest-high ramparts. In the centre stood the gold cross, fixed there at Godfrey's command as a proud standard. Dawn stained the eastern sky above the Mount of Olives. I could soon make out the portly shape of Eustace and the silhouettes of the other knights beside him. Then I could see their paraphernalia of war – the crossbows to be used in the approach, the long spears that would come into play as the tower neared the battlements, the grappling irons, the skins of water. I found myself hoping that there was some wine there too.

"Did you have the vinegar brought up?" asked Godfrey of one of his lieutenants, who answered briskly in the affirmative. "And have the scouts checked that the battering ram is burnt to ash? Are we sure that nothing blocks our passage through the curtain wall?"

Again the affirmative reply.

"Do we know how many mangonels they've been able to move to this sector? We'll be at most risk when we are further away. If we can get in under their range we'll be as good as home and dry."

The pale drawn faces now emerging in the thin dawn light looked less sure. I fingered my crossbow nervously, and checked that my helmet sat snugly on my head over my mail hood.

"There's enough light to make out any obstacles now. Let's move," commanded Godfrey.

Orders were passed down through the guts of the great tower. Then, with a jerk, we lurched forward. Like the battering ram which had prepared its way, the tower was furnished with ropes for pulling it forward until it came closer to the walls and the barrage pouring down became too much for the men in front. Then the task of pushing the tower on would fall solely upon those sheltering inside and behind the structure. The ground up to the walls was relatively flat, but the man-sized wooden wheels on which the tower rolled still bumped up and down so that the top swayed alarmingly from side to side. I had to grasp the ramparts in order to stand upright.

Behind, the mangonels began their covering fire. Beside, detachments of archers moved cautiously forward, as if to emphasise that the tower's fastest speed was less than their slowest walking pace. If the enemy had brought up catapults of their own to protect the breach in the curtain wall and to anticipate the attack, the lumbering tower would provide them with an easy target.

As if echoing my thought, a great rock crashed to the ground half a dozen paces to the right. I instinctively ducked my head. It was now light enough to make out that mangonels were indeed mounted in front on each tower beside the breach. The Moslems had been busy through the night. 'Oh my God,' I thought. Our tower was now perhaps one hundred paces from the walls and they began to get the range. One rock fell amongst the men hauling us forward. I peered over the edge and saw four crushed, others scattered. More ran up to take their place. Then the first projectile hit the tower with a dreadful thud, swaying it so that I feared it would topple. But the wattle screens did their job and absorbed the shock. We now came under a constant and ferocious barrage of arrows as the archers lining the battlements took aim. Sheltering as best I could behind the wall that surrounded the platform, I returned fire with my crossbow but with the movement of the tower it was hard to aim steadily and my quarrels flew well wide of their mark.

More rocks thundered against the superstructure. Their speed made the trajectory hard to follow, but I learnt to brace myself in readiness for the blow when the mangonel arm on the city walls kicked like a wild donkey to launch its missile. Then there would be a minute or so in safety before the arm could be winched back down, loaded up and thrown forward again by the ropes' twisted power. If I could hear the air-rush of the projectile, I knew it was perilously close. Once, I heard such a whistle and ducked my head. My face was spattered with sticky liquid. I looked up and saw that the knight next to Godfrey had been struck on his head by a stone twice its size. His skull had pulverised, scattering blood, brains and fragments of bone over those nearby. In disgust, I tasted human remains on my lips, retched, spat, and tried to wipe the gore off my face and out of my beard. Beside, Godfrey was doing the same.

"That was too close," he said with a grim smile.

The defenders did not have it all their own way, though. Their target was moving, albeit painfully slowly, but our artillerymen had a stationary mark. They were able to maintain an accurate bombardment of the top of the walls. Also, we had the advantage of three mangonels to the Saracens' two. Our fire concentrated on the towers containing the enemy machines, and we roared a great cheer when we achieved a direct hit, silencing one of the threatening engines of war.

The remaining mangonel now began to lob firebombs. These broke against the flanks of the tower, scattering burning pitch. But the carpenters had done their job well, and the flames could gain no purchase on the smooth water-soaked hides covering our front and flanks. The blazing material slid down and scattered harmlessly on the ground. More damage was done when a flaming missile burst on the platform, setting two men-at-arms alight like human candles. Quickly we swamped the flames in water. The platform was charred but safe. The two men, horribly burned, lay moaning and twitching behind me in agony. I tried to ignore their pitiful sounds.

Now we were close to the breach in the curtain wall. The teams tugging us forward dropped their ropes. The enemy's arrow fire had already depleted them so the tower's progress did not slow much. The advantage was ours, for we had passed inside the closest range of the remaining Saracen mangonel, whose missiles whistled harmlessly over our heads. And now we could pour arrow fire downwards onto the infidel ramparts. In response came the weapons that had been so effective against Count Raymond. A volley of fiery nailed mallets thudded into the side of the tower. The knights pouring down water to put out these fires panicked to see that they were having no effect. Flames began to lick upwards.

"Use the vinegar, for God's sake," roared Godfrey over the noise.

I seized a wineskin. I squirted down, pissing the vinegar into the flames, which faltered and died. Now it was the defenders' turn to be disconcerted. Their secret weapon had been countered.

I scrabbled for my crossbow again. I fired a quarrel down into the face of one archer on the ramparts. I saw my unfortunate target fall back, clutching at the feathered end piercing through his cheek. Then I threw down my bow to seize one of the long spears. I began roughly thrusting at the figures behind the battlements. Others beside me used grappling irons to pull the tower the last few yards and secured it against the wall.

Our mangonels had also been using flame as a weapon, hurling firebombs at the walls. The wood and bales of straw packed inside one of the towers to reinforce it had caught, and the hot wind began to blow thick smoke and flame out at the defenders in front of us. Temporarily they fell back, unsighted by the smoke, and Godfrey seized his chance. Hacking loose one of the protective wattles, he balanced it as a makeshift bridge to the ramparts, and waved to us around him to charge across. With a stentorian battle cry, swords and shields in hand, eager knights leapt over to seize a bridgehead. Godfrey himself followed, and I came close behind, wildly hacking and thrusting at any targets visible through the billowing smoke.

In their dismay unable to withstand the ferocity of the assault, the Moslem defenders were forced back. I pressed one

318

against the crenellations. A short spear pricked at me and I forced it aside with my shield, slashing again and again in a frenzy with my blade until the Saracen's body was a mass of blood. It slid to the floor, leaving a trail of gore down the stone behind. In the heat of the moment I gave no thought to the horror of my action. Perhaps I was anyway inured by all the brutalities that I had seen. Instead I turned to seek out another enemy to hack down.

Now our men held a section of wall and had cleared it of foes. Savage cheers went up as more troops charged forward with scaling ladders. They set them against the battlements, climbed up and began to pour over.

I raced along the wall toward the tower to the left, ignoring the arrows that were still dropping from archers further along the fortifications, and scarcely noticing the deep scratch made by one along my cheek. We had taken the tower containing the second mangonel, and our soldiers were pouring down into the street. The defence had broken and was turning into a rout. Down below I could see a brutal slaughter beginning, as fleeing Arabs were hacked down from behind without mercy.

In a crowd of knights I hurtled down the spiral stairway inside the tower, ignoring the fighting that was still going on in some of its rooms, and burst out with them into the lane. I slipped on the blood and gore which already smeared the street, and paused for a moment to catch my breath. I saw a savage glow in my companions' eyes, lit by their eager anticipation of the slaughter, rape and pillage that was about to follow victory. Maybe they could see the same bestiality in my own face.

Saint Stephen's Gate had now been thrown open and the main body of our force was pushing towards the main thoroughfare that led to the Dome of the Rock. Most of the Saracen troops were fleeing south in front of them down towards the Temple Mount. Some, hoping to find refuge away from their fellows, scattered down the maze of small alleys.

Few escaped. Their screams mixed with the higher, woeful cries of women and children, fleeing in desperation away from the ferocious tide of dreaded Frankish soldiers. Others hid in their dwellings, and their terrified laments rang out as the doors to their homes crashed down. They rose in pitch to ear-piercing screams and then ended with abrupt silence as hidden steel flashed.

I had to find one of the unfortunate inhabitants alive to tell me where in the city the House of Saint Anne might be. So I broke off down a narrow alleyway to find a dwelling whose occupants had not yet perished. The rule of right of conquest still applied throughout the army to noblemen and common soldiers alike, to prevent fighting amongst ourselves, so that whoever first entered and took a building and laid claim to it would have an unchallenged right to its contents.

I had to go a long way down the maze of alleys to find a home without a shattered door, without the bestial sound of rape, crashing destruction or shrieks within. The first two entrances through which I burst led into empty, deserted hovels. In the third I found a family cowering, a young mother and two children, who wailed and screamed at my approach as if their end had come. On her knees, the mother grabbed at my arm. She gabbled in Greek that she would let me do whatever I wanted if I would just spare her children. Her tear-brimmed eyes pleaded, but were empty of hope that her entreaties would meet with success. I tried to calm her – hysterical she was no use to me – reassuring her that I intended no harm, that I sought directions to the House of Saint Anne. Had she heard of any such place in the city? Now faint hope did enter her eyes but it was some time before I could compose her enough to understand that she was talking of a Church of Saint Anne. "It is just in this corner of the city" were the words I made out, "just in the little square at the end of this alley. I worship there." With a shock I realised that the woman was Christian, yet sheltering for her life from the soldiers of

Christ. Then my mind turned back to my own concerns. Perhaps this church was indeed what I sought. Perhaps in ancient times a church had been erected in honour of the Virgin Mary's mother on the site where she had lived. I resolved to investigate. Again in the poor woman's eyes I read terror, for now that she had given me her information she expected the worst. The terror turned to hope and surprise as I made the Sign of the Cross over the unfortunate family and turned out of their poor dwelling. I would have liked to have done something to help them but I had my own business, my own quest to solve.

Out of the door, and a little further along the alley, the narrow way did indeed open into a small square, at one end of which stood an ancient church. I could see that it touched the eastern edge of the city, for the walls loomed up behind, with the Mount of Olives above across the Kedron valley over which I had gazed in the opposite direction two days before. To my surprise, the small postern in the main church door swung open at a slight touch. It was unbolted. Was it left thus by some oversight? Or was it fate? Or was I somehow expected? Suddenly uncomfortable, I shook off that impossible thought and entered. The cool gloom of the interior made such a contrast with the hot patch of noon sun in the square outside that I felt that I had entered another world. I pushed the door to and shot the bolt home. Deep silence fell. The violent sounds of battle were closed out. I became cold as my sweat began to dry. I shivered as I walked between the columns down the dark aisle of the church.

SAINT LAZARUS' COLLEGE

The little column of mourners wound its way back towards the College from the nearby graveyard where Saint Lazarus Fellows were entitled to be interred.

"It was sad that he had no family there, no friends even, no-one from outside. The College was really his whole life." The Chaplain always felt a little low after presiding over a funeral, reminded of his own mortality, his faith briefly less secure. His eyes widened as he turned to the Master, walking beside him. "You don't think, when you told him he was going to have to leave, that he...that he did it on purpose?"

"Oh, don't be absurd. What a ludicrous idea." The Master resented the suggestion that his firm management action might have precipitated the tragedy. His mood was not improved by the two smallish boys who were running in front of the column of black-clad men, pulling faces and sticking out their tongues, before darting away out of reach.

Behind them, the History Don was walking with the Classics Fellow. "I've been doing some background reading on the topography of medieval Jerusalem."

He perhaps looked a little more excited than was quite appropriate immediately after a funeral – and than most would have thought the subject deserved.

"Once again, it seems our manuscript is surprisingly accurate. The north east corner of the city is known as the Muslim Quarter today. A Church of Saint Anne still stands there. But at the time of Jesus' ministry this whole area was outside the city walls. It was largely occupied by the Pool of Bethesda, which as you may know was the supposed location for a couple of miracles. Traditionally, Saint Anne, the mother of the Virgin Mary, had her home nearby. The buildings around the pool were razed with the rest of the city by the vengeful Emperor Titus, probably except for their foundations and the drains underneath. Later on, a church was built on top to honour the mother of Mary and the whole district was enclosed behind enlarged city walls. Isn't that interesting?"

The Classics Fellow murmured his assent but had actually been thinking what a shame it was that the funeral service was not still given in Latin.

The Professor of English was paired with the Best-Selling Author.

"I just love the language of that service. The vocabulary is so moving, the imagery so evocative."

His companion looked blank. Slow and tedious were the words he would have chosen.

The Research Assistant walked alone, trying to conceal his twisted face behind the upturned collar of his donkey jacket before those horrid little boys started making fun of him. He had not wanted to come to the service at all. He did not have the right clothes and was not sure how to behave. But he knew it would have looked odd not to be there.

A little distance behind came the Oxford Detective. He always made a point of going to the funeral in these cases. Partly out of respect for the victim, of course. But also for the opportunity to discreetly observe the suspects on an occasion when they were likely to drop their guard. He always sat quietly towards the front, but well to one side. Then he could watch the whole congregation without drawing attention to himself. These little tricks – they just did not teach them to new recruits any more. And what had he learnt? Well, any one of them could have done it. The Vicar – or the Chaplain, rather, that was what they called him – his smooth bland face had mouthed the words of the service with no emotion whatsoever. Sometimes it was quite moving, poetic even. But the Chaplain had made it sound utterly banal. The top man – the Master – had looked impatient even before the service began – anxious to be off – that could have been a sign of guilt, about something anyway. He wouldn't want to get on the wrong side of that one. Friends in high places, no doubt, and one of those cold, unforgiving tempers. Then the writer chappie, he'd obviously been uncomfortable in the church, an unbeliever almost certainly. That showed a lack of moral compass. And the other profs – English, History, Classics. Hmm. What a bunch of cold fish. Not a moist eye between them. Actually a couple of them had had their eyes shut for most of the service.

And then the last one, the bloke with the terrible mark on his face. Wearing that workman's jacket showed a total lack of respect for the man who, after all, had been his boss. And it was quite hard to tell with a mug like that, but he had looked very awkward. Very awkward indeed.

Chapter Nineteen

WHAT THE THUNDER SAID

What we search for is not always what we find.

"So you have come."

I started violently at the harshly nasal voice. My eyes, not yet accustomed to the unlit interior, struggled to make out an ancient dark-cowled monk standing in the murk near the altar.

"I have come," I replied. "I want to see the library here. Where are the books kept?"

In reply the shadowy figure cackled, and to my tautly stretched nerves there seemed something manic about that laugh. But I put it from my mind and struggled to catch the words of archaic Greek that followed.

"Ah yes. The library here. It is full of rare and precious books. But why would they be of interest to a man of war?"

Another cackle cracked from the cowled figure. I shivered again.

"I was a man of God, a monk like you, before I was a man of war. I believe you keep a rare volume here that I have not read before. It is known as the Gospel of Lazarus."

Again a burst of harsh mirth echoed around the vaulted

ceiling. By now I was standing in front of its origin. Under the cowl I saw hollow cheeks, and a livid red mark grotesquely disfiguring one side of a twisted face. The nose was half eaten by leprosy, and I started back. The leper's pouched eyes glittered with amused malevolence and he chuckled again.

My sword was still bloody and unsheathed. I brandished it angrily.

"Show me where the books are kept, or you will be sorry."

"Shame on you, young man, waving your weapon in this ancient house of God. Put your sword away. I was once as handsome and tall as you, but you now have nothing to fear from a weak old man like me...unless I come too close."

He took a step forwards. I recoiled, prompting more wheezy laughter.

"Very well, come, follow me."

The monk led me down a narrow curving stairway to the left of the altar. The steps were so deeply worn that in my agitation I stumbled and nearly fell headlong. At the bottom a smooth door of heavy stone stood ajar. My guide entered. I watched with suspicion as he took a tinderbox from beneath his robes and lit a wide church candle which stood on a stone table within. I had expected a crypt, but the room appeared to double as library and sacristy, for it contained vestments, chalices, reliquaries, monstrances, candles and all the paraphernalia of the Mass. One whole wall was lined with books. I looked aghast at the shelves of unmarked volumes, and my expression provoked that disquieting cackle again.

"The Gospel of Lazarus, yes, which one is it, I wonder? Oh dear, oh dear."

"You had better show me which it is, or you will suffer."

Threateningly I loosened my sword again.

"Suffering, suffering, so much pain and suffering," the monk crooned, "Now let me see..."

He reached bony fingers up towards a volume bound in

dark stained undecorated leather. He eased it from the shelf and laid it on the table.

"There. Read for yourself and see if it is the one that you want."

Greedily I grasped the book. I opened it and made out the correct title in Greek. I saw that once it had been a scroll, but that at some point it had been divided into pages and bound between leather covers. With a shock I recognised the script. It was identical to the papyruses I had carried for so long. Nevertheless, I thought I should read further to check that there was no mistake. I did not trust the leper librarian. I turned the book's stiff pages at random. The script was not easy to make out, but as I deciphered it I could detect that the volume indeed contained some sort of Gospel. Triumphantly I spelled out the name Lazarus again.

Utterly absorbed, I had forgotten the monk. I failed to notice his slow crab-like shift towards the door, until, out of the corner of one eye, I caught a sudden movement. The old man darted out through the opening with surprising speed for one of his age. Frantically I jumped after him, but before I could do anything the stone door had swung smoothly closed in my face. It thudded shut with baleful finality.

In mounting despair I hammered on the stone. I scrabbled at it with the broken fingernails of my dirty hands. I shouted, I yelled for help, I wept. I desperately searched around the door for some lever, some contrivance that might open it from inside. But the wall was totally smooth. The masons had done their job so well that I could scarcely see, scarcely feel, the crack between wall and door. I scratched round it with my dagger. Even its sharp blade could get no purchase and skated over the surface of the wall. What ancient ingenuity was this? What ancient ingenuity had closed me in this trap?

I froze as I realised that the door was probably as good as invisible from the outside too. My captor had moved it shut with just a gentle touch. The solid thump with which it locked spoke of some hidden mechanism, operated by a secret of which the old monk was perhaps the only guardian. Then, as my head cleared, I gave up my search for a lever. Surely, if the chamber could be opened from within, the old monk would have hidden inside it. There he would have been safe from any marauding Crusaders, and he would not have had to take the risk of luring me down into this tomb. That dreadful word – tomb – echoed in my head. I was in my tomb, buried alive. I would die there of thirst and hunger, or maybe first of suffocation if the sepulchre was sealed as hermetically as it seemed.

I sat with my head in my hands and shook bitter tears over the table. I had come so close. I had Hasan's book in my grasp but what good was that now? Nobody would look for me; Godfrey would just assume that I had fallen unobserved during the sack of the city. The Duke might regret my third passing for a few days, but there would be many others lining up to serve the man who could claim most credit for the capture of Jerusalem and was likely to become its first Christian king. Blanche would remain a captive and would forget me. Or worse, she would perhaps believe that I had betrayed and forgotten her, and end up in the arms of another. I shuddered at the thought. And I would die, my long and painful journey all in vain.

The candle burning down brought me back to my senses. At least I could keep the light going for a good while, for the stock of candles was large. I lit a new one from the old, and could continue doing so, and perhaps avoid dying in the dark.

I unbuckled my sword belt and laid the weapon beside my shield. I stroked the sheath, trying to rekindle the happy memory of its presentation to me at Bouillon. Then, inquisitive, I reached for the volume which had brought about my doom. With curiosity I considered the book again – *The Gospel of Lazarus* – why had Hasan wanted this so much? Why had the Abbot destroyed its twin so that its contents should be denied to others? With nothing else to do, I turned the page, and began to read.

'Others have undertaken to compile a narrative of the things which have been accomplished among us, just as they were delivered by those who from the beginning were witnesses and ministers of the word. Now, I wish to record an honest account for you, that you may know the truth about those things of which so much has been written.

'In the days of Herod a decree went out that all the people should be counted. To be counted, they returned each to their own city. So it came to pass that Joseph, who was of the royal house and lineage of David, returned to Bethlehem with his wife Mary, who was heavy with child and close to her term.

'At Bethlehem all the inns were full, for many had travelled there to be enrolled, and they took shelter in a stable. While they were there, the time came for Mary to be delivered, and she gave birth, and wrapped her baby in swaddling clothes, and laid him in a manger. And the baby, a boy child, was given the name Jesus.

'Now the royal house of David had kin in far off lands to the north, on the shores of a black sea. Three wise men travelled from those lands to pay their homage to their new kinsman, and they bore rich gifts. In that humble stable they fell down in worship and offered their treasures, a gold grail, myrrh, frankincense and other spices, and recondite recipes for their use.

'When Herod the King heard of these travellers he was

troubled, and he summoned them to him to know their business. At first they would not speak, but demanded to be free to pass on their way. In a furious rage, the King brought young children before them and killed them one by one, until in pity they were forced to speak to stop the slaughter. Thus Herod learned their secrets, but when he searched for Joseph, Mary, and the child, he found them not, for they had moved on.

'The family sought refuge from Herod in lands away from Galilee, in Egypt, and later settled in Nazareth, that the words spoken by the prophet might be fulfilled: "He shall be called a Nazarene." And so the child Jesus passed to manhood in safety.

'Joseph's royal lineage gave him proud ambition. He planned to use the magic of his northern kin to restore his House of David to its rightful position. But Joseph was old and ill, and so he thought that for himself the Magi's herbs would not serve. The grail must pass to his only son.

'Joseph loved his son. He could not risk his precious blood, the last of his line. And so he asked a cousin, by the name of John, to prepare the way for Jesus. John went with Joseph to a distant place in the wilderness of Judaea to be baptised and immersed in the sacred mysteries.

'John emerged from this trial a man of strength and vigour, and soon his voice was carrying loud throughout the land: "Repent, for the kingdom of heaven is at hand." Of him spoke the prophet Isaiah when he said "The voice of one crying in the wilderness: Prepare the way of the Lord, make his path straight."

'Then Jesus came from Galilee to the Jordan to John, to be baptised in his turn. And so Jesus was immersed and the holy spirit entered through his veins into him. After, Joseph said, "Thou art my beloved son; with thee I am well pleased." And Jesus spent forty days and forty nights in the desert with John, who nursed him.

'But now John's fame reached the ears of King Herod. Some said, "John the Baptizer has been raised from the dead; that is why these powers are at work in him." And others said, "It is a prophet, like one of the prophets of old."

'Herod sent and seized John and bound him in prison. He feared his power and wished him dead. So Herod had John beheaded. Herod ordered John's head to be placed in mockery on a grail, and paraded in front of his courtiers to please Herodias, his wife, and her daughter Salome, for now they thought that their line was safe from the threat of the ancient House of David.

'When Joseph heard the news he was dismayed. He withdrew with Jesus into Galilee and dwelt for a while in Capernaum by the sea. There Joseph and Jesus bethought themselves of a family who lived in Bethany who were dear to them. The sisters were called Mary and Martha, the brother Lazarus. It was decided that Lazarus himself should be baptised. And so the bath was prepared, and he underwent immersion. Thus the holy spirit entered into Lazarus' veins and strengthened him.

'Now it was time for Jesus to begin his ministry, to gather his disciples around him and to begin to teach. He showed

331

himself wise and many flocked to him and made him their rabbi. Joseph urged him to use the arcana of the holy spirit to achieve temporal power. But Jesus had greater thoughts. He would use the secret to rid the world of evil. If he could show that he could conquer death, he could found a cult whose beliefs would have the power to sweep away evil and make of this world a peaceful paradise.

'Others have written of Jesus' teaching. Wisdom poured from him as from no man before, yet all his words were touched by humility, and his gentle manner secured the love of all who listened with a pure heart. Great crowds followed him wherever he went and his fame spread throughout the land.

'At last Jesus decided that the power of the holy spirit should be tested, and that the task first set by Joseph for John should be fulfilled by another. So he passed unto Bethany to the house of Mary and Martha. They were fearful for their brother, whom they loved dearly, but Jesus spoke to them, saying, "He will conquer death and be glorified by means of his victory. Everlasting fame will be his."

'Near the house of Mary and Martha was a tomb, which could be closed by a heavy stone. Jesus entered the cave with Lazarus and Judas Iscariot, his trusted disciple. Lazarus was stripped of his robe, and a sharp blade was plunged by Judas into his side so that he fell down dead and a pale liquid flowed forth. They anointed his wounds and, binding him with strips of cloth, laid him gently down. They left the tomb and placed the stone across the entrance.

'Jesus went back to his teaching. On the fourth day he

returned to Bethany and ordered that the stone should be moved away. But Martha, the sister of the dead man, weeping, said to him, "Lord, by this time there will be an odour, for he has been dead four days." But Jesus said to her, "Did I not tell you that if you would believe you would see the glory of the holy spirit?" And so they took away the stone, and Jesus cried in a loud voice, "Lazarus come out." And the dead man came out, his hands and feet and side bound with bandages. Jesus said to them, "Unbind him, and let him go." '

I was so absorbed, bemused as I struggled to grasp all its implications, wondering whether I really understood correctly the ancient script, that I scarcely noticed that the candle was dying. Then, just in time, the flickering light caught my attention, and I hurried to light a new candle from the old. Then I plunged on with my reading.

'Judas Iscariot, who looked after the money box and used to take from it what was put in, was angry. "These spices, this secret, we should sell for many denarii." But Jesus said, "Let it alone, it must be kept for the day of my burial."

'As well as gathering together a great following, now Jesus had made many enemies, for his teaching threatened the Pharisees and the established order and gave hope to the poor and the weak. The Passover was approaching, and he knew the time had come to enter into Jerusalem and to confront his foes, so that his plan could be fulfilled.

'On the next day a great crowd heard that Jesus was coming to Jerusalem. They cut the branches of palm trees and ran out to greet him, laying the boughs before him as he rode on a young ass. Others laid out their cloaks and garments in his path. They cried "Hosanna to the Son of David, blessed is he who comes in the name of the Lord, even the King of Israel." And so the words of the prophet were fulfilled, as it is written, "Fear not, daughter of Zion, behold your king is coming, sitting on an ass's colt."

'Jesus entered the Temple of God. He flung over the tables of the money-lenders, and the stools of the pigeon-sellers, and drove out all who bought and sold in the Temple, saying "It is written that this shall be a house of peaceful prayer but you have turned it into a den of thieves."

'Then Jesus taught the people gathered in the Temple and told them many wise stories. The Pharisees demanded by what right he taught in the Temple, and to test him they asked "What is the greatest commandment in the law?" And Jesus replied, "You shall love the Lord your God with all your heart, all your soul and all your mind. And a second is of the same importance, that you shall love your neighbour as yourself." And the priests saw how the crowd hung on his words, and the sway he held over them, and they feared him. They dared not seize him before the crowd. And when Jesus saw how he had stirred the priests, he returned to Bethany, pausing on the way to teach another crowd on the Mount of Olives.

'Now the feast of the Unleavened Bread, the Passover, drew near. Jesus sent two of his disciples, Peter and John, saying, "Go and prepare the Passover feast for us, that we may eat it." And they asked him, "Where will you have us prepare it?" He said to them, "Behold, when you enter the city, a man will meet you carrying an alabaster jar containing all that I will need. Follow him into the house that he enters, where he will show you a large upper room; leave the jar there and make everything ready."

'And he sent another of the twelve, Judas Iscariot, to the high priests, in order to betray him to them in the absence of the crowd. "Tell them that they will find me in the Garden of Gethsemane in the hours of darkness after our Passover feast." And the priests were glad, and engaged to give Judas money.

'Peter and John prepared the Passover feast as their Lord had said, and when the time came he sat at the table, and his disciples with him. And they ate, dipping their bread into the dish that had been prepared for them. Jesus said, "All is ready. The betrayal has been prepared by he who dips his bread into the dish at the same time as me." And that one was Judas.

'And then he came out, and went, as was his custom, to the Mount of Olives, and his disciples followed him. He withdrew from them about a stone's throw, for he would be alone in his torment, and he knelt and prayed. "Oh my poor dead father, if only there were a way to achieve our plans without going through this suffering. If it be possible, let this grail pass from me." And his sweat became like great drops of blood falling down upon the ground.

'And then he gathered his strength and rose, returning to the disciples, and found them sleeping. He said to them, "Why do you sleep? Be ready. Rise."

'While he was still speaking, there came a crowd with swords and clubs from the chief priests and the scribes and the elders, and Judas was leading them. Now the betrayer had given them a sign, saying "The one I shall kiss is the man; seize him and lead him away safely." And when he came, he went up to him at once, and said, "Master!" And he kissed him. And they laid hands on him. But one of those who stood by drew his sword and struck off the ear of the slave of the high priest. Turning to his follower, Jesus said, "Put your sword back into its place; for all who take the sword will perish by the sword. Do you not remember my teachings?"'

I shivered in the cold silence of my tomb as I thought of the brutal weapons wielded by me and my fellow Crusaders and of the dreadful violence we had perpetrated in the name of this holy man of peace.

'And Jesus said to them, "Have you come out to me as against a robber, with swords and clubs to capture me? Day after day I was with you in the Temple teaching and you did not seize me."

'Then they led him away, bringing him to the high priest's house. When day came, the assembly of the elders gathered together, chief priests and scribes; and they bound Jesus and brought him before Pilate. And Pilate asked him, "Are you the King of the Jews?" And he answered him, "That is what my father would have had me say, and you have said it." And the chief priests accused him of many things. And Pilate asked him again, "Have you no answer to make? See how many charges they bring against you." But Jesus made no further answer, so Pilate wondered whether he wished for his own death.

'Now at the feast he used to release for them any one prisoner whom they asked. And among the rebels in prison, who had committed murder in the insurrection, there was a man called Barabbas. And the crowd came up and began to ask Pilate to do as he was wont to do for them. And he answered them, "Do you want me to release the King of the Jews?" For Pilate perceived that it was out of envy that the chief priests had delivered him up. But the chief priests stirred up the crowd to have him release Barabbas instead. And Pilate again said to them, "Then what shall I do with the man whom you call the King of the Jews?" And they cried out again, "Crucify him. Crucify him." So Pilate, wishing to satisfy the crowd, released for them Barabbas, and having scourged Jesus, he delivered him to be crucified.

'And the soldiers led him away inside the palace. And they clothed him in a purple cloak, and plaited a crown of thorns which they placed on his head. And then they began to salute him, "Hail, King of the Jews." And they struck his head with a reed, and spat upon him, and they knelt down in homage to him. And when they had finished mocking him, they stripped him of the purple cloak and put his own clothes back on him. And then they led him away to be crucified.

'And they compelled a passer-by, Simon of Cyrene, who was coming in from the country, to carry his cross. And they brought him to Golgotha, which means the place of the skull. Now the centurion in charge of the escort was named Longinus, and he was a disciple of Jesus. And he offered Jesus wine mixed with myrrh and other spices, and he took it. And then, at the third hour, they crucified him, and divided his garments among them, casting lots for them, to decide what each should take. And the inscription of the charge against him read "The King of the Jews."

'And with him they crucified two robbers, one on his right and one on his left. And when the sixth hour had come, there was darkness over the whole land until the ninth hour. And at the ninth hour, Jesus cried out with a loud voice, "Eli, Eli, lama sabachthani," which was a sign. And the centurion ran, filling a sponge full of wine, spices and myrrh, put it on a reed and gave it to him to drink. And when Jesus had received the drink, he said in a loud voice "It is finished" and he bowed his head.

'Since it was the day of Preparation, in order to prevent the bodies from remaining on the cross on the Sabbath, the Jews asked Pilate that their legs might be broken, and that they might be taken away. So the soldiers came and broke the legs of the first, and of the other who had been crucified with him, but when they came to Jesus the faithful centurion ordered them not to break his legs. Instead, he pierced his side with his lance, and at once a clear liquid flowed forth. I who have seen it have borne witness and I know that I tell the truth. And so the scripture was fulfilled, which says, "Not a bone of his body shall be broken," and again, "They shall look upon him whom they have pierced."

'After this, Joseph of Arimathea, who was a friend and secret disciple of Jesus, asked Pilate if he might take away the body, and Pilate gave him leave. And Nicodemus also came, bringing the alabaster jar of spices and myrrh. And they took the body of Jesus and bound its wounds in linen cloths with the spices. And they took him and laid him in a tomb nearby, whose entrance they closed with a rock.

'Now Judas Iscariot's greed drove him again to the chief priests and scribes. He told them of Jesus' plan to rise from his tomb, and how once he had conquered death, his power would be great. He told them too that like John the Baptizer, his life could be ended only by striking his head from his body. And for his pains, the chief priests took the traitor and hanged him.

'Next day, that is, after the day of Preparation, the chief priests and the Pharisees gathered before Pilate and said, "Sir, we have uncovered the impostor's plot to rise from the dead in three days time. Therefore order the sepulchre to be made secure until the third day, lest his disciples go and steal him away, and tell the people, 'He has risen from the dead'." Pilate said to them, "You have a guard of soldiers, go, make it as secure as you can." So they went and made the sepulchre secure by sealing the stone and setting a guard.

'So his disciples were unable to roll away the stone at the appointed hour and they despaired. Jesus woke in the tomb, and finding it still closed, he knew that he had been betrayed. Now this cave tomb had been chosen because a hidden passageway led from it. Jesus stripped from himself the bandages and made his way out through the passageway.

'Now after the Sabbath, toward the dawn of the first day of the week, the chief priests became impatient and they ordered the stone to be rolled away. And so, with a noise like thunder, this was done. But the guards trembled and became like dead men, for they found the tomb empty, save for the linen clothes in which his wounds had been bound.

'Mary Magdalene was also watching, and saw that the stone had been taken away from the tomb. So she ran, and went to Simon Peter and another disciple whom she loved well, and said to them, "They have taken the Lord out of the tomb, and we do not know where they have laid him." Peter then came out with the other disciple and they both ran to the tomb. At first they could not go in because of the guards, and they hid. But when the guards left they were able to go in. They saw the empty tomb and the bandages and returned to their homes.

'Mary remained weeping near the tomb. She turned round and saw Jesus standing there, but she did not know that it was Jesus for he was dressed like the gardener, wrapt in a brown mantle. Then he said to her, "Mary, it is I." And she said to him, "Rabboni!" (which means teacher). And he said to her, "Do not be dismayed. Go, tell the disciples and Peter that I will go secretly before them into Galilee, and that they will see me there.

'While they were going, behold, some of the guard went into the city and told the chief priests all that had taken place. And when they had assembled with the elders and taken counsel, they gave a sum of money to the soldiers and said, "Tell people, 'His disciples came by night and stole him away while we were asleep.' And if this comes to the governor's ears, we will satisfy him." So they took the money and did as they were directed, and this story has been spread among the Jews to this day.

'Now the eleven remaining disciples went to Galilee to the secret place to which Jesus had directed them. Because of his betrayal by the twelfth he could not show himself openly. He was seen by two friends on the way to Emmaus, but thereafter he took more care.

"And then Jesus went back into the rocky desert and we saw him no more.'

SAINT LAZARUS' COLLEGE

The Master pulled the key from his pocket and as usual looked at it with pleasure for its weight and workmanship. With a quiet sigh he bent forward and inserted it into the wine cellar door. The lock turned smoothly with a satisfying clunk and he reached for the handle.

When he had been Chairman of the External Security Committee, as a matter of routine he had been given some training in self-defence. Now, some sudden instinct, perhaps prompted by a slight breath of air on the back of his neck, caused him to pull the door hard inwards and step sharply to one side. The Research Assistant, a monkey wrench raised viciously over his head, hurtled past. The Master stuck out his leg, so that his assailant tripped and was carried by momentum head first down the steep wine cellar stairs. From the cry, the crash and the silence that followed, the Master knew that he had plunged to the bottom and knocked himself out. The Master closed the door and locked it before hurrying to his office to call the police.

Chapter Twenty

AMONG THE LOWEST OF THE DEAD

I now understood why my Father Abbott had destroyed the book at Cluny. Indeed, how correct he had been in warning me of the effect it would have on my shaken faith.

I closed the ancient volume and sat astounded, listening to my own thoughts in the silence. My head hammered as if it had been beaten by a mace. My brain flickered in turmoil like the candlelight round the walls of my tomb. Could there be any truth in this book? How was it possible? I could now indeed understand why the papyrus had described it as 'the book you fear'. Surely this book contained the heresy of all heresies and its contents could have strangled the Church at its birth.

Yet some things fell into place. How easy it was to believe the preaching of a well-meaning man of compassion, doing all he could to influence his fellows to make the world a better, gentler place. How hard it was to understand why an all-powerful, all-knowing God should wish to test His creation, and to punish His creatures when they fell short, as He knew they would. How hard to understand why His omnipotence permitted evil and misery to exist. How hard to understand why He inflicted pain and grief on His only Son when He could have simply forgiven the world its sins.

And the magic, that Lazarus called the holy spirit? How could that be? But even there much fell into place that I scarcely dared to believe. After all, I suffered an immersion like the baptisms described in the gospel; my veins too were cut and refilled with new fluid. I pensively fingered the scars at my wrists. And when I was wounded in Antioch, I healed faster than anyone could have predicted; when I had been surrounded by the plague, I had not succumbed; when everyone around had been suffering from famine, I scarcely felt hunger or thirst and it had seemed I could go almost indefinitely without food and drink. How different I had been before Alamut. I remembered my agonies toiling across the desert after Dorylaeum, my exhaustion then after a single day's march. Could it be that I was now one of those whose life could end only when the head parted from the body? I remembered from the skull in the Church of Saint Victor in Marseille that this was the method of Lazarus' death. John the Baptist too had died that way. What had happened to Jesus himself?

And if I was somehow long-living, even immortal – I scarcely dared to think the word – or at least stronger than other men, immune to disease – what did that mean for me and Blanche? Would I have to watch her age, wither and die, whilst I stayed ever-youthful and vigorous? Could she undergo the initiation too? Did it work for women or would their weaker bodies break under the pressure? If Blanche could be initiated would our children then inherit the same powers? These and many more questions fermented in my seething brain. I felt excitement but also alarm and fear. To spend more than a normal lifespan with Blanche would be heaven; to have her die while I was still young would be hell.

344

The candle guttered again and brought my thoughts back to my immediate predicament. I quickly lit a new candle from the dying wick of the old. So would I be relit again and again while the lifetimes of others burned out. I counted the candles that were left. Could I just stay in the crypt and wait for the leprous monk to open the secret door, expecting to find a corpse, dead of hunger and thirst? But what if the monk were to die, slaughtered in the violent sack of Jerusalem that was doubtless taking place above? And then...then I might spend the span of many lifetimes sitting in the dark of the crypt, in absolute silence, with only my thoughts for company, unable even to die. I shuddered. That would be hell indeed. I thought of an eternity bitter with guilt and self-reproach, turning over and over what might have happened to Blanche. How things might have been different if I had paid more attention to the old monk's movements. I would go mad – or perhaps the vile fluid in my veins did not even permit that release. I pictured myself desperately trying to hack off my own head with my own sword in the pitch dark. Frantic, I stood and scrabbled again at the door, trying to find a crack to push against, but now I could not even make out where the door ended and the wall began. I sat down again, my head back in my hands, in utter despair.

And then hope returned. What if the tomb had another entrance – an exit rather – like the tunnel they had started at the Cave Church at Antioch, or like the Holy Sepulchre, according to Lazarus? The air in the chamber was clear, not musty. The candle burned bright and undimmed. Yet fresh air could not possibly penetrate the door through which I had entered. Perhaps there was another way, unknown even to my leprous imprisoner. Suddenly I felt hope again.

Feverishly I felt round the high bookshelves. I began to pull out volume after volume – bibles, works of the saints, commentaries many of which were familiar from Cluny's library – piling them on the table, dropping them on the floor.

And then, there was one, from a shelf low down, which looked to have been gnawed by rats from behind, and another; now I felt the faintest breath of air. Or had I just willed it?

No, as I frantically pulled more books away, I saw a small gap, no larger than a fist, in a wall of rotten masonry. I grabbed a heavy candlestick and hammered at the wall, trying to enlarge the hole. Bit by bit the stonework fell away, and then the hole was big enough for my head, my shoulders. I lit another candle, held it through, and dimly made out a passageway. I levered out some more stones, making the hole wide enough to squeeze through, all the while praying that it might lead somewhere and not be a teasing dead end.

I had a moment of panic, for so many volumes were now heaped on the table that I thought I might not be able to identify the Gospel of Lazarus again. But then I found it and thrust it inside my tunic. I tucked a spare candle in beside it. I buckled back my sword and wriggled through the hole, holding the burning candle out in front. I stood up cautiously and found that my head did not touch the roof. It was true; there was a breath of air from somewhere, for I could feel a gentle draught drying sweat on my face. Oh, to be back in the desert offering the water on my face to the sun.

Holding up the candle in excitement and hope, and peering around, I saw that I was in a passageway with compartments on either side. Some were open, and brown skeletons lay there grinning at me in macabre mockery. My prison must have originally been the crypt entrance to a charnel house or catacomb, and had only later been blocked up and turned into a sacristy-cum-library.

I walked forward and in a few paces saw other passages radiating off on each side. Should I turn right or left? I chose the right. Then I was faced with the same choice again. This time I turned left, and then right, and then left again. And then I had lost all sense of direction. Anxiously I retraced my steps and with relief found again the broken wall. Some method was needed to make my way through the maze.

I wriggled back into the chamber and took a book from the table. I would tear out the pages, and at every turn would carefully lay the page on the ground facing in the direction I was going. The order and the direction of the pages would show where I had been. Then it would be easy to retrace my steps if necessary. I ripped out the first page, and saw that I had desecrated the opening of the First Book of Moses, Genesis. I thought in bitter irony that the Holy Bible itself was pointing my way through the maze; it had not been much use for anything else.

This time I walked straight as far as I could. I reached a blank rock wall and turned left, laying down the first page of Genesis in the direction I had turned. 'In the beginning...' read the opening sentence.

Again I walked as far as possible, passing several turnings to left and to right, but now I came to a dead end. I retraced my steps and took the first turning, now on the left, but originally on the right. I laid down another page and noticed that it began with the verse 'Let there be light...' Was I being mocked by the Holy Book? Perhaps deservedly so.

The next junction was in the shape of a T, and here I turned left, laying down the page that opened 'Let the waters bring forth swarms of living creatures...' A few steps further on, I saw red rats' eyes reflecting my candlelight, and a drain or a sewer carrying some sort of underground river, flowing from left to right. A pack of rats scurried along, splashing into the water. I backed away and went straight on at what had been the T, carefully placing another page at the junction facing in the direction I was now going. 'So God created Man in His own image...' the paper read. A few steps further on I came face to face with a skeleton sitting in a niche, its knees drawn up under its chin, its skull grimacing in malevolent contempt. Another dead end.

Shaken with disappointment I turned back, going left at the T and coming to one of the branches that I had passed. I tore out the next page and was about to place it on the ground when I read the verse 'a river flowed out of Eden...'

With a sudden thrill, it dawned on me that the rat-infested water must flow out somewhere. In rising excitement I turned and dashed back. I climbed cautiously down into the black water and found that it only reached up to my knees. I splashed forward, rats squeaking in front as they ran from my intrusion. I carefully checked that the precious book was inside my tunic safely away from the water, and as I was doing so I stumbled on an uneven stone. I put out my free hand desperately to stop myself falling and plunging with my treasure under the surface of the stream. But my candle dipped under the water and hissed out.

I stopped still in the pitch dark. In horror I realised that I had no way to relight the candle. What had I done? What could I do? Perhaps I could retrace my steps back to the chamber, feeling my way like a beetle through a dungheap. That would be better than standing knee deep in a rat-infested drain, but it would set me right back at the beginning. And I might be unable to find the way back, and wander forever among the skeletons. Or I could fumble forward, hoping to find a way out, but at risk of becoming ever more lost. I stood there in blank desolation, water running round my knees. I no longer even knew to what god I should pray.

Later I could not remember how long I stood there in anguished indecision. Then, bit by bit, I thought that perhaps I could detect some phosphorescence, some faint gleam of distant light. I inched forward, my hands on the slimy surface of the tunnel wall. I was sure now that I could feel a stronger movement in the air. I tried to contain my excitement, moving cautiously forward, anxious not to make the same mistake again and bring disaster with another stumble. The ground sloped gently downwards. The roof also began to slope lower, so that now I could no longer stand upright. Bent double, the water still up to my knees, I felt my way carefully forward. Then I thought I heard the rustle of leaves in the wind. Was I finally losing my senses? Now I could no longer stand in the tunnel. I took the Lazarus Gospel out of my tunic. I knelt. Holding the book beside my head just above the water, I crawled forward. What was I to do if the water reached the roof? I cursed my inability to swim on the surface, let alone like a fish beneath the water. But then I realised that if I could really hear leaves rustling in the wind, if I could really feel the breeze and make out some light, part of the passage must be filled with air and not with water. As I moved forward the water level fell; perhaps the moisture was seeping away into the dry soil around. Now I was in a hole the size of a large badger's earth, little more than a trickle of water running along its bottom. I felt a moment of alarm as the walls narrowed and pressed in on either side. Then the hand which I held forward with the precious book brushed against some thorny shrubs. My alarm turned to elation. I scrabbled at the earth around the opening, trying to widen it. Eventually I could squeeze my shoulders through. Ignoring the scratches to my face I pushed through a thicket of aromatic bushes, and found myself in a dry watercourse at the bottom of a steep valley. My nostrils filled with sweet dry air and I panted in relief, almost weeping. It was dark; night must have long since fallen, indeed for all I knew I might have been in that underground prison for days.

At first I was overcome by such emotion that I could not move. Then I began shaking with relief, shivering in my damp clothes in spite of the warm night. I crawled forward, sat up and started to take in my surroundings. Behind, above Jerusalem's soaring walls, red fires lit the sky, and I could hear the distant sounds of terror and celebration as the Christian sack of the Holy City continued. In front, up a steep rocky slope, silvery in the moonlight, loomed the bulk of a hill. This must surely be the Mount of Olives. It seemed that I had emerged on the eastern side of the city at the bottom of the Torrent of Kedron. Here in winter perhaps water flowed after rains in the surrounding hills; now in summer the bed was dry. From habit, I said a quiet prayer of thanks. Now my mind began to recover from the many shocks that it had suffered. Should I re-enter the city and return to my comrades? I thought of the awkward questions that I would be asked. Once I was back with Godfrey I would again become embroiled in his affairs. I found that I was still clutching the Gospel of Lazarus in my hand and I stuffed it back into my tunic. Or now that my quest was accomplished should I find horses and set off north towards Alamut? There was no purpose to hold me in Jerusalem, and everything to hurry me to Blanche as fast as I could go. I got stiffly to my feet and carefully set off northwards, boots squelching, turning west towards Saint Stephen's Gate and the point at which our siege tower had conquered the city walls.

I knew that there were horses picketed in my old camp. They had had no part to play in the assault. Stealthily I moved towards them. I knew too that few guards had been left. Those that were on duty were the least worthy soldiers, denied the chance to participate in the first wave of plunder. They would be distracted and disgruntled by their misfortune at being forced to stay in the camp, and would probably be drunk. Quietly taking two horses should be an easy task. Of provisions I had little need, and could pick up anything I needed along the way.

So I crept into the camp and heard the guards complaining to each other about their misfortune in thick winey voices. The horses started to move nervously and one near me whinnied. I put my hand over its soft velvet nose and soothed it. "So you have chosen to come with me," I murmured, and selecting another led them both away. I tethered them a little distance off and went back for a saddle. I chuckled at the thought that Duke Godfrey's trusted aide was now a renegade robbing his own camp. Then I mounted and rode hard to the north east, aiming to join the valley of the Jordan. I knew that a straight line to Alamut from Jerusalem led across the great Arabian desert. That was not a possible journey for one without camels or the knowledge of where water lay. I remembered Mohammed talking of the ferocious desert tribes and the unpleasant welcome they meted out to any who trespassed on their traditional lands. So I aimed to follow the Jordan valley up to the Sea of Galilee. From there, I would skirt round the great city of Damascus, carefully avoiding other travellers, and then cut an arc north-eastwards through the wild country that I had travelled in Mohammed's company towards Antioch the previous year. I would ride at night and shelter by day. I expected more trouble from wild beasts and animals than from human enemies.

And so I rode on. For all my impatience to reach my journey's end, I forced myself to travel with more care than speed. I stayed away from thoroughfares and cut through the wilderness. In the dark under whose cloak I rode, my progress was slow. I knew too that Mohammed and other Assassin *da'is* would be looking out for me. Perhaps they might attempt to relieve me of my burden and leave me lying by the wayside. Mohammed might have orders from his father to strip me of the book. I of course now knew that finishing me off would be harder to achieve than they might think; nevertheless I wished to take no risk of failing to reach my destination. I lived on my thoughts of Blanche, mixing memory and desire. I heard the inviolable voice of the nightingale filling the desert.

As I came further north, closer to Alamut, the summer turned to autumn. The minatory sounds of the waste land around rang out louder, the growls and roars of hunting predators echoing through the obscurity. Sometimes my horses would twitch and shy at unseen dangers and I would have to spur hard to drive them through the darkness. The desert nights became cold, and I chilled also with worry. When Hasan-i Sabbah had his book, how could I force him to keep his part of the bargain and set Blanche free? He would know all my secret when he had read the book. Then I shuddered – perhaps he already did, for I did not know exactly what was contained in the Colchean document that had governed my initiation, my baptism. Yes, Hasan, of all people, would know how to kill me if he wanted. But why would he do so? Perhaps I could be useful to him. Perhaps he would need my help to translate the book. Perhaps he would want me for other services. One like me could be a valuable and powerful servant. Perhaps, even if Hasan would not release Blanche, we could at least live our lives together at Alamut.

Thoughts of becoming Hasan's instrument troubled me and I began to be tormented about the use he would make of the information in the book. The Assassin was driven by an insatiable hunger for knowledge, that much he had admitted. But did he also plan to use the Gospel of Lazarus for some evil end? Would he endeavour to replay the Lazarus trick so that his Imam, his Mahdi, could be reincarnated and take the Moslem world by storm? Perhaps, having consolidated the Shi'a sects and after sweeping away the Sunni objections to his Mohammedan beliefs, he would turn his attention to the Christians and drive them from the Holy Land once again. Would the gospel add fuel to the fire of war; could it even be used to discredit all Christian beliefs? Was it an act of evil for me to deliver Hasan his desire?

And then, as my horse moved beneath me through those dark nights, I had dreams of power of my own. How could I use the book myself? Armed with my knowledge, could I become a great leader? Perhaps, strong and invincible in battle, I could persuade other men to follow me. I remembered the influence of my prowess on the wall at Antioch and the enjoyment I had taken from my fellows' respect. I remembered my exhilaration leading my troop of pseudo-saints over Mount

Silpius. But how could I tell of the secrets of the book? Who would believe the tale of the Lazarus Gospel? All the vested interests would deny it, brand it a fraudulent heterodoxy, and stamp what had been done to me as heathen witchcraft. I would be a pariah, an outcast. They would stop at nothing to destroy me, the only living proof of a cataclysmic truth. Death at the executioner's axe would be my fate.

These thoughts churned around in my head until I banished them with my picture of Blanche. Nothing else mattered, not power, nor wealth, nor knowledge. All I needed was Blanche and her love. Then fear turned my adoration to ice. What if I had been forgotten? One year and a half had passed. What if Mohammed had not delivered my message from Antioch? What if another had taken my place in her heart during my long absence? But then I remembered the passion of our love, the clear sincerity in her sad blue eyes, and I knew that I had nothing to fear, from her at least. I spurred on my horse, the optimism of love assuring me that I would find a way to deal with Hasan, that the Nizari could be made to honour his word, that when I saw Blanche again everything would be right.

Perhaps it was this state of lonely turmoil that drove me one cold night towards campfires in the distance instead of skirting safely around them. At least I had the sense to dismount and walk my horses quiet and unseen to the edge of the light cast by the fires. But then I was delighted to see that men of my own race were moving around in the warm welcoming glow. I remembered the pleasure I had taken even in the boorish company of Geldemer Carpenel, a familiar face when I arrived at Jaffa after long loneliness. Perhaps here were some old comrades from Antioch. Worn by solitude, and thinking with pleasure of some tasty rations and a draught of wine, I moved forward into the camp and made myself known to the sentries. They challenged me with suspicion, for they scarcely expected a lone Crusader knight travelling in the darkness, but they appeared impressed by my rapid improvisation of travelling north on a secret task for my master, Duke Godfrey of Bouillon.

"We'd better take you to our commander, then," they said, and led me towards the lavish tent at the centre of the camp. I waited outside as one of the men entered with nervous respect, showing that its occupant was a man whose moods were to be feared, to ask what should be done with the new arrival. Then from inside I heard the sibilant voice that belonged to the last man on earth I wished to see. But it was too late, and instantly I found myself standing before the serpentine figure of Baldwin of Boulogne, who was comfortably coiled on a luxurious silk-covered divan. He could not conceal his astonishment when he saw me entering. Amazement quickly turned to cruel delight. An unaccustomed smile split his thin mouth and his black eyes sparkled with sadistic amusement.

"Well, well, if it isn't brother Godfrey's little monk. Here I am, travelling south to witness the unwelcome spectacle of his triumph as *Advocatus Sancti Sepulchri*, Defender of the Holy Sepulchre. And now you turn up. What false humility on your master's part to turn down the title of King of Jerusalem! But I had no choice but to go. Even in Edessa they are beginning to mutter that I have failed to fulfil my Crusader vow to worship at the Holy Sepulchre. Are you bringing me a message from my beloved brother? No, I see that you are not. So you are deserting him. You are a renegade. What a shame friend Bagrat isn't here. He would have so enjoyed seeing you."

Baldwin's glimmer of humour was replaced in his expression with his habitual cold malevolence. He read plainly my discomfiture on hearing Bagrat's name.

"So you did have a hand in his death. I always suspected so. And do you have no greeting for me? You should pay the Count of Edessa due respect."

The men around me could sense Baldwin's antipathy. I felt

their hostility building. Furtively I glanced sideways to see if any were also veterans of Tarsus and Mamistra. Then, at Baldwin's gesture of command, they grabbed me on both sides and folded me down onto my knees, grating my head on the ground in obeisance to the Count.

Down in that position I did not see the first kick coming. I realised that Baldwin had given another sign to his henchmen, for a torrent of blows now began to pummel my ribs. They knocked the wind out of my lungs. I heard several bones crack. A brief respite came and I managed to suck in a breath of air, gasping at the stabbing pain in both my sides. Then I saw the finely stitched black leather of Baldwin's boots just in front of me. The Count joined in the fun. His first kick smashed my nose, so that it bubbled blood over my face as I struggled to breathe. The kicks to my head continued, and Baldwin's cruel laughter faded away into the distance. The others started again, moving lower down my body, kicking my genitals so that I doubled up in pain. From a long way off I heard Baldwin telling his men not to kill me, saying that he wanted to spare me for execution in the morning.

"I'll enjoy seeing the blood spurt from his severed neck," came the thick voice of one.

"No," hissed his master, "that death would be too quick and easy for this murdering renegade. We'll string him up and choke him slowly."

Relief washed over me as I passed into unconsciousness. But then I was immediately awake again, soaked with ice cold water. I shook uncontrollably in a broken heap on the ground outside Baldwin's tent. My left eye was closed and would not open; the right was swollen and felt crusted with blood, so that only a narrow slit showed me the dawn light. Rough hands pulled me up, and half dragged, half carried me toward a tree at the edge of the camp. A coarse rope was noosed around my neck. I sagged to my knees when my tormentors let me go. Only the cord stopped me from collapsing flat in the dirt again. My shaken wits told me that the other end of the rope must have been looped over a branch and held me up.

Through the slit that had once been my right eye, I made out Baldwin's baleful presence. With the best show of defiance I could summon I raised my head to meet his gaze. Baldwin sneered.

"Now you see the fate of those who dare to defy the Count of Edessa. This is what happens to people who murder his men. Beg me for mercy. Go on, beg. Maybe I will be merciful, or at least make sure that your end on that rope is quick."

I shook my head as firmly as I could, immediately regretting the movement as I retched and everything span round. Baldwin dealt me one last kick in the groin for good measure and barked the order to the men behind.

"Strangle him slowly."

The rope jerked me to my feet, and then raised me up, so that I dangled there, choking as my windpipe closed. I tried to suck air into my lungs through my battered lips, but could not. Nor could I stop the involuntary jerking of my legs, as with a mixture of shame and amusement I felt my priapus stiffening and rising in a mixture of pleasure and pain, the pleasure winning over the pain, the amusement over the shame. Then, for the second time that I could remember, everything went black.

"No punishment could be bad enough for him."

"I never liked him."

"I'd like to see him swing."

The Fellows were all venting their spleen on their murderous ex-colleague.

"I have never believed in the death penalty," said the Chaplain. "But he certainly deserves the most severe punishment permitted by the law."

"His attack on the Master was effectively an admission of guilt." The Oxford Detective looked very pleased that his case was solved. "And he has formally confessed to sabotaging the Maserati. My suspicions were aroused when my investigations showed that he had worked in a garage before coming here. He obviously knew what to do."

The Classics Fellow rolled his eyes. "To think that we nearly admitted a mechanic to the Senior Common Room."

"And I am sure that after a bit more interrogation he will own up to the attempted poisoning of the Master and to the murder of the Modern Languages Tutor. Of course, that is the big one we want to get him for. Attempted murder does not carry much of a sentence these days."

"Well, he certainly demonstrated how mindlessly malevolent he is when he ran amok in the wine cellar," said the Master. "He smashed pretty much every bottle in the place with that monkey wrench of his. In some ways though he has done us a favour. The insurance money will be welcome and we will be able to restock the cellar for the future. Quite a lot of what we had needed drinking or was past its best already."

"Talking of malevolence, what really surprised me was that extraordinarily virulent letter he seemed to be working on," mused the Classics Fellow. "It appeared to be a rant against everything – his old teacher, presumably meaning the Modern Languages Tutor, the Master, albeit he talked of you in rather strange terms! Perhaps by calling you 'assassin' he meant to refer to when you were chairing that secret service committee. He seemed to have a go at pretty much all of us, certainly you, Chaplain, and then God, and some ex-girlfriend. He was obviously still working on it, otherwise it would not have been on his desk. But to rewrite it so many times and craft it so carefully…it was done almost the way one would translate something."

"Maybe he was translating something," said the History Don with his usual interest in factual material. "Could he have dug another document out of the library somewhere? Was anything found in his rooms?"

The Chaplain shook his head. "Poor fellow, one does have to feel some compassion for someone who was so bitter and mixed up. He must have had a screw loose."

"That's not a bad way of describing a mad mechanic!" said the Best-Selling Author. "I must use that in my next book!"

Chapter Twenty-one

SOLITUDE IN THE MOUNTAINS

It is finished. Why did I forsake my God?

I awoke to feel Mohammed's dagger at my throat a third time. This time though, the blade pointed away from my skin to slice through the tight knotted noose. I managed to crack open one eye and saw a face blurring above me. My body burned with bruises, battered and broken surely beyond repair. The fear and shock that I dimly made out on Mohammed's indistinct face must have reflected my awful state. I groaned at the gentle efforts to wipe some of the grime and blood from my face, and moaned when my head was lifted so that my lips could be moistened with a little water.

"*Allahu Akbar*, so it is true," Mohammed muttered.

I summoned enough strength to inch my untied hands towards the pouch inside my clothes where I had sewn my precious package. Finding it still there I relaxed back into unconsciousness. When I next awoke the sun was past its zenith. I lay in the shade of a makeshift shelter constructed from a cloak and a couple of lances. I now saw that Mohammed had two companions with him.

I croaked out a question. My voice was so hoarse and

weak that Mohammed had to lean forward to catch my words.

"How long did I swing there?"

"We were close on your tail," the Assassin replied. "I lost you in Jerusalem but we rode north and picked up your trail after Damascus. It must have been midnight when we reached the camp. We guessed that you had joined your compatriots. Then, when dawn broke, all we could do was watch helplessly from a distance as you were hung out. But we had to wait until the *Franj* packed up their camp and left. They were in no hurry and it must have been three hours before they were out of sight. Only then could we safely come out of hiding to cut you down. I had hoped to find you alive, but I scarcely believed that it was possible."

I began to smile weakly but stopped as pain slashed across my face.

"So I hung there for hours. So it is true after all…"

Once more Mohammed moistened my lips with some water, and then lifted my head gently to pour something like porridge through my teeth. I tried to swallow, coughed, and felt a sharp stabbing pain in my side from my broken ribs. I leant back again and allowed my one half-open eye to close. I wondered again how much of my broken body would mend; what use would Blanche have for a cripple? These melancholy thoughts pushed me back into sleep.

When I woke again the sun told by its position that it was another morning. I looked up at its orb with both eyes open. Closing them in turn I found with relief that both worked. My ribs still hurt but the all-enveloping pain of the previous day had gone. I could distinguish separate aches. My overwhelming sensation now was itching; ants were crawling over my whole body – and it felt like they were not just over my skin but all about underneath, even inside my veins. I propped myself up on one elbow, cursing my companions for carelessly placing me on top of a termite heap, and ready to brush the tickling creatures away, but I saw nothing. Mohammed saw the movement and hurried over. I could now see his face clearly. Why was there a look of such astonishment written across it?

"It is extraordinary. Yesterday I thought your wounds would take days to heal but the marks on your face have almost gone already. Some bruises are left, yes, and some scabs, but the swelling has nearly subsided."

Now I realised that I could smile without feeling that my skin was cracking.

"I itch all over, but I suppose that is better than the pain. I feel hungry – is there anything to eat?"

Mohammed gestured over to one of his comrades who answered this request by bringing a dish of porridge. This time I was able to spoon it out for myself.

"When do we leave?" I asked. "I want to reach Alamut as soon as possible."

With a bit of help I was able to mount one of the pack animals. Mohammed's two companions avoided my gaze. I saw one surreptitiously making the sign against the evil eye behind my back. I found myself enjoying the awe in which I seemed to be held. That afternoon we covered only a short distance before I had to beg Mohammed to call a halt, but the following day I was able to survive a full day's ride at a gentle pace, and on the next I was back almost at full strength. Mohammed now also had wonder and respect in his eyes when he looked at me. My spirits rose as I began to imagine again all the great feats that I could achieve in my armour of invincibility. How proud I would make Blanche! And then my doubts returned about my reception by Mohammed's cruel father. I longed to ask what lay in store for me, but I knew that my friend could not have been back at Alamut since our encounter at Jerusalem. Not wanting to show unnecessary weakness, I held my tongue.

As the way led up into the mountains it became colder, and

361

we soon found ourselves riding through snow. I knew that Alamut must be getting close, for many wings of geese passed overhead in their V formations, doubtless towards the inland sea that lay just to the north of the Assassin stronghold. Mohammed's colleagues normally rode in front in silence, but now they jabbered excitedly to each other, pointing upwards. A peregrine flew high above one of the flights of geese, and then stooped like a falling stone on the rearmost bird which lagged behind the others. Keen hawkers, they stopped to watch the contest. The falcon's aim was nearly true, for it struck the goose's neck a glancing blow that knocked it down to the ground not far from where we stood. But perhaps scared by the human presence, perhaps already well-gorged, the bird of prey did not follow up its attack and instead spiralled back up out of sight. We rode towards where the goose had landed, thinking of a pleasant change of diet from the porridge that had been our staple for so many days. But its fall must have been cushioned by the snow, for at our approach it recovered and flapped back up again on its heavy grey wings. All it left in the snow was the imprint of its body and three drops of blood. As the blood sank into the white background, it brought to my mind the lovely colour of Blanche's perfect complexion. I sat there on my horse in a reverie until Mohammed nudged me and pointed to the other two riders now far ahead. I dragged my mind back to reality and followed.

And so it was that I came to Alamut the second time. In turmoil and trepidation I entered that long narrow valley and found it cold and grey, the crops long since taken in to winter stores. The eagle's eyrie perched there on its forbidding crag. I knew that we were watched, and imagined Hasan staring down from his nest. Our horses climbed slowly up the twisting road, their eagerness to be home constrained by the steep gradient. I also found myself pulling back on my reins, now unconsciously trying to put off my arrival. But with inexorable inevitability the pointed gate approached. The door swung open under its carved inscription and in we rode.

We dismounted.

"Now," said Mohammed, "give me the book. I must deliver it to my father."

He reached out his hand towards me. I stood there frozen. My friend looked tense.

"Come on, the book. Give it to me."

I made great play of feeling for it under my cloak. I watched Mohammed relax and eyed the curved sheath that he wore at the front of his belt. I threw myself at him, grabbing him around the neck and spinning him round to face away from me. In one fluent movement I pulled out the dagger that he had held to my throat so many times, and held it to his.

"Stand back." My order stopped Mohammed's comrades in their tracks. "One more step and your master's son is dead. Back off. Further. Which of you wants to be the one to account to the old man for that? You know that I have no fear of death. It cannot harm me. A bit further – that's right.

"Mohammed, my friend. I do not want to have to hurt you. But did you think that I am stupid enough to just hand the book over to you? Did you think I would I trust your father to free Blanche once he had the book? Would you?

"Now. This is what I want. I want fresh horses saddled and made ready. I want Blanche. I will ride back out of the castle with her, and with you. When I am a safe distance away, I will give the book to you. You will be able to ride back to the castle; I will ride away to my new life. Do you agree?"

I pressed the dagger a little harder against Mohammed's throat and I could feel his Adam's apple bobbing as he swallowed nervously.

"You know you can trust me. I saved your life once. I have nothing to gain by killing you."

"Hugh, please. My father will never agree to those terms. I cannot release Blanche. I do not even know where he is keeping her. He will insist on seeing the book; he will never let you go until he has seen it and made sure it is what he wants."

"If he must see it he can come here and see it."

Mohammed laughed grimly. "He won't. He will refuse. Since coming to Alamut he has never left his rooms. Once or twice he has been up to his roof. He will never come here to you. Never. Think what such humiliation would do to his *da'is'* faith in him. He relies on their fear and absolute respect for his power."

"I don't care. Send him a messenger."

"I'll send him a messenger, but I know what he will say. He would sacrifice me rather than risk losing the book and making a fool of himself."

My voice cracked.

"Send him a messenger, damn it. Those are my terms. Tell him."

"Very well." I felt Mohammed shrug. "Ismail, go to my father. Tell him what the *Franj* wants. Tell him that he will lose his son if he does not agree."

Ismail – one of the *da'is* who had accompanied us – hurried off. I backed against the nearest wall, dragging Mohammed with me, and leant against it to wait, glaring at the hostile semi-circle of Assassins in front of us. Their weapons were drawn, threatening, but none of them dared to approach lest they caused Mohammed's throat to be cut like a sheep. I felt Mohammed's weight sagging against me. I felt his desperation.

We stood there in silence for I do not know how long. Then I heard the approach of running footsteps, and Ismail burst out of the keep back into the courtyard.

"The Master will not come."

Mohammed grunted, and I felt him slump down a little more as if in despair.

"Instead, he says you must go to him. He will look at the

book, make sure it is what he wants. Then, if it is, he will give you Blanche. He guarantees you a safe passage out of Alamut. Anyway, you will still have Mohammed as hostage. He worries about his son. He told me to say that his son has served him well."

Ismail paused, as if he had not said the words quite right.

"No, I'm sorry. He told me to say that he loves his son, with whom he is well pleased."

I twitched at the familiar words, and felt Mohammed lighten in my clutch as he reacted to this news of his father's love.

"There is more. He told me to say that if you kill Mohammed he will take the book anyway. He may find it hard to kill you, but you will never escape with Blanche. And he can make her suffer. Oh yes, he can make her suffer. He told me to make sure that you understood how much he can make her suffer."

I stood in silence, thinking. 'If I do this, he does that. If he does that, I do this. And then he does that. And then...' It was like some diabolical game in which I had not had enough practice.

"Very well." Even to me, my voice sounded too loud, too high. "If the Old Man of the Mountains will not come to me and Mohammed, Mohammed and I had better go to the Old Man of the Mountains."

Now I was no longer taking any of Mohammed's weight as his hope lifted him. I felt his movement and was angry.

"Very well. Before we go, Mohammed, tell them about me. Make sure that they understand. Tell them that I cannot die. Make them understand that any attack on me in the corridors of your castle will fail. You will die. They will die. But I will live. So, no guards, no ambushes – they are pointless. We will walk together, you and I, to see your father. Nobody will interfere with us, and if they do...you will die. Those are my terms."

"It is true. He cannot die. My father's magic has seen to that. It is true, Ismail, isn't it? Tell them too. You saw him swing from that tree and survive. Most men would have died from the beating they gave him, let alone choking in that noose for hours."

Ismail acknowledged what he had seen, making the sign against the evil eye. Mohammed continued.

"So stand back and let us pass. That is what the Master wants. We must obey him."

"Back further, back," I barked at the ring of *da'is*. "Go down to the gate and stay there. If I see you move I cut Mohammed's throat."

They obeyed slowly and sullenly. When they were a safe distance off I began to back towards the keep, part dragging, part carrying Mohammed, my left hand around his belt and the dagger in my right always against his neck.

We passed through the gate into the keep and I made Mohammed close it and lower the heavy bar to secure it. Without releasing my hold, I now pushed him ahead of me through the labyrinthine corridors that led towards his father's chamber.

We rounded a corner. A few paces off stood two of the familiar white-lanced guards. They lowered their weapons and made as if to come towards us.

"Tell them to back off," I screamed. "Tell them."

Mohammed cried out in pain and alarm. I felt a trickle of blood running down the blade of the dagger where in my anxiety I had broken his skin.

"Back off, back off for the sake of Allah," he commanded, his voice shaking. "Otherwise I am dead."

The guards hesitated but then turned and disappeared down the corridor.

And so we came to Hasan's well-remembered door. This time I disdained the long talonned fingers of its brass knocker.

"Open it, Mohammed."

He reached forward and swung the door open. I pushed him into the room. Hasan, tall, turbaned, stood as I had seen him first, gazing out of his great window over the sharp mountains beyond. He was flanked on either side by two guards, who stood facing us, their spears at the ready. Anxiously I glanced round the room for a slender figure with blonde hair. She was not there.

Hasan swung round, the yellow circles of his hooded eyes burning with fierce intensity.

"So you have the gospel?" he said with greed and quiet menace. He put out his hand. "Give it to me."

I felt some strange force almost compelling me to reach inside my tunic.

"Let me see it. I must check you have made no mistake and that it is the book I want."

I pulled myself together.

"Bring me Blanche. Then you get the book, not before. Then I leave, with Blanche and Mohammed as hostage."

Just before Hasan spoke again, I caught the glimmer of cruelty in his eagle's eye. Every sinew in my body tensed.

"That would be difficult. That I cannot do. You see, she died in childbirth these two months past."

A cold numbness started in my stomach and spread from there throughout my body.

"What? No. It cannot be. What about the child?" I asked automatically.

"The child is dead too."

And then my chilled brain began to work, to calculate.

"Just two months ago, no surely not. I have been gone for almost two years. One year and two months you must mean."

A mirthless smile split Hasan's sharp face.

"Do you really think that you were the only one?"

He threw back his head and laughed cruelly.

"When my *da'is* are initiated here, I drug them and let them wake in Paradise. They find themselves in a world of pleasure, surrounded by beautiful courtesans and every luxury. After they have enjoyed bliss for a while, every pleasure they desire, they are drugged again. Next time they wake, so it seems to them, they are back in the bitter reality of this cruel world of ours. Their foretaste of Paradise removes all fear of death. Indeed, they can hardly wait for death to return them there. The lovely Blanche was one of Paradise's main attractions. I think you can yourself understand why."

"You devil, how did you make her do it? What did you do to her?"

Hasan's cold smile frosted forth again.

"Oh no, we did not have to force her…she was very willing. Very willing indeed. It seems that her talent for the art of love was matched only by her appetite for it. Did you really think that she treated you differently to the others?"

I screamed obscenities and leapt forward, my dagger outstretched, to strike down my tormentor. Hasan laughed in triumph.

"Seize him now!" The four guards grabbed me and held me back, although it took all their strength to do so. I twisted and wrenched in their grip. Try as I might, I could not wrest myself free. Behind me, I sensed a movement. Mohammed brought some heavy object crashing down onto my head, and I lost consciousness.

When I came to my senses I found myself back in the small stone turret room where I had started my first sojourn at Alamut. Empty, broken, drained by anger, bleached by sorrow, I stared through the window slit at the vicious pointed mountains frozen in the distance.

'If only I had died on the wall at Antioch. If only I had remained locked in my sepulchre in Jerusalem. If only Baldwin's noose had done its proper job. Anything would be better than this bitter pain of betrayal.'

Now I stand alone, staring down the long dark tunnel of time. The knowledge I have gained has shivered all the beliefs on which I once relied. The love that replaced those beliefs has been utterly shattered by betrayal. All I have left to me is time...

EPILOGUE

The Fellows of the College of Saint Lazarus were gathered once more in the Senior Common Room. A new Honorary Fellow, the Best-Selling Author, sat proudly in their midst. The room was full of light and air, touched by the evening sun of a perfect English summer's day. The soothing smell of newly mown grass wafted through the generous Georgian windows.

Leaning forward in his comfortable wing chair, the Master looked almost avuncular as he patted proudly the pile of gaudy paperbacks on the beeswaxed table beside him.

"Well, they may be a little slimmer than the volumes we are accustomed to send to be published from this ancient college, but they certainly sell a few more copies, eh."

A polite titter of laughter greeted his sally, and partially disguised the discomfort on the Fellows' faces. A cloud passed over the sun outside and suddenly the room was cold and gloomy, the gleam banished from the dark oak panelling.

The Chaplain launched the first assault.

"I really don't think I can live with all that Bible parody stuff. And the book still seems to me to raise Islam above Christianity. Not that it has much good to say about either religion. I am still absolutely sure the reasons for the First Crusade were not as venal as they are portrayed."

The History Don attacked from a different direction.

"Actually I would stand by my earlier statement that most of the historical facts and the chronology are pretty accurate. I'm impressed by some of the research and the contemporary colour. It's the characters that are distorted beyond all recognition. To portray Godfrey, such a saintly knight, as a drunken lecher, and his brother Baldwin, the first great King of Jerusalem, as some sort of sadistic monster…"

He shook his head in dismay and as his voice faded away the Professor of English took advantage of the breach in the conversation.

"I know that I have had a go at improving some of the prose. But it is still pretty crude in many places."

"And whatever you say about Eliot blending Roman myth with the grail legend in the real *Waste Land*, I maintain that the way Ovid has been used in the story is both far-fetched and disrespectful," charged the Classics Fellow.

"My issue is that there are just too many literary references and too much history," gloomed the Best-Selling Author. "God knows I've fought a few battles to keep the thing readable."

The Master's sharp voice stabbed into the room.

"Well, I'd stop complaining if I were you. We are top of the best-seller list. The College coffers are in better shape than they have been for a long while. What is more, we have not come to the end of our friend Hugh de Verdon's memoirs. We can't leave the poor fellow languishing miserably in his cell after all he has been through. We must get started on the next volume.

"In memory of our Modern Languages Department, I have come up with a title. It will be called 'The Flowers of Evil' – '*Les Fleurs du Mal*'. Rather apt for the bilious state of mind our hero must now be in, I thought."

The Professor of English's eyes lit up. "Master, if I may say so, that is inspired. The cross-reference to *The Waste Land* is a stroke of genius. '*Hypocrite Lecteur – mon semblable – mon frère*'. Absolutely brilliant."

The Best-Selling Author groaned under his breath. But the cloud outside passed and suddenly the Senior Common Room filled again with light.

BIBLIOGRAPHY

Ashbridge, Thomas, *The First Crusade, A New History*, London 2003

Augustine, *Confessions*, Translated by Albert Cook Outler, 2002

Augustine, *Concerning the City of God against the Pagans*, Translated by Henry Bettenson, 1972

Barber, Richard, *The Holy Grail, The History of a Legend*, London 2004

Barnes, Jonathan, *Aristotle, A Very Short Introduction*, Oxford 2000

Billings, Malcom, *The Cross and the Crescent, A History of the Crusades*, 1987

Boas, Adrian, *Jerusalem in the Time of the Crusades*, 2001

De Boron, Robert, *Merlin and the Grail*, Translated by Nigel Bryant, Cambridge 2001

Buchan, John, *Greenmantle*

Caner, Ergun Mehmet and Emir Fethi, *Christian Jihad*, 2004

Chadwick, Henry, *Augustine, a Very Short Introduction*, 1986

Cobb, Paul, *Usama ibn Munqidh, Warrior Poet of the Age of the Crusades*, 2005

Comnena, Anna, *The Alexiad*, Translated by E.R.A. Sewter, London 1969

Constable, Giles, *Cluny from the Tenth to the Twelfth Centuries*, Princeton 1999

Daftary, Farhad, *The Assassin Legends, Myths of the Mohammedis*, 1995

Eliot, T S, *The Waste Land*, 1922

Frazer, Sir James, *The Golden Bough*, London 1922

Gabrieli, Francesco, *Arab Historians of the Crusades*, Rome 1957

Haleem, M A S Abdel, *A New Translation of the Qur'an*, Oxford 2005

Harris, Jonathan, *Byzantium and the Crusades*, 2003

Hill, Rosalind (Ed), *Gesta Francorum, The Deeds of the Franks and the other Pilgrims to Jerusalem*, 1962

Hoyt, Robert, *Life and Thought in the Middle Ages*, Minneapolis 1967

Hughes, Ted, *Tales from Ovid*, 1997

Hunt, Noreen, *Cluny under Saint Hugh 1049-1109*, Indiana 1966

Jones, Peter, *Learn Ancient Greek*, London 1998

Konstam, Angus, *Historical Atlas of the Crusades*, 2004

Krey, August C, *The First Crusade: The Accounts of Eyewitnesses and Participants*, Princeton 1921

Lacey, Robert, and Danziger, Danny, *The Year 1000*, London 1999

Lewis, Bernard, *The Assassins, a Radical Sect in Islam*, Princeton 1967

Ibn-Munqidh, Usamah, *An Arab-Syrian Gentleman and Warrior in the Period of the Crusades*, Translated by Philip Hitti, 2000

De Nerval, Gerard, *Les Chimères*, 1854

Nicolle, David, *Crusader Warfare Volume 1, Byzantium, Europe and the Struggle for the Holy Land 1050-1300 AD*, 2007

Ovid, *Metamorphoses*, Translated by A.D. Melville, Oxford 1986

Peters, Edward, (Ed.) *The First Crusade, The Chronicle of Fulcher of Chartres and Other Source Materials*, 1971

Python, Monty, *Monty Python and the Holy Grail*

Ralph of Caen, *Gesta Tancredi, A History of the Normans on the First Crusade*, Translated by Bernard S Bachrach and David S Bachrach, 2005

Rider Haggard, Henry, *King Solomon's Mines*

Riley-Smith, Jonathan, *The First Crusade and the Idea of Crusading*, 1993

Robert the Monk, *Historia Hierosolimitana*, Translated by Carol Sweetenham, 2005

Runciman, Steven, *A History of the Crusades*, Cambridge 1951

Scott, Sir Walter, *Ivanhoe*, 1814

de Troyes, Chrétien, *Le Roman de Perceval ou Le Conte du Graal*, c 1180

de Troyes, Chrétien, *Perceval, The Story of the Grail*, Translated by Burton Raffel, Yale 1999

Tyerman, Christopher, *God's War, A New History of the Crusades*, London 2006

Virgil, *The Aeneid*, Translated by C Day Lewis, Oxford 1952

Weston, Jessie, *From Ritual to Romance*, Paris 1919

THE FLOWERS OF EVIL

The Flowers of Evil is the sequel to *The Waste Land*. It takes up the story of Hugh de Verdon in the early years of the Twelfth Century, a turbulent period when the victorious First Crusaders fought to hold on to the lands that they had won in Outremer. Unfinished business from *The Waste Land* takes Hugh on a journey of vengeance and fulfillment to Aleppo, Damascus, Petra and Jerusalem. He battles his old adversaries Baldwin of Boulogne, now King of Jerusalem, Hasan-i Sabbah and the Assassins, and meets the Templars.

Hugh's story is once again translated and edited by the dons of St Lazarus' College, Oxford. They have been delighted by the commercial success of their first volume and hope to repeat their achievement with *The Flowers of Evil*. This has unexpected and sinister consequences for them.

Do not disappoint the dons! Buy *The Flowers of Evil* when it is published in 2011.

Visit www.charlwoodbooks.com for further information.